The Isle of Rebels

Willa Holmes

To my friends and family, who have supported me since page one

Copyright © 2022 Willa Holmes
All rights reserved.
ISBN-13: 9798835699834

Part 1- It's unfair, this life

A declaration

Effective immediately: all young offenders will be transferred to the country's new human-made island penitentiary, the Offshore Youth Rehabilitation Facility.

Inmates shall be classified in accordance with the severity of their crime. They will be treated with fairness and housed in an environment where they are safely isolated from society and assessed for reintroduction.

Visits, calls, and any other form of outside contact will not be permitted.

All criminals, regardless of birthplace, who commit malevolent deeds within the borders of Sykona are affected by this law.

Any person under the age of fourteen or over the age of twenty-five is exempt. For a complete list of exemption eligibility, please visit the government website.

Any questions can be answered by your area's official representative.

Emry McLeod

Unanticipated moments

It was never my intention to become a criminal. Even on my worst days, I would never have gone so far as to call myself a rebel, like the tough guys you see in high school hallways, decorated in bruises and black eyes. I had always kept a safe distance from trouble, and the only sticky situations I had ever gotten myself into were the ones that found me, not vice-versa.

I had never been anything more than an average guy, scraping by on a low budget and equally low self-esteem, the way any poor fourteen-year-old kid would.

But I guess the police didn't realise that because they shipped me off to the Isle of Rebels anyway. All because of a package of beef jerky and a loaf of cheap convenience store bread.

It was a Tuesday after school when it happened. The dramatic arrest, the big showdown. There had always been something about Tuesdays that I just couldn't stand, and on that particular day, I was finally able to put my finger on it. Monday's exhaustion was brutal enough, but having to repeat it all over again? That was Tuesday for you. Pure torture for a bored soul, carefully disguised in Monday's shadow.

The sun beat down on my back as I walked home from school, lost in my idle thoughts of Tuesdays and troubles, homework and helplessness. I hugged the sidewalk with my head held low, crossing my fingers that no one would pass by and force me into social interaction.

The muscles in my shoulders were sore again, over-exerted from a long walk with my heavy bag. Generally, my teachers were pretty lenient when it came to homework coming in late, but the textbooks they assigned weighed about two tonnes.

Academically, however, I was nowhere near in danger of falling behind. My grades were less than stellar, but people expected that of me.

I lived in a dodgy neighbourhood, and my classmates, let's say, weren't among the best and brightest. Any grade above a B got you flagged as a nerd, and while I could probably do well if I tried, there was no point in spending long hours studying only to get beat up as my pleasant reward.

I scrunched up my nose, lifting my head. The streets were narrow, squished together by squat apartment complexes and run-down shops. An occasional car whirred by, skidding dangerously over the uneven asphalt.

Among the usual stench of burning rubber, there was a new smell. I puzzled over the scent, sniffing again.

Grilled chicken.

My stomach grumbled, and I turned my head back to the ground, shaking my head in dismay mingled with the faintest traces of envy.

Someone in the neighbourhood was clearly having a barbeque, a rare occurrence in such a place. An odd time for it, too. It was way too hot and way too dry to be around open flames. If a lowly spark landed in the right place, it could cause the entire row of houses to light up, burning down each and every crumbling structure.

Not to be overly bleak, but the neighbourhood already looked apocalyptic enough. It didn't need another scar to remind people of the war fought on these streets, the buildings bombed on this block.

After the war, everyone had rebuilt quickly enough, but the slums were the only places still crawling with visual reminders of the multiple conflicts our nation, Sykona, had been wrought with.

"Stupid battle," I grumbled, voicing my thoughts aloud. I had only just been born when the most recent war had wrapped up, but it had brought some significant changes down on the country. If you could even be so brash as to call Sykona a country. Sykona had a complicated history, but even before the civil war, we had been the laughing stock of the world with our laughably tiny population, over-inflated egos, and lack of financial security. I didn't pay enough attention in social studies class to know the rest, but the point was, the fighting had been a big deal.

And while the world was constantly reminding us of the peaceful way things had supposedly ended, it sure turned a blind eye to us suckers caught in the aftermath.

I shook my head, clearing my mind. My eleven-year-old sister and seventy-two-year-old grandma were waiting for me back home. They'd worry, and they'd have reason to do so, if I was late. I had to pick up the pace.

About to make the final stretch, settling into a steady jog in spite of the heat, I was suddenly struck with a revelation. Well, more of an idea than an epiphany, but it was one of my better ones.

Partially thanks to the appetising aroma of the grilled chicken across the street, I was famished. And, while I couldn't count on my own house to provide me with a filling snack... I could do something about my hunger via other sources.

Rerouting my mental GPS to a new destination, I decided that my family could wait a little longer. When I came back with a snack for my sister, the grin on her face would be sure to eliminate any anger brewing in my grandma's head.

Back at the house, we were running tight on food. We were always running tight on food, but lately, the situation had gotten particularly dire. My grandma worked hard to provide for my younger sister and me, but she could only do so much with the limited pool of money our parents had left us with.

My parents weren't ready to handle children, so they had put me and, four years later, my sister in her care. Actually, the exchange went more like 'here are our children, take 'em or leave 'em,' and since then, we hadn't had any contact with our parents whatsoever.

I didn't mind. It was a little awkward being the only guy in the house, but I loved my grandma, and she was the sole real guardian I had ever truly had. The only thing I knew about my parents was that I had inherited my dad's ugly mop of straight red hair, along with his crooked nose and lousy vision. I had tried fighting with my permanent tangle of greasy locks but had eventually given up, letting it grow past my shoulders. I looked like a ginger metalhead. On the other hand, my sister had been handed all the attractive traits. My dad's bright eyes and my mom's cute freckles (which looked significantly better on her than they did on me with my thick-framed glasses) made her look as though she came from an entirely different family.

Maybe if we'd stayed in our old, much nicer neighbourhood, we would have seen our parents more often. But due to our suddenly plummeting financial situation, my grandmother had been forced to sell our decent-sized house and move to the dumpiest place in the city.

I didn't blame my grandmother for her choice, but there was something unnerving about going to school with a bunch of shady kids who snuck vapes onto school grounds and smoked between periods because they had nothing better to do with their lives. Not that I could point fingers at them. They were probably in the same situation as I was.

I veered left, making for the convenience store. The buildings, all painted the same uniform shade of dusty brown, seemed to close in even tighter in this part of town. Every establishment was in various stages of decay, but as I walked deeper and deeper, the damage seemed to increase, and the power lines began to droop.

My mouth still had the faint taste of morning breath, even though it was late afternoon. Slipping my hands into my pockets and cracking my knuckles, I turned my focus to the task at hand.

There were very few things I knew how to steal. And, in hindsight, it was probably a bit of a stretch to say I 'knew how to steal' in general. But I had shoplifted before, and I had boiled it down to three basic steps.

Locate, grab, and go.

The spot where I would best put those three principles to work was my local convenience store. The workers, for the most part, didn't pay me much mind, used to this thing all the time. The other kids, like myself, were too preoccupied in their own shifty business to snitch, and the non-human factors, i.e. the security cameras, had been beaten up years ago. The last time I had… permanently borrowed a few objects from those shelves was just last week, and it had gone smoothly enough. Sure, my grandma gave me a disapproving glance as I stepped through the door with a few bags of trail mix and an energy drink, but she was the only one who had seen through me instantly.

I resolved only to take something small. The convenience store wasn't exactly a struggling business, but I had to be rational. I felt my pockets, gauging their size. My lips turned downwards, shaping into a frown. I was wearing jeans, and anything I stuck into the pockets would stick out like a sore thumb.

I'd have to use my backpack, homework inside and everything. Doubtfully, I fingered the straps, questioning my clumsy fingers. In theory, it sounded easy. But the item's journey from the shelf to the backpack had a lot riding on it, and I wasn't quite certain I could see it through.

Like I said, I had never been a criminal. Not really.

Second thoughts swirled around my headspace. Who was I kidding? I was about to save a couple of bucks and impress my family in the process. Theoretically, I could do this without difficulty. But still, despite those reassurances, I was fighting hard not to tremble.

I clutched my hand into a fist as I passed through the door, calming my racing heart. I was fine. I had done this before. Locate, grab, go.

It was simple.

The door chimed as I stepped inside. I steadied my breathing as I walked in, wrinkling my nose at the stench of cigarettes. My worn sneakers tapped on the linoleum tile floor, shuffling awkwardly as I made my way around the aisles. The overhead light flickered. The dude at the cash register- an older guy with a greying handlebar moustache- eyed me suspiciously. I flashed a toothy grin at him on instinct before turning immediately to the ground, a flush rising to my face. What did I think I was doing?

I was so caught up in that exchange that I didn't even notice the dark grey, very functional security camera watching me intently behind its mechanical eye.

I browsed through the rows in the most casual manner I could muster, pausing to carefully examine items whenever someone walked by. In reality, I already knew exactly what I was looking for- beef jerky. It was my little sister's favourite snack, and it was also easy to pocket. My eyes were set on the brand and flavour, which I kept sneaking glances at as subtly as possible.

When I came to the end of the row, there it was. My eyebrows went up at the price. They had ramped the cost up even higher.

I snuck a glance at the cash register, only to immediately wish I hadn't. Moustache guy was watching me like a hawk.

Ducking behind the aisle, I slipped two packages into my pocket, then resurfaced, humming along with the song on the radio. Too late, I realised that said song was laced with profanities and had no right to be played on a loudspeaker in any context whatsoever. With my charade crumbling from under my feet, I continued down the aisle. Initially, I had planned to make off with a more extensive haul, but if I hadn't utterly blown it already, I was sure as hell about to.

I prepared myself to make a beeline for the door when a second sight caught my eye. Bread. My gaze shifted between the door, the cheap loaves, and the corner of my bag. I bit my lip, paying the door one last glance. I gulped. Making sure to avoid the glare of the moustache guy, I snaked around the aisle, slinging my backpack off my shoulder. I shoved the textbooks away, crumpling up a history assignment to make room for a squishy, soggy loaf of white bread.

Too late, the contents jostled, and my heavy binder toppled to the ground. As it fell, the air below it made a loud whoosh, intensifying as my eyes widened. I swooped down to catch it, my fingers grazing the edges but slipping from the sides, grasping at thin air.

"Shit!" I screamed, my knees smashing to the ground at the same time as the binder. I clapped my hand over my mouth as the catastrophic boom echoed across the store. I wasn't sure which had been louder- my scream or the slam of the plastic binder.

I scampered up, sweeping up the binder with one hand and booking it out of there, sprinting for the door. I swore under my breath, just about slamming into the wall. Panting, I recovered, dashing outside for the taste of sweet freedom.

The saddest reality was that I almost made it. My feet would've come into contact with the pavement in just a few more inches, allowing me to take off like a shot and run home free. But the fundamental principle upon which the entire world revolves can be described, in plain terms, by this simple sentence- it's unfair, this life.

I was almost out the door when a meaty hand grabbed me by the strap of my bag, stopping me in my tracks and knocking the wind out of my lungs.

"Not so fast," a gurgly voice chortled from behind me. I whirled around, my backpack tugging at the skin underneath, producing the nerdiest kind of rope burn. Moustache guy wrapped his greasy hand around my bag, staring at me with the cold glare of a man with no mercy. "Kids like you," he grunted, tightening his grasp. "Always thinkin' they're smarter than us. Smarter than the adults who built this country." He yanked me closer, maintaining firm eye contact. His breath smelled of garlic and crushed souls. "But you kids? You kids are always, always wrong."

"Please," I squeaked, struggling for air. "I don't want any trouble."

"Oh yeah?" Moustache guy scoffed, topping it off with a loud snort. "I'm sure that's what you would've said last time you stole from my store. Or the time before that. Or the time before that. It's three strikes and you're out, kid. That's how you play it anywhere else, and that's how you play it here."

Technically, if you counted this one, I had struck four times, but I wasn't about to correct him.

"How-"

He pointed up at the wall. I followed his finger to a tiny security camera nestled in a shadow-draped corner. The red dot below the camera was on, casting its reflections in the man's glossy grey eyes. My heart sunk, collecting at the bottom of my gut, where it pooled with a lump of dread, bile, and the aftermath of an idiotic mistake. I flitted my eyes back to moustache guy, who curved his lips up in a twisted smile.

"Rebels like you might not've killed anyone, but you're bad in your blood. I've bagged four of you this week, and the government pays me for it every time. I'm sure you've heard of the new Declaration. I work for the system, and the system works for me. And from what I've heard, they're looking for one more punk like you to tie off this month's shipment."

An icy jolt spiked through my bloodstream. "You can't-" My pubescent teenage voice jumped an octave. "You can't possibly-"

The man smirked. "Why not? It all works out for me. I rid the streets of one more criminal, I get the money for turning you in, and…" he paused, as though I was supposed to already know the answer to that one. "You stop robbing my store."

The first pack of beef jerky clattered to the dirty floor seconds before I was off, tearing down the street and out of moustache guy's grip.

"Get back here!"

I dodged past a kid on his bike, leaping over potholes and narrowly escaping gaping cracks in the sidewalk. My heart sped a hundred miles a minute. I didn't know where I was going, only that I had to put as much distance as possible between myself and moustache guy. Dust, crumbling off the narrow buildings and skiffing off the ruined path, snaked its way into my eyes, rimming my periphery with a foggy sheen.

Moustache guy tailed me, following close behind. I sped up, skidding down an alleyway. Gravel clouded at my feet, shooting behind me in violent wisps. Part of me wanted to look back, but the diminishing logic centre in my brain urged me to focus on the task at hand. Panting, I swerved down another corner, nearly losing my balance. How was this happening?!

My orange-red hair flapped like a flag, the wind hissing in my ears. I could taste the acrid stench of asphalt mixed with the giddy tang of exhilaration. My knees strove forward, half-tempted to buckle under the weight and give up entirely. This had to be some sort of misunderstanding.

I was Emry McLeod. Even my name wasn't threatening.

There was no way I was being chased down an alley, no way I was getting punished, let alone getting arrested. Zero chance. Probability? Nada. Zip. Zilch.

I was fourteen years old, for goodness sake. They couldn't *arrest* me.

Midway down the alley, I realised moustache guy had stopped. The street had gotten eerily quiet, each of my panicked footsteps initiating their own little echo. Finally, I brought up the nerve to turn around, sneaking a glance behind my shoulder. Not a single person was in sight. Confused, I stopped running, catching the breath that hitched in my throat. Where-

The last thing I could register before I blacked out was the uniform of a cop and a searing hot pain burning through my right shoulder.

***

I sat, slumped over the barred window of a shipping trailer, contemplating my life choices. Screams came from outside. My grandma. My sister. Moustache guy. The cops. I had stopped paying attention to the conversation a while ago because the verdict had already been decided. Ever since my first case of shoplifting, I had been sentenced to the Isle of Rebels.

Apparently, I had been a walking target from the start. This had simply been the day someone had been lucky enough to hit the bullseye.

My right arm felt like it would split off at the joint, cracking from the sheer force of the pain radiating through it in waves that were getting progressively worse instead of better.

Printed into the soft flesh of my upper right forearm was a crimson-red 1. A metal branding stamp had been slapped onto it brutally and without much precision, leaving the deep burn at a slight angle. I could almost catch the sight of smoke or steam trailing out of the wound, my arm's pitiful way of rebelling against the canvas it had been turned into. The deep mark was like a crater on a strange planet, but the journey I was about to embark on was a lot less exciting than a mission to Mars.

Unless, apparently, you were a masochist like me who had walked straight into captivity.

Frozen in place and sick with dread, I followed a fat, black fly around the tight quarters. I stared down at my white sneakers. The shoelaces had been sawed off, leaving me with nothing but a bare sole flapping uselessly with every step. I felt like I was going to hurl. The soft pink paint, a colour specifically designed to make prisoners feel weaker, was peeling off the sides of the wall. My left arm, which ached slightly less than my throbbing right one, found a sagging curl of paint-sloshed wood and ripped it down, wrenching it all the way to the floor. Splinters bit at my hand, but I didn't care. My entire arm could fall out of its socket if it got me out of this trailer. I let out a low groan, fighting back an onslaught of tears.

How could I have been so damn *stupid*?!

The door of the trailer opened. A tall cop stepped in, a rifle slung around her shoulder. The gun was an old-fashioned style of rifle. Not the kind that dated back to just before the war, with a million fancy buttons and different variations that I couldn't even begin to pronounce, but the kind that slid into the category of an even *older* brand of 'old-fashioned.' The newer guns had been banned from use throughout Sykona ever since the dust from the war had settled, which seemed pretty pointless to me, considering the prison guards still continued to carry giant assault rifles. The particular one this guard was holding had a wide neck and a black leather shoulder strap. It looked like one of the weird-ass soviet rifles they used in the 1940s, with a couple metal shoots poking out of it. A general rule of guns was that they were all pretty menacing, but this one was on a whole new level of intimidating weaponry.

The guard herself bore the standard uniform of a police officer, the long sleeves made of thick navy-blue fabric. The bronze buttons lining the front were crisp and polished, as firm as her stone-cold expression.

"Emry Terris McLeod," she said in a pinched tone, spitting the words out like a stiff cough. The rifle on her back looked as though it were purely for show, although I wouldn't be willing to bet my life on that fact. I was sure that anything involving criminal arrests involved a lot of defences. Then again, the 1 burned into the soft flesh of my exposed shoulder indicated that I wasn't much of a threat. They likely wouldn't need to physically restrain me. Numb and in shock, they had herded me here easily enough after I had come to my senses, temporarily blinded by the jolt of pain from the boiling burn.

I thought back to moustache guy's words. I wasn't a threat now. I shuddered, pressing my eyelids shut. Maybe if I blinked hard enough, the fabric ensnaring me in this awful reality would fall, and I'd wake up to find that this whole ordeal had been a dream. A really, really shitty dream.

"You have been sentenced to a year-long stay at the Offshore Youth Rehabilitation Facility," the cop continued, "your current status is that of a Level One prisoner. Your behaviour at the Isle may elongate your sentence or shorten it, depending on your obedience."

"Listen-" I stuttered, my eyes flitting madly around the empty room. "This has to be some kind of mistake. I'm not a criminal. You can't send me there! I didn't even get a trial!"

"The moment your skin was stamped, your rights to a trial were revoked. And I don't care about what you did. In the eyes of the law, a crime is a crime, and crimes need to be stopped. That's why we have the Rebel Tier system."

"This is ridiculous!"

"This is justice."

I started to pace, getting up and walking back and forth through the small space in my pink cell. "You've seen the neighbourhood I live in! I had no warning! People just do that stuff around there! It's how we... it's how we survive!" Playing the 'survival' card in the face of a stern-faced officer might have been pushing it, but I was thoroughly out of options.

"If you're trying to win my pity, Mr. McLeod, you're not going to get it. And I can assure you that any other individuals caught doing the same things you have are waiting in a carriage like this, awaiting a sentence like yours. That'll be all, Emmy."

"It's Emry!" I screamed to her back as she shut the door behind me. I stormed back to the thin slab of bench, crumbling onto it with a loud huff. I felt the wood strain, but it didn't give.

I pressed my nose through the bars, trying in vain to get a good look at what was happening outside of the truck. The searing metal stung my cheeks, and the shapes, shadowy blobs behind the mesh screen covering the window, resembled my family. Occasionally, wails and cries of objection would ring out, flames that were rapidly quenched by the guard's condescending tone.

Suddenly, one of the shapes broke free, running closer. An aged, creased hand ripped the screen away, shoving her arm through the bars.

"Grandma," I was able to muster, clutching her wrinkled fingers.

"Emry!" She screamed, sucking up a noseful of snot. Her usually strong, calm, and collected face was a mess, torn up by tears. "How could you let this happen?!"

"I-"

Her grip tightened, and her stringy grey hair that was usually tied back fanned out in front of her face. "How *could* you?!"

And just like that, she was pulled away again, with the screen dropped between us. The shreds of my life, and my sanity, were erased in mere moments due to a fool's mistake.

The door to the truck opened two more times that afternoon. Once to deliver an ironed set of prison wear, consisting of a short-sleeved blue-and-white striped shirt and a pair of light grey sweatpants with a blue 1 emblazoned on the side. The second time, they came to transfer me into the overseas transport bay. Only then, with home slipping far behind me, did the shock disappear and the reality of the situation start to sink in.

All because of an unprecedentedly crummy Tuesday, a pack of jerky, and a loaf of bread, I, Emry Terris McLeod, was no longer a human being.

Emry McLeod

The People Who Surround You

Even among other prisoners wearing the exact same striped uniform, I was out of place. I was sandwiched like an animal between two other new arrivals, both of my bony arms squeezed to my sides. Pressed up on either side of me was a teenage girl so gaunt she could probably disappear into thin air, and a tall sweaty dude who was hyperventilating and reeked of B.O. All I wanted to do was bury myself in the crowd of striped shirts and disappear forever. I had already dug my own grave. There was no point in letting it sit empty.

There were approximately 25 criminals packed into the metal arrival chamber. Some were carefully nurturing the 1s burned into their shoulders, while others crossed their arms, retreating to the fringes of the crowd. They varied tremendously in age, height, colouring and physical build, but one thing remained the same- all of them breathed out fear.

And none of them were dumb-as-dirt redheads. Except me.

Never before had I felt so insecure with my long, oily hair and grime-covered freckles. My shoulder had a heartbeat of its own, and the number branded into it was swelling with a crimson blister. The inside of my cheek was bloody from twenty minutes of nervous gnawing, and I had an overpowering need to use a restroom. If they even *had* restrooms on the island. Based on the kinds of horror stories I'd heard about the place, it was likely that people did their business smack in the middle of the roads. If they even *had* roads. We were probably about to be hauled into a giant cell, left to sit with nothing but iron bars and scary people as companions.

My knees trembled, and goosebumps crept up my arms even though it was sweltering inside the tinny chamber. A giant panel of glass separated us from a podium, where an old man with thinning grey hair adjusted a microphone. He cleared his throat, testing the sound. Something about his features was slightly familiar. I narrowed my eyes, zeroing in on his face. It took me a second to pick out the resemblances. The man was Jezmon Tylor, Sykona's head of military defence. After the war had come to a close, the position was purely ceremonial, but it was enough to make my heart skip a few beats. What was *he* doing here? Or, more accurately, what was *I* doing amid a crowd that his presence was needed to settle?

"Greetings, inmates," he said, in the dull monotone I was sure he'd rehearsed hundreds of times in front of groups no different than this one. "You're quite the large bunch. Allow me to give you a brief orientation of the Isle."

"This is barbaric!" A kid in the back screamed. "I didn't *do* anything!"

Jezmon promptly ignored her. "You are all tagged as Level One prisoners. You are only allowed to stay within your designated quarters and associate with those at your level. Disobedience will add time to your sentence, whereas a swift following of the Isle's rules will deduct time. Lights out is at 21:00, and wake-up call is at 06:00. The Guards will lead you to your quarters. You will stick to the designated path, and you will obey their directives. No exceptions."

With a clunky series of ear-splitting scrapes, a massive door slid open behind us. We whirled around, and the tall guy to my right whacked me in the face with his long, slender arm, grunting out an apology. Uniformed guards, which had been positioned at each corner of the room, brought up the front and rear. The blue edges of the uniforms cut into the bright sunlit backdrop as though they were navy knives, closing in on us like we were nothing more than old vegetables due to be scraped off the cutting board.

Each guard wielded a rifle tucked firmly under their uniformed shoulders. They assumed the stance of vigilant snipers, but past the narrow-eyed concentration, there was an underlying layer of formality about the way they held their weapons. They matched the others in perfect symmetry, their equidistance only adding to my mounting nerves.

We were marched out of the room in a slow procession, allowing us plenty of time to adjust to the blinding rays of hot sunlight. I drank in the salty breeze, forcing it into my lungs and savouring it while it lasted.

I looked behind me at the arrival centre, blinking rapidly against the bright sheen of light that reflected off the open sea. The structure I had just been pushed out of stood nestled at the edge of the coastline, emerging from a small building painted with lazy, beige brushstrokes. Underfoot, a shiny metal walkway slithered up to a tall gate. It consisted of various steel panes nailed together in a sloppy frankenstein of a dock, a series of loud clanging noises vibrating off it with every step. The cargo ship that had been used to transport us to the Isle stood in the loading bay, reminiscent of a gigantic iron beast ready to trap us beneath its jaws once more.

The shore was massive. Spanning as far as the eye could see, the coastline was grey and rocky. Reflective orange signs with the number 1 were positioned along the stretch.

The guards took up the front, rear, and centre of our steady march, driving us forward with their menacing stares and firm nudges. I was half-tempted to go rogue and make a run for it, springing into the ocean for the sharks to take me. As if they could read my thoughts, two guards on either side of me sent a death glare my way. "Keep moving."

I gulped, doing as they bid.

An immense gate encircled the entire island, made from thick poles of steel and topped with some nasty-looking barbed wire. The leading guard stopped at the end of the walkway, punching in a long code. At the sudden, jarring halt, the tall dude, now in front of me, sprung back, causing me to lose my balance.

A hand shot out, grabbing me by the forearm. I teetered off the edge of the walkway, dangling over the rocks. A small gasp emanated from my strangled lungs as my line of vision flitted to the walkway, to my feet, to the rocks I had just about fallen on, to the sea-green eyes of the person in front of me.

The fingernails of a small girl had been embedded deeply into my skin. I stumbled forward. The girl's grip was awfully strong, and the skin where she had caught me had blanched and was starting to trickle out blood.

"You're welcome," she said, unsticking her claw-like hands from my arm. She pointed at a piece of what looked like harmless plastic jutting out from the beach.

"What's that?" I asked, my tone distant as I surveyed the scratch marks on my forearm. The girl had saved me the embarrassment of tripping in front of everyone, but she might as well have let me fall. Her hand had injured me more than the rocks would've.

"Land mines."

My blood froze. "I'm sorry- *what*?"

"I'm Lizabeth," the girl said, changing the subject. "What about you, Sir Inmate The Clumsy?"

I gulped, feeling a deep red blush rise to my cheeks. My face bent towards the ground. "Please don't call me that. I'm, uh, Emry. Emry McLeod."

"Nice to meet you, Emry."

"Nice to meet you too, uh, Lizabeth."

Lizabeth raised her eyebrows, surprised that I had gone along with the niceties despite my distant tone. "So. What are you here for?"

I gulped. I wasn't sure whether to attempt to keep my cool for this strange girl or admit defeat and gain her utmost pity. Torn between both, my mouth let out a little squeak. Lizabeth nodded as though I'd just recounted a long and detailed version of my past endeavours.

"I understand. You don't have to tell me if you don't want to."

"I- I stole some stuff from a…." I swallowed, not wanting the truth of my lameness to be broadcast on full display, "...place. Three times. Well, technically four."

Lizabeth smiled grimly. "I'm a thief too."

I was afraid to ask, but the guard was having trouble with the gate, and it didn't look like I'd have an excuse to get out of this conversation any time soon. "What did you steal?"

"Nothing. It's what I *almost* stole that they locked me up for."

"Okay… what did you *try* to steal?"

"The entire contents of a person's bank account."

"A rich person? Cash or crypto? The universal currency, or Sykona's?" I spit-fired the questions as though I were the host of a TV show, hoping any curiosity about the topic would make me appear knowledgeable enough to scrape by.

"Is any of that relevant?"

I nodded vigorously as though I understood completely. "I see."

Then and there, I made an important mental note. Lizabeth and whatever crew she attempted to pull that kind of heist off with were the very kind of criminals I was trying to avoid. The kind I could *never* become, no matter what the burn engraved on my shoulder read.

As soon as I could, I was getting off the island. And if that meant turning into the Isle's equivalent of a teacher's pet, then so be it.

The gate clicked open and slid to the side with a mechanical whirr. One by one, we were ushered onto a vast stone plateau extending across the base of the Isle. A second, smaller fence was posted behind it, low enough to step over. On top of that fence, the same reflective signs were posted at even intervals. Beyond it, the buildings rose. The structures dotting the horizon looked nothing like prison cells, instead resembling wood cabins. Each one was drab and rectangular, sculpted with rich, dark brown wood. Red paint was swabbed on the outside walls, numbering the structures. Starting from 1-1 and continuing on to 1-2, the buildings went on and on.

I caught sight of the windows, filthy panes of glass caked with dirt and dust, and immediately wished I hadn't. Peeking out of the yellowed frames dotting building 1-1 were several rows of faces. Their features were disfigured by the tint of the windows, but I could feel their eyes.

Suppressing a shudder, I turned away. Simple black street lamps decorated the smooth stone pathways, which were turned off now, but had shimmering solar panels stationed on the top of each. It looked like a military version of my old block, polished so thin it was too good to be true. I hadn't expected the Isle to be this put-together, but more so, I had never expected it to be so open.

The guards weren't running a prison. They were running a civilization.

"Form a single file line," one of them barked, pulling out a clipboard. Her raven-brown hair was tied back in a tight bun, and the uniform she wore was evenly pressed and free of stains or wrinkles. She looked more like a robot than a person.

One by one, she called up names, hand at her gun. No one was dumb enough to attack her, but several gave off nasty glares, topped off with middle fingers and the certain kind of swear words you only hear in dark alleyways or online forums. Each person was assigned a building and given a laminated QR code.

"This is your meal card," the guard explained. "At the wall to the Isle's inner circle, there's a food station where you can scan it. Do so at the beginning of each day to receive your rations. You can also scan it at the washing station to clean your uniform. Your backup change of clothes is located on your bunk. Those are the only clothes you will get, and the only clothes you will ever get. Likewise, there are no replacement meal cards."

Again, my mind drifted back to the beef jerky. All that to get put on a diet consisting of prison rations anyway.

"Emry McLeod," The guard's firm tone snapped me out of my self-pity. Knees trembling, I walked up to receive my paper. My shaky fingers slipped while receiving it, sending it pinwheeling to the ground. I caught a snicker in the back of the thinning crowd as I bent down to pick it up.

"Building 1-3. Unit 97."

I ducked away, moving my feet as quickly as possible. Although I was practically sprinting, the next name was called before I had time to disappear from earshot.

"Lizabeth Merrin. Building 1-3. Unit 98."

Great. Just *great*.

***

I stood outside the building labelled 1-3, eyeing it doubtfully. The red paint that labelled it was faded and sun-bleached. The whole structure was slumped over as if the very walls were depressed, and the windows watched me with scrutinising eyes. Cinder block steps led up to a door. At the bottom of them, my feet stopped. Any mental GPS of mine was swung entirely off-kilter and, at this point, utterly broken.

Lizabeth stepped in front of me and twisted the knob, holding the door open and gesturing for me to step through. I breathed out hard through my nostrils. How could she be so calm, so collected? We had just been sentenced to the worst place on earth. No, not sentenced. *Shipped*. Like products. I hadn't heard a word regarding my release ever since we'd arrived, and the thought of spending an entire year on the island twisted my stomach up in knots.

I stepped up to the entryway, gritting my teeth. Moustache guy, the guards, the police officers. They had all made a big mistake. I would show them who I really was, show them the harmless coward buried inside me, and they'd *have* to shorten my sentence.

The door tapped shut behind us, leaving me in darkness.

"Hello?" I called, stopping in my tracks. Every nerve ending flared to life as I prepared to flee, readying my reflexes for some sort of ambush. "Is anybody in here?"

An overhead light blinked on, revealing two rusted rows of metal bunks. Each of them carried an intently-gazing prisoner. Adrenaline lit up inside me, and I jumped back, lifting my hands above my head to defend against the oncoming threat.

Lizabeth coughed, glancing at me with her eyebrows raised. I glared at her, slowly lowering my arms. My cheeks matched the colour of my hair and steamed as hot as the sun outside. My time in building 1-3 was not off to a great start.

An awkward moment of silence radiated across the chamber, officially crowning itself the worst set of seconds I had ever experienced.

A man dropped down from his bunk, making his way over to us.

"Welcome to the Isle," he said, holding out a welcoming hand, "the name is Joe. Consider me the overseer of every event in the Level One sector. I am pleased to make your acquaintance."

The man, Joe, was by far the oldest of the bunch. He looked to be in his early twenties, but the creases on his face indicated that he'd seen more than a lifetime's worth of hardships. His head was fully shaved, with tiny black dots of stubble poking out of his hairline. His olive skin was lined with a sheen of sweat, and he towered well over the both of us. Around him, the others ranged from my age up, forming a collective array of intense glances.

But it was the walls that held my attention. They were gruesome pieces of art, with designs etched in and drawn over in what looked like blood. I tried to pick out individual scenes amid the twisting mass of veins, each breathing life into the room and connecting at its heart. Few of them formed actual pictures, but they stretched so far that it would be impossible to deny them a purpose. I didn't understand them, and I didn't want to, but even to me, they were inescapably *there*.

The roots sprawled all the way up to the bunks, where they ended subtly, fading off to nowhere. On the empty wall opposing the bunks stood a coat hook, a water pump, and a bucket. The hook was open, relatively useless on an island with a warm climate. As for the silver water pump, I liked the idea of drinking out of a tin bucket like a farm animal even less than I liked the idea of being in prison in the first place.

"My name is Lizabeth," she said, cutting to the introduction. "And this is Emry. Which bunks are units 97 and 98?"

Joe pointed to a set near the back, one on top and the other on the bottom. "I'll let the two of you take a few moments to settle. We'll all be out of here in-"

A speaker positioned in the corner of the room crackled on, startling me once more. Jezmon Tylor's scratchy voice boomed through it. "Attention, inmates. The newest shipment had been organised and counted. You are free to exit your quarters."

Nobody moved. The prisoners lining the bunks continued to stare at us, surveying our puny forms as though we were pieces of prey. I backed up a few paces, holding in a breath.

"As I was saying," coughed Joe, clearing his throat. "You two get yourselves sorted."

Promptly, he left us, slipping out the door and abandoning Lizabeth and me in the crosshairs of building 1-3.

Cerina Rayz

Tasks to fill the time

Every month or two, a new batch would come. They would come hard and fast, with no prior warning. Some came in bloodstained uniforms, thirsting for vengeance and freedom. Others arrived mortified, trauma written all over their faces. Most were downright terrified.

Amid all of the varying facial expressions tossed between the new arrivals, the bottom line was this; all of them wanted to get out. But none of them ever would.

I grunted, taking a breather from the push-ups I'd been occupying myself with for the last fifteen minutes. I got to my feet, resting my back against the cabin's back wall and massaging my sore muscles. I had come to the conclusion that our band wouldn't be growing any larger this time. It was the most likely scenario, considering each spot in our building had been filled up, but surprises tended to come out of nowhere, and I had been rehearsing the speech I delivered to new members.

I had made it to the top, after all. Being a leader meant having to be prepared, even if that meant partaking in extra hours of dull tasks in readiness for situations that may never come.

I caught my breath and dropped back to the floor. Adjusting my hands, I got into a suitable position and continued the workout. The ground was a minefield of wood chips, a carefully-laid bed of wooden knives. I gasped, just about cutting myself on a splintery patch of sloppily-built flooring.

Everyone in building 2-7, the room I shared with approximately 25 others, whom we classified as family members, had agreed that forced chitchat was an agonising, unnecessary procedure. It was far too formal for our scruffy group and far too dull to have much impact. Actions spoke much louder than words, and no one knew that better than the Level Two sector. Here, appearance was everything.

I was never a steller giver of advice, but I had learned plenty after a long, arduous year on the Isle. Everything about living as a prisoner involved a maze of charades and skirmishes, wins and losses, but knowing your ability was the most crucial part of everything. Thanks to the laws of nature, I was physically incapable of sprouting as big a six-pack as lots of the guys in my building. But a shrewd wit and swift reflexes could make up for that tenfold. The vast majority of the guys, not just in my group but on the entire Isle, were arrogant, cocky, and ended up getting themselves hurt. I had known from the start that I possessed enough willpower to get me far up the social food chain, and I had put that willpower to good use.

"31, 32." I counted my number of push-ups aloud. Sweat beaded on the dark brown skin of my arms, and I pushed a strand of black hair out of my face. I gritted my teeth, drawing in deep, measured breaths.

In the Level Two sector, people sorted themselves into groups called Families. Most of the time, the Families formed in the cabins. After all, the clusters we were sorted into based on the endings of our last names were generally the most convenient ones.

That was what had happened in the case of building 27. Our allegiance with one another was both a blessing and a curse, especially considering the purpose the Families of the Level Two sectors served.

For the most part, the Families existed for one purpose- to fill our violence-craving hearts by fighting one another and rising to the top. They fought over one item, and to possess it was to both rule the Level Two sector and have a giant target taped to your back at the same time.

Currently, said item was sitting at the bottom of my satchel.

The speech I gave to the rookies of building 2-7 was a revised version of the one I had received so many months ago from the former leader of our Family. It spewed a bunch of nonsense about courage and perseverance, self-worth and self-proof, and it was supposed to involve a sweeping muscle demonstration, which I evidently omitted.

A few months before, the former leader of the building 2-7 Family had been tagged as a Level Three, the most dangerous and mysterious class of Rebel. He had been taken away by the guards to the great unknown. I couldn't care less about what happened to him, though, because his absence left an empty spot that I'd had my eyes dead-set on filling.

"Attention, Inmates." The announcement stopped me in my tracks. I stood up once more, swinging up to my bunk to grab my satchel, the most useful thing I owned. It was made from scraps of my backup uniform, joined together by bits and pieces of packaging from meal rations. Each person's satchel varied in size and composition, but everyone in my Family had one. "The new shipment has been organised and counted for. You are free to exit your quarters."

I heaved a sigh. My right arm stung, and I shut my eyes, embracing the brief moment I was allowed to do so. I squinted down at my shoulder. The jagged 2 burned into it was bleeding again.

"About time!" Irabella, my most trusted bunkmate, called, thudding to the floor. No sooner had she said it than the door was kicked open, revealing two teens, the sleeves ripped off their blue and white uniforms in the evident fashion of one of our many rivals- building

2-8 and a few stragglers from 2-9. They were a more prominent Family than we were, but they were far less stable. If memory served correctly, they called themselves the Shattering Daggers.

Many of the Level Two Families had gone overboard when it came to dramatics. Most adopted a signature look to differentiate them from the rest, and others had named themselves after something they deemed 'edgy.' And so names like the Shattering Daggers were born- titles that seemed cool on the surface but logically... didn't quite fit right. Although, I supposed the 'intact daggers' wouldn't have been as popular a choice.

"Rayz," one of them snarled, bringing me back to attention. I was being last-named. I had to admit, being addressed with such menace was quite flattering.

The girl in front of me was sturdily-built and sun tanned, her fists clenched into tight knots. I was sure she could knock my entire set of teeth out if I let her. I had to give her credit for that much, at least.

"We know you have it," she announced. "Give us the key."

I jumped down from my bunk, shrugging my satchel over my shoulder and meeting her grey eyes. She stared back, venom in her gaze.

"I appreciate the sentiment," I said, "but I'm afraid that isn't how things work around here. I'm sure you're aware that people in this world give and take. Obviously, I'm not just going to hand the key over, which means you might as well go home because there's nothing for you to bring back."

"You don't have a choice. I respect you, Rayz, but you're no match for us. Either we take it the easy way or the hard way."

I scoffed, hating how snobby that made me sound. I made a subtle signal behind my back, and I caught Irabella's nod in the corner of my eye. Not breaking my confidence, I faced the girl. I felt pity for her, but I would never dare let that show in my gaze. Instead, I settled with another option, facing the coming conflict directly in the eye.

"I'd like to see you try."

I ripped off my satchel with one abrupt motion, tossing it into Irabella's capable hands. The girl prepared to attack, crouching down and readying herself to spring. She skidded forward, about to collide with our defences.

A hand shot out, pulling her back.

The second figure, who had been patiently biding his time in the entryway, stepped out from behind the door frame, dropping the girl's uniform.

"Fuck you, Zane," she grunted, stepping back for him to steal the thunder. "I had that situation in the bag."

The boy, Zane, whose features I vaguely remembered from a previous encounter, looked at her with a wary eye. "No, you didn't."

He dipped his head out the door, grabbed something, and swung back into the cabin. Inside his hand was the balled-up collar of a limp figure's uniform. I identified the hostage immediately by his wrinkled eyebrows, scraggly white hair, and the dazed smile on his face even as the air was being squished from his lungs.

"I don't understand your fondness for this old man, but I'll snap his neck in a heartbeat if you don't hand over the key," Zane spat. His messy swach of black hair hung over his forehead, overgrown like everything else in the Level Two sector. His scarred ears poked prominently from the strands, a calculated move. Rumour had it that Zane had cut them up himself to increase his coolness factor.

My gaze didn't falter, my breath didn't hitch. It was all talk, theatrics, and swearing when it came to him and his bunch. The only thing Zane targeted were his insults, and even then, they rarely made marks.

"Arvin?" I said, curious but veiling my surprise. The old man in Zane's arms looked up, squinting at my face.

"Yeah?" He grunted, his words coming out in wheezy puffs.

"Are you alright?"

He shrugged as though he was completely oblivious to the situation. Every single member of building 2-7 knew he wasn't, but his madness, both feigned and real, had made him seem like a low threat to any other Family. In reality, he was anything but.

Arvin was not supposed to be on the Isle of Rebels. He was well past the age cutoff, and his mere presence was a huge risk to both himself and others. But most of his personal information had been lost to time, and the guards had decided he wasn't worth the hassle of relocation to a new facility. Which suited building 2-7 fine. Arvin was our most valuable spy, and he was far more intelligent than he let on.

"I'll answer that for you," Zane sneered, "people generally aren't *okay* if they're about to *die*."

"What the hell were you doing outside, Arvin?" I spoke calmly, mainly stalling for time. I took a few steps back, and the two people at the door inadvertently moved further inside, making themselves all the more vulnerable. "The guards demanded a total lockdown for the new shipment."

Arvin coughed, croaking out the statement to plead his case.

"Outside is where stuff happens. It's where drama unfolds and scenes shift. Inside, the little ghosts lodge up in my ears. But out, they fly right through."

Zane laughed. "Was that supposed to be an excuse?"

I didn't let my eyes betray me as Irabella danced in my peripheral vision, slowly slipping in behind the two Shattering Daggers, who stared at me in wait for my reaction.

"That wasn't safe, Arvin," I explained as I would to a child. "New arrivals might not join us 2s often, but you'd be strictly punished if a guard were to see you."

"Yeah, Arvin," Zane spat, "Bet your old bones couldn't take the beating. They'd shatter into dust. Now, Rayz, give us the key."

Snapping my fingers behind my back, I gave the rest of my building the signal they needed.

Irabella slammed the door to the building, joined by two more who pushed up against the wooden frame to block the onslaught of Shattering Daggers outside, who had been positioned in wait for Zane's move. Arvin escaped the headlock in one swift motion, kicking Zane square in the stomach. Two more 2-7s lept at Zane, muffling his screams with their toppling body mass.

The girl looked torn for a moment, evaluating whether she should help her fellow building mate or make for the key. A blur of agile movement careening in her direction made the decision for her. It was Irabella; two satchels swung over her shoulders.

The girl dodged the attack, rolling onto her side. She groped for Irabella's bags, her fingers catching on the strap of one of the satchels.

I sprung into action, grabbing the girl's arms and swinging them behind her back, kicking her knees in both at once. She struggled against my grip, but her kicks came in vain. The girl was pinned. I shoved her head down to the floor for good measure, leaving her nose-to-nose with the dirt.

"Alright, Rayz," she fumed, craning her neck to look me in the eye. "You've won. Again. Just don't make it bloody. Please don't leave a stain."

I thrust her head up, escorting her to the door. "Wasn't that easy?" I swung the exit open, gesturing for the others to bring Zane, screaming a string of curses, up to his feet.

"To answer your question," I tried to keep the groan out of my voice as I recited the classic spiel to conclude my grand performance, "I won't waste your blood on such a needless cause. Just as long as you remember your place."

I promptly shoved Zane and the girl out of building 2-7 before either of them could spit out a retort.

"Yeah!" Irabella cried, applauding my performance. "We rule this Isle!"

The others joined her in a chant while I slipped off to my bunk, reclaiming my satchel. I sighed, fingering the items inside. Every day was the same in the Level Two sector. Fight. Defend. Repeat. And so little of it was actual fighting, either. If these people really wanted to go to war, they would be rallying up against the guards, battling for their lives. Not for a stupid metal key.

Said key, a tiny bronze item carved intricately in a swirling pattern, brushed against the two other things sharing its living space in my satchel. My meal card and the silver chain bracelet I had slipped onto the Isle each made a distinct sound as they tapped against it. Those two items had no value to anyone but me, but the key, by contrast, had value to everyone.

That was how it had worked when I arrived, and that was the game I continued. However much I complained about it, that was how things were, and that was how things would remain.

The key itself belonged to a former mess-hall type area tucked next to the shore. The interior wasn't all that attractive- bare tables, white-painted walls. But it had luxuries that couldn't be found anywhere else on the Isle. Decent electricity, bathrooms that didn't smell like piled-up shit, and, more importantly, the tools left in the kitchens. All the knives had been removed for obvious reasons, but some severe damage could be done with a fork and a rolling pin.

And, of course, there was the prestige. Really, that was all anyone cared about. The Family that gained control over the hall was known by the title of Head Chefs. Even if you lost the key to a rival Family down the road, your name would forever be emblazoned into a golden hall-of-fame. In theory, you were supposed to be looked upon with reverence, but the rival Families had interesting ways of showing it. Lots of them knew better than to cross me, but a lot of them had made it their goal to knock me down a peg and ridicule the Family I represented in whatever way possible.

I should have been satisfied with my position. After all, there were many people, not just on the Isle but in my very building, who would've killed to be in my shoes. But I couldn't ignore the purpose our elaborate games truly served.

The guards let us run rampant because, for the most part, things never escalated past bumps, bruises, and hard language. It helped them root out which rebels they would tag as Level Threes- who would be taken and never seen again- and it gave us something to do. Because with the impossibility of escape and the tightness of security, a revolution was never going to happen.

It wasn't building 2-7 that ruled the Isle of Rebels. It was Sykona, and it always would be.

***

Soon after, we headed to the mess hall, our fortress, to celebrate the week. Not only had we bested both the Shattering Daggers and the Bloodsoakers, two of the most egocentric, over-the-top Families around, but that day also marked the two-month-long anniversary of my possession of the bronze key.

We walked down the desolate block of the Level Two sector in a large cluster. Irabella and I held up the front, with Arvin and the other, more vulnerable group members stationed around the middle. Logically, it would have made more sense to put me in the centre of the formation- I had the key with me, after all. But I was the figurehead of building 2-7, which automatically put me first.

Everyone we passed recognised us immediately, scampering behind the uniform rows of buildings to make way for our procession. I could hear Irabella laugh every time someone darted out of the way, but I kept my eyes to the ground.

"You look deep in thought," Irabella said, snapping me out of my withdrawn focus. As we arrived at the mess hall, I didn't respond, pulling my satchel open and sliding the key into the door. The building was squat, and its white walls were mostly mud-encrusted, but it was a palace compared to the cabins.

I held the door open for the others, a gesture that gave me a disapproving frown from Irabella. Once everyone had rushed inside, I bolted the lock behind me, tucking the key back to safety.

There were a couple of plastic folding tables in the centre of the mess hall, each surrounded by a good number of chairs. I took a seat at one of them, and Irabella joined me, heaving a sigh. My thoughts threatened to plunge into the morbid realities of the system once again, but Irabella waved a hand in front of my face, the whoosh of air grounding me to the present.

The air conditioning, yet another perk of the mess hall, whirred from the fan above. The room itself wasn't much to look at. It consisted of a barren counter, a window to the mostly-empty kitchen, and smooth wooden floors.

I swatted Irabella's arm away, placing my hands on the plastic table. Its surface was covered in grooves and nooks, burns and dents. I traced the lines with my fingernails, not missing Irabella's eye roll.

"You have no right to be acting so depressed," she said. "It's all thanks to you that we're the new head chefs. Enjoy it!"

I nodded, but the bitterness of the gesture didn't slip Irabella's notice. She pouted, and I put on a tight grin. Irabella scoffed at the awkward excuse for a reaction.

"The whole team helped," I said, reinforcing my facial expression, "without you, Arvin, or any of the others, we wouldn't have stood a chance against the adversaries we've faced."

Irabella beamed with pride, and my false grin gradually seeped into a real one. Irabella had been the first friend I made when I arrived on the island, and at this point, I knew exactly how to tell her what she wanted to hear. Still, there was always a great measure of satisfaction that came with saying the right thing.

"Come on, Cerina. You have to celebrate with us!" Irabella tugged at my hand, pulling me to my feet.

Giving in, I allowed myself to get out of my seat. A few Isle-related questions were on my mind, but I pushed them down my throat, following Irabella across the room where the rest of the building was gathered, feasting on meal rations like a grand buffet.

My building mates quieted as I went to join them. The only one who continued to speak was Arvin, engaged in a lively story about either a contagion or a dead bird, possibly both.

"Cerina!" Arvin shouted, cutting his tale short to introduce my arrival. "Come to join us?"

Irabella nodded, giving me a slight shove in Arvin's direction. "I'll get the drinks."

Of course, the only thing to drink around here was water, but in glass cups, we might as well have been sipping fine wine. Shut off from the world with the members of building 2-7, we could fantasise to our hearts' desires at no cost to the Family. We could be in a mansion. We could rule the world.

Irabella passed out a set of water cups. Some people downed them immediately, nearly choking on the stream of liquid. A few others retained enough courtesy to wait, listening attentively as Irabella made her classic toast.

"To Cerina Rayz!" She cried, "the keeper of the key!"

"Cerina Rayz," a few people mumbled, "keeper of the key."

The water tasted bitter on my tongue, but I savoured the taste. If we could rule the world, we could rule the Isle.

So what if it was an illusion? The way things were was the way things were. We could choose what to make of our reality, and here, if only for a second, I decided to enjoy it.

Things wouldn't change tomorrow, but today didn't have to be a stain.

"Cerina Rayz," I muttered against the glass, "keeper of the bronze fucking key."

Lizabeth Merrin

The bigger picture

There were three styles of climbing that the local gym used to offer. And I say 'used to' because, while the establishment continued to operate, I was long gone from the neighbourhood and its climbing wall, so to me, it was a thing of the past. But back when I was a frequent visitor, I had gotten to know the place quite well. The options it offered consisted of top-rope climbing, lead climbing, and bouldering.

I loved the top rope course. Some of my friends thought it was too easy. It might have been on a high wall with tricky twists and turns, but the thing about top-rope climbing is that you're attached to a rope and a harness. And sure, there's some measure of preparation you have to do on your part, but mostly, it's your belayer, the person manning the rope below you, that you can count on. If you fall, it's okay because the rope will catch you. Every time. When it came to top-rope climbing, you could always count on someone else to keep you safe.

But the other two were different. Bouldering was its own struggle. It took place on a low wall, but there was no rope, nothing to stop you if your fingers slipped or your weight shifted the wrong way. And while there was a mat below you, if you landed incorrectly, you were done for. Bouldering had never been my cup of tea. I could force myself to do it, sure, but it took courage.

I could never lead climb. Doing so required a lot of skill- skill I possessed but was never brave enough to put into effect. You still had a belayer, but a lot of the climb was on you. You had to clip your rope into the hooks on the wall. You had to lay out the steps to your path, and when you fell, you dropped. If you screwed up, then, well, you screwed up, and it was all over.

If you fell, it was your fault.

And, thanks to my negligence, my forgetfulness to secure myself into a good place in life, I had fallen hard.

Standing in the predatory gaze of every member of building 1-3, I gulped down a wash of bile and tried to refrain, to absolutely no avail, from getting flustered.

"Hi," I squeaked, feeling the room grow hotter. I looked to my side, at the boy I had caught on the deck. The only difference between our two expressions was that he had maintained the sense to keep his lips sealed.

"We're, uh, Lizabeth and Em-"

Emry nudged me on the shoulder.

"You already said that," he rasped, his voice a jagged claw inside my ear.

"Right. Let's find our bunks."

Emry kept his distance from me, training his eyes on the ground as we made our way to the end of the room. I turned away from the rows of people, but keeping my head down didn't help. Hearing nothing but their breathing and the heavy, rhythmic pounding of their heartbeats was almost worse than watching their eyes.

Emry slid into the bottom bunk before we could hold a debate on who was supposed to go where. I swung up the ladder, testing the rungs. My new living space was small and cramped, with a wooden divider separating my bunk from the one next to me.

I turned to my bunkmate, spotting their meal card propped against the barricade. *Hannah Megany*.

"Hey," I ventured, "I'm-"

"Lizabeth," the person cut me off. "You've mentioned." My new neighbour had an overgrown pixie cut that spilled over their forehead, the dark-blond

39

strands reaching almost to their eyelashes. A black streak ran through their hair, starting from the top left and stretching to the bottom.

"Hannah?" I guessed, gesturing to their meal card. Hannah frowned, snatching up the card and folding it in half. I caught a glimpse of a small section on the side. Previously, the word female had been shaded in by a soft pink, but now, the entire square was furiously scribbled out by a black sharpie.

"That's not my name anymore. Call me Haven." They folded up the meal card, sticking it in their pocket. I held out a hand, shaking Haven's outstretched palm.

"Pleased to make your acquaintance, Haven Megany."

"Likewise." Apparently satisfied with my introduction, Haven swung down from the bunk, their loose work boots connecting with the ground with a loud smash. The laces trailed behind them as they crossed the floor, hopping up to a bunk on the other end of the room. One of their friends, a brown-haired boy with a similar streak, reached out a hand to help Haven up.

"Come on, weirdos!" Haven shouted, a scoff in their tone. "Give the newbies some privacy!"

I turned away, 'getting myself sorted' as Joe had instructed.

Once again, I tried not to stare as the members of building 1-3 began to leave, but I could hear their feet hitting the ground and feel their presence slip from the room. Everyone lost complete interest in us except for Haven and two other inmates standing in the corner together, talking in hushed tones.

There were two reasons I disliked the top bunk. Primarily, I hated heights. Anything that required a railing on the side of it made me uneasy. Not only that, but top bunks usually had windows. I couldn't sleep in anything other than pitch-darkness, which meant that while others would jump at the chance to get a shaft of moonlight, I hid away from it like a nocturnal owl.

I felt the mattress, running a hand over the rock-hard fibres. The sleeping conditions said a lot about a place. A fancy home with a bed as stiff as bare bones might not be as inviting as it appeared. Likewise, a prison island with soft, comfortable bunks might have had a sweeter spot, a sunny kind of hidden depth.

Unfortunately, this was not that kind of prison island. The mat might as well have been made of metal. The fibres were rock-hard and lumpy, much denser in some places than it was in others.

The bunk rattled below me, and Emry stepped out, glaring daggers at the remaining prisoners.

"Yeesh. Could you guys maybe stop staring at us? It's creepy."

As if on cue, Joe re-entered the cabin, a subtle announcement that settling-in time was over. Emry sighed. I slid down from my bunk, joining him on the floor. He gave me an odd look, and I stepped back, wishing I had stayed put. Clearly, he didn't want my pity.

Then again, it wasn't like he could stop being pitiful. Don't get me wrong, I was in the same situation. In fact, it was solidarity I was looking for with him. But clearly, he had already slid into the ideology that prisons weren't ideal breeding grounds for friendships.

"Have you guys gotten sorted?" Joe asked, looking around. Emry's bed was untouched. Clearly, he had only tested his mattress with a quick glance. Not the most thorough approach, but I couldn't blame him. Sitting on a big pile of rocks wasn't a hot item on my to-do list either.

"Well enough," I answered for the both of us. Emry nodded, though his eyes indicated otherwise.

"Fantastic," said Joe. "Do you want me to give you a tour of the sector?"

I started to nod, but Emry cut me off.

"No. We'll look around ourselves."

Joe's face fell, a bit surprised. Clearly, his offer wasn't usually declined. He shrugged, making his way back out the door.

"Well, then," he called, his voice trailing off, "I'll leave you to it."

Briefly, I paid a glance at the trio whispering in the corner of the room. Finally, their gazes were otherwise diverted as they talked amongst themselves, gossiping as though the two of us had disappeared.

Something about how they talked so easily made my eyebrows furrow. Being put in the spotlight was uncomfortable, but being outright ignored was worse. It made it feel as though we had disappointed their expectations.

I caught Haven's eye from the centre of the room. Their irises glimmered a unique shade of dark blue, like the deep sea rather than the salty, turquoise beaches.

I glanced at Emry. "Why did you decline Joe's offer?"

"Isn't it obvious?"

I didn't respond immediately. "You don't trust him," I said after a long beat, the pieces taking a second to click into place.

Shame crept into my cheeks. I had always be͏͏ gullible.

So far, my mission to earn respect and meet new people was not going well.

"They don't just assign you a welcome committee when you land in jail. This guy is clearly a snitch. Or a serial killer."

I bit my lip. "Maybe. But what's the worst that could've happened? I wouldn't want to be stumbling around here aimlessly. A little bit of guidance would've helped."

A cough sounded from the other end of the room. I turned, facing the group. They had quieted down, and we were, once again, engaged in a tense staring contest.

Haven stepped forward.

"The redhead has a point," they said, gesturing to Emry. "But you should start exploring. It won't be long before this scene fades into monotony, just as all things do. Might as well enjoy it while it's new, right? The only time things get interesting in this place is when we run our yearly talent show."

The friends on Haven's left and right were both a little shorter, with matching hair streaks. On the left was the brown-haired boy, his arms crossed and his eyebrows fixed into a permanent scowl. The girl on the right, however, looked much more jovial. Her heart-shaped face was dusted with tiny freckles that stood out against her honey-brown skin tone, and long auburn hair hung past her shoulders.

"So... you do talk," Emry stated, standing up a little straighter.

"Indeed I do. A little too much, one could say."

I tugged on Emry's sleeve. "Come on," I said, "We should check out the Isle."

He followed me, albeit hesitantly.

"Who are you?" he called behind him, inching towards the door but facing away from it. "Or are you going to keep that a secret?"

"Names are nothing to hide. Mine's Haven. Behind me are Max and Adrienne. I think we might've gotten off on the wrong foot." Haven held out a hand, but Emry didn't take it. "Come on," Haven said, "we're not going to shake hands like civilised people?"

I'd had enough of this. I was a patient person, but I didn't like where this was going. I pulled on the door, propping it open with my foot.

"Emry. Are we going to check out the Isle or not?"

He muttered, following me out.

***

"Those guys were weird as hell," Emry commented once we were out of earshot. I suspected Emry didn't care whether or not they heard us, but I was grateful we had left them behind.

"Do you think the centre circle is nearby?" I asked, "I want to see how the meal system works."

We paused outside of building 1-3, evaluating our next options. There were two rows of buildings in front of us, each one connected by a stone path. They all curved in the shape of a semicircle, starting from the beach and spanning beyond my line of sight.

Emry shrugged, "I'm going to find a washroom."

I started to follow him, but he shoved me off, speeding up.

"I don't need you here. Go look for the inner circle or whatever."

I didn't stop. "I think it's best if we stick together," I offered, "wouldn't you say?"

Emry stopped, whirling on me.

"I've had a pretty bad day, okay? I get that you're trying to be nice, but we are not friends. Got it?"

I sighed.

"Emry-" he stalked off in a random direction, veering to the left before I could follow. I gnawed on the inside of my cheek. There was no sense in being mad at him, and there was no reason to feel bad for myself. After all, I certainly didn't deserve pity. Maybe Emry had a sixth sense. Maybe he could tell, just from our first encounter, that if he was going to get close to me, he was going to get hurt.

Still standing, dejected, on the steps to building 1-3, my mind drifted to Melanie. Mel for short. She was my girlfriend, but she had also been much more. I didn't know where we stood now, separated by miles of sea.

I grit my teeth, walking to clear my head. The island was shaped like a circle, and I was on its fringes. The centre should have been dead ahead.

Each time I passed another person, I shuddered in my oversized uniform. The legs of my pants dragged behind me like two stubby tails, trekking dirt into the ankles. I'd have to use the uniform-washing station before my first day on the island had even come to a close.

I scanned every face I walked by with a careful intensity. Most people were in packs, either working out, conversing amongst themselves, or simply watching the world in silence.

There were two people I was looking for but hoped to never find.

I hurried down the block, my short hiking shoes clattering against the blocky pavement. Each row of buildings was identical- a basic set of wooden structures bare of decoration or frivolity. They increased in number the further down I went.

Building 1-19. Building 1-20.

How many prisoners did they keep here, free to roam as they pleased?

Once I had passed the final row of grey tiles and brown panels, the buildings abruptly stopped. The tiles faded into a new scene, disappearing underfoot.

In front of me, on the last aisle of the street, was a gaping field. It spanned the length of the entire block of buildings, the shrivelled expanse of grass spreading far in the distance. A silver speck dotted the centre of it, and I squinted to better make it out.

The glimmering structure resembled a fortress. A single, circular wall stood firm and proud in the middle of the grassy plain, the details of which I couldn't quite decipher from so far away.

Undoubtedly, this was the centre circle. I looked from my current position to the structure, gaging the distance. Setting foot on the scraggly layer of grass, I began the jaunt, keeping my pace at a steady jog.

More people were gathered here, their heads speckling the plain. I sped up, feeling distinctly out of place.

Panting, I skidded up to the walls, surveying them with a timid eye. The iron blend encircling whatever lay inside was thick, topped with a menacing tangle of barbed wire. As I approached, I caught sight of the gate cut into the wall, firmly closed and only faintly visible. There were two guards posted outside of it. At the sight of them, my blood froze.

The two of them lounged on either side of the gate, staring at the sky with their eyes glazed over. My muscles relaxed as I registered their boredom. Their uniform looked like that of the cops, with a few slight differences to distinguish them from average officers. Their cuffed sleeves were tipped with the same grey colour of the barricade, and a small strip sewn onto their wrists indicated their rank, which was either very high or very low.

One of them blinked lazily in my direction. The panic seeped back into my bloodstream. The guards might have been exhausted, but they still carried rifles.

And I had no doubt in my mind that they wouldn't use them.

"Stations are over there," he slurred, waving to his left. He sounded drunk, half-awake. But that didn't make his gun any less dangerous.

I bobbed my head up and down, scurrying off to the leftmost side of the wall. In the middle of the field, beginning at the centre of the curve, was a short fence that split up the Isle into two semicircles. Sticking out of the top of those fence posts were huge, unmistakable signs that sent goosebumps crawling up my arms.

Against a reflective orange backdrop, a single number was stamped on the sign.

2

The fence came up to my hip. The bars were somewhat spiked, but that was hardly a deterrent. I could easily leap between the gap, and even someone with larger hips would undoubtedly be able to shimmy through without much difficulty.

You must only associate with those at your level.

They might as well have been asking people to cross that fence, begging them to break the rules. It was so easy that I would have laughed if it didn't place me in immediate danger.

What kind of prison was this? It seemed we were all filed by our last names, but any organisation ended there. Based on my rudimentary knowledge of jail, I had at least assumed that the guys and girls would have been separated. I had *definitely* assumed the Ones and Twos would be separated.

The meal station consisted of a small slit in the metal wall with a scanner attached. Below it was the uniform washing station, a large box with a similar scanner on the lid. Technically, the setup was located on the Level One side, but it teetered dangerously close to the fence.

I knew someone who would be glad to crack a puzzle like this and take on the challenge of decoding an entire system.

But, of course, thanks to a bridge I had foolishly engulfed in flames, that person now hated my guts.

I was still staring past the fence, down the stretch of field that looked identical to ours, when I realised I had stopped trembling.

With a huff, I flipped back to the food station. I had never been one of those stone-cold 'hide your emotions' type-people, but, at least for now, I had to do my best to conceal my fear.

Once again, against my will, I thought of Mel. I had given up my social life, the network I depended on, all for her. The least I could do was stand and survive. Pep talks didn't usually work to motivate me, but this raw feeling was a source of inspiration I couldn't put into words.

I would serve my sentence on the island, and I would pay for what I had done without objection and without protest.

With no further encouragement needed, I went to fish out my laminated barcode from where I had tucked it inside my stiff, waterproof shoe.

I rubbed my heel against the back of my hiking boot, searching for the reassuring stab of the plastic card. None came. I frowned, pulling my foot out. The bare sole was the only thing to greet me.

"Looking for this?"

I whirled around, and even though I was in a wide-open field, all the air disappeared from the area. My breath tangled my vocal cords, knotting up in the back of my throat. The words triggered my gag reflex, and I gave a pathetic little cough as I scanned the figure in front of me. Not that I needed my eyes to recognise the person in my path. I would recognise that voice anywhere.

Although waves of panic, shame, and guilt were doing somersaults in my gut, I couldn't help but feel the tiniest shard of relief.

The person in front of me went by the name of Jakson Veer. His parents were highly ambitious business people who appreciated two things in life- productivity and efficiency. Due to this, they had cut out the 'c' in his name to make it sound crisper, more to-the-point. No sense in having a pointless consonant elongating his name but adding nothing to the pronunciation.

I knew that detail because we had been best friends for eleven years.

But looking into his eyes now, it seemed as though I were staring down a total stranger.

Amid the swell of sympathy and meaningless apologies, I found the courage to hold my tongue, standing my ground.

Jakson was, from a technical perspective, the lesser of two evils. But when I saw the pain in his gaze, all logic vanished away. Sure, he certainly had the brains not to beat me up here and now with guards in the immediate vicinity, but the two of us had a history. A history that I had ruined.

"Jakson," I warbled, my voice up a few notes too high. He looked eerily collected, but then again, he always did. With his analytical blue irises that were many shades lighter than mine, something about his complexion always made him look one step ahead of everyone else. Even after transportation to the island, his blond hair was smooth, shiny, and put together. In third grade, he had gone through a hair gel phase, but that had ended abruptly after he'd realised the gel made him smell like hand sanitizer. In high school, he had hit a growth spurt, which was around the time he became recognised as 'the hot math guy.' He had grabbed the attention of almost every male-attracted person roaming the halls, but none of the relationships he got himself into ever truly lasted.

At least those kinds of break-ups could be cured with a mountain of ice cream and the right friends. The ones that cut a bond forged since kindergarten and landed you on the Isle of Rebels went a little deeper.

"Lizabeth," Jakson said, his voice as cold as ice. "You dropped this on the field." My laminated card was pressed between his thumb and index finger, hanging loosely between those two pressure points.

My brain commanded my feet to step forward, urging my hand to snatch up the piece of plastic. But all I could bring myself to do was stay put, completely frozen in place.

After a painful three seconds, my senses finally returned to me, and I took the card from his hand, flinching when our fingers brushed. I dug the sharp edge into my palm, unsure of what else to say. Jakson didn't move, staring at the ground.

"Why did you do it, Lizabeth?" he asked, his tone low and fragile.

"You know why," I mustered.

"No," he said. "I don't."

"I had to."

Jakson looked to the ground. "I understand that part. What I don't get is why you saved your girlfriend from the heat of it but didn't spare a second thought to my future. To Darby's future. To your *own* future."

"I didn't know what would happen."

"No. You didn't." The words possessed a sharp bite, and an expression of hurt flashed over my face. Jakson turned away, shuffling his feet in the opposite direction. "Darby and I are both in building 1-10. Learn what's good for you and stay away."

Tears stung at the backs of my eyes.

"Wait!" I called, but Jakson didn't stop. "You have to understand. You were my best friend, Jakson! I'm fucking sorry."

"'Sorry' won't get me back into school."

It took everything in me not to come on the defensive. Every brain cell was screaming at me to call him out on his condescending tone and remind him that I was no idiot. But he was hurting too, and he would get over it, as would I. I might have dug all of us into a low spot, but someone had to be the bigger person.

50

Jakson's form faded farther and farther away. A part of me half-hoped he would look back, apology in his eyes. Not wanting to risk the disappointment of seeing him disappear back into the row of buildings, I glanced down at my plastic card. The edges I had dug under my skin had forced my fingers to blanch.

Making a fist, I stalked over to the food station's scanner and swiped the card in a downward-pointed fury.

"I really am sorry," I whispered.

If only someone could hear those words and understand how truly I meant them.

Emry McLeod

An obscured lens

I wiped my dripping hands on my sweatpants, shaking my palms back and forth. Droplets of water scattered midair, dotting the tiles underfoot with dark-grey splotches. The water I had washed my hands with had been tepid at best, but it had provided plenty of relief in the searing heat and dry summer air.

After a long sprint around the entire Level One sector, I had finally located a washroom. Sandwiched between building 1-5 and building 1-6 was a small shack that matched in colour to the surrounding sleeping quarters. Based on its rustic look, I hadn't had high hopes for what I'd find inside. If the sleeping quarters resembled cabins, the ramshackle shed resembled a summer camp's outhouse.

Honestly, it wasn't that bad. There were two stalls and one long lineup. Apart from the wait, there was only one con in a sea of pros. The privacy factor.

The creaky doors hung on rusted hinges, squeaking in greeting every time someone had finished up. They shut well enough, but they didn't lock. I wasn't a fan of non-locking bathroom stalls at the best of times, but on a prison island, the whole idea seemed out of the question. This island was either invented by a psychopath or a moron. At every turn, it seemed there was a perfect setup for someone to be hurt at their most vulnerable.

Whether it was intentional or accidental was up for debate.

A dingy shower was fastened to the wall behind the bathroom, releasing a steady stream of wasted water through a valve that never fully closed. It collected into a murky pool at the structure's base, the breeze sending ripples over its glossy surface.

Evidently, no one used it to clean themselves due to its inconvenient placement. I turned my nose up at the unhygienic state of things, but I soon came to realise that it wasn't all bad. The bathroom package didn't include the luxury of sinks, but the disused shower stall provided a solution to that problem.

I had cranked the water as cold as it could go, then rinsed off my hands, feeling quite satisfied with myself. The line behind me continued to move forward, and the thought of an organised system keeping things under control put me at ease.

We might have been prisoners, but we were still civilised.

I froze, puzzling over my last thought. I had used *we* in reference to the Level Ones. Not *them*. *We*.

Using the walk back to my sleeping quarters to ease my mind, I convinced myself that uniting myself with the others was a mistake I wouldn't make again, even in the furthest reaches of my mind. I was Emry, and I was getting out of here. I had to set myself apart from every prisoner, even Lizabeth, or else I would become one of them.

Lizabeth.

Guilt settled in my stomach as I recalled my last words to her, replaying the angry outburst. She had told me she was going to the centre circle. I had to find her and apologise. We might have been two very different people who were brought here for very different reasons, but I had screwed up.

"Lizabeth!" I called, jogging ahead. "Are you still here?"

I blew by the steps to building 1-3, ducking around the corner. "Lizabeth? Where-"

A warm hand set itself on my shoulder. The texture of the palm wasn't what I had expected, but in this weather, in these uniforms, everyone was dripping with sweat. "Lizabeth, I-"

"How do you know that name?"

I froze. This voice was deep and gravelly, a sharp contrast to Lizabeth's smooth, measured pitch. Could it have been creepy Joe? Creepy Haven?

Slowly, I turned around, peeling the hand off of my shoulder. The figure behind me was *definitely* not Lizabeth.

The first thing that stuck out to me about the guy was his blue-tipped hair, the coloured ends shining like a beacon in the sunlight. He was about my height, but his build was much stockier, both of his broad shoulders quashing any thought of escape. His narrowed eyes were a swampy green, and rage radiated off him from every angle. If his pure, seething fury could burn any hotter, it would be strong enough to boil a kettle.

"Well?" He repeated, clenching his hands into tight fists. "*How* do you *know* that *name*?"

"What name?" I squeaked, feeling my knees start to tremble. To be quite frank, I was disappointed with my fear reaction. For some people, adrenaline turned them into overpowered maniacs, the fight-or-flight instinct giving them superhuman abilities. But unfortunately, the same thing had not occurred in my case. My reaction had two parts- the first; going slack still. And the second? Blurting out the most random shit I could think of.

I racked my brain for everything I knew about self-defence. I could punch him in the nose, scratch his face up a bit. If my grimy fingernails really hit home, maybe I could actually do some damage. Enough to cause a bit of surprise. Building 1-3 was close behind him, and he was a giant wall preventing my access to it. If I struck that wall, maybe I could slip away before he could retaliate.

Blue-haired guy caught my hand just as it was flying up. He clutched my wrist in a death grip, and my face settled into a wince as I felt the bones gnashing against each other, crumbling in the tight vise.

"Wrong move, kid," the guy snarled, "wrong move."

My arm exploded with pain, but my panicked rush hadn't come full circle yet. I still had quite a lot of humiliation left to go.

"My name isn't 'kid'!" I spat. What had seemed like a fully coherent thought got horribly distorted on the way to my throat, mangled up into an idiotic exclamation that I voiced with a hideous amount of false bravado. "I'm fourteen!" I cried, not helping my case any further. "My name is-"

"I don't give a crap about what your *name* is. How do you know Lizabeth Merrin?"

"Lizabeth? Doesn't ring a bell."

"Don't play dumb. I heard you call her name. Now tell me where she is, or I will *make* you." All of a sudden, I felt something being lifted off of the bridge of my nose. My other hand flapped madly while the blue-haired boy wrenched my glasses from my face, fingering them with his free hand.

It was as though a vast veil had descended over the world. Dizziness struck me like a blow to the gut, and I staggered backwards, my eyes adjusting to this new lens. The blue-haired guy sneered.

"Will you be more willing to listen to me if I dull your other senses? Will you finally hear me if you can't see?"

Technically, his statement wasn't quite correct. I was nearsighted, which meant that I only had problems when it came to things in the distance. In other words, I could behold the dreadful sight before me on high-resolution TV, but with my arm still hopelessly pinned and my depth perception struggling to get a hold of itself, the only thing I could do in response was sit back, chew my popcorn, and watch the show.

With one fell swoop, blue-haired guy flung the glasses to the ground and flattened them into a million tiny pieces, grinding them into the stone tiles. They made a sickening crunch as they split in two, the snap of the glass and metal grinding into the cement reverberating through my ears.

"Stop!" I cried, though it was no use. My glasses, now reduced to blurry scraps of useless wire, were beyond repair. My shoulders slumped in defeat. There was one last defence left at my disposal, and I really, *really* didn't want to use it.

"Now. Where-"

I kicked the guy between the legs before he could continue, ripped my limp hand from his grasp, and ran like the devil itself was on my tail.

My wrists nearly shattered as they careened against the door to building 1-3. I ripped the thing open, not daring to look back at my giant pursuer. Once inside, I slammed it shut, pressing my back against it. The wood dug into my spine, but the nagging pain was a small price to pay. I braced for impact, jamming all my weight on the wooden board. My eyelids scrunched, ready for the worst.

Five seconds ticked by.

Ten.

Twenty.

Slowly, I peeked through my eyelashes. Nothing had happened.

It was a freaking miracle.

Three shapes, craning their necks like giraffes, were staring at me intently.

"Outside wasn't your jam?" the girl with the brown hair guessed as I slowly opened my eyes. I grasped for her name. Addy… Ariana…

"Come on, Adrienne," said Haven, answering my question, "outside isn't *anyone's* jam." They paused for a second, looking at my panicked expression. "What happened to you? Didn't you used to have glasses?"

I scowled, crossing my arms over the door. I had three new least favourite people. "Why should I tell *you* anything?"

Haven shrugged. "You don't have to. But the three of us all know what it's like to come in here, fresh off the streets, unfamiliar with this world. We can help you."

"I don't want your help."

Haven was spewing bullshit. The three of them were nothing like me. They never had been.

"Okay, then. Step away from that door."

I placed my foot below the crack, keeping it shut, and slowly pulled my hands off.

My fingers had only drawn back a few inches when I immediately planted them back in place. What did I think I was doing? If I were to let go, blue-hair guy would bust in, and we'd all get beaten to bloody pulps. Haven thought that by being weird and confusing they were being smart, but, really, I was doing them a favour.

"Can't do it, can you?" Haven said, tapping their foot with impatience. Max stepped to the wall with the pump and the coat hook, producing a doorstop from behind the bucket. Wordlessly, he placed it beside my foot.

"You might not want our help," Max said, "but you're going to need it."

I stepped away from the door, eyeing the trio carefully. The cabin's features started to blur past the bucket, which meant that their attentive, calculating facial expressions were crystal clear.

"If your guidance is so important, why are you offering it freely? You guys are too…." I struggled to find the word to describe them. 'Weird' and 'creepy' were too broad of terms. 'Lurk-y' would be a more suitable adjective. "Distant," I settled with. It wasn't the word I had been looking for, but it fit the bill. "You guys don't strike me as nice people. I mean…"

"We're in prison uniforms?" Adrienne said. "Way to stereotype."

"I wasn't-"

Haven cleared their throat. "Come up to my bunk. I don't think we've quite gone through the proper introductions. When Lizabeth gets back, she can join us."

Hesitantly, I followed Haven as they crept up the ladder closest to the wall, settling on the bunk tucked tightly in the corner. Max and Adrienne fit on the padded mat well enough, but if three was a crowd, then four was a freaking mob. And there was no room for 'freaking mobs' on a tiny bunk bed. I shuffled clumsily up the next ladder, eyeing the door. The doorstop was firmly fixed into place, but there seemed not to be any strain against it.

Blue-haired guy seemed to have given up. Or… he had paused to strategize.

What had I been thinking? This guy was looking for Lizabeth, and I had led him straight to her.

"Are you coming?" Haven asked with impatience.

"Yeah," I gulped, scurrying up to the top. I sat on the bunk beside Haven's, keeping a safe distance from the trio.

With the bars between us, the setup looked more like an interrogation than a casual chitchat, which put me even more on edge than I already was. I felt off-balance, unsteady, and not just because of my missing glasses.

"So, Emry," Haven said, "what do you like to do?"

The question wasn't at all what I had expected. I had been anticipating them to pry for personal information and dig for some kind of leverage. But this seemed… unnaturally casual.

"What do you mean?" I said, propping up onto my knees.

Adrienne looked at Haven, then back at me. "I don't know how much clearer sh- er, they can make it." She fumbled with her words, and Max visibly winced.

A long moment passed, the long silence stretching twice the length of my school's running track. Except, in this case, there was no finish line you could cross, only a boundary I was too afraid to break.

"Look," I exclaimed, throwing my hands in the air, "your question is dumb. Who cares what I like to do? I'm in prison. It's not like we can start up our careers behind bars."

"Need I remind you that said bars you mention are purely metaphorical? No matter the circumstance, we can never forget our passions." The words flowed off of Haven's tongue like a perfectly rehearsed script. I wondered how much of it they meant, how many of their words they truly believed in.

Our passions? I didn't have a passion unless you counted 'scraping by' as a leisure activity, which I certainly did not.

"My favourite subject at school is- well, was- science," I mustered weakly. Mostly because my teacher was prone to falling asleep in the middle of class, but I neglected to mention that little detail.

Haven nodded, though they didn't appear quite satisfied with my answer.

The situation's awkwardness seeped into every part of my skin, making my face flush red. I didn't even know why I was blushing. When it came to words, I drew blanks all the time.

"What do you guys like to do?" I had barely spoken above a whisper, but Haven heard me perfectly.

"We're artists," they answered. "I'm a poet, Max is a painter, and Adrienne is a performer."

"Did you just alliterate? I respect people with talents for words, but I swear, if you purposefully just *alliterated-*"

Haven laughed, a surprisingly high-pitched squeak, "there is hope for you yet, Emry. There is hope for you yet."

Just like that, the layer of tension blanketing the room was lifted off, a gust of refreshing air blowing specifically for us as we began talking, kicking off a real conversation.

It was only small talk, sure, but social niceties were good foundations. And, maybe, in spite of the situation… Haven, Adrienne, and Max were no longer my least favourite people. In fact, they had been bumped quite a few places up that list.

Eventually, our talk was interrupted by a swift rap on the door. For a second, I froze, anticipating blue-haired guy. But the familiar voice on the other end quelled the tide of anxiety.

"It's Lizabeth! Can someone let me in!"

Max hopped down, swinging the door open. I caught a brief glimpse of the outside world from the sliver of light. Behind Lizabeth's silhouette, the sun was begging to set.

She burst into the room before she could question what I was doing, launching herself at her bunk. Her eyes were swollen red, and tear streaks ran down her pale cheeks.

Without a word to us, she crossed the room and disappeared behind her tiny barricade, crumpling up on the bed sheets.

The thick cloud of suffocating silence filled up the room once more. I slunk down from the bunk, not wanting to meet anyone's gaze. I could feel the weight between each movement, each momentary bout of eye contact.

All it took was one presence to turn a tide. One cryptic teenager. One blue-haired prisoner. One crying girl.

What had I just walked into?

Emry McLeod

The only way out is in

I woke up the next morning exhausted and sore, with a grumbling stomach. When nine PM had come, I wasn't even close to tired, but the decision had been made for me. As promised, the power had cut at exactly 21:00, plunging us into a darkness that was smothering but peaceful all at the same time.

In the end, it was Lizabeth who woke me up.

"Emry?" She called, shaking my shoulder. "Don't tell me you've gone comatose after your first day."

I groaned, rolling my neck. It made a horrific cracking sound, the result of sleeping bunched up in an awkward little ball. How many hours was I out? Four, at most. I climbed out of bed, whacking my head on the board. I yelped, and everything came back to me. My outstretched hand stopped groping for my glasses as the memory of the sadistic blue-haired kid flooded back.

Clearly, Lizabeth, sporting a cheery morning grin, had gotten over whatever had happened to her the night before.

The lights were already on, and an annoying buzz sparked from the intercom. "What's with the whirring sound?" I asked, rubbing my eyes. My spare uniform was bunched up against the wall of my bunk. I took it out, spreading it over the firm mat and doing my best to pound out the wrinkles.

"How am I supposed to know?" Lizabeth countered. "I know as much about this place as you do. Probably even less."

'Because you're an actual criminal,' I almost said. Before I could flat-out burn a bridge that was only newly under construction, Joe came to my rescue.

"I've noticed you still haven't picked up your meal rations... um, what was it again? Eddy?"

"Emry," I glowered.

"My apologies! I can show you to the food station if you'd like."

I didn't 'like.'

"No," I refused, folding the uniform up into a neat pile, "Lizabeth went yesterday. She can show me."

Haven materialised behind Joe, flipping their meal card between their fingers. "Come on, Emry. Let Joe give you a tour. He's not going to strangle you in the middle of the street."

"Plus," Lizabeth added, "I still have my meal from yesterday. I don't need to go with you." Keeping my back to Lizabeth, I raised my eyebrows.

"If you're turning down extra food," I said, "I'll take it." I folded my spare uniform shirt again, flattening it into a tight square. Haven sighed, wrenching the fabric from my grasp.

I whirled on them, annoyance written on my scrunched-up forehead.

"Go with Joe," Haven demanded.

I shot Lizabeth a pleading look. She crossed her arms, making it clear that I wouldn't be getting any help from her. Defeatedly, I turned my focus to Joe, who was waiting patiently on Haven's right.

"Fine," I grumbled, "lead the way."

Joe clearly didn't appreciate my tone, but he said nothing of it as he took me past the cabin and out onto the street. Only then, in the fresh air, did I notice how much everything reeked. Evidently, the lack of available showers had taken its toll on the island, and a layer of stink, clouding the atmosphere like smog, lay thick over the Level One sector.

We passed several people who were already out and about on our way through the simplistic web of interlocking paths. As we moved further into the island, the gaps between the buildings felt like they were shrinking, pushing tighter and tighter. When we finally broke free, my stomach dropped. The wide field was like a blow to the gut, the discombobulating sense of open space messing with my head.

"Are you okay?" Joe said, picking up on my dizziness.

"Of course," I snapped.

"If you say so." Joe kept walking.

"Wait!" I shouted, holding my arms out to steady myself. "Do you think I could talk to the guards about getting new glasses?"

Joe raised his eyebrows as though I'd just asked him the dumbest question on planet earth.

"You could try, but they wouldn't give you a second thought, let alone a new lens prescription. You'll have to be more careful next time."

I was about to snap at him again, but I held my tongue. I couldn't identify our destination, and the thought of getting stranded in the middle of the broad plain made me queasy. Like it or not, I'd have to stay shut up and hope that I wouldn't get stabbed in the back.

I kept my distance from Joe, observing him for any sign of suspicion. He strutted along in the most typical fashion possible. His hands were out of his pockets, and his head was held high. Desperately, I wanted to blame him for all of this, but he was as normal as a person could get.

It was infuriating.

The sun had only freshly risen, and I was already sweltering under my uniform. As we approached the thick metal barricade, a sense of dread burrowed under my skin. I was afraid to ask what went down behind those walls.

A mechanical gate came into view, with a guard who eyed us suspiciously. A shudder coursed through

64

my body. My arm hairs sprung on end as I felt the guards watching my every step. The muddled image cleared as I got closer to the scanning stations, de-fuzzing as I half-hid behind Joe to get out of the guards' field of vision. My fingers fidgeted, and I peered over to the other half of the circle.

The Level Two sector. If it was so strictly off-limits, then why did it look so easy to hop to the other side?

"Scan your card here," Joe instructed, snapping me back to reality. A sheet of paper had been fastened to the wall, but the fine print was too tiny for me to read. I stepped around the uniform washing station, placing my card under the red beam of the scanner.

"What does the sign say?" The machine answered me with a quick ding, and I pulled back my card, fidgeting with the edges.

"It's a warning about the beach. It's mined, you know. Not only do you get blown to bits, but a big show is made of it, too. 'Big group tried to get out a few weeks ago. It didn't end well." The slot on the wall clanked open, and out slid a brown paper bag. I caught it with both hands, and the contents jiggled.

"When you're done with the bag, there's a trash can in the washroom," Joe explained, changing the topic before I could pry any further about the Isle's security measures. Ah, the washroom. I wasn't eager to return there, but my mouth was parched with thirst. I would have to face the dreaded stall once more, and with the threat of blue-haired guy, I began to consider that maybe having Joe with me wasn't such a bad idea after all.

I felt the soft handle of the bag, careful not to tear it. Many holes were punched into the flimsy pouch, a clear deterrent to anyone who thought smothering people with bags was a fun pastime.

My next goal was to figure out how to get on the guards' good side. The cop who had arrested me had been very vague about how I could my sentence, but I was sure I could find a way.

However, I didn't love the idea of going up to the guards at the gate and asking them how I could help out. Not with Joe here. Not with blue-haired guy on the loose.

If I were to become some sort of snitch, I wouldn't last a day.

"I just don't get it," I said to Joe, collecting the items into one hand. "Why are you being so nice to me?"

"You had many assumptions about this place, didn't you?"

There was no rhyme or reason to the idea of lying, so I nodded.

"I'm not saying the Isle of Rebels, sorry, the *Offshore Youth Rehabilitation Facility* is a great place to spend your time," Joe said. "But it all depends on mindset. If you hang out with the right people, you might just find that we aren't so bad."

I picked out one of the cans, unsticking the lid and examining the contents. Beans. I pulled a few out with my fingers, slipping them into my mouth. They were freezing cold, but they were tasty and filling in the summer heat. I had to fight the urge to immediately start feasting on the whole can.

"If you don't mind me asking," I said, "what are you here for?"

Joe sighed, swiping his card to collect his own meal. "I was sent here early on, many years ago. Now, I've devoted myself to helping this sector. Specifically when it comes to newbies."

My grandmother had told me once that if you stayed quiet in a conversation, it invited the other person to keep talking. I had never really had the patience to try out that tactic, but I was willing to wait a few seconds if it would satisfy my curiosity. I leaned against the wall, counting back from ten in my head as Joe picked up his food.

I had reached four when the man spoke again.

"If you really must know," he said, "I was framed."

This piqued my interest. "By whom? For what?"

"I was accused of burning down a classmate's garage. The target had a lot of enemies, and I was one of them. In terms of motive, the cops had enough. Despite the lack of proof, the second people started pointing fingers, it became apparent that somebody was getting sent here. I was just unlucky."

"I could hardly call getting put in prison 'bad luck.'"

"Oh? Then what happened in your case, Emry the shoplifter?"

I froze. My hand on the bag tightened, crunching the paper beneath it. "How do you know about that?"

"Lizabeth let it slip to Haven last night. Haven told Adrienne, and Adrienne told me. Gossip moves through the walls of building 1-3 the same way it moves through anywhere else. Don't worry, though. I won't tell anyone else if it embarrasses you."

"It's fine," I mumbled. "I don't really care anymore."

I wondered what was happening back at home. How my class would whisper about my empty desk, how they would react to the similar absences dotting the classroom. If they asked the teacher, what kind of answer would they get? A pinched smile, an awkward grimace? Few of them knew me enough to deserve the truth, but they'd figure it out sooner or later.

And what about my sister? What would she say when her friends came over and asked about her brother's whereabouts? Would my grandmother be hopeful, counting the days until I returned, or would she fall into despair? Or was I being ridiculous? The beans that had moments ago been so flavourful now felt sour in my mouth. How could I be away from my life for a whole entire year?

My presence touched so few people I wondered if it was best for everyone that I was shipped to the island. The best they could do was forget about my non-notable existence and go on with their crime-free lives.

"LEVEL 3 TRANSPORTATION. PLEASE CLEAR THE FIELD IMMEDIATELY."

I jumped, dropping the bag onto the ground. I fumbled to pick it up as the announcement blared over the loudspeaker jutting out a metre above my head.

"Come on, Emry! We have to go!" Joe tugged my hand, but the can of beans was still loose, rolling on the grass. A clanging sound echoed through the field as the gargantuan gate screeched open, letting loose a flood of guards.

"LEVEL 3 TRANSPORTATION. PLEASE CLEAR THE FIELD IMMEDIATELY."

Joe was grabbed from behind by a guard and yanked out of the way. A gunshot was fired, and I searched for the source. The guard at the gate was now pointing their rifle in the air, firing a warning shot. But to whom-

Two guards leapt over the dividing fence, kicking me in the back. I hugged the food to my chest and crumpled to the ground, struggling to get back up. On the Level Two side of the dividing line, three prisoner-shaped blobs were surrounded by four times the amount of guards. Each officer held a rifle, and each one was not afraid to use it.

"LEVEL 3 TRANSPORTATION. PLEASE CLEAR THE FIELD IMMEDIATELY."

One of the prisoners swung a fist at a guard, shattering the cartilage in their captor's nose. A second guard retaliated with the butt of their rifle, smacking the prisoner in the shins. The inmate screamed, their punches flying madly. The second prisoner delivered a powerful kick that incapacitated another officer. The third stood, motionless, watching the scene unfold.

"We need backup!" someone shouted, dashing right past me. The short sleeve of my uniform caught under a guard's knee-high boot as I jumped up, tearing the thin fabric. Midway to the gate, the guard stopped, grabbing me by the scruff of the neck as though I were a sick puppy.

"Get out of here, kid!" Spit flew from her mouth, and she shoved me back, knocking my skull against the metal. Stars swirled in my path, and I staggered forward. Black spots danced in my vision as the guards continued to pile around the prisoners, tugging them toward the fence.

"What's going on?" I called after the guard who had shouted at me, staggering after her. I hopped over the fence, barely paying it a second thought as I surged forward. "What are you doing?"

"LEVEL 3 TRANSPORTATION. PLEASE CLEAR THE FIELD IMMEDIATELY."

The guard glanced back, her eyes flitting to the loudspeaker. The announcement had explained everything to me. I doubled back, panting. The world spiralled, the ground swaying under my feet like an earthquake.

The next second, I was running. The cans of food dug into my ribs, but I didn't care. The lines in front of me blurred, and my head throbbed. I shut my eyelids, relying purely on sound. The noises of the fight drew farther and farther away as I kicked at the grass. Clutching the food bag with my other arm, I stuck out my hand as a guide.

The blare of the loudspeaker continued to sound far off in the distance. I paused, skidding to a complete halt. I risked a squint through my eyelashes, peering through the grey-clouded screen.

I was on the field's far edge, just a few feet from the bordering fence. Panting, I re-oriented myself, stumbling in the direction of the buildings.

"Joe-" I called hoarsely. "What happened-"

The stone tiles returned underfoot, and as I stepped, I felt one of them crack. I looked down, taking note of their disrepair. That was strange. I could've sworn the cobblestone pathways were in perfect condition, almost too neat. "Joe? Where'd you go?"

Somebody coughed, though I couldn't place the source. I wandered in further, holding the bag out protectively. "Joe? Anyone?" I picked up the pace.

"Lizabeth?" I tried, leaving the field behind me. I squashed the growing worry budding in my chest. There was no reason to freak out. I had been separated from the others. That was all. But still, a sensation of unease nagged in the corner of my mind.

Down the second row of buildings, I stopped short. A man who was far too old to be in the Offshore Youth Rehabilitation Facility was positioned against the side of one of the quarters, prodding at something on the ground with… a fork?

"Excuse me, sir?" I tried. "Have you seen Joe?" The man didn't look up, stabbing at the ground with his culinary utensil. "In his twenties, about this tall?" I held up an arm way above my head, hoping to provide some sort of indicator that didn't truly put my insignificant height to shame. I held my arm there for a good minute before the guy spoke up.

"There wouldn't be a Joe anywhere on this side of the island." The man's voice was strained and gurgly, and as he spoke, his knee moved aside to reveal his work. My breath hitched. On the ground was a dead bird, barely the size of a robin. In fact, it very well *may* have been a robin, but any possible identifiers had been masked by the stream of blood decorating the bird's body, pouring from a jagged wound in its chest.

In a separate pile lay a set of stringy lumps that I could only describe as 'bloody bird guts'.

My stomach churned, and acid rose to my throat. I covered my mouth. I was going to hurl. I stepped back, finally taking into account the number peeking out of his arm. He picked the fork back up with his thumb and forefinger, proceeding to smash the pile of bird organs to bits. On his wrinkled shoulder was a long scarred-over burn. *2.*

I stepped back, but I wasn't fast enough. I thudded into someone who had taken a stance behind me, and my arms were immediately pinned behind my back. I coughed, feeling the bulge of vomit clawing at my oesophagus. The shapes painted on the side of the building behind the old man blurred in and out of focus. *2-7*, I managed to read.

"Nice job, Zane." The voice behind me was distinctly female, high-pitched but bearing a raspy undertone. "Sending a spy from the Level Ones. I think you'll have to teach him the concept of sneaking next time."

"What is this!?" I shouted, writhing against her grasp. "I- I don't wanna fight! Please just let me go! I'm visually impaired!"

"Shut up, kid," the girl rasped. "What should we do about this one, Arvin? And *put that thing away*." The old man nodded immediately, stepping in front of the brutal scene.

"Take the little carrier pigeon to Cerina," the man spoke, his voice a squeaky, slurred rasp. "She'll know what to do. If not, I'm sure I can put him to good use. Both the birds are instruments. If we play them accordingly, we can fit them to our purposes. Even this one." He held up the fork, pointing it at my head.

"*Shut up, Arvin*," the girl snarled, tugging me along. The old man, Arvin, apparently, collected the bird remains, guts and all, making room for the girl to shove me up the blood-soaked steps. I thrust against the girl's powerful arms, to no avail.

"Next time," the girl rasped, her voice ringing in my ear. "Your small-brained boss better send someone a little more competent to do his dirty work."

Cerina Rayz

Pointless Questions

I had never loved surprises. A few of my building mates found that odd, considering the element of surprise was a tactic I used to my advantage all the time. When they asked about it, I would tell them all the same thing- that you didn't have to adore a skill to master it.

But truth be told, I had never held mastery over the shock of others. I was an amateur strategist, but I had a wealth of tools at my disposal. Including Arvin. The ultimate expert of spontaneity.

I was sitting on my bunk, waiting for the old man to finish locating a better hiding spot for the bronze key, when Irabella brought in the first surprise of the day.

"We've caught a spy," She announced proudly, holding the kid up by his stringy red-brown hair. The boy winced.

"I'm not a spy," he groaned. "I'm not even supposed to be on this island!"

Irabella laughed. "We'll see about that. Tell us, how are the shattering daggers paying you? Extra rations?" She smacked the food bag out of his arms, and two cans, one of them open, rolled to the floor. An expression of pure horror crossed the boy's face.

"No!" He screamed, as though his most prized possession had been thrown into a bonfire. "Pick those up! They're mine, rightfully, rightfully mine!" He stuttered, lunging for the can of beans. Irabella put a stop to his efforts, amused by how little effort it took on her part. "Nice try," she said. "But you're as bad a liar as Zane. You might be proud to wear the trademark of the shattering daggers, but here's the first lesson in spycraft- don't show off your allegiances in front of your enemies."

The boy's Adam's apple bobbed. "I swear, I didn't align myself with any of you-" Irabella tugged harder on his hair, bringing tears to his eyes. "I swear!"

"That's enough." I swung down the ladder and swatted Irabella's hand off the boy's scalp. His kneecaps, knuckles, and forehead were caked with dirt and grime. His joints stuck out of his body like sharp pieces of a barely-functional machine, yet he wasn't particularly skinny. Not in a stealthy way. Even for Zane, this was a new low.

I picked up the can on the floor. Not many of the contents had spilled out, yet the boy looked heartbroken. I didn't have time to analyse whether or not the food belonged to him, but I knew one thing. Only one of his sleeves was torn, and underneath it was the trademark burn scar of a Level One prisoner.

It was unclear who he worked for, but either way, this kid obviously had no idea what he had gotten into.

"How long have you been on the Isle of Rebels?" I asked, peering into his eyes. They darted this way and that, not seeming to hold focus on any singular point in the room.

The boy gulped. "A day… and a half."

Ah. So Zane was preying on the newbies. "And how long have you been working for the Shattering Daggers?"

"Zero hours, zero minutes, and zero seconds. I don't know who the hell you're talking about, but trust me, I'd die before I ally myself with a Level Two. I want to get out of here as fast as possible, so, *please*. Let me go."

I narrowed my eyes. Genuine terror was written all over his face, but that wasn't necessarily a show of his allegiances. He could easily be lying, I reminded myself.

"What happened to your shirt?" I softened my tone, feeling a tide of sympathy for the pitiful prisoner.

"A guard stepped on it. The sleeve ripped."

I lifted up the sleeve, examining it. Sure enough, the faint treads of a boot print were stamped on the frayed seam. I turned to Irabella, who drummed her fingers on the rungs of a nearby ladder, waiting impatiently for my decision. It was true. In the same way that the members of building 2-7 carried satchels over their shoulders, everyone who allied themselves with the shattering daggers had torn up the already-short sleeves of their uniforms to show off the trademarks of the Family and Level they stood for. But bringing Level Ones into the Families was a risky business. I looked the kid over, scanning for attributes that could have made him a valuable recruit.

Outside, I caught the snatches of a noise that was distinctly Arvin's, a yelp that fell somewhere between a victorious chant and a moan of pain. I could only hope that wherever he planned to hide the bronze key was as good a place as he said it was.

"You don't know who I am, do you?"

The boy shook his head vigorously. "Please. I just want to go back to my side of the Isle. I'm in building 1-3. I can prove it to you!"

I raised my eyebrows. For the most part, building 1-3 kept to its own affairs. However, at least two people, maybe three, had formerly joined forces with a different Family. Not just any rival group, either. The previous Head Chefs. After I had stolen the key from them, the members had gone their separate ways. But perhaps they were back in business.

"What's your name, kid?" I said, keeping an even tone with the boy, who was so on-edge that the drop of a pin would probably send him into cardiac arrest.

"Emry," he murmured.

"Irabella," I commanded. She snapped to attention, ready to obey my coming request. "Take Emry back to the border. Make sure none of the guards see you. And tell Arvin to hurry up out there."

Irabella's eyebrows furrowed. "Are you sure about this?"

"Just go. Do it before he learns anything else."

Irabella nodded, grabbing Emry by the arm. "Right. Whatever you say."

"Wait!" Emry exclaimed, breaking out of her grip. "What were they doing back there? Who were those prisoners? Who are you?!"

"A word of advice," I said, handing the boy his bag. "Don't ask pointless questions. The important things will become apparent soon enough, and everything else will make you look like an idiot."

Emry looked confused. "Isn't that what every teacher in every school tells you not to do? Not gonna lie, that sounds like pretty crappy life advice."

"On this island, you'd do well to listen to it."

Emry's lips tightened.

"You look like you want to say something. Spill."

"But it's another question."

I sighed. "Just spit it out, then go home."

"Okay…" Emry paused, sucking in a huge breath of air. "Who's the guy sticking out of the window, and why is he rifling through somebody's bunk?"

Everyone snapped to attention, whirling around to find a head halfway through the upper window, hand patting my bunk bed. I jumped up the ladder in a flash, snatching my satchel away from his arm in the nick of time. I grabbed the thief by the hair, and a heavy puff of air blew out from his lungs.

"Not again," I muttered. It seemed like everywhere I looked, there was another plucky kid with their heart set on the bronze key. This one, at least, didn't belong to Zane's band.

At that moment, Arvin thrust the door open, a blood-soaked bird carcass dangling between his pointer finger and his thumb.

My stomach flipped.

"I've found the perfect little nook to stash our precious prize!" The man bellowed, oblivious to the fact that we had an enemy, possibly a second, in our direct vicinity. He scanned the room before clamming up completely, dropping the dead bird onto the floor. "Oh," he whistled, the hairs of his thin white beard bristling.

I used one of my callused hands to pin the intruder down, burying his skull against the mattress. The other, I brought up to my own forehead, drilling it against my skull.

"Irabella, take the Level One boy home, now. *Arvin*, get your bloody science experiment off this floor. And you, whoever the hell you are-" I pinched the guy whose torso was still firmly stuck in the window frame, "Tell the buddy that hoisted you up here to stay the fuck away from building 2-7."

I glared down at Emry. He probably didn't deserve the epitome of my scoldings, but I wasn't having the best day.

"The same goes for you, kid."

Jakson Veer

Inner Workings

I knelt down, running a hand along the thin line where the bordering fence sprang out of the ground, closing in around the sector.

There was a small gap between the stone tiles and the thick metal posts where the ground was laid out with coarse dirt. I was able to fit two fingers in that space, feeling the gravelly soil beneath them as though within it lay the groundwork of my own roots. The area was small, but to me, it was a promise.

Most people missed the plants that grew in that space, the intricate fibrous roots embedded deep within that sanctuary. But for me, the three green strands poking out at the bright afternoon sun were the most stand-out element of the island.

Well, *green* was a bit of a stretch. With so much sunlight and so little water, there was only a small window of hardy species that could survive in the desolate conditions of a gap between a slab of concrete and a prison island's fence. And even amid that small selection, no life of any form was designed to reside in such a place. The world of nature was fascinating, but the Offshore Youth Rehabilitation Facility was human-made. It housed teen prisoners, not plants.

I cupped my hands over the tiny sprouts, letting a few muddy droplets of water trickle out of my fingers. The ground moistened, the water sinking deep into the soil.

"You're welcome," I muttered, shaking my hands clean. Plant cells couldn't feel gratitude, but I took pleasure in the feeling of accomplishment. Even if, right now, in my bubble of solitude, the only kind I could get was brutally one-sided.

Yes. The world of nature was fascinating, but moreover, it was *distracting*. Distracting from the world around me. Distracting from my lack of future. Long ago, I had learned to substitute the expression 'I feel like' with 'I think' whenever I needed people to take me seriously. This was a little like that. If I could run my emotions through a translator, turning them into nothing more than impartial statements, I could substitute them with facts easily enough.

Temporarily satisfied with myself, I stood up, gazing down at the plants. By the looks of them, I would need to pay them another visit tomorrow. I would only see results after about a week, but that was barely a factor anymore.

As far as I was concerned, I had all the time in the world.

My hands were already drying, the bright sunlight beating down onto my palms. It was funny. My parents had hoped for a mathematician, and while I excelled in that field, my true interests lay within the realm of ecology and botany. When my parents asked about my hobbies, I was deliberately vague, giving them an answer somewhere along the lines of 'the general field of science'.

"Not like those things matter much anymore," I muttered to myself, voicing aloud the thoughts I struggled so hard to wrap my head around. "Not like any of it matters."

I sucked in a deep breath of the salty sea breeze, pulling the air into my lungs. I did so because it was a grounding force, a means of survival. I did so to accept that I was here and I was alive. I was nothing if not human. And since I was human, I could be no one else for the rest of my years.

It was that day, however, that I learned about second chances.

"You like plants, do you?" I whirled around, searching for the source of the sudden noise. My eyes landed on a figure standing in the shadow of building 1-10. Their eyes were deep blue, peeking out behind a curtain of sandy hair with a black streak running down the strands, which had clearly been coloured in with a sharpie.

Embarrassed, I stepped in front of the tiny sprouts. "Well-" I stammered.

The person put out a hand. "Relax. I'm not here to deliver a blow to your masculinity or whatever. In fact, I was wondering if you could help me."

Normally, I would have declined the offer immediately. But something about that person made me pause. If they had drawn the colour into their hair with a marker, the touch-up job would have had to be recent; otherwise, the streak would have long faded. And based on the worn-out, grass-stained state of their uniform, I could guess that they had been on the Isle for quite some time.

That meant that they had snuck a marker onto the island. Sure, that was a small thing on its own, but with every small thing came another, larger one. It might have only been a hunch, but if this person could sneak items onto the island, perhaps the marker was only the tip of the iceberg.

I raised one of my eyebrows, a skill I had practised to perfection. "What do you want?"

"Right now... a line for my poem. What's the first thing that pops into your head?"

Bewildered, I frowned. "I'm going to need more context than that."

The person shrugged. "Tell me the first thing that comes to mind. I'll find a way to work it in."

"I'm still going to need more context. What is your poem about?"

"'I'm still going to need more context, what is your poem about,' written by Haven Megany. When I said I'd find a way to work this in, I assumed I'd have more to work *with*."

"Hey," I said, "you were the one who asked for my help."

Haven held up a hand, suddenly struck by inspiration. "That's better! Much, much better. You were the one who asked for my help. Now that can be put to several uses. What's your name? I need to co-credit you, after all."

"Jakson," I said, "without the c."

"I bet a lot of people misspell that."

"You have no idea."

Haven laughed. "I know a thing or two about people getting your name wrong. Do you have any friends here, Jakson? Because you look like someone who doesn't have any friends."

My brows knotted, a low grumble tickling my throat. "What makes you say that?"

"You're standing here, behind your sleeping quarters, talking to a plant. That doesn't strike me as the behaviour of someone with an active social life."

I bristled. "Is there something I can actually help you with? Because if not, then I'll be on my way."

In silence, we stared at each other for a moment. Nothing about this person was trustworthy; I could already tell. They had an affinity for words and liked to play with them. Of course, words couldn't speak for everything. That's when I would turn to numbers. But someone like them, for whom words were their life essence, would certainly seek more destructive means of expressing what they felt they needed to get across.

Haven reached behind their back, producing a tiny clay pot. They held it out, gesturing for me to step forward. "Do you know what plant this is, Jakson?"

I moved closer, peering down at Haven's hands. A minuscule seedling was poking out of the dirt, stretching itself out to catch the rays of sunlight. The oval-shaped leaves were pale green and strongly ribbed, with the makings of a bud forming on the end.

"Deadly nightshade," I stated, tossing a glance from the sprout and back to Haven.

"Very good."

"How did you acquire it?"

"That's for you to find out. If you're willing to take care of this bad boy, that is."

I narrowed my eyes. "What's in it for me? Why should I help you?"

A smirk befell Haven's face. "Because, Jakson, I sympathise with lonely people. I took a risk in trusting you. The least you could do is return the favour."

Slowly, I felt Haven's fingers slipping from the pot. I clutched it in my hands, stopping the plant from crashing to the ground. Haven put their palms in the air, holding them in a gesture of surrender. I looked down at my own fingers, clasped firmly around the tiny pot.

"Consider that a first step. Now come on. There are some people I'd like you to meet."

***

At first, I couldn't quite tell where Haven was leading me. All the buildings looked the same, and while the building arrangement retained some organisation, the vast majority of the groupings were scattered at random. Starting from building 1-1 and ending at building 1-5, the first wave of prisoners were sent and sorted by alphabetical order. Building 1-1 housed last names A-D, building 1-2 housed last names E-H, building 1-3 housed last names H-M, and so on. But the weird thing was, only a couple people were included in this first wave. It ended abruptly at Z in building 1-5 before starting back at A with a new, random set of prisoners in building 1-6. I supposed this was so that they didn't all fill up, messing up the sorting system whenever one bunk reached capacity.

Altogether, there were 30 sleeping quarters lined up across the Level One sector. Each one looked more or less identical, the roofs seeming to sink lower the further into the sector they were located.

Suddenly, Haven stopped in front of a set of cinder block steps. They led up to building 1-3.

"Now," Haven said, "we wait."

We shuffled to the side of the cabin, watching as a crowd trickled out to empty the building for whatever uses Haven saw fit. The potted plant was still clutched in my hand, surprisingly heavy in my arms. As the tail end of the group was escaping, I caught sight of something all too familiar.

I was able to pick Lizabeth out of any crowd. We had gone to the same school from elementary to tenth grade, and navigating those busy hallways required an acute goal and a straightforward plan of action. I knew the back of Lizabeth's head like the back of my own hand, which was probably as creepy as it sounded but had proved helpful in many situations.

My stomach dropped when her familiar streak of dusty blond hair blew by. In a way, I was relieved- she was walking away from the building while I was walking toward it. But as we crossed paths, if only for that brief moment, I found myself holding my breath. Lizabeth exited the cabin tentatively, searching the streets for someone to accompany her. I ducked even further behind the building's wall. The view from behind the quarters- the barbed wire fence and grey-speckled shore- was much more pleasant than the one I had to face on the streets of the sector.

"All clear," Haven said as the final stragglers wandered out, leaving building 1-3 vacant and ready for use. "The others should be arriving shortly."

The interior of the building was, initially, the identical twin of my own quarters. With the exception of the magnificent walls. The ink that formed the lines running through the building looked almost *bloody*, but the red stains only outlined a pre-carved scratch. These people would have needed something sharp to create such an indentation.

I was relieved that I didn't know which bunk Lizabeth occupied, but in a way, not knowing was worse. Who had she talked to? Did she even feel sorry? Of course she did. Who was I kidding? It would have been so much easier to hate her if I didn't know she was hurting just as much as I was.

"Allow me to introduce Adrienne and Max," Haven interrupted me from my bout of self-pity, gesturing to the only other two in the building. "Guys, this is Jakson."

The girl, who I could only assume was Adrienne, hopped down from where she was nestled in a top bunk. Immediately, she held out her hand, shaking mine with a firm grip. "Nice to meet you. I suppose we have ourselves a newbie?"

Max was a little more sceptical. He stayed back, eyeing Haven doubtfully. He crossed over to the centre of the room, whispering a few words into Haven's ear.

"What is this?" I asked, furrowing my eyebrows.

"Well, first things first," Haven began, "like you said. I owe you a bit of context."

Suddenly, the door burst open once again, and two girls, arm in arm, stepped into the building. The girl on the left only had one free hand, the other of which was tied up in a beige sling. I narrowed my eyes at the cast. A few lumps were poking out behind the fabric, and I found it very hard to believe that the only thing stashed inside the sling was a fractured bone. The girl herself was about an inch shorter than I was. Her hair was dark brown, almost black, and tied in a messy bun above her head, a few loose tendrils hanging over her eyes to rest on her soft brown cheeks. Her chin was pointed, and her joints stuck out at bizarre angles, self-consciously tucked at her sides. She stuck close to the other girl, eyeing me apprehensively. Recognition flashed in her eyes, and I realised with a bit of a start that I remembered her from my own building.

The second girl's crimson red hair was long and flowing, billowing behind her like a fiery cape. Her pointed chin was held high, and she half led, half dragged the other girl toward the bunks.

"Haven," she began. A thick French accent was in her voice, muffling the 'h' so it sounded more like 'aven'. "We have…" she trailed off, turning her head to me, "who is this?"

"Amélie, meet Jakson. He can take care of the plant."

Amélie raised one of her thick red eyebrows. "Are you sure about that? That thing is on the verge of death."

"I can do it," I assured, "but whether I want to or not depends on what you're going to be using it for."

Haven stepped behind me, making sure the door was firmly closed. "There's a security camera in the corner of this building, below the loudspeaker," they said, "it's supposed to be hidden, but Max stumbled upon it a long while ago. You don't have to worry about it because it's broken, and the guards couldn't come in to fix it without revealing to everyone that they have hidden cameras in their quarters. When you take that plant into building 1-10, you will have to be mindful. Because the one over there is almost certainly still intact."

I turned around in a full circle, the five people inside the building taking a stance around me. Sucking in a deep breath, I spoke.

"What do you want from me?"

"I thought you would've figured it out by now," Haven said, "come on. I'm not just going to tell you. But no guess is out of the question."

I glanced between each person. Surprisingly enough, the gaze I settled on was Farrah's. Her eyes darted to the ground before I could meet them, drifting absent-mindedly to the window. And that was how I got my answer.

"You can't possibly…." I said, the air slowly beginning to drain from my lungs. "You're trying to escape the island."

Adrienne brought her hands together, clapping ferociously.

"We have a winner! Congratulations, Jakson!" Her cheers died down, and she drew in a deep breath, launching into a story. "We used to be in league with a Level Two Family. The Families on the Isle have one goal- to gain possession of a single key and declare themselves the 'head chefs' of the Isle. The Family that had taken us in had managed to acquire said key, which unlocked an old mess hall. We made our mark on this room with the forks inside the hall. Of course, about a month ago, Cerina Rayz, the Level Two at the top of the food chain, stole the key from Haven, who had been entrusted with it by the former Head Chefs. But we didn't give up there. Us Level Ones split off from the Level Twos we had let down and formed our own little club."

I cut her off, holding up a hand. "You have quite the ambition, I'll give you that. But your mission is pointless. Unless you want to get yourselves killed, your escape plan will amount to nothing. No matter how many poisonous plants you have on your side."

"My entire family lives in France," Amélie grumbled. "I'd do anything to join them again, and I'd rather die than stay here." The others, with their eyes, echoed her statement. Amélie's French ancestry surprised me. At one point, Sykona had been a part of the United Kingdom. But after the first war, where all of Europe had broken into conflict over the rise of cryptocurrency and the crumbling of many social constructs, Sykona had carved itself from Britain and appointed its own officials. It was the rebellious, problem child of Europe. Only, unlike most disagreeable teenagers, it had an army at its command.

"I hope this doesn't sound rude, but how did you end up here if you used to live in France?" I asked Amélie.

"I was travelling and ran into some trouble." She said with a slight glare.

The girl with the cast shook her head slowly, muttering under her breath. "Definitely a newbie".

I crossed my arms. "Why? What did I say?"

Haven sighed. "What Farrah here means is… that's not the kind of question you're supposed to ask around here. You know how you never ask a person their salary unless you're interviewing them for a job? Well, on the Isle of Rebels, you never ask a person what crime they committed unless you want your neck snapped."

I gulped. "Technically, I didn't ask-"

Amélie rolled her eyes. "Forget about it, Jakson. The point is, are you joining us or not? Farrah, Max, Adrienne, Haven and I have presented you with an offer. You can accept it or reject it, but there's no in-between."

"Like I said, I appreciate your ambition, but this is too risky, too dangerous. You might as well wait out your sentence."

Haven shook their head sadly. "I'm afraid that's not how it works. Adrienne, Max, and I were sent here for one year. This is our third. The thing about the Isle is that it's unfathomably lazy. We prisoners are all treated the same. You come in for whatever reason, and the only way out is through death. Or being tagged a Level Three, which gets you taken to who knows where."

I sighed. "Do you have a plan?"

Haven broke into a grin. "I'd thought you'd never ask."

Before they could launch themself into a detailed speech, I, once again, stopped them before they could start.

"I'm still not convinced just yet. I'll need time to think about this, after all. But I'll take care of your plant, and I'll hear you out. You have my word on that."

Haven held a hand out for me to shake. I clasped their palm in a firm hold, shaking it once.

"Now," Haven said, "let's make you a member of our little group."

Farrah shoved her left hand into the sling binding her right and pulled out a sharpie. It only took a second for me to connect the dots between it and the black streak in their widely-varied hair colours.

"Oh, no," I said, stepping back. I slammed into the wall, and Haven grinned.

"Oh, yes."

Emry McLeod

The walk of shame

I protested as Irabella grabbed me by the wrists, practically dragging me out of building 2-7. The old man with the bird flipped his head to watch me intently, his crusty yellow bug eyes bulging from their sockets. I was forced to look away from the mysterious girl, who was somehow capable of restraining someone and ordering three other people simultaneously.

Irabella wasn't kind in her shoving. "You might not be a spy," she huffed, "But you still don't belong here."

"I couldn't agree more."

Irabella glared, avoiding my eyes and tightening her hold on my upper arm. "You don't have to escort me there," I snapped. "It's not like I intend to stick around this place."

"Famous last words. You claim you ended up here by accident, yeah? You should be lucky Cerina isn't dumping you out here to die."

"Cerina," I repeated. "So that's her name."

Irabella huffed. "You were bound to learn it eventually. And next time you hear it, you had better be scared."

"Who are you to tell me what to be scared of?"

Irabella fumed, shoving my arm away from her. "Just shut up, idiot. We're almost at the border. Then you can go do whatever dumb shit Level Ones occupy the time with."

We walked in silence, and I stared at the ground. The stones lining the streets of the Level Two block were cracked and weathered, much unlike the clean-cut squares paving the paths around building 1-3.

"Just walk normally across the border," Irabella advised. "You're not supposed to be on our side at all, but the guards don't give two shits about who hangs out where. 'Course, if you look suspicious, you might as well be asking for a beating."

My eyes widened. "Do they really beat people up?"

Irabella smiled wickedly. "I guess you'll find out."

She slid back into the shadows, and the hairs on my arms shot up. I crept down the stretch of grass, feeling too exposed on the open field. I tried my best to heed Irabella's advice, sticking to the edge. Nobody glanced my way. I looked about as suspicious as a person could get, but the people I walked by didn't exactly look innocent, either. I guess in a world where everyone looks up to no good, the ordinary people are the ones who stand out.

"Hey! Stop!" The shout of a guard halted me in my tracks. I sped up. I was almost at the dividing line. If I could get back to my sector-

"Good! Now, drop it!"

I skidded to a stop, turning to the source of the noise. On the other end of the field, a Level One prisoner was facing the centre circle, looking down the barrel of a rifle. I willed my legs to keep moving, but my feet stood planted in the jagged grass, my attention pulled to the scene by the uncontrollable tug of curiosity.

The prisoner held a towering stack of containers, the silvery cans piled high. Some were tucked in his shirt, bulging against the fibres of his uniform. The rest were in plain sight, reflecting the searing sun. He, along with his items, could be seen for miles.

He had stolen food. That much was obvious. But what was he doing with it? Clearly nothing that involved sneaking.

The man stood still, but he didn't drop the food, nor did he cower in fear. He held his head high, staring defiantly into the face of the guard.

I wasn't sure if he was brave or stupid.

"Make me," the guy sneered, "I'm sick to death of this island. Sick to death of you. So much so that death has become a close companion of mine." The man readjusted his arms, holding the cans between his elbows, popping one of them open. He tipped the food into his mouth, burping loudly and discarding the still-full can at the guard's feet. "That's waste, now," the guy said, "like us. Based on what you've done with the prisoners, I bet you're going to keep that can around for a while."

The answer to my previous question came to me the second I started running, my survival instincts getting the better of me.

The man was both brave *and* stupid.

"You think you're invulnerable because you're useless?" The guard scoffed, "It's shameful how much you don't know. Soon enough, you'll see what we do to waste."

The air stood still.

I shut my eyes, sinking my teeth into my bottom lip. The island itself seemed to buzz, thrumming and pulsating with electricity. The atmosphere was a live wire wrapped around my throat. I hated violence, but I had seen enough of it to know what would happen next. All of a sudden, the arm holding my bag of food felt very, very heavy.

The bang of a gunshot split the silence like a knife, echoing across the expanse of field. The ring of the rifle burrowed in my ears, drumming over and over again inside of my skull.

My fingers loosened, and the brown paper bag crumpled to the ground.

A whoosh of air slammed against my side, a warm-bodied presence cutting a path down the stretch of grass. I peered through my eyelids and, through the squint, noticed the silhouette of the man with the food disappearing into the row of buildings.

Confused, I turned back around. The guard was back against the wall, but his weapon was still raised. I smelled the faint tinge of smoke and a heavy stench I could only describe as burning plastic.

There were ten, possibly twenty, cans of dropped food at the guard's feet. One of the cans had a bullet hole blown through it, the contents spilling out the side.

The guard nestled the gun at his shoulder. "Inform the Level One prisoners that the meal station is out of service for the next few hours," he called, gesturing to me with a flick of his chin. "That's an order."

Nearly stumbling over my own feet, I tripped and scurried to the row of buildings, my heart hammering in my chest.

I wasn't sure if I should have been relieved or downright terrified.

As soon as my feet touched down on the stone tiles, the thoughts of my tour guide were called to memory. Amid all the other chaos, I had completely forgotten about Joe.

I dashed down the block in search of him. Many people were milling around, shooting me an odd look here and there. This time, I decided I didn't mind their stares. They could blab all they wanted. I just needed to regain some normalcy. After a frenzied burst of hurried searching, I came to a halt at the end of the outer street. I was about to run past the buildings again, a little slower this time, when I caught a glimpse of neon-blue hair out of the corner of my eye. I had to suppress a heavy groan. Just when I thought this day couldn't get any worse, the psychotic destroyer of glasses had to come sulking down the street.

I wasted no time diving behind the nearest building, hurtling across the narrow space between the wire fence and the sleeping quarters. My lungs gasped for the air I had neglected to inhale in my mad dash to escape the crazy blue-haired guy.

I nearly collided with Lizabeth, who had hidden out of sight against the wall of the same building.

Dodging at the last second, I crumbled into a half face-plant, half knee-slide. Lizabeth swerved, jumping almost a foot in the air.

"Emry?!" She cried, "watch it!"

Gravel bit at my kneecaps, tunnelling under my skin. I swore through gnashed teeth, an ugly ripping sound tearing out of my chest. My hands slid forward to protect my face, colliding with the gravelly path just in time. Dejectedly following the natural rhythm of gravity, my arms slumped over, leaving me splayed out like a starfish.

No. Starfish were supposed to look nice. I resembled more of a beached whale.

"The hell are you doing here?"

I huffed in response, digging my fingernails underneath my skin to extract the tiny rocks. Getting back to my feet, I glanced at the number on the side of the building. *1-10*.

"I could ask you the same question," Lizabeth said, "are you okay?"

Heat rushed to my cheeks. This blush felt more like a slap in the face than the gradual augmentation of body temperature. It was spontaneous, incurable, and very, very noticeable.

"I'm fine," I grunted. The tears nipping at the corners of my eyes betrayed me instantly. My face darkened to an ugly purple as I descended to an even more awkward phase of blush-dom.

"Are you sure? You look like… you don't feel well."

"Nah, I'm good. I just… saw something. That's all. What are *you* doing creeping around the corners of buildings?"

"I'm not creeping. I'm walking. You, on the other hand, looked like you were running for dear life. I take it the tour didn't go so well?"

Right then and there, I wanted to tell Lizabeth everything. The words were on the tip of my tongue, but I bit them down at the last second. I still wasn't sure what impact my actions had made, but I could be sure that if word got out that I ended up in the Level Two sector, I would never be back there again.

And although the place was downright terrifying, Cerina's face kept popping up in my mind. Her collected, commanding presence. Her furious stare. The agility with which she had pinned down the intruder.

I collected everything I knew about her into a box in my mind- she was protecting some sort of key, she lived in building 2-7, and she was one of the most powerful people on the Isle of Rebels.

That wasn't much to go off of, but I would be back there.

"Want to head to building 1-3?" Lizabeth suggested. I nodded, shooting one last glance behind me to make sure the coast was clear.

"Lead the way."

I followed Lizabeth, but my steps were only half-hearted.

I would go back to the Level Two sector. I would see Cerina again.

I was sure of it.

Lizabeth Merrin

Recruitment Business

The lights blinked off methodically, shutting off in perfect timing with the closing of my eyelids. I pulled the itchy blanket to my chin. Sounds circulated the room, mainly those of people snoring and sliding into late-night conversations. I tugged the blanket higher, covering my ears. The sheet slid off my now-bare feet, exposing them to the cold outside. Glaring at the faint shadow of the grey fabric, I shoved the blanket back down, declaring my efforts pointless.

I supposed we never could truly get what we wanted. We just had to make do with what we were given.

"Lizabeth?" Haven's voice came from beside me, startling me out of my lapse of self-pity. "Sorry," they continued, "I apologise if you're trying to sleep."

"No, no, it's fine," I assured them, "I've accepted that sleeping is futile in this place."

"You'll learn to deal with it," Haven said, "trust me. You'd be surprised by how effective morbid thoughts are at lolling someone off to bed."

"Are you sure about that? Every sleep article I've read, well, ever, advises against that."

Haven laughed. "It's *worrying* that distracts you. The uncertain. But the thought of inevitable, unchangeable doom is actually quite comforting."

"Define 'comforting.'"

Haven yawned. "Depression isn't your thing. I see. Y'know, that's pretty admirable, considering most people like to brag about how sad they are. As if their misery could win them an award. If bleak thoughts don't float your boat, I'd suggest hope. I'm leading another meeting tomorrow. The future is on the horizon, and I, in this dazed little nine-PM dream of mine, will be the one to lead the way."

Puzzling over their words, I let the noises of other chatter engulf the bunk. "Haven," I asked, finally, "what do you mean by 'a meeting?'"

Haven didn't respond, didn't stir. I tried again, but it was pointless. They were out cold.

***

"Emry… it's wake-up time."

Emry groaned, rolling to the side and colliding with the wooden barrier. "…why…"

"Because you're on the Isle of Rebels, and it's 06:00. At this point, more like 06:10. Come on. We did this yesterday."

I led Emry, lethargic and half-zombified, out of building 1-3 and into the fresh air of the Level One sector. From the corner of my eye, I spotted Haven watching us closely. *I'm leading another meeting tomorrow*. A meeting of what? With whom?

I had to admit, I was relieved when we were outside the walls and into the morning sun. The sky still held traces of a pink and orange sunrise, the streaks running through the sky like watered-down swashes of paint.

"What should we do?" Emry asked, pacing back and forth in front of the steps, "The centre circle is out of the question."

"I couldn't agree more." Emry had briefly recounted the incident he'd run into with the guard and the food thief, but all the details leading up to that were pretty hazy. Still, it wasn't like I could pry without inviting further questions involving *my* whereabouts.

After all, if Emry knew about building 1-10, it wouldn't take him long to figure out that I'd been trying to spy on Jakson and Darby. And if Emry learned about Jakson and Darby, well, there was no going back.

The last few members of building 1-3 trickled out along with us. I craned my neck to peer inside the building, but the door was pulled shut before my eyes could focus on anything.

Emry and I cleared the steps, making way for two girls approaching the building from different directions. They met at the base of the stairs, ignoring our presence as they strode up to the door.

The girl who had come from the right, in the direction of Jakson's building, only had one free arm. Her entire right one was fixed into a beige sling from the bicep down. The bones of her elbows poked out like sharp knives, coated by a thin layer of light brown skin. She walked shyly behind the other girl, stepping in her shadow.

This second girl breathed out confidence. Her head was held high, and her ruby-red hair billowed behind her, announcing her presence for miles. The way she rested her shoulders indicated that her presence was one to not only acknowledge, but one to respect.

The two of them strutted into building 1-3, and, instead of being turned out as I had certainly expected, they were hastily greeted and ushered in by Haven.

Emry and I were still standing there, attempting to glimpse what was going on. Haven shot us a brief glance before they closed the door once more, disappearing before I could get in a word.

The clamour of voices began to travel from the gaps in the doorway. I stepped up to the cement blocks, pressing my ear to the wood. Inside, I could hear Max addressing a group of people.

"... we've broken it up into sections... no, he should be coming back... whether or not he does, we need that plant." Other voices joined in agreement. I turned to Emry.

"What do you think is going on in there?"

Emry shrugged, taking my spot against the door. He pressed his cheek to the wood. A few seconds later, he resurfaced from his concentration, shrugging.

"Sorry," he said, "maybe we can check the windows?"

We made our way to the side of the building, where the only glimpses into the interior were the high panes of glass.

I was average height… for a fourth-grade student. But even if I were tall, there was no way I could see past the wide windowsill blocking any view from the bottom of the structure.

"It's pointless," I said, eyeing the ledge doubtfully.

Emry shrugged once more. "Maybe we could climb onto the overhang?"

"Don't be ridiculous. Do I look like a good climber to you?"

"Actually, yes."

"We're not climbing the windowsill," I resolved, "I'm going to try the door again."

Emry and I both positioned ourselves on the top step. Few words reached us, but gradually, Haven's voice started to rise.

"We have to take measures," they said, "to prevent threats to our operation. Such as guards," their tone continued to mount, "obstacles," their voice grew louder and louder. It was almost as though they were stepping closer, speaking directly from the other end of this door- "and spies."

The door swung open, knocking me back. Haven stood in the frame, a bemused smirk on their face. "Y'know," they said, "you two could've just come in. Saves you the hassle of eavesdropping."

Emry's cheeks burned red with shame. I managed to hold myself together, embarrassment tugging at the corners of my lips, turning them up into a miserable excuse for a grin. A 'coping smile,' as I liked to call it.

"What are you guys doing in there?" I asked, getting straight to the point. Haven smiled.

"I dunno. How 'bout you come in and find out? Door's wide open."

"I'd rather not."

Haven sighed. "Lizabeth. Would you mind coming in here for a second? There's something I'd like to discuss with you."

I looked at Emry. Or maybe it was Emry who looked at me.

Either way, both of us put our feet forward.

The second our words were safe behind the walls, Haven flew through the introductions. "This is Farrah and Amélie. We have another member who's supposed to be joining us, but he's a little late today. You've already met Max, Adrienne and me."

My mind drifted to the security camera next to the loudspeaker, staring down at us from its high perch. Clearly, we weren't supposed to have noticed it, but it was hard to miss the unblinking eye constantly watching my every move with my bunk next to it. Haven followed my gaze.

"Oh," they said, "don't worry about that. The camera in this building has been broken for years."

"That's a bit of a security problem, don't you think?"

Haven shrugged. "There are lots of security problems on this island. But the funny thing is, as long as everyone *thinks* measures are ship shape, they're easily deluded into following them without protest. We, on the other hand, like to be a bit more creative when it comes to who we blindly obey."

Emry glared, gazing between each crowd member, his eyes resting on the black streak coloured into each person's hair. "What are you doing here, Haven?"

"Something that doesn't interest you unless you find out about it."

"The hell is that supposed to mean?"

I couldn't take this any longer. A hunch, an unlikely but possible hunch, bubbled at the front of my thoughts. "They're trying to escape the island," I blurted. Every eye in the room turned to me, and Emry, a bit disappointed that I had stolen his thunder, turned his mouth down in a frown. "And," I continued, "I want in."

Haven smiled. "Clearly you *were* wide awake last night."

"I think you were, too. I know how to spot a fake sleeper when I see one. You wanted me to come here."

"And what," Haven asked, "would lead me to do so?"

"I don't know yet."

Haven gave me a smile that was supposed to be warm but looked more sickly than sweet. "I'd tell you the plan," they said, "but I wasn't counting on the fact that you'd bring a friend along with you."

Emry bristled. "Hey! I want in as well."

"You weren't *invited* in, I'm sorry to say. I offer my apologies, Emry, but we don't have an on-site optometrist. If you can't see, you can't help."

Emry gave Haven a blank look, somewhere between hurt and disbelief. "What do you mean? You want Lizabeth, but I'm entirely useless to you?"

"Yes," Haven said "You summed it up quite perfectly."

I stepped in front of Emry, giving Haven a cold stare. "What's the matter with you?" I said, "if you're going to let me in, you'll let him in as well. There's no reason for me to join you. For all I care, Emry and I could go off and escape by ourselves."

"Don't do that," Haven said, "we have supplies, allies, and plans. You could be a valuable asset. This isn't an opportunity you want to turn down."

Emry grumbled under his breath. "It's fine, Lizabeth," he muttered, "go do your thing. It's not like I can help, anyway."

He whirled around, flinging the door open. He stalked off, disappearing behind my line of sight.

I turned back to Haven. "Seriously? What's your problem?"

"I don't mean to be a jerk. No, I am not someone of malevolent intent. I'm only doing this for his own good. He isn't suited for the team."

"But I am? You barely know me. What makes you such an excellent judge of character?"

Haven shrugged. "I suppose I'm an empath."

I scoffed. "Last time I checked, empaths were supposed to have *empathy*. Now, look at what you've done. You haven't thought this through in the slightest."

"Oh, I thought it through a lot. Except for the new guy, each person here had something to say on the matter of your entry."

"That reminds me," interrupted Max, "where has the other guy gone off to?"

"Is he even coming?" Adrienne asked.

"He was supposed to."

"Did you tell him when we were meeting?"

Max started to talk before pausing, cutting off a gasp of air. "I forgot."

"Great. Does anyone know which building you handed our... ahem, hidden advantage to?"

A pause.

"Great. Fantastic. I'll go ask around, I guess."

Adrienne spun around in a dramatic twirl. "I'm not joining you guys unless you let Emry in. Got it?"

Haven shook their head slowly. "That's not how it works. *You're* the one who is supposed to prove yourself to *us*."

"I thought I already had."

The girl who had been introduced as Amélie stuck her hand in the air, waving it wildly. "Tell her about the plan, already!" She cried. Her words rolled with the clips of a thick French accent, clunking together in an impatient string.

"I don't want to hear it," I said, stepping back. "Not until you show me this is a group I want to be a part of."

"Come on. We don't have time-"

"You said it yourself. Your sentence is never going to end. You have all the time in the world. So, for the sake of example, tell me. What do all of *you* have to offer?"

"Well," Haven began, their tone bordering on anger. "Adrienne is a natural extravert and isn't afraid to talk to new people. She's an incredible liar and can easily twist her way up the social ladder and into the guards' inner circle. Max is detail-oriented and can spot the tiny cracks most people miss. Plus, he's good with locks. Amélie is the most efficient person I know. She's a fast learner, a fast runner, and she has a way out of any situation. The new guy can resurrect our dying hope for this plan, and Farrah... Farrah remembers everything. From numbers to names, to dates, to faces. She can look at a place once and remember it exactly for ten years."

"And you? What can you do?"

Haven's annoyed glare faded into a smirk. "I started this group; therefore, I am the leader. Do I really need to make a grand ego display?"

At that moment, the door burst open. On the other side was Emry, an expression of cold resolve on his face. "Just so you know!" He wavered, his voice loud but shaky, "you guys are making a mistake!"

Haven raised their eyebrows. "And what mistake is that?"

Emry clenched his hands into tight fists. "You'll see. I'll prove it to all of you." With that, he took off.

I leapt up, springing to action. "What have you done? We have to go. Now!" Haven eyed me thoughtfully, hopping up onto their feet.

"I didn't realise-" they trailed off, watching the door swing on its hinges with an expression that I could only describe as pure, unrivalled bewilderment.

Of course, it had to be that moment when Adrienne returned, flush-faced, to building 1-3. With their newest recruit in tow. My heart dropped even further.

"Jakson…" I said, staring into his clear, astonished eyes.

"Lizabeth-" the last thing I heard before I flew out the door after a runaway Emry McLeod was the sound of Amélie scrambling to catch the clay flower pot before it came tumbling to the floor.

Cerina Rayz

Battered and bruised

Irabella rarely got into fights. She talked her big talk, more so than anyone, but as violent as she pretended to be, few people had tried to lay a hand on her ever since her arrival on the island.

Perhaps it was because she was friends with me. Or maybe her confident, strong personality deterred anyone with bad intentions.

Either way, it came as a surprise when she returned to building 2-7 early in the afternoon with her eye swollen shut and a welt on her cheek.

Arvin and I had just finished hiding the key, doing so in the most discreet manner possible. I was sceptical of Arvin's solution, but he had been very stubborn about the hiding spot. We had just returned to our building when Irabella stumbled in, leaning against the bunk beds for support. Arvin and I had been talking, but my words died on my lips as I caught sight of Irabella's state.

I dashed over, holding out a hand. She staggered forward, wrapping her fingers around my forearm.

Getting a hold of herself, she regained her footing, her dizzy eyes popping back into focus. She let go of me, stalking off towards her bunk, one of the upper ones located next to the door.

"What happened?" I followed her up the ladder, trying to make eye contact. She ignored me, scurrying up the rungs and fixing me with a cold glare.

"Nothing," she grumbled. "I'm fine."

"No. You're not." I was instantly relieved that we were the only ones in the cabin. Apart from Arvin, there was no one else who could see this. Irabella's face burned red from her injuries, but more than that, it steamed with shame.

"It's nothing," she affirmed, "how's the key? Did you hide it okay?"

"That's not important right now. You're hurt. Here-" I shrugged off my satchel, weighing the thin fabric between my hands. I tore off a long scrap of it, enough to be fashioned into a bandage, and held it up to Irabella.

"Here. Take this. Your arm's bleeding."

"I don't need your help. Like I said, I'm fine, alright? What did you do with the key?"

I didn't move my hand, holding the fabric out in front of me. "Can you at least tell me what happened?"

Irabella sighed, snatching the bandage. She wrapped it twice around her hand, where her knuckles were split open and trickling crimson. "A few guys spotted my satchel on the way to the centre circle. From the Bloodsoaked Thorns, I think. They cornered me and tried to get me to hand over the key." Irabella scoffed, "idiots. I'd die before betraying 2-7, and I told them that too. They beat me up pretty badly, but it's nothing compared to what I did to them. They'd be stupid to go after you again."

I pursed my lips. "You're wrapping that wrong. It's going to come undone. Here, let me help you."

Reluctantly, Irabella shuffled to the side while I hopped up to the bunk, peering over Irabella's shoulder. I pulled the makeshift bandage out of her hands and re-wrapped it, tucking the loose end snugly underneath the rest.

"Here. This will hold better." I backed away, turning to look Irabella in the eye. "Thank you, Irabella. You showed bravery."

Irabella shrugged. "Oh… uh, it was nothing. Anything for 2-7, am I right?"

I nodded, though my heart wasn't in it. "Right you are."

"Thank you, too," Irabella stammered after a long pause, holding her head down bashfully. She fingered the bandage, running her hand over the split-open skin. When I had first arrived on the island, I had received harsh treatment as well. But from my current position, I had almost forgotten how bad things could get when people acted on their threats.

I had almost forgotten what differentiated the Level Twos from the Level Ones.

Briefly, my mind went to the boy who had stumbled into our sector. Emry. It was probably pointless, but I hoped he was holding up well enough. The thought of those terrified eyes saddened me all the more.

"It's no problem," I said, placing my hand on top of Irabella's. "What else am I here for if not to take care of the people I lead?"

Irabella scoffed, but her gaze softened. "You better not tell that to anyone else that lives here. Their pride would be so hurt that they'd kick you out of the building."

A knock sounded on the door. "Open up! We want the key!"

Now it was my turn to laugh. "I'd like to see them try."

Emry McLeod

The worst way to measure self-worth

Honestly? I had no idea I was desperate to join the gang of rogue wannabe prison escapees. I had no idea I was even brave enough to step over that dividing line again to see the face of the elusive Cerina. But, of course, when your self-esteem comes into play... weird shit happens.

I tore down the field like my life depended on it, which, in a weird way, it kinda did. I'd probably starve to death or catch an odd mutation of the bubonic plague if I was forced to stay on the Isle of Rebels for over a year. I had woken up that morning with a pounding headache, but I wasn't going to let that stop me. I was in a full-blown rage- of the oddest sort.

Once I broke into the Level Two sector, it wasn't hard to find building 2-7. The sleeping quarters were arranged in the same way the Level One quarters were, with the higher numbers close to the inner circle and the lower numbers filling the outermost ring- but there was a sense of great foreboding around the area. It was the place all the Level Two passersby snuck a glance toward at least once, debating where, when, and if they should strike.

It was also the place where the fighting noises came from.

I snuck around the buildings. Well, I *tried* to sneak around them. The big blistering 1 on my shoulder stuck out like a sore thumb, but the shadows were still long and dark, providing, at the very least, a bit of concealment. Though I couldn't say the same about the huge crowd milling in front of Cerina's building.

It didn't take me long to find her. She stood at the centre of the mob, her very presence expelling command over everyone and everything. She made an announcement that was lost in the breeze. I stood still for a moment, mesmerised by the sight of her. My pitiful eyesight turned her into a blurry splotch, but the radius of her command touched me even at a distance.

I wanted nothing more than to clasp her hand and draw myself closer, partially blinded and everything.

What was I thinking? The entire population of Cerina's building was outside, restraining a group of Level Twos with identical red splotches oozing over their hearts. I thought the blood was coming from the prisoners for a second until I realised it was some weird symbol of allegiances, like the black streak in Haven's hair.

But either way, building 2-7 was empty. Normally that would've been great for me if the crowd wasn't right in front of the door.

Then and there, I wanted nothing more than to drop to the ground and declare my presence. Cerina would be confused as hell, but at least she'd notice me again. The sound of her voice- even though it was nothing more than a distant murmur, laced with the threads of the other day's memory- calmed me and frightened me all at the same time. It was like being on the edge of your seat at the movie theatre. You're pulled in by the action, but at the end of the day, you're still sitting on a very soft cushion.

I braced myself to run, getting into a position I was 60% sure would help me sprint. 60%, because my main goals of every phys-ed class I ever took were to a) run away from the ball, and b) avoid the tough kids at all cost. One would think that would've helped me run better, tightening my focus on the gym teacher's instruction, but in fact, it had done quite the opposite.

Good thing I was *great* at impulsive decision making. I wondered if that counted as a skill worthy of initiation into Haven's group.

I ran like the wind behind building 2-7, landing in a painful knee-slide that looked way cooler on TV than it felt in real life. Winded, I got up, pulse-pounding. I had made it past the giant clump and was now behind the unguarded building. But what now?

I looked up. The windows were high above the ground, newly covered by a torn fabric that resembled an old tablecloth. Clearly, the dude who had shimmied up to Cerina's window had received some help from the ground. Help that I, the breathless Level One, wasn't going to get.

Squinting and stepping closer, I noticed something resting above the window frame on the back side of the building. A tiny bird lay there, motionless, hugging the wall. It was tucked firmly in a small nook between two seams of the aged wood. I wouldn't have paid it a second thought, considering it a minor casualty of life on the Isle. An insignificant animal that had probably starved to death before it had the opportunity to make a nest.

My mind flashed back to the old man on the steps. *I've found the perfect little nook to stash our precious prize!* Wasn't that what he had said, dangling the revolting thing from his hand? My eyes zeroed in on the teeny corpse. There it was, unmistakably. Covering the wings was a red blob of dried blood. This bird didn't starve. It was brutally gutted by the creepiest old guy in the Level Two sector.

But why was it *there*? Why wasn't the old guy using it to perform some weird voodoo, burning incense and laying out its vital organs in a little bowl? With the ground as rocky as it was, there weren't many places ideal for burial, but leaning on top of a window wasn't what I would call an optimal resting place by any means.

The perfect little nook to stash our precious prize.

I had no idea what could be so special about a dead bird, but if it was important to Cerina, it would be essential to Haven and the others. Bile rose in my throat at the thought of touching the thing, but it was a small price to pay for a life on the Isle of Rebels.

My fingers slipped into the little grooves where the wood panels met, fastened down by rusty nails on the verge of snapping apart. I surveyed how high up the window was. It was way above my head, far enough to be slightly blurry but clear enough for me to identify the bird.

But the key point was this- unless, unbeknownst to me, I had become a 7-foot tall basketball player overnight, there was no way I could reach the windowsill easily. Lizabeth had mentioned she was good at climbing, hadn't she? Looking up at the jagged wall, I came to the conclusion that even she would have difficulty with this task. For the slightest moment, I recalled her chasing after me. She'd probably had the sense to turn around at the border. Good for her. She wouldn't have to touch bird guts.

Tucking the fingers of my left hand into a little gap just above my head, I folded my knees, taking a deep breath. My legs kicked off the ground, and, using my trapped hand to hoist myself up, I shot off the ground and into the air.

The tips of my fingers grazed the window, making the jump but failing miserably to get a hold of the smooth windowsill.

My fingers bent on the way down, getting pinched between the wood. I howled in agony, wrenching them out of the wall. They were bright red, throbbing and half-numb, but not nearly numb enough.

Tears from the unpleasant surprise stung the corners of my eyes. I wiped them away, focusing on the goal. I just had to grab the windowsill, then somehow hoist myself onto it in a position that would be comfortable enough to knock the bird to the ground. I grunted, preparing, again, to leap. The windowsill was broad and covered in accessible handholds. I could do this… maybe?

I furrowed my eyebrows and went for it once more. This time I got too carried away, coming at it at an awkward angle. My head smashed into the board, and I fell, splayed out, onto my back.

"Shit!" I screamed through gritted teeth. "Shit, shit, shit, shit, *shit!*"

My head felt like it had a heartbeat of its own, but still, I got off my knees. Maybe the third time was the charm. Above me, the bird dangled from the ledge, teetering in mockery. At least it was closer. Maybe the bashing of my skull hadn't been the worst thing in the world unless, of course, my brain had become completely discombobulated, and I was seeing things.

This time, I was prepared. I sucked in a breath, and without thinking twice, I soared. My outstretched hand latched onto the windowsill, tightening for dear life over the wood. It took everything I had to keep from crying out in triumph. A pinched smile forced itself onto my face. I gripped it with my other hand, slipping my fingers into the grooves. Walking up the wall like a stubby-legged spider, I pulled my feet up, bending in an incredibly awkward, lung-crushing position. Panting, I steadied myself, pressing both hands against the window frame. I teetered dangerously off the tiny ledge, which had seemed so huge from the ground, but barely counted for anything when I was attempting to sit on it.

Jaw clenched, I swung a hand to the top and flung the bird to the ground. It landed with a satisfying thud, and sure enough, out of its torn-open chest flew a single item, about as long as my pinky finger. It was a uniquely-designed key that looked like it belonged in an antique shop way more than it belonged on a prison island. I swung down from the window, plopping onto the pavement with a *whoosh*.

My hand travelled over the key. The top of it looped in a circle, a good enough size to fit around my finger like a ring. The bottom was cylindrical and narrow, splitting off into two ends. It was light in my hand, and the sunlight reflected off the bronze surface. Before I could puzzle over what it was, I tightened my fist around it. If it wasn't worth anything, I swore to myself that I would toss it onto the beach out of rage, letting it go off to its death like the land mine it would be sure to ignite.

I flew past the crowd again, exhausted from the leap but not entirely burnt out yet. Filled with frenetic energy, I was able to slip out below the notice of everyone but Cerina Rayz and her watchful eye.

Breaking away from her exchange of words with yet another rogue Family, she cut her way through the tangle of people and sped off, startling everyone in the cluster.

But I didn't hear her with the wind in my ears, my attention diverted by the triumph in my smile. Whatever it was, I had just managed to steal an item from the Level Two sector. Maybe it wasn't worth much, but I could snag *dirt* from the Level Two streets and it would get me respect. That much I knew.

As I dashed forward, the dividing line in my sight, all I could hope for was that whatever in my hand was worth   it.

Cerina Rayz

Planning and precision

It had been entirely on a whim that I had ditched the parlay at the door- this time, with the bloodsoaked thorns- and run after Emry McLeod. In fact, when that streak of red hair had blown by, I had only been half-sure it actually belonged to him. That wasn't the part I had noticed. Truth be told, my eye had been captured solely by the way he was walking. He ran, correction, *escaped* with a telling gait that I had seen countless times in the Level Two sector. It could only be described as the stride of a person bent on a mission to make a quick getaway, half-paralysed by fear but still alive enough from the initial adrenaline rush to pick up their feet and hightail it out of there.

At a closer distance, when fatigue finally caught up with him, I was able to see that Emry had something clutched in his hand. And that something was nothing other than the bronze key.

The damn kid was a spy, after all.

He sensed my arrival, speeding up. I swore, lunging forward and tackling him to the ground. He stumbled, and we tripped and rolled onto the centre of the border, arms and legs flailing every which way. I got him pinned, pressing both of my hands to his wrists. His fists opened. Nothing. I scanned the area. About a metre away, planted in the dirt, was the bronze key.

Emry whimpered, mid-wheeze. "Let me go," he pleaded. "I need that-"

"You don't need it. You *want* it. There's a difference."

Breathless, Emry went limp. "Please? I bashed my head to get that thing. Now I feel like I might-"

"You might... what?"

Emry lurched forwards, a torrent of vomit flooding from his mouth. I scurried back, letting go of Emry as I took notice of the three people sprinting from the Level One sector. The short girl in the middle ran with haste, her long blond hair whipping behind her. The person beside her sported a jagged pixie cut, urgency written on their forehead. Something about the short-haired person seemed familiar, but I wasn't able to place it until they had drawn closer.

Behind that duo was a second girl, following with hesitation. She walked with uncertainty, stealing a nervous glance behind her.

The girl at the front of the group snatched the key from the ground. "Emry," she growled. "You are the biggest idiot on this island."

"But-" the second person stepped up, a black sharpie in their hands. That was when I recognised them. It had been two months since we had last crossed paths, but our last interaction wasn't one I would soon forget. They were the Level One who had been entrusted the bronze key by the former Head Chefs. It was supposed to have been made to look like a sneaky move, but they had made it all too easy for me to slip through the Level One sector and snag the key right under their noses. The person's name was Taven if I recalled correctly. Maven, possibly?

"You, Emry McLeod, have just made off with the biggest prize of the Level Two sector." *Haven*. That was it. They lifted a vomit-soaked Emry off the ground, raising their eyebrows in an impressed look. "You're more than worthy of this."

Without further adieu, a dark streak was marked onto Emry's filthy mop of hair.

"Mind telling me what this is all about?" I asked, fixated on the key in the girl's hand.

The third person caught up, stifling a short gasp the moment she saw me.

"We're actually running a recruitment operation," she spoke, her words flying a mile a minute. She reached out a hand to shake before immediately pulling it back. "The name's Adrienne. This is Haven, and that's Lizabeth. We are so honoured to be in your presence-"

I arched my eyebrows. "Please. There's no need for any of that." I turned to Lizabeth, eyeing the key in her palm. "Now, I'm going to make this very simple. Give me the key. *I* don't want to hurt any of you, but if you don't hand it over right now, the key and its legacy will do you great harm."

Lizabeth loosened her hand. "Forgive us, er, ma'am. Here, the key is all yours." She held out her palm, but before I could make my move, Emry leapt up, snatching it.

"Lizabeth, wait," he stammered, putting himself between the group and me. "We're running a recruitment operation, no? I think we have a perfect recruit right here."

Haven stalked forward, grabbing Emry by the wrist. "Absolutely not. Hand her the key, Emry. You don't know what you're dealing with."

"You're the one who's trying to escape the island," Emry swatted at Haven's arm as they attempted to pry the key from Emry's grip, digging their fingers into Emry's fist. A spectrum of emotions flooded over Haven's face, ranging between anger, surprise, and shame.

"I'm going to stop you right there," I butted in. "You *can't* escape. It's impossible."

Emry coughed. "I knocked your damn bird off the window. Anything is possible! Especially if we have you," Emry cheered weakly. The guy had definitely hit his head.

"Do you guys not realise how little chance you have? Do you know what the probability is that you'll make it off this island? Zip, zero, zilch. Now, if you don't *mind*," I sprung at Emry and Haven, snatching the key from both of their grasps. "I'll be on my way. If you know what's good for you, you'll stay on your side of the line."

I whipped around, stalking back to the Level Two sector.

"Wait!" Emry grabbed me by the wrist. He reeked of sweat and puke- both things that covered him from head to toe. "Please. We, I mean, you, you guys have a plan. Right? You said you had a plan? Are we a *we*? Is that a thing?"

Haven massaged their temples, breathing out a deep sigh.

"Whatever it is, it's not going to work," I said. I was fully prepared to turn back around when Emry pulled out his last defence, stopping me.

"So you'd rather stay here?"

His face was hopeful, along with the expressions of all of his fellow Level Ones. It was maddening. In theory, I was supposed to have built up an immunity to this. But maybe I wasn't as invincible as I was made out to be.

"Follow me," I grumbled, "you desperately need to get washed up."

***

Irabella would probably call me a traitor to host a band of four outsiders in the old mess hall. It wasn't my ideal plan either, but Emry reeked, and his friends didn't smell so great themselves. Don't get me wrong, I didn't have the pettiness to let that bother me, but with the luxury of the shower in the mess hall's bathroom, you forget about what it's like to have to get your drinking water from a tap sticking out of a cabin's wall.

A collective gasp descended over the four Level Ones, namely the two older prisoners introduced as Adrienne and Haven. Emry didn't look that impressed- after all, it was nothing but a bare room dotted with tables and chairs. Even the kitchen, the door to which stuck out of the right-hand corner, was pretty drab, with most of the drawers bare, their contents long raided by the previous head chefs.

Still, he definitely didn't object to the clean bathroom awaiting him in the left corner of the mess hall.

Even though I had never technically given them permission, Lizabeth, Haven, and Adrienne began to line up in front of the door. The sound of the shower's turbulent jet of water trickling down the drain came from the locked bathroom, putting longing looks on everyone's faces.

After five long minutes, Emry stepped out of the shower, his hair wet and sticky but sharp and clean. With his prison uniform drying on top of the radiator, the only thing to cover him was a massive pile of towels, each one used to cover every inch of his skin as though he were an overstuffed marshmallow. I had to stifle a laugh when I saw him emerge from the washroom fully prepared for a freezing blizzard.

Lizabeth stepped back as Adrienne and Haven scrambled to take his spot, engaging in a full-out wrestling match to determine who would make it inside. In the end, it was Adrienne who won, ducking in behind the door before the others could stop her. The group reminded me of my own bunkmates.

But as Level Ones, they still retained some measure of innocence.

Unlike me.

I drew in a sharp breath. "So," I began, "let's hear it. What's your plan, and why do you need me for it?"

"Our plan is still in the works," Haven admitted sheepishly, tossing an annoyed glance in Emry's direction, "but, clearly, *some* of us have a *ton* of brilliant ideas."

"I think it should be obvious why we want you to join us," Emry said, ignoring the barb, "You're respected, strong, brave-"

Haven nudged Emry in the shoulder. "What he's *trying* to say," Haven explained, "is that he's an idiot who doesn't know what he's talking about, but he fears you like everyone else on this island. In exchange for your kind treatment and your silence regarding this issue, we owe you and the members of building 2-7 a debt. However we are to pay off said debt is up to you."

Emry audibly gasped. "We can't just pass this opportunity by! We have a Level Two with us! There's-" Haven blinked, slowly. They bit their bottom lip, retreating from the conversation to rap sharply on the washroom door.

"Adrienne!" they called, "if you haven't started your shower yet, would you mind giving up your spot in line to teach Emry here about who Cerina *is*?"

The door opened, and Adrienne sighed, casting a longing look at the clean shower stall lying in wait. She pulled Emry aside, taking him into the kitchen and leaving me alone with Haven. I couldn't hear what they were talking about, but I could only begin to guess what types of rumours the Level Ones liked to spread about the other half of the island.

"You owe me nothing," I said at last, "no one is to hear about our encounter. As far as I'm concerned, nothing ever happened. Understood?"

"Are you sure? I insist-"

"No compensation is necessary. You have done me no harm; therefore, there is nothing to compensate *for*. And even if there were, I have no use for you. Building 2-7 is perfectly capable of minding to its own affairs."

"Understood," Haven said, topping it off with a curt nod. We were about to shake on it when Emry reemerged from the kitchen, bursting our agreement wide open.

"You're still coming with us!" He cried.

Adrienne chased after him. "Are you out of your mind? No!"

Emry skidded to a halt in front of me, whirling to stare down a red-faced Adrienne. "Don't you see?" Emry shouted, "this is even better! She's the most powerful person in the Level Two sector! You've heard about what she's done as the keeper of the key. Now imagine what would happen if she had the *guards'* keys!"

Haven winced, gritting their teeth. "This is *really* a conversation we should be having in *private*."

I fought back a laugh, not wanting to embarrass these two even further. "Look. I admire your cause and your determination, I really do, but this idea is out of the question. I am willing to ignore you if you ignore me, but this is a step too far."

"You don't think we can do it?" Emry challenged.

"No. I don't."

"But it's better we try than do nothing. I don't want to waste away here for my whole life, and I don't think any of you do. Even the worst-case scenario presents two options. Either we get out and die fighting for freedom, or we die *here*. Now I'm not going to make any judgments because, quite honestly, I'm genuinely curious. Which fate would *you* prefer?"

Haven opened their mouth but had nothing to object with. Adrienne, as well, was drawing a blank.

Emry made a pretty damn valid point.

"If I'm really going to consider this," I said. "Then I have two things to say. First of all, I'm not adopting your trademark hair streak- there's no way I'd allow myself to look like I'm from another Family. And as for the second thing... there's someone else we should bring along."

My terms were fair, and my words were confident, but the only person who looked indefinitely certain was Emry.

He thought he had all the answers, but he was sorely mistaken. I glanced at Adrienne, and she rapidly looked away, shrinking under my stare.

She had neglected to mention one crucial detail to Emry. One vital slip of information was on the top of everybody's mind, gnawing at their certainty like a swarm of termites.

It was the clear distinction between a Level One and a Level Two. Getting sent to the Offshore Youth Rehabilitation Facility was one thing, but the number on your shoulder was the true identifier. Haven and Adrienne stared at me with a mixture of dread, shock, and fear. It was as though they were staring at a monster.

And they weren't wrong in their judgement. How could they not be scared when I, Cerina Rayz, had been sent to the Isle for murder?

***

"Where on earth have you been?" Irabella paced back and forth on the floor of building 2-7, fretting as I shut myself inside. "The key is missing! We've been looking everywhere! Discreetly, of course. But nobody has it! I don't know-"

I reached my hand into my satchel, pulling out the tiny object. "Relax. It's right here."

Irabella's eyes widened. She stalked across the floor, ripping the key from my hand. "Could you *maybe* have thought to *tell us* that you had removed the key from the hiding spot? The last hour has not been pleasant."

"I apologise. I suppose you could say I got a little sidetracked."

"Sidetracked how?"

"That's none of your concern."

Irabella raised her eyebrows. "Oh? You're playing that card?"

I assessed the crowd I had in front of me. Most people had gone off on Irabella's wild goose chase, but a few members had stayed put to hang out in their bunks. Arvin, I saw with relief, was among them.

"We're changing the hiding spot," I announced, "the bird fell. From now on, the key stays with me."

For once, Irabella didn't seem so sure about my decision. "Fine," she agreed after a long moment. "But you have to stick with us next time. And alert us of any sudden changes."

"I certainly will."

I hung my satchel onto the coat hook, transitioning the key to my front pocket. Irabella followed me up to my bunk, where I was about to dig into my lunch.

"Come on," she pressed, "can you at least give me a hint about what you were doing?"

"I told you," I said, "that's none of your concern."

"Seriously?!" Irabella huffed, "how bad could it have been? Did you beat someone up? Get into a fight, make it all bloody? No, you're not injured." Her eyes suddenly widened. "Are you seeing someone? Damn, Cerina. Of all the places to hook up-"

"I was not *hooking up*. Got it?"

"You better not have been. This place is freaking revolting, not just in terms of hygiene but in terms of *material*. Seriously, Where were you?"

"How many times do I have to say it? It's none of your business. Now, go. Call off the hunt for the key. Do *something* instead of bugging me about my personal life!"

A hurt expression passed over Irabella's face. She hopped down from the ladder, crossing her arms.

"Fine." She huffed. "I thought we were friends, but if you want to give me orders, I'll follow them. Bye, Cerina. Or, should I say, *ma'am*?"

"Irabella, wait-"

Before I could finish, she was out the door.

I sighed, walking up to Arvin, who had been watching the whole scene unfold. "Arvin," I whispered, "there are some people I'd like you to meet."

The old man arched one of his white, bushy eyebrows. "You come to me, of all people? Now *this* has captured my attention."

"Good," I said, not wasting any time, "this is going to sound stupid, and I'll admit, I don't have high hopes. But what would you say about trying to escape the Isle?"

Arvin gave me a half-smile. "Good luck with that."

Jakson Veer

Eager words

The plant, let's just say, had seen better days. The pot had struck a hard landing when it had toppled from my hands, and now, the clay fragments were bound together by a few of Farrah's tensor bandages. I wasn't sure which one it resembled more- a mummy or an ER patient. Perhaps a bit of both.

Despite its look, the sprout itself was actually doing quite well. Under my care, it was thriving within days, and while I didn't like to brag about something so simple, the green leaves were probably the only things capable of making me smile on a day-to-day basis.

Unfortunately for me, however, the plant's welfare was the least of my problems.

Thanks to Haven, Emry, Lizabeth and Adrienne, I now had to deal with three unbearable people. An old friend (Lizabeth), a partial psychopath (Cerina), and a deranged old guy (Arvin) had all busted into my life with next to no prior warning, and it didn't appear as though they were making plans to depart any time soon.

In the shadows of building 1-3, a deal had been struck. When it came to Cerina, things were simple enough. At least, that was the way she sold it. However, the plan she laid out, which none of us had the power to contradict, left her with much more say in matters than any of us did. We would meet every two days, and during that time, we would discuss strategy. Cerina could join us as she pleased, and she had veto power over every decision. Not only that, but she brought Arvin with her.

The plan was simple for us, but it clearly bothered Haven. They readily caved to Cerina's every whim, but more than once, I had picked up an angry word, a raised voice, and a furrowed brow targeted in her direction. Quite frankly, I couldn't blame them. I didn't trust anyone on the island, but I trusted Cerina even less than the prison guards. And it didn't take a genius to realise the feeling was mutual.

I kept as far away from Lizabeth as possible, and with both of us stubbornly refusing to ditch the group, we had no choice but to continue meeting in the same room. We hadn't spoken directly ever since our first day on the island, but her voice, even when directed elsewhere, bore the agonising tones of nails on a chalkboard.

Amélie and Farrah did their own thing, as did Haven, Adrienne, and Max. We had all pretty much divided ourselves into our own separate sub-groups. Except for me, of course. But how could I complain? I had a plant to keep me company.

As soon as Cerina and Arvin were on board, we had completely wrapped up the recruitment operation. Our first official meeting, with everyone accounted for, was held in building 1-3.

"We should call ourselves the Escape Artists," Adrienne had suggested to open us up, sitting down on a nearby bunk. It was a shadowy evening, and lights-out was fast approaching. It wasn't a good idea to be meeting at such a time, but there was no choice but to cut it close. Cerina was busy in building 2-7, and we had to abide by her schedule.

"Whatever for? There's no time for silly business in a tough case like ours." Everyone turned to Arvin. Cerina kept him close by, occasionally reaching out to grab his uniform as though it were a leash.

"Arvin," Cerina said, "have patience, please."

"Oh, I'm plenty patient," the old man objected, "we just gotta think seriously. And that name sucks." Arvin spat up a thick wad of saliva, which sent everyone reeling backwards in repulsion.

"Okay," I said, bringing us back to the present. "We don't need a name immediately. Or, for that matter, at all. What we *do* need is a plan." Truthfully, I had already been told the plan. Farrah and Haven had met up in private at Farrah's bunk in building 1-10 earlier that morning, and I had presented a lot of my input. After giving Haven some suggestions, I had to admit I was eager to hear what they had turned our ideas into.

Everyone nodded in agreement, leaning in.

"Here's what we've got," said Haven, dropping their voice. "The escape plan has three parts- and I need all three of you for each one."

"Step one," Haven explained, "We tap into their communications. We cut off the line to their head of military defence, Jezmon Tylor, and disable the links between the high-ups on the Isle and the mainland. In order to do so, we'll have to gain access to some tech. And in order to do *that*, we have to deal with the guards, which is where the poison comes in. Once we're done with that step, we can proceed to part two."

Everyone nodded along with the plan thus far. Even Cerina muttered her approval, allowing Haven to continue.

"Secondly, we have to steal our identities back. Once we've gotten into the online software, we can shimmy around in those records. But nowadays, thanks to the technology risks brought on by the wars, most records are physical, and ours are probably being stashed in a filing cabinet somewhere in the inner circle."

More nods.

"And finally, once the technical stuff is sorted out- we run for it."

Carina was the first to object. "That sounds great in theory, but you can't steal a person's identity from a guard's walkie-talkie. How do you plan on tapping into the Isle's security? They don't just have personal files floating around for anyone to come by and steal."

"We break into the inner circle."

"Yeah. Because *that's* a simple task."

I had known this was coming- I had even helped Haven plan the entry. Ideally, it would be a simple in and out job. A survey, followed by an assessment of the risks. If it was all clear, we'd make off with a laptop. If not, well… we'd have to improvise.

"We'll sneak in through the food chute," I stated.

"That won't work," Amélie said, "it's way too small."

"Not necessarily. I've taken measurements into account. It will be a tight fit, but there's one person who can make it."

Everyone turned to Lizabeth.

"No. No way. Absolutely not."

"It's the only way," I muttered awkwardly, staring at the ground. It wasn't like this was my first choice, either. "All you have to do is take a peek inside. If all goes according to plan, you'll get out of there safely and below the guards' notice."

"No. I can't go in there. What if there are people right outside? What if the machine has a mechanical crusher, or I end up trapped? There are too many uncertainties. You might as well be sending me to the wolves."

Her point was fair, and none of us could contradict it. It surprised everyone to hear Emry, of all people, be the first one to speak.

"Maybe we can get in another way?"

Amélie regarded him with scepticism. "And what, do tell, would this 'other way' be?"

"When the Level Three inmates are taken to the inner circle, the guards kinda freak out. I didn't see much when I was caught in their midst, but the gate was open for quite some time after all the guards had fled to help keep the Level Threes at bay. What I'm saying is, if we could anticipate the next Level Three transportation, we'd have a clear shot at getting inside."

I hated to shut down his idea when his face was so hopeful, but his plan wouldn't work. "It's not a bad proposition, but it's also not going to happen. The gate is heavily monitored, and there will doubtless be guards inside. It's the most active area in the inner circle. We don't stand a chance."

"There will also be cameras on the other end of the shaft," Lizabeth countered, "and at least with the gate, we know what we're looking at. More people can get inside, as well."

"It could be months until the next Level Three is tagged. The guards catch them at random."

"Exactly. It could happen next year, or it could happen tomorrow."

"We can't prepare for tomorrow, and we can't wait for next year."

"If we wait in secret, the guards are unlikely to suspect a thing. They don't care about us. And don't forget they switch shifts," Lizabeth pressed, her determined gaze unrelenting.

"But what if they do, suspect us, I mean?"

"Look. I'm not going through a food shaft. Got it?"

"Oh, because the last time you made a decision on our behalf, everything worked out great." The pointed remark flew out before I knew it was coming. A hurt look flashed over Lizabeth's face. The others stepped away, glancing between each other.

"Get out," Lizabeth bit, "this isn't your cabin."

"It's not yours, either."

"Either way, there's only room for one of us."

Lizabeth and I were positioned on opposite ends of the room. The door was to my back, whereas Lizabeth hugged the other wall, shrinking away from my presence as though I were some sort of disease.

"I'm staying," I said, "I have more to offer. And, not only do I want to get out of here, I *need* to get out of here. The only thing you need is a reality check."

"Has it ever occurred to you that maybe we *need* the same thing?"

Emry shuffled closer to Lizabeth, eyeing the both of us nervously. "What is happening?" He rasped. Both of us shot him an intense glare, clamming him up with due diligence.

Our gazes then began to refocus. Lizabeth stood resolutely, fixed against the wall. Her stance was firm, but her eyes wavered. She was about to give up. From the start, I thought I wanted that. But now, I was watching my own expression reflected in her eyes.

Her eyes. I had never been able to tell whether or not they were blue or green. And even now, I was fuzzy on the distinction. In spite of everything, that small, insignificant fact remained unchanged. How funny.

I pursed my lips and whirled around, storming out the door.

What had just happened? I had never been on an athletic team in my entire life, but I could now relate to the losers of a sports game- sullen-faced, angry, and sad. But the worst part about losing was having to face the winning team, a group of people exactly like them, but proud, happy, and victorious. The stiff handshake at the end where neither party knew what to say was the sentiment radiating throughout building 1-3. Snippy arguments could say plenty, but there is only awkward silence when the dust settles.

I walked, hunched over, back to my cabin. My mother had always been uptight about posture, but I could slouch all I liked without her to watch over my shoulder- both literally and figuratively. I cursed the smooth stone of the Level One sector. According to Cerina, the Level Two grounds were cracked and chipped- hazardous. How could our living quarters be so filthy yet so neat and tidy? Everyone on the Isle was broken. The ground below us had no right to be whole and put together.

My cabin was momentarily occupied. Inside, a very happy couple was taking advantage of the space, making out with an uncomfortable level of aggression. They promptly ignored me as I slipped by, keeping my eyes on the ground.

I pulled up my pillow and took the tiny potted plant in my hands. The itty bitty leaves were green and sufficiently moisturised, but I knew that wouldn't last.

"At least I still have you," I muttered. "You barely-germinated seedling."

"Hi."

I spun around, nearly dropping the pot a second time. Farrah stood behind me, a stone-cold expression on her face. In the corner of my eye, the couple kicked their kissing up a notch, and I struggled not to gag.

"Hello," I stammered, deciding then and there that, of all places, the ceiling was the safest place to look.

"You were being a jerk," Farrah said. I caught traces of an accent in her soft voice, but I was unable to place it.

"I know," I admitted.

"Are you sorry?"

Something strange, dangerous, and albeit terrifying welled up inside of me. "I don't know."

"Then I don't know if I forgive you," Farrah said, sitting next to me. I flushed, taking notice of our close proximity.

"Look," I explained, "you don't get it. It's kind of a long story."

Farrah looked at me with undaunted understanding in her icy stare that somehow reflected a hidden part of myself. She slipped her hand into her cast and pulled out a small item.

"It's a sweet," she said, "caramel. You probably don't deserve it. But I 'get it' more than you think. And in a world where no one gets what they want, the least a person could do is give someone what they need. And needs go beyond the fundamentals of 'deserving' and 'righteousness.'" To strip someone of their basic necessities, social, emotional, or otherwise, is to strip them of their humanity. And *nobody* deserves that."

"How…" my voice warbled, and I coughed, clearing my throat of phlegm. "How did you get that here?" The sound was too high. To Farrah's ears, I seemed just like a petty four-year-old trying to get a nonsensical point across. Not a sixteen-year-old, not a fucking *high school student*. What on earth was my problem?

"I store things. It's safe; anything with sugar preserves itself."

"Did you give one to Lizabeth?"

"No. She looked like she didn't want one. But I've never really been able to tell those things from a surface glance."

A bitter laugh escaped me. "Same here."

"Are you trapped in the past?"

"I guess."

"Ah," Farrah nodded, a faraway look in her eyes. "I think I understand that. Do you think you can try to work things out?"

I had no idea what I was agreeing to, or if I was even agreeing to *anything*, but I took the potentially disease-ridden caramel in my hand and chewed it up, even though I had never been fond of sweet things. "I'd like that." I forced the candy down my throat in one swift gulp. It was the sentiment that mattered, and sometimes, you have to take what you can get.

"Great," Farrah said, "now go apologise."

"Me? What do *I* need to-"

"It has to start somewhere. I don't know what happened between you two, but you can't fight forever."

"Look. You don't know what you're talking about."

"I don't know the details. But maybe that's what you need."

The couple that had previously been deeply enamoured with each other departed from the room, leaving us in silence.

I moved my eyes away from the ceiling, cautiously bringing them up to Farrah. She caught them in her gaze like a net, drawing them closer and encircling them like mesh webbing.

Farrah nudged me on the shoulder. I sighed, getting back on my feet.

"*Fine*. I'll try, but I can't make any promises."

Lizabeth Merrin

Miss Popular

"What was *that* about?" Emry asked after the meeting had drawn to a close. For a change of scenery, we had moved outside, leaning against the wall. I was starting to like Emry as a person, despite his impulsive behaviour, but right now, I just wanted to be alone with my thoughts.

"I don't want to talk about it," I admitted.

"That's fair. But seriously, what's up with Jakson?"

"What part of 'I don't want to talk about it' did you not understand?"

I didn't wait for him to respond, pushing off the wall and stalking off towards the field. I didn't know where I planned on going. Anywhere but here would suffice.

It seemed as though the meal station was back up and running. I had lost my appetite, which meant that there was no reason for me to be circling the grassy field.

I didn't care. Pacing back and forth, I wished I could bite back my words. *Get out. This isn't your cabin.* I was supposed to make everything better. Setting things right might have been a distant possibility before, but with the way I was acting, I had the same probability of making up for what I had done as the sun did of spontaneously falling out of the sky.

My teeth gritted against each other in frustration. "Stupid island. Stupid Jakson. Stupid *me*."

"Stupid Darby?" I whirled around, a jolt running up my spine the second I heard the familiar voice. I had called Darby's face to mind several times since my arrival, but nothing was comparable to seeing him in person, with his victorious glare zeroed in on my trapped expression.

Darby's neon hair truly put the blue in his uniform to shame. He looked exactly the same as when I had last seen him, watching as the three of us were separated and slammed behind the bars of the shipping trailers.

His arm only newly stamped, he had clawed at the window and sworn that he would make me pay.

The same expression was on his face right now. I took a few steps back, holding my hands in the air in a gesture of surrender. What good it would do. He was here to uphold his promise of vengeance.

"Considering you doomed us all," Darby continued, "it's sad you didn't include me in your speech."

I bit my lip. "I don't want to fight with you. Okay?"

"No, no, no, you don't want to fight with *anyone*. It's why you chickened out, isn't it? Why you sent us here?"

"Oh please," I said, unable to contain the flood, "you had booked your ticket to this island the second you found your target for the job."

Darby advanced, his hot breath streaming down my throat. "Doesn't mean I had to board the plane, dumbass. You kicked me in head-first, thanks to the idiotic stunt you pulled. And I'm not going to forget that easily. I won't kill you, but I'll give you what you deserve. You can bet on that."

"Please," I begged, eyes darting back and forth for an escape. "You can't hurt me. If you do, you'll be tagged as a level 3. You'll be taken into the inner circle and killed. I've heard the theories tossed around the Isle. I'm sure you have, too."

"Good," Darby said, sporting a twisted grin. "I've always wanted to be the worst of the worst. But I can't do that very well in prison, can I? If the only way out is in there, then I want out. And I'm taking you with me."

He seized me in a headlock, pinching my arms behind my back. "Y'know, I always thought you were kinda hot. 'Shame you had to waste your talents on that girlfriend of yours. What was her name again? She'll be awfully sad when she hears how you went out."

"Her name is Mel," I choked out, struggling against his giant arm.

"Pretty name. I'll be sure to remember it as the last word you ever uttered."

His grip tightened, cutting off the air to my windpipe. I kicked, writhing around, desperate to escape. Darby had always been a ticking time bomb, but this…

"You… are… a *psycho*…." I coughed out. "I want… those to be… my last words."

Darby pulled tighter, glaring at me with a pure, undying hatred. Black spots eased their way onto my vision, playing with my thoughts. The panic danced on the fringes of my world, slowly ebbing as my entire world faded into blackness.

When I met Darby, I was with Jakson and Mel. We were all freshly off school- taking advantage of the weekend by meeting up and discussing our shared goals, needs, and plans for the future. We all went to the same high school, and we were all facing our own set of challenges. Jakson was strained from the academic program he was in, and while Mel and I weren't under as much stress from homework, we still had to deal with all the jerks that turned up their noses when they saw us holding hands in the hallways.

But that was nothing compared to the stress of our financial situations. Things weren't looking up, so we had to, shall we say… force them up.

I had been on smaller jobs with smaller groups before, but this time it was different. There was no big guy in charge with a husky voice and a gun at his waist like the kinds of things you see on TV. It was just the four of us. Jakson Veer, the biggest brain in school, Darby, the young anarchist we had somehow managed to sway to our side, me, of course, and Mel, my girlfriend.

We all needed the money. Jakson's parents owned a business of their own, but they pretended to be a lot more well off than they actually were. Every penny of theirs went to their outward appearance, to the point where they didn't have enough money left to provide their son with the basic essentials. My father had thrown all our cash away on a drunken trip to the casino, and Mel had gotten her bank account hacked. Darby just wanted an excuse to break things, and the heaping pile of dough he would wind up with in the process was just an added bonus. The plan was that we'd split the giant sum of money four ways, each one enough to get us through our tough spots.

Our financial dilemmas weren't uncommon in Sykona. Two wars had been wrought on the country- the Sykonan war, which had created our country in the first place, along with the more recent civil war that had many hazy details surrounding its cause and outcome. Amid all the conflict, anyone in good financial shape in Sykona was a rare find.

One such find became the target of our operation. The four of us were robbing a wealthy family.

Nobody likes snobs. And I could be a patient person, but I was no exception. However, the target of our assault wasn't *that* kind of rich kid. Don't get me wrong, we all had a certain level of resentment towards the upper class, but even still, the thought of taking money from someone undeserving made me nauseous.

I would have gone through with it if Darby's grudge hadn't come into play. Darby, oddly enough, didn't have a lot of enemies. Everyone steered clear of him because his rage was lethal. Deep down, he had a bit of a softer side, and once you got to know him, he could truly be a fun guy. But the thing about Darby

Olson was that he had a strange, obsessive fixation with loyalty and payback.

Jakson and I were always careful around him, and we were correct to do so. When we saw who our target was, we began to understand just how far Darby's grudges could go.

The target was a quiet guy named Harold. Mel and I had nothing against him- for the most part, he kept to himself. But, a while back, he had caught Darby stealing school lunches, which got the guy suspended for a week. It wasn't the suspension that ticked him off, though. Getting caught knocked him down a few pegs on the social ladder. Now, he was just another student who was just as vulnerable to getting punished as anyone else was.

Unwittingly, Harold had just pinned himself in the crosshairs of an unstoppable grudge.

It was Jakson who navigated the web of technical stuff. He dealt with the account we would use to store the money, something that couldn't be traced back to the four of us. He couldn't get any passwords, but that was okay. That was our job.

Mel and I were working together on the strategy and the risk assessment. There were plenty of valuable items in Harold's house, but we decided that our main goal was the money. Once we had our hands on that, we could be unstoppable. We spent long hours into the night thinking about what we would do once the heist was completed. We could run away, to a different town, to a different country. We could leave everything behind.

Darby took care of the 'brute force' aspect. He went alone, against our wishes, and managed to wrangle the bank information out of Harold and his family. As soon as the numbers started to go up in our offshore account, I panicked.

Jakson and Darby were in too deep to get out of the storm, but Mel had played it safe. When we met afterwards to discuss, I texted Mel in secret, telling her to run and to run far away. Just as Jakson started to clue in, I called the cops.

I didn't know about the Isle of Rebels. We lived in a small town on the country's border. I didn't know where the boundary lines started and ended amid the chaos of the new government and our own personal struggles. For some reason, I didn't think the rules applied to us.

But the thing was, even after seeing what had happened to Jakson, Darby, and *me*, I would do it all again. I hadn't chosen correctly. Nobody who had ever decided anything in the history of the world had chosen correctly because when you make a choice, you leave the alternative in the dust.

Looking back on it then, I realised that maybe the other alternatives had been far behind to begin with.

***

My eyes shot open.

"Let go of her, now." A familiar voice rang out. I gasped at it like a lifeline before jamming down the tide of hope. It was just a hallucination. One final push before my body ran out of oxygen and I was completely done for.

The hands closed around my throat were wrenched off in a huff of hot breath, sweat and tears. Tears. My eyelashes were sticky with them. I inhaled a choked gasp, relishing the taste of air running down my throat once more. I wobbled, steadying myself.

Jakson stood eye-to-eye with Darby; his knuckles turned utterly white from clutching the flower pot in his hand.

Darby stared at Jakson, pure terror in his expression. "You…"

That's when I spotted it. Sticking out of Darby's leg was a tiny shard of the pot protruding from the flesh. Blood gushed out of the wound, spewing all over the grass. A guard leaned against the gate of the inner circle, watching the scene play out as though it was some messed up form of quality entertainment. They fidgeted with their tight uniform, blinking lazily in the sun. The guard wanted to weed out the Level Threes, I realised. They watched us to see if we were the brutal murderers who would be sent to the inner circle to face execution.

"Jakson-" I breathed. "You-"

Were we? We had come here as outsiders, but had that only been decency's plea with me? Were *we* the monsters?

As if he could read my thoughts, Jakson spoke venomously. "The wound isn't fatal. It'll bleed a bit longer, and then it'll calm down. But I can do worse, and so can she. Stay away from us, Darby. Or you will regret it."

Darby turned and fled. Jakson and I faced each other, a million unsaid things floating between us. I nodded once, as a thank you, an apology, an acknowledgement.

"Are you…" I said, unsure of how to finish that sentence.

"You should stay away too. If you can forget, so can I."

His words came with a pang, but I agreed with every one of them. "There's room for you in building 1-3," I said, "but that doesn't mean we have to share the space."

"Understood."

As satisfied as we could be, we turned back to the Level One sector, making our return to building 1-3.

The guard looked on, adjusting their rifle. On their face was an expression of mild disappointment. Nothing more. Nothing less.

Emry McLeod

Temporary Solutions

Lizabeth returned to the cabin with her head held down. The meeting, at that point, had mostly broken up. Our initial goal had been finalised, and the framework of our plan was settled.

"Hey," I began, "are you finally ready to spill the tea about-" she tilted her head up, giving me the deepest glare I had ever seen. Her cheeks were bright red, and tears pooled at the bottom of her eyes. My words died instantly. "Lizabeth? Are you okay?"

She shoved past me, setting her hand on the doorknob. "I'm fine." She pushed on the door, but it wouldn't budge. Screaming in frustration, she slammed her fist against the wood. "Open up! It's Lizabeth, dammit!"

I set a hand on her shoulder, which she immediately swatted off, digging her fingernail underneath the back of my palm.

"Hey, dude!" I cried, gripping her arm, "stop! What do you think you're doing?"

"I'm getting into my cabin, Emry. Piss off."

"Seriously, hold it for a second. I know you're angry-"

"Did you just call me 'dude'?"

"Excuse me?"

"Earlier. You *totally* called me 'dude'." The rage in her expression started to subside, replaced with a bemused smirk.

"Um… yes, I suppose I did… er, dudette?"

She laughed, an airy sound that fell somewhere between a cough, a snicker, and a guffaw. "Do not call me a 'dudette' ever again."

"Understood. Bro?"

"No."

"Ma'am?"

"Ew."

I sighed. "Lizabeth Ramona Merrin?"

She smiled. "That one's acceptable. How did you know my middle name, though?"

"Your meal card fell out of your pocket." I pointed to the plastic square with my toe, tapping the corner. She huffed, bending down to pick it up.

"You can read that without your glasses?"

"No," I admitted, a little sheepishly. "I saw your meal card beforehand. On the day we arrived."

"Stalker."

"Hey, it's not like it's my fault! If anything, blame the pockets. Everything falls out of them. *Everything*."

"These pockets do suck."

The door cracked open, and Haven peeked out from the other end. "Is everyone okay?" they asked, "the meeting's over. Do you two want to come in?"

I gnawed on the inside of my cheek. Briefly, I met Lizabeth's eyes.

"We'll be out here for a bit. Sorry about that."

Haven shrugged. "No worries." The echo of the door tapping behind us filled the silence for a measure of moments, radiating throughout the streets as Lizabeth stepped down from the stairway, resting against the side of the building. She stared, far off in the distance, folding and unfolding her laminated plastic sheet.

"I almost died today," she breathed. "Well, I was told I wouldn't get killed, but accidents happen."

My ears perked up. Her tone was light, but her subject was heavy. I couldn't tell whether or not she was joking. "Do tell," I said, playing it safe.

And she did. She told me everything. From the crime that put her here, to the sacrifice she had made, to her encounter with Jakson.

When she had finished, I didn't know what to say.

"Shit," I said, putting it plainly. "That sucks."

She gave me a look, only emphasising that I had just stated the obvious. *Is this the best you can do?*

"You're not totally in the wrong, though," I continued. "Is Darby the guy with the blue hair?"

Lizabeth nodded.

"He broke my glasses. I have to say, he seems like a pretty bad dude in general. You were only doing what you thought was right. If this is anyone's fault, it's his."

Lizabeth looked at me as though she were considering it. She seemed surprised, impressed even. But that didn't succeed in masking the solemn undertone to her expression.

"Pinning the blame on other people won't help anything."

I shook my head, drawing in a long, slow breath. "Well, we're all on the same stupid island. It's not like it really matters how we got here and what terrible deeds we used to pave the way. Our predicament sucks just as badly, no matter what we've done. You might as well enjoy the moment."

"Just out of curiosity, how did someone like you end up on the Isle? You said you robbed a convenience store?"

I bristled at the phrase 'someone like you' but nodded along anyway. "Simple as that. My family's short on money, and I needed to provide for them. It was stupid, really. The way I got caught."

"There's no reason to beat yourself up about it," she said, "after all, it's like you said. It sucks just as badly either way."

I chuckled. "I guess that's true." I waited a long moment before continuing to speak. "Have you ever thought, Lizabeth..." I tested, "that it doesn't have to suck?"

Lizabeth leaned her head against building 1-3, shutting her eyes and breathing a wistful sigh. "I wonder every day."

***

After Lizabeth's fight with Jakson, it took the group a few days to bring up the issue again. It was on everybody's mind, yet nobody had anything close to a solution. Even worse, Cerina and Arvin hadn't shown their faces once. We could talk strategy all we wanted, but everything was pointless if we couldn't get Cerina on board. For the most part, our planning strategies were like my old bedroom in the sweltering summer time- they stank to an indescribable degree. And without input from the most valuable asset the Isle had to offer, well, surprise, surprise, they stank even more.

"Alright," Haven said, kicking off another equally tense meet-up. Everyone was spaced out, tense silences filling the gaps and deepening already-gaping craters.

Jakson and Lizabeth were like two magnets, both expelling the natural force of repulsion. Jakson held his back to the door while Lizabeth was positioned on the other end of the room, shuffling as far back as humanly possible. Haven stood in the middle, with Max and Adrienne at their side. Amélie paced around, and Farrah stood next to Jakson. I stood a couple inches away from Lizabeth, keeping my mouth shut.

At the sound of Haven's announcement, we knew what was coming. I think Haven half-hoped Amelie would continue their sentence for them, but she stood silently as if telepathically communicating that Haven was completely on their own.

"I know we've all given some thought to how we're going to orchestrate phase one of the plan," they began, "and none of the options are ideal. Also, let's be honest for a second- nobody wants to climb through a food chute, and it's risky and impossible to sneak through the main gate undetected. So, with that said, we need a new plan to cut off communication between the Isle's security and Jezmon Tylor. Once we do that, there's the whole second phase of our plan to contend with. Phase one only sets things up. We'll have to act fast between the two."

The more the plan was re-explained, the more I realised how improbable our chances of success were. It was like Cerina said. It worked. In *theory*.

"I have an idea," said Max. "But it won't be easy. There's an antenna on the gate of the inner circle. The gate is a thick steel wall, except for the tangle of barbed wire on the top. That's where the antenna is hidden. It's positioned behind the wire, with a little white light blinking on and off. In the daytime, it's pretty easy to miss, but at night you should be able to pick it up."

"Do you think that's how all their communications get through?" Jakson paused, phrasing the question shyly.

"It's the only antenna on the island. They have to connect across the sea somehow, and I think that's how they do it."

"Would the gate be high enough?" I asked, with a lump of dread in my throat. I didn't like where this was going.

"It doesn't need to be very high at all," Max explained. "It's smaller than I had thought it would be, but it must be capable of sending out a pretty good signal."

"Why do we even need to break the antenna anyway?" Lizabeth blurted. I turned to her, a bit baffled. She looked a bit nervous, flustered. It took me a second to notice how hard she was trying to change the topic.

"Because," Haven explained, "when we steal our identities back, they won't be able to call for backup. When we blow this joint, they won't see it coming."

"But they will, though, that's the thing. Once we cut the comms, it's all-out war. We're being too obvious."

Adrienne spoke up. "Escapes can only be done subtly up to a point. If we want things to happen, we can't shy away from change."

"They'll tighten security."

Everybody paused. "How about we do it all at once?" Amélie suggested. "We could conceal the escape with an event. How about a talent show, like the one you ran last year? We could bring the entire Level One sector into it. You wanted an explosion, right? If we do it this way, something's gonna burn."

"You know..." Jakson, Haven, and Max all said simultaneously. "I kinda like that idea."

A talent show between a group of prisoners. Now that was something I didn't want to miss.

***

When lights-out rolled around, I couldn't sleep. I tossed and turned on my bottom bunk, rolling over and over. The room had gotten stuffy, the pitch darkness fully closed in. Each direction felt like the edge of a black wall, suffocation expelled from all sides.

I didn't want to wake anyone, but I couldn't stand this.

"Hey," I tried, "is anyone awake?"

No response. It was probably in vain.

I tossed my head to the side. I was in dire need of the washroom, but I didn't want to risk breaking the curfew. Who knew what the guards would do to me if I got caught?

"Hey, Emry?"

The voice came from above me. I placed it as Lizabeth's.

"Lizabeth?" I called out, a bit wearily. "Can't sleep either, huh?"

"Nah. But it doesn't bother me anymore. Is there anything I can do to help?"

"Unlikely. Unless you, by any chance, have sleeping pills on you."

"Sorry. No can do."

A groggy groan sounded from the top bunk. "What's going on?" It was Haven. I had woken them.

Lizabeth snickered faintly. "I suppose we have another insomniac."

Even in darkness, I could vividly picture Haven's face and the expression that befell it. "You can count me out. Good night."

"It's actually closer to morning at this point," I remarked.

"Good *morning*, then," Haven retorted. I heard them turn over, burying their face into their pillow.

"Morning, Lizabeth," I repeated.

"Morning, Emry. Sweet dreams."

I rolled my eyes, even though it was completely pointless in the darkness.

Then again, the smile on my face was pointless too.

But it still helped.

Cerina Rayz

The bird's message

To the surprise of no one in building 2-7, demand for the bronze key had gotten even higher. Each day, it seemed, I was faced with a new set of enemies and their attack plans, which were getting progressively worse. To Arvin's glee, the key was still being stashed inside the bird carcass, although I had placed it on the roof this time. Based on how laughably bad the latest key-theft attempts had been, though, I might as well have framed it in front of building 2-7 and stuck neon lights around it.

Few people actually looked for the key. They simply relished the thought of getting a free excuse to beat somebody up.

Until one day, when the fighting stopped.

"They must be planning something," Irabella theorised, gritting her teeth. "Arvin? Have you heard anything? You're out all the time on those spying trips. Did you pick up any word of an alliance?"

I bit my lip, hoping that Arvin would do the same. Guiltily, I scratched at a growing red patch on my arm. Even now, Arvin and I were missing an important strategy meeting hosted by the escape team. It was only Irabella leaning against the outside wall of the cabin with us, but we weren't inside the safety of our building, and whispers spread far in the Level Two sector.

Not to mention Irabella couldn't keep a secret for the life of her.

"Nothing, not a peep," Arvin said. "Old ears get rusty. And rusted hinges creak! So loud, they can be."

Arvin winked not-to-subtly in my direction. I pretended to ignore him, dismissing his words the way Irabella would- the mutterings of a crazy man.

"Perhaps you're right," I turned to Irabella, drawing her focus away from Arvin and the roof, which she tossed glances at every now and again, a dead giveaway. "The other Families must be banding together. The key has never been in a single building's possession for so long. They're growing impatient. If we don't let up soon, they'll tire of the game and seek other methods to use theatrics and bloodshed."

"So, what should we do?" Irabella pressed. The tension in her voice heightened, a clear indicator that she hadn't been talking as much as she would've liked to today.

"We hang onto the key until things escalate. Then we denounce our status as an active Family."

Irabella gaped. "Wh- *what*?!"

"This game of ours keeps the others occupied. That's why the guards allow it. If people get bored of it, however, things get violent, and people start getting hurt. I don't want that. For the sake of this sector, I will willingly give up the bronze key if tensions mount."

I might as well have told Irabella that I was about to jump off a bridge and take building 2-7 along with me.

"But you *can't* do that!! It's- it's-" she stuttered, at an utter loss for words.

"I'm not going to hand the key over to just anyone," I reassured. "And believe me, stepping down is the last thing I want to do. But if anything gets bloody, I'm not going to be a part of it. If you don't agree with that, you can join another Family."

That very suggestion clammed her up completely. "Understood..." she trailed off, though the panic hadn't faded from her expression.

"Come on, Arvin," I led the old man away, taking a pause on his primary habitat- the front step. I closed my eyes, basking in the sun's rays. I coughed a few times, clearing out my throat. Maybe it wasn't a great idea to tell Irabella, queen of drama, about my plan.

But it would ensure that my ragtag but loyal team kept anyone from getting seriously injured, which was what I really wanted, above all else.

Right?

A pang resonated through me as I thought of how I had dismissed Irabella the other day. I was stuck. From the start, I had been debating telling her about the group in the Level One sector. But it was too risky, too uncertain. As much as I wanted her on the team, I had to think rationally.

The sun covered my face in a warm blanket, and I breathed out a sigh. It took everything in my power to keep my legs up, to stand unwavering. I was exhausted.

"Hey, Rayz." A pubescent teenage voice, a threat on it that I knew all too well, interrupted me from my moment of rest. I groaned, keeping my eyes shut for a long moment. "You know what we want," the voice pressed.

"Not… again."

I forced myself to blink open. Once again, the Bloodsoaked Thorns had all assembled in a big clump, brows furrowed and fists clenched. Each one bore their signature trademark- a red splotch of their actual blood painted over their hearts. The dude who had spoken had a hideous amount of flaming red acne. I vaguely remembered that his name started with an R. He stood beside a ratty-looking girl with a dishevelled swash of hair and a brow crowned in a thick layer of filth. The two shared the position of leadership since the Family was so big- reaching over two whole buildings.

And yet they hadn't managed to get their hands on the bronze key. And that was really pissing them off.

"So," Zit-face squeaked, narrowing his eyes into slits. It was supposed to be intimidating, but it looked more like he had been staring at the sun for too long. "We gonna do this the easy way or the hard way?"

"Not," I grumbled. Arvin was spaced out, not even bothering to take notice of the giant group surrounding the cabin. I gave him a gentle slap behind his head, snapping him back to reality.

Zit-face frowned in confusion. "Whaddya mean, *not*? 'Fraid I'll hurt ya, girly?" His slimy tone set my nostrils aflare, bringing back a dark memory.

I didn't hesitate before kicking him square in the shins. He doubled back, screaming a string of insults. "Get her, Rosette!"

The other leader, who looked like she had just rolled through a mud puddle, took a swing at my jaw. I guess I had been wrong about the names- it was *hers* that began with an R.

I dodged her punch, pinching her wrist and swinging her arm behind her back, locking her in place with her head pointed firmly at the ground. "What are you doing, you idiots?" She grunted. "Attack her!"

All of the Twos behind her exchanged a wary glance. They varied in physical build, age, and mental capacity, but they outnumbered me to a point where any of my fighting abilities were irrelevant. In close combat, the winner would be obvious.

They realised that seconds before I did. The frontmost line of them surged forward, taking me by surprise. I dropped Rosette, yanking Arvin by the arm and whirling around. I ducked around the building, sprinting and gasping.

"Old bones-" Arvin gasped, "Can't run-"

I swerved down the stretch that separated the buildings from the fence. I could manage easily down the narrow space, but the Bloodsoaked Thorns were trapped, compressing themselves into an awkward blob to avoid crushing themselves. I took advantage of their stumble and shoved Arvin off to the side, hauling his flailing body into a slight dip in the ground. The wind whipped at my face, and I sputtered, choking on the air. What was going on with me today?

I had left two big sleeping quarters in the dust when my brain flipped into strategy mode. What kind of plan was this? I had to get back to building 2-7.

Back on track, the Bloodsoaked Thorns gained on me, hot on my heels. I still maintained a considerable lead. The whole group had packed themselves into the narrow gap instead of splitting off to corner me later. I supposed I could count myself lucky. I didn't crave adrenaline anymore, but they provided the sort of risk-free rush I used to search for. Until, of course...

I couldn't think about my past in the middle of a chase.

Once again, I swerved, en route to my building. I hoped that Arvin hadn't been trampled by the angry mob that fanned out across the street, dispersing over the square. I picked up the pace, tapping into a store of energy reserved only for mad rushes. Silently, I cursed my idea to put in blinds for our building. It seemed like a good idea at the time, but with them blocking the view, there was no one to see me coming, no one to help me inside.

That was fine. I had never needed anyone else, anyway.

I hurtled down the block, fixated on my destination. Twenty feet. Ten feet. Five feet- I tucked in my knees, preparing to make the leap. I barrelled over both steps at once, sticking my legs out and positioning my arms to wrench the door open. My heart raced with the anticipation of victory. My heel buckled, and the jolt within me turned to one of pure terror.

The bottom of my foot collided with the top of the step, bouncing me back. I landed smack on my tailbone, sucking in a lapse of overpowering pain.

Each member out of breath, the Bloodsoaked Thorns caught up to me, laughing between wheezes.

"Well-" Zit-face huffed, "Well-" another inhale, "*well.*"

My shoulders slumped, weighing me down. The back of my skull connected with the cracked stone, receiving only a wince from me, completely absorbed in a raw, throbbing ray of agony. Looking up at the cabin, my eyes drifted to the roof. A sudden panic seized my heart. The bird was gone.

The door to the cabin swung open. On the other side was Irabella, looking down at me with something that resembled shame. In her hand was the dead bird, which she clutched protectively. The others reeled back in disgust, oblivious to what sat inside of it.

"Cerina," Irabella said, her voice the lowest and most serious I had ever heard. "You are banished from building 2-7."

My senses returned to me with a sudden slap. I laughed morbidly, heaving myself back up. "Nice try."

"You don't understand," she rephrased. "We voted. You're kicked out."

"You can't *kick me out* of this building. I sleep here."

"No," Irabella continued. Her words were heavy and clunky, very different from her usual confident, upbeat tone. "We can't kick you out of the Isle's pre-existing sleeping arrangements, but we *can* kick you out of our Family. And building 2-7 is included in that package."

Zit-face whistled, sneering down. "Guess little miss tough guy isn't so strong after all."

I got up, unable to bear the shame of being looked down upon. Heat rose to my face. "You can't do this. You need me."

"Look, I'm sorry," she said. "But that's what the vote came to. And you've made it very clear that you don't need us, so if that's the case, then prove it."

"May I ask where *your* vote stood?"

Irabella blushed, "that doesn't matter."

Rosette coughed. "It's nice to see your precious Cerina knocked down to where she belongs, but y'all owe us a key. Hand it over."

"I don't owe you a living shit," Irabella snapped. She then turned to me. I met her eyes, standing red-faced with my throat swollen and my body aching. "Hand me your satchel. It doesn't belong to you anymore."

Any sorrow or confusion dancing at the tip of my tongue melted away in a burst of hot anger and the weight of shame. I tore my satchel off my shoulder and ripped the thin fabric to shreds. My meal card and the silver bracelet wrapped around it tumbled to the ground. I demolished the last of the satchel before picking up my belongings and stomping the tatters into the rocky crevices.

Rosette and zit-face backed away, smirks on their faces. My eyes met Irabella's, but she tore away instantly, fixated on the ground.

Before she found me, Irabella was a lonely, aggressive gossip girl without a home. I made her what she was. I was here before her, and Arvin, who I had carelessly shoved out of my way, was here before me. My eyes found the bird. Inflating in my chest were the words I so desperately wanted to utter. *The key is inside the bird. Take the thing. Take it.*

But I sealed my lips with all my might, battling the surge of pettiness that consumed me, engulfed me.

"Good luck, Bella. I hope you know what you're doing."

One last barb, and then I whirled. The crowd parted, snickering in my humiliation. I shoved past them. Zit-face jeered in mockery, and I stuck a fist in his face without even looking. I was sore and tired and angry, but I ran; I ran as fast as my legs could carry me, wherever my legs could take me.

Part 2- It's sickening, this ideology

Emry McLeod

A minor issue

I'd mentioned many times that I had never been a lucky dude. I wound up on the Isle of Rebels. My glasses were broken by a psycho. I had been hit with the genius idea to wander to the Level Two sector without any planning or protection. And, of course, the one planning meeting where we actually started to get some actual planning done just *had* to be the one where Cerina Rayz barged in on us and demanded hospitality.

It was the day after we had settled on the groundworks of the plan, and things had actually been going fairly smoothly. Sure, there was an unmissable absence of Cerina's presence, which I wasn't sure how to feel about, but for the first time in a long time, I was getting the sense that my ideas were actually being listened to.

Max, Lizabeth and I had eagerly taken the floor when the door was flung nearly off its hinges. Everyone jumped, scampering back as Cerina barged in with an unceremonious huff. Her chestnut-brown hair was sticking out in every which way, and her face was flustered. The little bag she usually wore across her chest was gone, and she walked with a limp. Her knees were scraped, and the holes in her trousers were caked with blood.

I rushed over to her. "Cerina? What happened?"

Cerina slammed the door shut, a jagged crack shooting up the doorframe. "I've been kicked out of building 2-7."

"Pardon?"

"I *said*, I'm-" she broke into a coughing fit, leaning an arm against the wall. "I've been kicked out of building 2-7."

Lizabeth cleaned and filled the glass of water for her, and while Cerina drank, occasionally pausing to clear her throat out, she recounted her story.

Amélie inched forwards, "what are you going to do?"

"For the time being? I need a place to stay."

"You can have my spot!" I volunteered before I was even aware of the words escaping my lips. Cerina scratched her arms absent-mindedly.

"What about the old guy?" Amélie interjected. Cerina froze.

"Crap. Arvin." Immediately she whirled, making for the door.

Jakson shot out a hand. "Wait!" he cried. "You're sick!"

Cerina stopped, hand on the doorknob. "What are you talking about?" As if to prove Jakson's point, she brought her elbow up in front of her mouth and doubled over in a heavy, hacking cough.

"That doesn't-" she spat, "prove anything."

But it did. On her arm, a blistering scarlet rash had bloomed. She picked at it feverishly, digging her nails down into the raw flesh.

"Don't scratch," Jakson said. "Is this the first onset of symptoms? Have you-"

I stopped listening, rushing to Cerina's side. Jakson held out a hand, stopping me in my tracks. "Stay back,

Emry. We don't know what she has. It could be highly contagious."

"Seriously?" I said, "she coughed, what, twice? Please explain how that sets us on a course to imminent death."

Frankly, I was surprised that Lizabeth had ever gotten along so well with this Jakson guy. Effortlessly, his words had weight. He was annoying as hell, a bit condescending, yet somehow, he had a say over everything.

"Sicknesses have happened," Cerina said, her tone mildly irritated, as though this were only a minor issue in a sea of significant problems. "They're not uncommon, actually. I mean, we live in utter filth. There has never been a deadly Isle-wide outbreak, though. It's probably just some new branch of the flu."

"Or you need to clear your throat," I said. "I don't know what you're getting so worked up over. It's nothing."

I felt tempted to swat Cerina's hand away as she continued to pick at her rash. She really wasn't helping her case.

Farrah, on the other end of the room, began to sweat. She did not hold the same composure. "Is there anything," she whispered, "that may have caused the ailment?"

Cerina didn't hear her, instead eyeing Jakson.

"Did you hear what she said?" Jakson repeated, "is there anything, a waste product, a shared space, a dead organism that could have brought on a virus?"

Cerina's face paled. "Well..." she trailed off, "there is one thing...."

I thought I had a pretty good idea of what she was referring to.

"The bird," I whispered. Cerina nodded, confirming my suspicion.

"It's probably fine," Cerina assured. "Haven, Max, Adrienne, Farrah, Amélie, you've all been here for a while. You must remember some of the diseases that have come upon the Isle. None of them have resulted in any major fatalities."

"That isn't reassuring," Haven said, their face pinched in deep concern.

"Like she said, it's probably fine," Amélie interjected. "We should go get Arvin. It's just a cough. No big deal, right?"

Oh, so Amélie would listen to *Cerina*, but *I* was being overlooked?

Farrah shook her head. "No. This is a problem."

"If that's the case," Cerina said, "then I have to go warn Irabella- um, the new leader, I'd assume, of building 2-7."

Haven stepped in front of the door. "No. If the disease came from your building, it'll be placed under guarded quarantine until the sickness blows through. You'll be trapped."

"Arvin will be too. It was him who cut the bird open in the first place. I need to get to him- I made a mistake. I shoved him. He might've gotten hurt."

Jakson cleared his throat, putting everyone on edge. "I don't think you're taking into consideration the other issue at hand-"

Cerina coughed again, ignoring Jakson's advice and clawing aggressively at her arm.

"Cerina is sick," Jakson continued. "We don't know how bad it is, but I don't want to take any chances. Cerina can't stay here unless we all want to catch whatever bacteria hopped into her immune system. And, Emry... the same goes for you."

"Me?! But why-" the rough texture of the bloodsoaked bird feathers flooded back to memory. "Oh."

157

"But where will they go?" Lizabeth argued. "Cerina just got booted out of her home. You can't be suggesting we do the same to Emry."

Jakson put his hands up. "We're not booting anyone out of anywhere."

"I'm going to get Arvin," Cerina huffed. "I'll be back right away. Don't follow me. I want a decision to be made by the time I'm back."

"I'm starting to like Cerina," Amélie said with approval.

Adrienne plopped down on her bunk. "Great. Now what?"

"The solution is obvious," I grunted. "You guys can't get sick. I have to get out of here; in fact, I have to do that right now."

"No!" Lizabeth exclaimed. "You're one of us, Emry. We haven't even confirmed if or if not Cerina's contracted anything. For all we know, she's caught a small bug, and everything is fine."

Voices rose in disagreement. Everyone yelled at once- even Farrah had something nice and loud to say. The clamour drifted up past the cabin walls.

The door swung open once more, putting all of our collective thoughts to an immediate standstill. The silhouette in the door frame was a giant brake pedal, the screeching of a broken record over our discussion that had suddenly turned into an impossible shouting match. I had trouble distinguishing facial features at that distance, but their voice's deep, if not parental hum, was instantly recognizable.

"Is everything alright?" The figure asked. "I heard some shouting."

"Joe!" I said with a smile that felt way too forced. I hadn't had an actual conversation with the guy since I'd meandered over to the Level Two sector. "How's it going?"

Lizabeth nudged my shoulder. I winced.

"We're all good," Haven took over the conversation, maintaining a neutral tone. "It was just a little disagreement. Nothing you need to worry about."

Joe nodded, but he didn't look convinced. "There's been word of some sort of disturbance in the Level Two sector," he said, "I just don't want any of you getting hurt, okay? That's my job."

Did whispers really travel that far, that quickly?

"We'll let you know if anything seems weird," Haven shrugged. "See you around."

Joe nodded, going back out the way he came.

"Why haven't we recruited him?" I asked, if only for the change of topic.

"He's a busy guy," Max explained. "It's all thanks to him that the Level Ones don't split off into Families like your friend Cerina's sector has. That, and the fact that we're not all murderers."

Something within me skidded to a halt. "Excuse me… what?"

Max crossed his legs, teetering off the edge of his bunk.

"You mean you don't know? That explains a lot, doesn't it."

I scrunched up my forehead. "What don't I know?"

"Maybe you should ask her. Just a few minutes ago, you were jumping at the chance to sacrifice your spot in this building for her. If the two of you are such good pals, she'll tell you herself."

Immediately, I rose to a sudden defence. "Don't make this about her. She's had a rough day."

"So did the person she *murdered*. But that doesn't change the fact that whoever she killed to get here is a cold corpse."

"What are you talking about?"

"Haven't you ever wondered what differentiates a Level One from a Level Two? Or are you as dumb as you look?"

I pretended to ignore his last insult, folding my arms resolutely. "I've wondered. But, recently, I was taught not to ask pointless questions."

Max scoffed. "By Cerina herself, I'm guessing? It's not surprising that she didn't want you to pry. After all, she wouldn't want you to find out that all the Level Twos got sent here for the same thing."

"And, what, do tell, is that?"

"Look around, dummy. There is one thing and one thing only that makes a Level Two a Level Two. This friend of yours… is a killer."

Adrienne said something, but the sound didn't process. All I could register was the movement of her lips, the sound waves bouncing off my ears as though my head had been placed inside a fishbowl. I staggered back, a visceral reaction adding another layer of dizziness to my already-blurry surroundings.

"That can't…." I muttered, voicing my thoughts aloud, "that can't be."

Max continued to speak, paying me no mind.

It was at that moment when Cerina returned with Arvin. The old man had never struck me as frail, with his passion for animal gutting and all, but as he leaned on Cerina's shoulder, limping slightly, I couldn't help feeling a pang of pity for him.

Clearly, I had been inside that stuffy room for too long.

"Before you start bickering like disgruntled puppies, I have an idea." Was it just me, or did Cerina's voice sound a little scratchier than usual? Maybe it just sounded different now that I had been faced with the truth of what was behind it.

I couldn't look at her.

But I couldn't look *away* from her either.

I bent my head down, my eyes continuing to look up. Haven shot me an odd look as they watched me make a double chin, fighting with myself. What was wrong with me?

"Let's hear it," Amélie pressed. "Because so far, everyone else's ideas have totally sucked."

"Not entirely," Jakson reminded her. "Speaking of which, we have to catch her and Arvin up on the escape plan."

"A problem for another day," Amélie shoved the issue aside, helping steer Arvin into the room. Clearly, she wasn't too worried about getting sick. I grimaced. My hands were rash-free, but it was only a matter of time if I had the contagion brewing inside. A gross, sluggish feeling stirred at the bottom of my stomach. Normally, I didn't mind a minor cold because it meant I'd have a free excuse to slack off at school and kick around at home. Sure, it wasn't the ideal way to spend a few evenings, but laziness didn't always have to be a bad thing. But on the Isle, where sanitation was a living nightmare and scary people loomed around every corner, I had a few other things to say.

Mind you, illnesses were the last thing on my mind when I had two murderers standing in front of me.

Cerina didn't bother making herself comfortable, keeping a safe distance from us. An arm was wrapped around Arvin's shoulders, ensuring he did the same.

"I'm going to take Emry," her hand was already on the doorknob. It seemed like it would be difficult to argue. "We're going to break into the mess hall."

"Excuse me, *what*?!" My pulse sped up, and I could avert my eyes no longer. Cerina's expression wasn't menacing, her eyes deep in thought. But I was a deer in headlights, and I looked like it too.

"You heard me. Everyone is so busy chasing the damn key that they're seldom occupied by the thought of what it opens. I guarantee you that the spot will be unoccupied for at least the next week. And if quarantine is implemented, even better. We can discuss the plan in private."

Jakson frowned. "But it's likely that everyone in this room already has the sickness. What's the point of isolating Emry?"

"If any of you get symptoms, you can join us. If this outbreak is like any of the other ones we've faced, the second Emry develops symptoms, building 1-3 is going under quarantine. That won't be very helpful, considering half of your little club comes from elsewhere on the Isle."

Amélie nodded, but the doubtful expression on her face didn't match the gesture. "What about Arvin? If anyone has any disease, wouldn't it be, oh, I don't know, the guy who was rummaging around a dead bird's-"

"I'm not sick," Arvin interrupted, "I've been on this island for a long time, and I've never been caught ill. And even if I were, I can't come with them. My breaking and entering days are long gone."

"That doesn't mean he's immune," Jakson said, struggling to keep his tone even, "you can't possibly be suggesting that he stays with us!"

Arvin pulled up the collar of his Level Two uniform, burying his face into the fabric as though it were a mask. "I'll... keep my distance," he said, his words muffled.

"Arvin can sleep outside," Haven ordered, "Emry and Cerina have to go now. And we will stay here and resume business as usual. If nothing happens within the next day, Emry and Cerina will return, and we'll give them a recap of the plan. Got it?"

Reluctantly, Cerina led me out of the door and into the crisp evening air. My heart slammed against my ribcage. If it could beat any harder, it would fly out of my chest and land smack onto the stony pavement.

Even if it pulled all my arteries out with it, it probably wouldn't make me look any paler than I did now.

"Just so you know," Cerina clarified. "I'm not into this plan either."

***

I didn't say a single word until we were against the wall of the abandoned mess hall. Fearful of what I would see within them, I hadn't met Cerina's eyes the whole way there. An invisible string tugged my gaze in her direction, but I resisted the pull, focusing instead on my barren surroundings. The building was surrounded by a layer of gravel that dug into the soles of my sneakers, spreading clouds of fine dust. For the first time, I noticed that Cerina was in bare feet, her toes firmly calloused over.

I tried not to stare at her quick, agile, and very deadly movements as she shot up along the side of the grey cement, slipping a thick chain-link silver bracelet over her knuckles. In one stroke, like a viper, she smashed the back window of the mess hall, planting a hand on the windowsill and ducking away from the torrent of shattered glass.

We both took cautious steps back. Cerina dropped the chain, double-wrapping it snugly around her wrist. Broken glass lay everywhere, speckling the ground in icy fractals. A huge hole was punched into the mess hall, its borders sharp and jagged. Satisfied, Cerina gave a terse nod before erupting into another coughing fit.

"Pick up the glass," Cerina said, though it sounded more like an order. One I wasn't about to contradict, anyway. Cerina ran her fingers over the jagged edge while I bent over, collecting the window pieces in partial disbelief. So much for Jakson's poison. Now we had a whole pile of weapons.

"Follow my lead, and be careful. The glass is sharp." Cerina wasn't thin and nimble like Lizbeth, but her muscular structure moved in perfect sync, hopping onto the windowsill and sliding through the jagged gap without so much as a scratch. I nodded, as though she'd just given some thought-provoking lecture, and dumped the pieces of glass in through the window. Cerina sighed, clearing them away from the floor.

"How do I get through?" I asked, looking from the ground to the wall to Cerina's remarkably unfazed expression.

"Here," Cerina offered, holding her hand out. "Grab on. Once you get a solid grip on the windowsill, manoeuvre through the hole. You'll have to take it slowly."

"*You* didn't do that."

"Yeah, well, I've been here longer than you have."

"And I take it breaking and entering comes with the Level Two job description? I wonder how that looked on your resume."

"Just shut up and climb. Someone's going to see us."

I obeyed, moving my hand in nervous skips as though I were about to touch hot coals. My nails latched onto Cerina's palm. It was ice cold, rough, and bone-crushingly strong. I planted my other hand on the windowsill, swinging a leg up. I teetered on the edge, dangling there for a moment or two. Cerina huffed, impatiently sustaining my entire body weight with her one arm.

The words of an apology materialised in my mouth, but I shut them down at the last second. Apologising to a killer. That was an item I would save for my Ultimate Idiocy bucket list.

Cerina grit her teeth. "Use your other hand to grab the top."

"Right! Sor- I mean, thank- never mind."

Not unlike the time I had knocked down the dead bird, I steadied myself on the window frame and climbed inside, head-first. Cerina dropped her grip, and I plunked to the floor. Taking in my surroundings, I had to suppress a shudder. I wasn't a big fan of low-light areas, especially with my foggy eyesight.

"Mind getting the light switch?" I fumbled with my words, almost tripping over the pile of broken glass. A retort was on the tip of Cerina's tongue, but she was, thankfully, too exhausted to say anything. She crossed the hall, fading in clarity. The overhead light blinked on, illuminating the familiar folding tables. I stared outside, at the sun that had begun its course of dipping below the horizon. It was nowhere near peak sunset yet, but faint lines of blue and dandelion-yellow blurred together in the sky, an oil painting that hadn't completely dried.

"I don't want to question your methods, but, uh… won't this be a little obvious?"

Cerina didn't reply, stalking off to the kitchen. She came back hauling an empty oak shelf behind her.

"That's the point," she grunted, hauling the thing to the window. The back of it was black and dusty, a sharp contrast from the light brown wood on its front side. The thing probably hadn't left the wall in years. Cerina heaved the shelf so the darkened side faced the window, looking into the night. She gave the stand a final, relieved shove.

"Now, do you see why old Arvin couldn't come with us?"

I nodded, swallowing.

"There's a broom and some duct tape in the supply closet. I put up a doorstop to discourage anyone from using the stuff inside, but all you have to do is knock it out of the way. Go bar the front entrance while I stack the folding tables in front of the shelf."

The closet was damp and musty. It reeked of wet dog, even though all the water from the mop bucket had evaporated away ages ago. I brushed away a tangle of assorted towels, soap-buckets, and obsolete models of vacuum cleaners. My hand found the splintery handle of an old broom and a near-depleted roll of duct tape. A knot of cobwebs was spun overhead, which I made sure to steer clear of.

Once I had located the objects, I was more than ready to sprint out of there. But something made me pause in the entryway. I shoved the mob of assorted cleaning supplies aside and faced the white plaster wall. Something about it- the cracks, the way it had aged and splintered and flaked off- didn't seem right. It felt... incomplete. Unfinished. I ran a hand over the surface. It was smooth and chalky.

I tugged my hand back. The mark where my hand had been left an enormous dent in the wall, despite the fact that I had barely grazed it.

"Cerina!" I called, "come take a look at this!"

She arrived behind me a moment later. The cuffs of her pants were hiked up, a crown of sweat painted on her brow. It looked like she had just gotten back from a hard day at the gym. Immediately I turned my eyes to the ground.

"What's up?" She asked, a little confused. "If you need me to kill a spider, I swear-"

"Have a look at this wall."

I stepped back, giving her room to peer at the surface. Her brows furrowed. "Go. Block the door. It's probably nothing."

My head bobbed up and down with devoted, fear-mingled loyalty. I raced to the front entry, securing the broom to both ends of the doorframe with the silvery tape. Giddy energy bubbled up inside. I was alone with none other than *the* Cerina Rayz, and I had just accomplished some acts that would have been considered seriously illegal if I had not been on the Isle of Rebels. I had broken into a building with a murderer.

No, I realised. An *alleged* murderer. I grasped onto a shard of hope as my heart leapt to my throat. Rumours weren't always true. And Cerina was much more than a label.

Eagerly, I bounded back to the supply closet.

"I did what you-"

I skidded to a stop. My breath hitched, and my eyes widened. My knees trembled at the sight of what was inside the supply closet, begging me to turn around and run.

I didn't run. All I could do was stare. Into the deep black stairway that had, minutes before, been a solid wall. At the trail of blood running down the shadowy cement steps. And at the body lying at the bottom of it- a tangled and blurry, yet beautifully elegant shape. Dark brown skin coated in fresh red blood, with long, chestnut hair wrapping around it like a veil, a noose, a shroud.

At the bottom of the steps, Cerina let out a low moan before convulsing, retching all over the darkened ground.

Someone pounded on the door. My thumping pulse reached up to my ears, building in my blood. I think I might have screamed.

Outside, I heard a cough, then I heard nothing.

Lizabeth Merrin

Chosen moments

The entire night, I worried about Emry. I would never have admitted it to anyone, and, frankly, I had trouble admitting it to myself. Because worrying was a sign of caring, and I didn't want to care. But when it came down to it, I had no choice. The worry ate up my thoughts, nagging at the corner of my mind. No. Not at the *corner*. It was all I could think about, and I hated it.

When the sun rose the next day, there was still no word from the guards, Joe, or Emry. I tried not to let that bother me. It was still early. Anything could happen in a day because anything could happen at all, and a day was an obscure measure of time.

Adrienne and Max cornered me as I left my bunk, walking me outside. Bewildered, I glanced between the two of them. I wasn't sure whether or not they were there by choice, and it was highly probable they had been sent out of pity. I'd caught Haven shooting me a sympathetic gaze in the morning, and based on Max's strained expression, I could tell that this was just as awkward for him as it was for me.

Adrienne, on the other hand, was optimistic as always, practically dragging us to the space behind building 1-3. Too late, she realised that was where Arvin was sleeping. The man was curled into a small ball on the side of the cabin, continuing to doze even as the sun was rising. Adrienne made the decision to ignore him, strutting towards the shiny metal barrier.

"I can't wait for the talent show," she said, twisting her fingers into the chain-link fence. From a distance, it looked easily bendable, but the stuff was as sturdy as the thick steel gate surrounding the centre circle.

"Why?" Max's face scrunched up like a shrivelled fruit. "It's the event that'll kick off our escape. Aren't you nervous?"

"No," Adrienne laughed. "I'm excited as fuck. My life has been far too boring lately. I'll be counting the days until I get to make some sort of impact. You can't get very far when it comes to looks in these drab uniforms, for example. I can't wait to be *seen* again! Plus, my uke hasn't seen nearly enough light lately."

"Hold up," I cut in, "'uke' as in… ukulele?"

"Yup," Adrienne announced with pride, "my joy in life. I snuck it onto the Isle, but I haven't been able to use it since the *last* talent show. My calluses are starting to wear off. It sickens me."

"How did you get it past the guards?"

Max whistled. "You do not want to ask that question. You'll never hear the end of it." Adrienne punched Max in the shoulder, scowling.

"To answer your question," she said, immediately brightening, "it actually wasn't that hard. When I got arrested, I had the baby with me. I saw the guards, and, obviously, attempted to run. Max and Haven were running at my side, and the two of them were slower. No offence. Once the two of them were clapped in chains, I knew what was going to become of me. Haven still had the door to their carriage open, screaming at the guards about freedom or whatever, and I took that as an opportunity. I slipped it in under the guards' noses. Smart, right?"

"In other words," Max grumbled, "it was mostly thanks to Haven's diversion, but she still takes all the credit."

Adrienne glared, a seething beam. "That is *not* true. First of all, it was not a diversion. Have you ever seen Haven pass up the chance to scream at authority figures? Plus, even if you *had* managed to sneak the ukulele in without me, there's no way on earth you could play it. When we escape, I will sign with a record label if it's the last thing I do. That'll show 'ya."

"You won't be able to," Max contradicted, "we'll be in hiding. Making a musical debut isn't exactly a subtle activity."

"So you say. I think I can pull it off."

"What about you, Lizabeth?" Max asked, snapping me out of my distant ponderings. "Are you worried about our escape plan? Or are you a clone of the undaunted Adrienne here?"

"Pardon me?" I stuttered, shooting back to reality.

"Are you nervous? Excited? Both? Neither?"

I gulped. I wasn't sure I was ready to answer personal questions with so much tumult going on around me. Not on a morning when I was disconnected from everyone I was just starting to care about.

"I don't know," I mustered.

"You don't know? Come on, Lizabeth," Adrienne pressed. "We're being nice to you, but *you're* not even trying."

Max elbowed Adrienne in the shoulder. "Shut up. She's thinking."

"Honestly," I admitted, still fixated on the rolling waves. "I already told you. I have no idea what to think. I guess the important thing to do is focus on the present."

Max shrugged. "The present isn't exactly the most fun place right now."

"It might not be great, but there are varying degrees of terrible. It doesn't have to be all bad, don't you think? Now, Adrienne. Would you mind showing me your ukulele?"

Adrienne's face lit up. "A million percent, yes!"

Max eyed her doubtfully. "You sure about that? If the guards find out where it's hidden, they could take it away."

"Since when do the guards so much as bat an eye in regards to what we do?"

Max heaved a sigh.

"Alright. But if anything goes wrong, let the official record show that this wasn't my idea. And if anything happens to your dumb instrument, don't say I didn't warn you."

Adrienne smiled. "Thanks for giving me all the credit for this brilliant show. And *don't* bring the uke into this."

"If you call it a 'uke' one more time, I will personally smash that thing to pieces."

Adrienne darted to the front of the building, carefully avoiding Arvin's crumpled form.

"Stay out here," she instructed, "I have it hidden in my mattress. I'll be back in a second."

Max and I stood still, staring at the ground while we waited.

"How long have you known Adrienne?" I tried. Max shot me a cold look, killing any hope of a conversation.

After a minute that seemed to stretch an eternity, Adrienne reemerged with a small brown instrument, holding it by the neck. She got down on one knee, propping it on her leg and tuning the strings. She winced as she held her ear up to the base, cranking the knobs on the end.

"This clearly hasn't seen the light of day in a while," she grimaced, "it sounds like a dying animal."

As she re-tuned the instrument, a small smile began to creep up her face. She gave it a quick strum, deciding that it met her satisfaction, before standing up once more.

"So," she said, "what do you want me to play?"

I shrugged. "I'm not picky. Anything will do."

"You've gotta give me more than that. I don't know what you like yet, so I can't pick something for you."

"If you can't play for me, then play for yourself."

Adrienne scoffed, giggling under her breath. "That's not how it works."

"What do you mean?"

"I mean, it's never as simple as picking something you like and crossing your fingers that everyone else will like it too. At this stage, where I'm just starting off, everything has to be calculated, or else no one will like you. If you pick what you share based on your tastes, they won't be accepted, and you'll undergo an identity crisis because what resonated with you turned out to be the wrong choice. I wrote most of these songs, you know. I'm not just going to share them uninvited."

"But I *did* invite you to."

Max let out a loud huff of air. "For such a social butterfly, you sure are overthinking this one. Play her the instrumental piece you played me a while ago. I actually remember it, so that has to be a good sign."

"It's too depressing. Lizabeth doesn't seem like the kind of person who likes depressing things."

"I can decide what I like for myself, thank you," I said. "Come on, Adrienne. You were so excited about this a moment ago. What changed?"

Adrienne slung the black strap of her ukulele over her shoulder, breathing out a deep sigh. "*Fine*. I'll play you that one. But it sucks."

She leaned against the wall, propping the instrument up in front of her. At first, the chords were choppy, her fingers dancing along the strings in an irregular, indecisive rhythm. Briefly, she glanced up, meeting my eyes. I saw a surety there that I hadn't noticed before, a glimmer of something vibrant that I couldn't quite describe.

Her music rang louder, and the sounds described it for me.

The notes didn't travel very far, but a few curious heads glanced our way. A small crowd gathered, which didn't bother Adrienne, feeding her instead of pushing her notes away. She continued playing, the sorrowful melody echoing across the streets. I tried to discern the different reactions on peoples' faces, but each one was different. We were hearing the same song, but it struck differently with each person.

That wasn't something to be ashamed of, to shy away from.

It was beautiful.

Adrienne finished her song, beginning another one that was more upbeat. This one had lyrics, and while her voice was excellent, she didn't overdo it on the singing. It was perfectly balanced. Of course, my conception of perfection was only relative to what I knew. But I stuck by the motto that there could be many perfect things in the world coexisting simultaneously.

For once, my mind was far away from Emry and Cerina, drowned out by the tune.

Adrienne kept it short and sweet. She cut off the music after her third song, beaming widely. The others clued in, starting to clap.

Applause shook the buildings like an earthquake. The group was tiny, but they knew how to shout. They cheered and snapped, a couple even going so far as to cry out for an encore.

And on the fringe of the audience was none other than Darby Olson. There was a gash in his pant leg, and his blue hair blew around in the breeze. He clapped along with them. For a brief second, his eyes met mine. Panic leapt to my throat before giving way to something else entirely. Maybe I was naïve to think so, but I thought it resembled understanding. We held a gaze for a moment longer before Darby turned away, walking with his head held low.

I furrowed my eyebrows and glanced at Adrienne. The Isle would never stop confusing me.

People ran to us, giving Adrienne high-fives, fist bumps, and pats on the back. She was completely and utterly glowing. Revelling in the attention, she shook the hands of her brand new fans, bringing Max and me into the mix. The clump smelled like the rest of the island- old, filthy, and reeking of rot and body odour. But, in the weirdest way, it felt comforting.

The comfort only lasted for a solid four seconds.

A gasp emanated through the crowd. The three of us froze, and the group parted, jumping away. Face red, not just from rage but from a huge, blistering rash, was Haven. They raised an arm and pointed to Adrienne. I squinted. A red patch had bloomed over her forearm, surrounding the *1* burned into her smooth skin. It looked innocent enough, like a minor infection from the burn that would clear up in a few days.

Until she let slip a tiny little cough.

"Nice job," Haven wheezed, blood rushing to their head. "You got noticed."

Without further adieu, they tumbled to the ground face-up, unconscious.

Jakson Veer

Patient Zero

Amélie and Farrah sat with me beside building 1-10, giving my little seedling its daily dose of sunlight. I was uneasy. My restless legs begged to return to building 1-3, but I held them in place, resisting the pull. More people crowding the area would only make things worse. I didn't want to talk to Haven, not to mention isolated Arvin, but I couldn't stand waiting, either.

Both Farrah and Amélie looked to be in the same position. Amélie was standing up, stretching her arms and fighting back bored yawns, while Farrah looked deep in thought. She and I were crouched down, surrounding the pot while it absorbed a small helping of water. I tried not to stare at the odd way Farrah's knees jutted out, the bones strongly defined against the fabric of her trousers.

"We should give the plant a name," Farrah suggested softly.

"You can if you want," Amélie said, "but I don't see much point in naming inanimate objects. The main use of names is to scream them at people. If you're not going to yell at it, there's no point in *calling* it something you can yell."

A few days ago, I probably would have said something similar, with the exception of the screaming affinity. But the little guy had really started to grow on me. Its leaves were beginning to peek out as though they were yawning in the morning light.

"You don't yell at strangers," I said, "but they still have names."

Amélie raised her eyebrows. "Are you kidding me? I yell at strangers all the time. And maybe they have names, but I don't need to know 'em."

"Let's split the difference. I'm naming the plant, but you can feel free to cover your ears. Let's go with…" my mind drew a blank. So far, I was on a roll when it came to non-awkward social interactions, but just the thought of coming up with something creative came to me as the harbinger of death. "Uh… Bob?"

"You're kidding me," Amélie scoffed. "If you're going to name a plant, you have to at least name it something original."

I wasn't about to leap to the defence of the most overused name in history, so I swallowed a gulp. "If you're the expert, how about you name it?"

"Fine," she shrugged. "I'll name it. *Paul la plante*. Happy?"

"Paul the plant?"

"Ew, no, you obviously have to say it with the accent."

"You do *not* want to hear my attempt at French."

"Well, I can teach you. I taught Farrah."

Farrah shook her head. "I already knew how to speak it," she said, "If it weren't for border security, I would've liked to travel to France someday. Amélie just criticised the way I pronounce my *R*s. What was it? Clipped, not-"

"Rolled, not clipped! Have you learned nothing?!" Amélie snapped. "The accent might not seem like a big deal, but it's the most important part. Your grammar could be spot on, but the only way you're going to convince people that you actually have linguistic skills is if you sound like you do. Plus, with a good accent, you can easily garble the words and talk so fast that people will just nod along if you mess up. Idoitwithenglishallthetime."

"We could name the plant Adira," Farrah suggested, steering us back to the original topic, "I had a friend back at home with that name. It means *strong*."

"I like the name, but I'm not sure that something sentimental is our best bet," I said.

Farrah bit her lip, turning to the ground. A long beat of silence ricocheted off of every surface, striking me in the gut as though it were a tangible enemy.

"Something new, then," Amélie grinned. "I like the sound of that."

Ideas flew every which way.

"How about Gerald?"

"*Non*."

"Adelaide."

"Jaques!"

"Carmen."

I held a hand up, silencing the flood of potential names. "I've got it," I announced proudly. "JJ."

"What does that stand for?" Farrah said, cocking her head to the side.

"Jakson Junior."

"I mean, you do you," Amélie scoffed. "But I think that Jaques is by far the superior choice."

A shouting sound rose up to meet us, coming from the field. I stood up. "Should we go check that out?"

"You can if you want," Amélie said. "But I'd rather stick around here."

I sat back down. "When we escape, I don't know what to do about my education. In theory, I'll have a fake ID, but there will still be holes in my life story. There's no way I'll be able to apply for university." After dragging myself through the social dead zone known as junior high school, I had learned that conversations were like boats on a stormy sea. There was always one person who had to take the wheel, but if the crew was well suited to each other, the position could shift before the captain got tired and gave up. But sometimes, when you were on a voyage with less tactful people, someone could always overstep and steer the ship right into a topic the size of an iceberg.

And the annoying thing about life is that sometimes, you just don't have time to bring lifejackets.

I held a tense breath, already starting to feel the icy waves engulf me. What had I been thinking? The last thing anyone wanted to talk about was home-

"I had a similar problem even before I got here," Farrah admitted, speaking before I could drown in worries. "I'm hopeless in maths and science, but I love history. I was in this crazy gifted program, hence the advanced French classes, but I was torn. I had to decide which was more important- my academic achievement or my happiness. I couldn't choose between either, and one day, I snapped. After vandalising my school and running away from home, I wound up here. It served me right, honestly."

"I don't think we have a similar problem." I could sympathise, but the two were one and the same for me. I could never picture myself going on such a rebellious streak, especially not against the world I had lived for my entire life.

"I disagree," Farrah stated. "Your life isn't a grade. I learned that the hard way. My parents never learned it. They always wanted a successful child because they never got to be successful themselves. I have a genetic disorder that makes my bones more brittle, and since they are easily broken, I couldn't exactly go down an athletic path. That meant that my only future was an academic one. My parents were incredibly stringent."

"I'm sorry to hear that...." I mustered, "that must have been a lot of pressure."

"Don't be," Farrah said. "I'm not angry with them or anything."

"How? How aren't you angry? My parents were… enthusiastic, but they didn't confine me to one path. I had room to pursue my personal goals, even if I was a bit embarrassed by them." I shot a quick glance toward the plant, looking back at Farrah's warm eyes.

She put her hand up, stopping me. "They had their faults. Sure, they were nowhere near perfect, but the thing is, they regret their actions. Just because someone isn't willing to apologise doesn't mean they're not worth forgiving." Amélie stopped shuffling anxiously on her feet. She seemed just as curious about Farrah's words as I was.

"You can forgive them that easily?" She asked in partial disbelief.

"They love me. I can tell they mean it. I've never held a grudge against them, and I never will, even though our interests and plans differ. When I escape, for instance, I won't be going back to school."

"But then… how will you get by?" I tried hard to hide the sputter in my voice.

"I'll write about the Isle. I'll make it known that I've escaped and truly illustrate how unjust this policy is. I want my words to have power, but more than that, I want to stick to my values. And faking my way back into a stuffy classroom isn't my driving force. School ends eventually. And I don't want to serve this country in any way whatsoever. This world is brutal, but it doesn't have to be."

My jaw just about fell off my face. Amélie started clapping.

"Couldn't agree more!" She shouted.

"I-"

"You don't have to declare rebellion, Jakson," Farrah said, again, at a near-whisper, "but you've been marked a rebel. It's by no means an opportunity, but when you've seen how awful things truly are, you've opened your eyes to changing them."

Suddenly, I noticed how close we were, the way our kneecaps bumped against each other. Each of my defences fell, and I sat in the sunbeam, cradling JJ's pot in the crook of my arm. I saved that snapshot in my head, tucking it deep in the corner of my mind. Much later, I would return to it, examining it like a dust-covered photo strip after the blush had faded from my cheeks and the sun had sunk beneath the sky.

And, though I could go back to it time and time again, watching as a mere spectator, my role in the scene, my time in the freeze-frame had to end.

Because, after all, it was a known fact that those moments could never last.

***

Arvin was the first red flag. He came barrelling down the street at a shockingly rapid speed, with his long, scraggly beard trailing behind him like a cape, his ancient lungs bellowing out his presence to the entire Level One sector.

"Patient Zero! Find patient zero! They're looking!" He screamed the chant over and over again, garbling the phrase into a mashed heap of sentence fragments.

The three of us exchanged a glance. We all shot up at once, Farrah moving with a more careful delicacy. I held the plant protectively at my side, keeping Arvin's bouncing silhouette firmly in my periphery.

"We should probably go see what that's about," Amélie said, echoing the thought on all of our minds. The shouting that, now that I listened to it, sounded more like *singing*, continued to grow. Amélie broke into a run, and I tailed her, snaking between the buildings. A sinking feeling settled into my gut as I realised where the noise was coming from.

Behind building 1-3, a vast assembly was gathered. And at the front of it were Adrienne, Max, and... Lizabeth.

I braced myself. Managing big groups had never been my thing, to say the least. By that, I mean I liked to avoid them entirely.

Fortunately for my antisocial tendencies, Haven had gotten there first. Amélie gasped. On the back of Haven's neck and arms was an angry red rash. They stormed up to the front and pointed an inflamed finger at Adrienne. I craned my neck to get a better look at what was going on and noticed Darby in the sea of bodies. As soon as he caught a glimpse of me, he turned and ran.

I happened to notice that the wound on his leg hadn't quite healed.

Haven delivered a line, indecipherable from this distance, that made the others rear back in shock. Satisfied for the time being, Haven marked the occasion by crumbling to their knees, passing out in the dead centre of the show.

Lizabeth scampered forwards. "Help them!" She cried, her shrill voice alight with panic. But she had lost the public's interest. The crowd dispersed, promptly ignoring the shouts of Adrienne and Max.

Amélie sprang into action immediately, lifting Haven's calves. "Come on! We have to take them back inside!"

I hesitated, the thought of getting infected giving me pause. Max, Lizabeth, and Amélie picked up the unconscious Haven, carrying them away. I ran ahead with Farrah, who held the door open for the crew. Once inside, the transportation team's arms gave out, dropping Haven not-so-gently onto the wooden floor of the majestically decorated cabin. Haven's chest heaved up and down. It was too rapid, too jarred, but at least they were breathing.

Joe, the only audience member who had cared enough to stick around, rushed after us. Panting in the doorframe, he surveyed the scene.

"What do we do?" Adrienne panicked, pacing in little circles.

"Everyone stay calm," Joe burst into the centre, placing a hand on Haven's flaming brow. A heavy line of sweat dampened their blond line of hair. "What happened?"

"She's contracted an illness," Adrienne explained. Max nudged her in the shoulder, hard. A little too hard. "I mean, *they've* contracted an illness! I mean, what illness? I mean, we don't know anything about this!" Joe frowned, and Max buried his face into his palm.

"Is there something you aren't telling me?"

"No," Max attempted to cover, but his charisma didn't quite match Haven's.

"If something is going on, you have to let me know about it," Joe urged.

Haven moaned. Their eyes shot open, and they lunged forward. Their cheeks puffed out, filling with bile that they managed to contain at the last second. They rolled over, getting up in sharp, angular motions and spitting a thick wad of what had been this morning's breakfast onto the floor.

Then they screamed. It was a deep, guttural wail. The veins running through their neck bulged, their scarlet rash exploding like an angry red fire. The sound reverberated off the painted walls of building 1-3, infusing our eardrums with the cry of utter misery.

Joe put a hand on Haven's shoulders, but they shoved it off, huffing and panting and giving everyone the deadliest glare I had ever seen.

"Lizabeth. Max. Adrienne," they fumed, a sharp growl in their voice. "What the *hell* were you fucking idiots *thinking*?!"

Max stammered. "It wasn't my idea!"

Haven wrenched Max forward by the collar of his striped shirt, a blend of vomit and saliva flying onto Max's face. "DO I LOOK LIKE I CARE WHO PLANNED IT?!"

They gave Max a hard shove backwards. His head connected with the base of one of the top bunks, smashing against the wood. Max stared, eyeing his friend with the fear of a total stranger.

"Haven," Joe commanded calmly. "Relax. You aren't yourself."

Haven laughed, a gurgly, gruesome sneer. "How can *you* say that, Joe? You're trying to be my parent." Haven strode ahead, pressing their face next to Joe's. They were nearly eye-level. "You aren't my father."

Haven pushed by Joe. No one stopped them as they made for the door, head bent low in determination. "I need... I need to find them."

"Where are you going?" Adrienne sprung after them. "Haven!"

"Ahem," Joe muttered, stopping us from giving chase. "You all have a great deal of explaining to do. And where is Emry? I thought he hung out with you, Lizabeth."

Lizabeth stuttered. "Um, yeah, well, the thing is-"

Fortunately for her, Arvin came to the rescue. Following Haven and Adrienne's sudden departure, he came barreling into the building like a battering ram. "PATIENT ZERO!" He bellowed. "WHERE IS PATIENT ZERO?!"

Joe opened his mouth. His gaze landed on the faded 2 scarred over the old man's arm. He clenched his jaw, drawing in measured breaths. "What is a Level Two doing here? Max, Amélie, Jakson, Farrah? Lizabeth?" he eyed each of us, and shame rose to my face. I was surprised he knew me by name, considering we had only met briefly, but if he was the parent of the Isle, what parent didn't know the names of their children?

"Nasty little trial! Winner kills! Their minds are not right; their minds are not clear! Winner kills! Patient

Zero! One... one goal!" Arvin spoke in shrill, choppy breaths. A great urgency was in his eyes.

"Someone get him out of here," Amélie demanded.

"Wait," I said. Arvin was panicked, but not for himself. "The first case! The first death!" He cried, shaking back and forth.

"I think he's trying to tell us something," I stated, stepping closer to the blundering man. His wrinkly arms were bare of rash, and though his breath came in wheezes, he hadn't coughed a single time. "He isn't sick...."

"I already *did* that trial," he spat, as though it were the most obvious thing in the world. "I have immunity. You'll get it soon. After the first case dies! After they are killed, stomped, crushed, obliterated, squished into the very void that surrounds us and annihilated to utter ruin!" He paused, then, overcome by a sudden revelation. "Cerina," he choked out. "CERINA."

"What about Cerina?" I asked softly, looking into Arvin's wild eyes. They were dull grey and bloodshot, with hints of yellow peeking in.

"Cerina..." I said, "was the first patient. And everyone who got sick... is looking for her?" Bewilderment swirled around my brain. Was such a circumstance even possible?

"YES!" Arvin screamed. "Don't you get it?! It's the trial! When the worst wins, you want to come in third place."

I turned to the others, trying my best to ignore Joe. He'd learn about this soon enough, and he'd try to stop us. That issue just wasn't particularly relevant at the moment. "Where did Cerina and Emry say they were going?" I asked.

"The Level Two sector," Lizabeth answered. "They're breaking into the old mess hall." Joe held up a hand to cry out an objection, but Arvin silenced him with his next dazed ramble.

"So are the rest! They know! They see more when their senses are heightened. They're angry. They're in pain."

Adrienne gulped, her eyes darting back and forth over the red patch that was rapidly growing in size beneath her burn. "How do you make it stop?"

"We can't stop it. Only *they* can. You can only end what you begin, after all. It's only fair. And this is a game like any other. No cheating allowed."

Lizabeth lunged to the door. "We have to go help them!" She exclaimed. Adrienne followed her, as did Max, albeit a smidge reluctantly.

"You can't go out there," I urged, "if it's going to be a bloodbath, then there's nothing we can do. You have to stay back."

"If I only have a few hours before becoming a murderous rash-faced psycho," Adrienne countered. "Then I'll spend those hours beating the snot out of *other* murderous rash-faced psychos."

The three of them, plus Arvin, were out the door instantly, leaving Farrah, Amélie and me alone with a very baffled Joe.

"You three have a lot of explaining to do."

Emry McLeod

The Tomb

9 Hours Prior-

Smashing sounds erupted from outside. There wasn't one, but many people surrounding the building, forcing themselves at the windows, pressing against the door. And then there was Cerina, spitting blood and vomit at the bottom of the dark stairwell. I shut my eyes, squeezing them tight enough to crush something, to crush my problems. I had to do something, and I had to do something soon.

But sometimes, things looked better when completely removed from view, obscured and cast aside.

At least, in this case, the blank screen seemed to do the trick. My mind snapped back to attention, and I crashed down the stretch of the hall, yanking up a shard of broken glass from the pile on the floor. I was about to rush back to Cerina's side when the remainder of the mound pulled my gaze back. Hurriedly, I dumped the rest of the shards into a trash bin, scampering back to the supply closet.

The spiders dangling on the ceiling, completely oblivious to all the fuss, were the last things on my mind as I took the shadowy steps two at a time, nearly tripping over myself to get to Cerina. She had stopped vomiting, but it was hard to decipher any other sign of well-being in the low light. I hefted her shoulder up, barely able to support the weight with my tremendously out of shape chicken arms.

"Cerina!" I gasped. "Please, *please* be alive!"

Cerina rolled over, steadying herself into a crawling position. "Emry-" she breathed. "What-" her head shot up to face the pitch-black hallway. My eyes adjusted to the light. I could barely see Cerina, let alone the horrors before us.

The piece of glass dug into my palm, drawing a little blood. The pounding outside was faintly audible even through the empty hall. In minutes, they would be inside, whoever *they* were. We were trapped. As much as I hated the thought of the dark unknown-

"We have to shut ourselves in the closet," I warbled, my voice trembling.

Cerina heaved herself up, gulping down a tide of bile and answering with a nod. She stumped forward, staggering up the angular cement staircase. Gashes from the jagged stone ran down her back, and she winced with the effort. Shaking like a lead, I followed, holding a hesitant arm out behind her. I wouldn't do anyone much good if she fell, but I prepared to catch her anyway. Sending a red blush to my cheeks, a fantasy of saving her in the darkness leapt to mind. Shaking my head, I shoved the daydream away. What the hell was wrong with me?

I shuddered. Cerina got to work hastily, gesturing for me to hand her something. With a start, I realised that the roll of duct tape was still wrapped around my wrist. I shrugged it off, and she moved with sharp, decisive motions. In minutes, all kinds of doorstops, brooms, mops, and buckets were fastened securely to the closet door. The only light came from the old incandescent bulb, the ripples of heat pulling beads of sweat up to my forehead.

We were thoroughly trapped, but so were they.

"What do you think is going on?" I asked, struggling to keep from hyperventilating.

"I don't know," Cerina coughed. "One minute, I was feeling the fake wall, and the next, I was at the bottom of those stairs. I don't feel well-" as she swayed to the side, unsteady on her feet, her eyes widened. "Oh shit. The glass."

"Don't worry," I said, beaming with pride. "I chucked them in the trash."

Cerina frowned, but there were traces of relief in her expression. "It's not a great solution, but no one's first instinct is to rifle through the garbage. Most likely, they'll pass right by them."

"Who would want to break in here in the first place?" I wasn't sure I wanted to know the answer.

Cerina snickered. "The entire Level Two sector. *This* must be what they were planning. And unless Irabella's announced her leadership over building 2-7 in the span of thirty minutes, they all have one target."

"You," I finished. I snuck a glance at the bottom of the stairwell, half-expecting something to jump out of the depths at any moment. Cerina let out a shaky breath. We were both looking at the same place. "I don't want to go down there," I admitted.

I expected Cerina to laugh at me, mocking my inner chicken, but instead, all she did was nod. "You know," she said. "Neither do I. But it's not like we have much of a choice. The unknown, after all, is always the scariest enemy."

Goosebumps crept up my arms. Faintly, I could hear the sound of screaming.

"Are you afraid?" I asked. Instantly, I wished I could bite back the words. It was a hideously stupid question. Cerina Rayz, the Level Two, wasn't afraid of anything. "Sorry."

"I'm afraid every day," Cerina said, cutting me off. "Not of the Families. But of the island. I can play the social game, but the game is just a construct. The real demon is beneath us, invisible but always present. I feel stupid, sometimes, because, just like everyone else, I've turned a blind eye to it. I think it messes with us. Toys with our fragile existences, like a test. If this were a test, I would have failed long ago. You haven't, though. You admit your fear. When you aren't running around like a moron, I actually think that's pretty admirable."

"Me?" I stuttered, "admirable? I... I've never been called that before. I've never been *admired-*"

"Give me the glass," she interrupted, before I could make an even bigger idiot of myself. I handed her the shard, feeling vulnerable without it. She gripped it solidly, wielding it like a familiar blade, and stepped down the first block of the stairway. I didn't budge. She continued, two more steps, three.

"Well?" Cerina called, "are you coming?"

I scampered after her. "If it's any consolation," I muttered as we began our trek. "If this is a death trap, I'll be the first to go down." As if to prove that theory, I stumbled over a sudden step, staggering backwards to recover from the jolt. Even in darkness, my thrown-off vision was still a problem.

"Good to know," Cerina replied. "But as long as you keep that mouth shut, nobody's going to die today. Not on my watch."

We had reached the landing. The air was icy and damp, and a heavy stench that I hadn't noticed in my preoccupation with Cerina wafted its way to my nostrils. It smelled, undeniably, like death. Not in a traditional way, like rotted flesh and dried-up blood and a bunch of other morbid scenery, but the way *I* remembered death. Like the too-strong air fresheners of funeral homes and the bouquet of fragrant roses they placed over the casualty's corpse. It smelled of all the pretty things they used to wipe up a spill. Supposedly, it was supposed to soften the blow. All it really did was trick you, though. When you clean up blood with roses, all the blood does is stain them.

This particular example bore the smell of decaying lavender blossoms.

"Stop," I said, not liking where this was going. Cerina didn't listen.

"You want to get this over with, Emry. Follow me."

"I appreciate that you're being a decent person right now, but something is wrong. I don't like-"

"Oh!" Cerina announced. "I think I found a switch-"

A blinding overhead light blinked on, knocking me a step backwards. I blinked a few times, adjusting to the glare. Cerina stood still, expressionless. I followed her eyes to the end of the cement-lined hallway.

I screamed.

At the end of the hall was a body- old, ancient, but barely decomposed. The cement around it had cracked, starting from where the body lay and reaching its long talons all the way to the walls. The corpse was tucked in a prominent crater, the cracks spreading like long talons. Blood, dry and flaky, was splattered everywhere. The figure was slumped over, head to the ground, long hair pushed in front of their eyes. At least the face wasn't visible. A balding scalp was a little less human than the sullen eyes of a carcass.

All around it, sprinkled in a circle, were piles and piles of lavender, each one brown and long shrivelled up.

Jagged strokes were etched into the wall, but I couldn't read them from where I stood.

"It's-" I gasped. "It's a tomb."

Cerina, undaunted, stepped forward. Her feet touched the lavender, brushing it aside, but she had the courtesy not to disturb the body. She looked up, analysing the writing.

"Wh-" I stammered. "What does it say?"

"Arvin..." she read at a quiet rasp. "Arvin Rayz. Winner of the trials. Casualty of war."

Confusion mingled with the terror running through my system. I must have misheard. "Can you read that again?"

"I don't... have to," Cerina said. "You heard what you thought you did."

The casualty was clad in a torn and tattered prison uniform. They looked about Joe's age, with sallow skin that had shrivelled up like a raisin. A wide gash lay over their heart.

And on their shoulder, the burn as bright as ever, preserved in the dank tomb, was a scabbed-over *3*.

A crash exploded from behind us. We whirled. The entire door to the closet, kicked off its rusty hinges, clattered down the narrow stairwell. A mob flooded in, trampling the door to a splintery ruin. At the front of it was a furious figure, clutching the bronze key so tightly her hand turned stark white. She paid no mind to the body, dismissing it as though it were an everyday occurrence. Her eyes, instead, went to Cerina. Behind her was an army of Level Twos, smaller than I had expected but large enough to wipe me out in seconds.

"Irabella," Cerina said, not a trace of fear in her voice. "Building 2-7."

Irabella eyed the glass in Cerina's hand. "You," she snarled. "You started this."

Cerina raised her eyebrows. "If I remember correctly, *you* kicked me out of the Family."

"Not *that*!" Irabella sprinted up to us, stopping with her nose inches from Cerina's. "This!" She raked her fingernails down her face, tugging at the fiery rash. Four wobbly trails of blood poured from the cuts, raining over her. She smiled. "Now you're going to stop it. And *I* am going to stop *you*."

Cerina's expression faltered. "What are you-" Irabella yanked the shard of glass from Cerina's hand and raised her arm. Cerina grappled for it, lunging, but her reflexes were slower under the sickness. In one sharp motion, the blade was destined for Cerina's heart.

But it never met its target.

Instead, Irabella fell to the ground, spitting curses and regaining her footing. *I* was in front of Cerina, my fist extended, flaming with the impact of Irabella's jaw.

My eyes wide, I stared down at my split knuckles, shocked more with myself than the girl on the ground, a bright bruise fresh on her chin. Irabella screamed, but Cerina had already grabbed the glass from her. Irabella grimaced. "I don't want to do this, you know. But there's only one way. One way to win."

The other Level Twos had collected at the bottom of the stairwell, forming a human wall in front of us, teeth bared.

"We can't take them," I rasped. Cerina gave me an annoyed glance.

"I *know* that. Just follow my lead."

Irabella kicked at Cerina's shin, but Cerina jumped back, anticipating the move.

"I don't know what the hell has gotten into you," Cerina spat, "but you are going to stay here until you've come to your senses. Your intentions are unpredictable, but your moves aren't. I know you too well, my friend."

"You might... know me...." Irabella coughed, "but you don't know *them*."

I barely had time to process what that meant before the Level Twos surged forward.

I swerved to the side, caught under the grasp of an angry member of Cerina's building. My back slammed against the right side of the wall and screams lit up everywhere. My fists flew, my meagre defences carving a path back to Cerina.

Just as I was able to push through the thick knot of confused, angry, and driven Level Twos, a single sentence reached my ears.

"Sorry about this, Irabella. But you're not yourself."

Cerina grabbed a fistful of lavender and shoved it in Irabella's nose. She spat and coughed and writhed but, seconds later, fell limp in Cerina's outstretched arms. I watched, standing still in pure confusion, attempting to connect the scattered fragments of what I saw next. Cerina pulled Irabella's mouth open. A frothy foam bubbled out of it, mixed with blood. Plunging her hand in, Cerina came back with two of Irabella's molars.

Had my punch, a gesture of pure, impulsive defence, knocked the teeth out of the second scariest person on the Isle of Rebels?

Cerina bent her knees and jumped up, hurling the two teeth at the large silver button on the wall. The one that controlled the overhead lights.

I had just enough time to reach down and grab myself a healthy dose of shrivelled plant poison before we plunged into darkness.

Fists and feet flew everywhere, elbows connecting with faces and knees jamming into stomachs. Only hoping Cerina would do the same, I made a run for it.

Flashes, glints of metal, and demonic eyes toyed with my vision, fringing on what was real and imaginary. A small shaft of light drifted from the stairway, but it was nowhere near enough to brighten the room. Silhouetted in the beam stood a single figure, scanning the crowd.

"Cerina!" I shouted, steering my way through the throng. The tiny points of her eyes met mine in the dim stairwell. "Help!" I choked out, yelping as someone slammed into me, knocking me further back.

The figure in the stairwell turned. As she went up, I made out her features. Her figure was muddled by the distance between us, but it was unmistakable. The shape was indeed Cerina. And like the Level Two she was, she was leaving me to die at the bottom of the steps, surrounded by her former allies and accompanied by a rotting corpse.

"Hey! Cerina!"

She continued to stand there, with her back toward me. My voice was hoarse, and my pleas barely carried over the sound of the fray.

"Over here! Help me!"

The light at the top of the stairs blinked off, and a hollow, empty feeling settled in the core of my very bones.

A fist collided with my right cheekbone, but the sting barely registered.

"Cerina…" I wheezed, the air whimpering its way out of my mouth like the shallow squeak of a deflated balloon.

A hand gripped my wrist, and my eyes were pulled to a shadow that had suddenly materialised beside me. I had trouble distinguishing her features in the darkness, but that grip was all the identification I needed. I could hardly believe it. Cerina had come back for me.

"…is about to save your ass, idiot," she rasped, finishing off the sentence my dejected muttering had begun, "now follow me! Unless, of course, you *want* to be mauled to death by the stage rush to my accidental performance."

We pushed our way through the crowd hand-in-hand. Cerina carved a clean path that I followed with a timid gait, my surroundings fuzzy and a few stars swimming in the corners of my eyes. The bizarre plant poison surrounding the corpse must have finally gotten to me.

Cerina let go of my hand once we reached the stairs, zooming up with determined energy. I followed, wobbling on my unsteady feet and nearly slipping on the last step. Cerina caught me by the arm before I could tumble back into the darkness, tugging me out of the closet.

We slammed the door behind us, resting both of our backs against the board. I planted my feet on the floor, pressing my body weight onto the wall.

"This isn't going to hold," Cerina said, "we can't stay here."

I looked around the near-bare hallway. "We could run for it," I suggested, "I bet we could make it back to building 1-3 before lights-out."

"I think we're too late for that." Cerina held a hand, pointing to a small shape at the far end of the hall. It was an old maintenance ladder, propped in the back corner and covered with so many shadows and dust bunnies that it blended into the backdrop almost too well. "Sorry to make you do this," she said, "but this isn't over yet."

Lizabeth Merrin

Idealistic goals

I didn't like to rush into things. It wasn't like I was an intense overthinker like a certain Jakson Veer, but every time I considered an action, I asked myself the following question- which did I prioritise more: my own safety or the completion of the action in question?

In this case, the answer was obvious. Because I wasn't the only person for whom safety was at stake.

"What happened here?" Adrienne gasped. I had never been on the Level Two side, but its resemblance to the Level One sector was unsettling with the cracked pathways and streets teeming with malicious prisoners. But the old mess hall was the most frightening scene of all. Outside, one window was shattered, blocked off by a black slab, and another one was on the verge of crumbling in on itself. The door was kicked open, the handle and hinges wholly splintered. Arvin had ditched us halfway there, which meant that Adrienne, Max, and I were left to brave the Level Two sector all alone.

Max stepped inside, taking a peek behind the dangling door.

"There's no one there," he said. "But you might wanna take a look… up."

I glanced at the roof. Passed out on the grey shingles were two figures, splayed out like crustaceans washed up to the shore after high tide. Soaking in the sun were Emry and Corina, a few strands of Emry's red hair dangling off the roof.

"Well," Max said, "What do we do?"

Adrienne tensed her jaw. "I say we wake Emry up and leave Cerina here. There aren't many places a Level Two can hide, and if people are looking for her, it's only a matter of time before they show up. It looks to me like they already have."

Max nodded. "I second that plan. Anyone got an idea as to how we can go about waking up one person but leaving the other sound asleep?"

I took a few steps forward, surveying the building. Leaning against the side was an old maintenance ladder. The wood was split in two, but the rungs that remained intact seemed to be in pretty decent condition.

"We can't just leave Cerina to die," I said, picking up the two halves of the ladder.

"It's what she deserves," Max sniped, "she's a killer. If we leave her like this, we won't have to worry about taking care of her later."

"You couldn't possibly be implying-"

"Oh, I'm not implying anything. As long as we get back to the Level One sector, that is."

I set the ladder down, crossing my arms. "Cerina isn't my favourite person either, but we need her help. Even *you* can't deny that."

Max spared a glance at the roof. "She has a weapon. Look. She's holding a glass shard."

Sure enough, a shard of glass poked out of Cerina's hand. Even in sleep, her arm wasn't limp, gripping the weapon protectively. I wondered if she was dreaming. I wondered what kind of things she dared to dream *about*. "We won't get any answers if we beat around the bush," I said, reluctant as I was to smell the morning breath of Cerina Rayz. "I think we should wake her up."

"And how are we, sorry, *you* going to do that?" Max asked, slumping against the side of the hall. He kicked the ladder to the side, sending it clattering to the ground.

Adrienne spiralled into another coughing episode, absent-mindedly picking at her shoulder. "Cerina!" She screamed hoarsely once the fit had run its course. "Rise and shine!!"

Neither of the shapes on the roof stirred.

"Do you think she's dead?" Adrienne theorised.

"No, both of them are breathing," Max said. "Wait- why am I helping you? Forget I said that. Forget I said anything. Just- bye." With that, he whirled around, his point made.

Seconds later, he was back. "Okay," he re-stated, catching his breath. "Forget what I said. Again. Be quiet-" everyone stopped silent in their tracks, picking out sounds. In the distance, the sound of shouting, chanting, and fighting was audible. Not only that, but over the white noise was the blare of the central circle's loudspeakers.

"LEVEL 3 TRANSPORTATION. PLEASE CLEAR THE FIELD IMMEDIATELY."

I shivered, even though it was a searingly hot afternoon. "They're not just looking for Cerina anymore, are they?"

"All of a sudden, everyone is really angry. Why? I don't even know. But on this side of the Isle, when everyone is *already* too pissed for their own good... what do you think that means?"

He didn't have to elaborate.

I spared a glance at the rash on Adrienne's shoulder. The rash that *had* been on her shoulder. Now, it covered her entire right arm.

"I'm climbing up there," I said before I could backpedal. My stare hardened as I thought back to my extensive gymnastics lessons and hours upon hours of phys-ed classes. Glinting on the side of the wall were two flimsy hooks for the ladder to clip onto. I stood below them, gaging the distance.

Carefully, I tested the strength of the remaining pieces. The ladder had been reduced to a pile of guaranteed slivers, but it was thick- enough to support my weight, anyway.

The hooks, like the ladder, were old and flimsy. But if I played my cards right, they could cut it.

The longest piece of the ladder stood at my eyebrow- the equivalent of Max's shoulder height. I cursed my shortness. Ideally, I would get Max or Adrienne to climb, but I didn't want to risk the ladder snapping under their feet.

I balanced the ladder between my shoulder and chest, getting a feel for the weight. Adrienne and Max watched me- Adrienne with urgency and Max with scepticism. I ignored their stares of both scrutiny and hope and threw the wooden series of rungs in a perfect arc.

It bounced off the wall, flopping defeatedly to the ground.

"Try it again," Adrienne begged, her voice hoarse and gravelly. "*Please.*"

Once again, I took a few steps back. The throw was too low, but it went in the right direction. I picked the ladder back up, readjusting the angle.

I hefted the bars just below my chin and chucked the ladder over my head once more.

With a satisfying clatter, the top rung caught on one of the hooks. The ladder teetered unstably, but it held itself in place. I gave the wooden object a half-smile.

I took a running jump, leaping up to the dangling bar. I gripped it with two hands, and the ladder slid down the hook. My stomach dropped, but though I swung violently, I managed to hold on. I closed my eyes, focusing on the wall instead of the ground, where Adrienne cheered in triumph.

I pressed my feet to the wall, tightening my core and closing a hand over the next rung. I gasped, just barely sliding my fingers around the wood. My second hand joined it, and I tucked my knees below me, resting them on the tilted first bar. Two down. Three to go. I heaved a sigh, thinking of Mel.

It wasn't a good thought, but memory lane was a better place to be than at the bottom of this ladder, crashing onto the pavement and drowning in a pool of my own blood.

The third rung was easier to reach, aided by the stability of my feet. The ladder quaked, but I scaled it with ease. It was just a ladder. This was nothing more than a shelf that was too high up, a minor inconvenience. My eyes flitted downward, and my stomach churned.

My heartbeat spiked, sweat pooling around my collar. Just one more to go-

The hook snapped. I screamed, leaping and grasping. My fingers flailed, but the only thing they clutched was air. The ladder tangled around my legs, dragging me down with it.

Miraculously, my hand found the roof, clutching it for dear life. My nails dug into the rough shingles, sliding as though they were greased with oil. The friction from the jagged tiles burned like a fraying rope. I bit my tongue so hard it coated my teeth with blood. My right hand slipped off, flinging into empty space.

I opened my eyes. As if in slow motion, I took in the scene through the blurry screen of terror-induced tears. My left arm throbbed, but against all odds, it held me. The ladder twined between my knees bent my legs at awkward angles, tangled between each joint. A shaky sigh heaved its way out of me.

"Get your other hand up!" Adrienne shouted, holding her arms out below me like a safety net. As if that would break my fall. The only thing it would break would be both of our necks.

I gulped, my ribcage near the point of exploding. I turned back up. The sun had moved along the horizon, sinking its way into my eyes. Against the blinding flash, I squinted. My hand, drenched with sweat, started to slip. I grit my teeth. I wasn't going to die this way. I had never acquired a taste for drama, but there was no way I would let myself go with so many words left unspoken, with my unmourned body rotting on the Isle of Rebels.

I swung my other arm up. Shimmying myself to the side, I got my upper torso onto the roof, with only my hopelessly tangled legs hanging freely. My nails dug into a crevice, and I used my momentum to slide into a side roll. With my upper legs sitting in a secure enough position, I reached a hand out, detaching the ladder from my knees.

When the ladder fell to the ground, smashing into an even smaller shard, I didn't jump. I let out a shaky sigh, standing up and getting my footing on the uneven ground. Adrienne whooped and cheered, and even Max announced relief. A faint smile crept to my lips.

I stepped over to Emry first, and gave him a gentle shake on the shoulder. He was dangerously close to the side of the roof, his head resting on unstable ground.

"Emry!" I whispered, "wake up!"

No response. I tried again, louder this time. "Emry? It's me, Lizabeth. *Please* wake up."

Beside Emry, a small groan escaped Cerina's mouth, downturned in a frown. I stepped away as she toppled forward, rising in a lethargic motion.

I had a million questions burning on the tip of my tongue, but I swallowed them all in one big gulp. Cerina had been through some sort of ordeal, and a bombardment of aggravating curiosities wasn't going to help anyone.

"Lizabeth," Cerina spat. Her rash had died down, but her uniform was in tatters. "Have you, too, come to stick a knife up my throat? Did you find the glass shards? Or do you prefer hand-to-hand combat?" She lifted up her face, revealing a black eye.

I stumbled back, getting myself out of arm's reach. My hands flew up, palms against the wind. "I don't want to hurt you! It's just... seeing someone out cold on the rooftop of the most sought-after location in the Level Two sector is bound to pique one's curiosity."

Cerina smiled slightly. "Finally, a bit of sensibility. Keep your hands in the air. You couldn't hurt me if you tried, but it looks like I have a bit of a target on my back. Wouldn't want anyone's finger slipping on the trigger, would we?"

It was then that a piece clicked. "What happened to you last night? What happened to Emry?"

Cerina gave Emry a firm kick in the shins, knocking him way too close to the edge for comfort. He groaned, raising an arm in front of his groggy eyes. I dropped my hands in relief, and Cerina adjusted her hold on the glass shard.

"Hands back up."

Emry rolled to the side, getting onto his knees. "Lizabeth," he grumbled, "how did you get... onto the roof...."

"Probably the same way you did," I said. "Are you okay?"

"Never been better."

"Do you mind telling me what you're doing unconscious?"

"I'm not unconscious *anymore*," he corrected, "and that's a bit of a long story. Cerina, I think you're the one who tells it best. After all, I'm the bystander, not the target."

Cerina eyed me with a suspicious frown. "I suppose if you had come up here to kill me, you would have done it while I was asleep."

She explained her predicament in such a breezy way that I almost mistook her distant expression for nonchalance. But after she had finished, I could read the concern written in the lines of her brow. She was genuinely worried.

I spared a glance at Emry. Was it him she was scared for? The elusive Arvin? No, there was more than that. She was worried about Irabella.

An inkling of sympathy, an uninvited but heavily-pronounced pang, nipped at the inside of my chest for her. Emry nodded, echoing her statement.

Was this what he felt for her? This shred of humanity that escaped past her stone-cold expression? It was a dangerous light, but the fact that it was small and hard to find made it all the more appealing.

"So," I said, wrangling the most sensical words I could, "we need to figure out three things; how to get off this roof, how to help Emry, and who on earth Arvin is?"

Again, the time had come to ask myself a question of priorities. Despite my flood of emotions, what was done was done, and the real anger management was fixing it.

Cerina nodded as though my entire train of thought had been broadcast to her via high-quality radio. "I think I'm starting to like you."

Emry McLeod

Acquaintances

"If I'm gaging the distance correctly, we could survive the fall," Cerina estimated. We had been pacing on the roof for the last ten minutes and were running short on creative solutions. "As long as we land right, that is. It isn't too far off the ground."

"You can do that if you want," Lizabeth squeaked, her voice a whole octave higher than usual. "But I'm not in love with that plan."

Cerina paced along the edge, dangerously close to spiralling off the side of the building. "Toss what's left of the ladder up to the remaining hook. I'm going to give it a shot."

Max picked the fallen ladder piece off the ground, winding back to throw. It missed by a mile, but Cerina managed to swerve into its path, catching it between both arms.

In a single swift motion, the ladder was fastened to the hook, and Cerina was lowering herself down. It sagged dangerously under her weight, but she paid it no mind. Dropping her feet and gripping the bar with only her hands, she let go of the wood and landed to safety.

"I suppose I owe you a thanks, Lizabeth," Cerina dusted her hands off, squinting up at the ladder. It hadn't budged. "Are you going next?"

Lizabeth didn't nod, looking down wide-eyed. Was she surveying a route? Figuring out the fastest way down?

Lizabeth shook her head. "Emry, you go ahead. I'll go last."

My eyes flitted between the ladder and Lizabeth. "You sure about that?"

"Yeah, by all means. I'm good with waiting."

I kept my eyes away from the ground as I stepped down the ladder, the wind biting at my back. I swayed a bit with my unreliable depth perception, gripping the bars for dear life. The air was knocked out of my lungs when my feet hit the ground, giving out under me as I landed into an awkward sitting position.

I looked back up to Lizabeth, shooting her a thumbs-up. "You're good to go!"

She stared at the ground, completely petrified. I tried to meet her eyes, my confusion apparent.

"I can't," she refused, crossing her arms. "It's not going to happen."

"Come on," Cerina urged. "It's not as far as it looks. Just lower your feet and make the drop. Easy as that. Here, I'll spot you."

Lizabeth gulped. "I told you. I *can't*."

"If you got *up* there, you can."

Out of the corner of my eye, I spotted two shapes. My blood froze. Approaching the building was a group of guards.

"Uh, guys?" I shouted, the urgency in my voice shining through, "we've got company."

Lizabeth walked away from the edge, plopping down resolutely on the shingled tiles. She glanced to the side, spotting the threat on the horizon. "You guys have to go on without me. I can't jump down. No way. Absolutely not."

I narrowed my eyes, focusing on the guards. They had stopped at the corner by the entrance, paying us little attention. They were holding something, it seemed, fidgeting with an unknown item.

They tossed something through the door frame before picking up their feet and turning back around. A single sentence drifted toward me, caught by the wind's intricate net.

"...apologies, soldier… your resting place has served us well…."

205

Cerina clued in a few seconds before I did.

"If you want to die on the top of the roof, I can't stop you," she shouted. It might have just been me, but I was catching faint undertones of panic in her tone. "But we have much bigger fish to fry than your fear of heights."

Lizabeth blushed, her face turning beet-red. "I'm not afraid."

The flames began slowly at first. But what I had dismissed as the ashy layer blanketing the Level Two sector soon began to turn into another problem. Starting from the door and billowing up into smoky plumes, a fire was growing. The flames licked the side of the building with hungry, vicious laps. Lizabeth continued to stand there, the smoke drifting to her nose. Slowly, she turned. I watched alarm spike through her, sudden shock making all of her limbs jolt up.

"If you're not scared," Cerina said, "then prove it."

With that, Cerina turned around, gesturing for us to follow. I stole a glance behind me, where Lizabeth eyed the ladder in panic. "You can't just leave her there!" I cried, pushing to Cerina's side.

"Relax," Cerina said, keeping her sights on the path ahead. "She'll be here in a matter of minutes. Mark my word."

We began to walk, picking up the pace.

Sure enough, before we had even left the cluster of buildings, Lizabeth came panting behind me, sprinting down the street. Corina smiled.

"I told you that you could do it."

A shudder that could have scored a 10 on the Richter scale shook my arms as I heard the fire crackle behind me, signifying the conquest of the vicious, deadly flames.

Cerina Rayz

Long time no see

We stuck to the edge of the fence, winding our way back to the Level One sector as subtly as possible. There were little to no areas we could hide behind in the clearing, but once we reached the buildings, the shadows provided a good amount of concealment.

"We have to find Arvin and Haven," Lizabeth said, a wall of distance in her voice. She kept tossing looks my way- first an onslaught of glares, followed by squints of confusion, fading into the infamous side-eye.

"Where did you last see them?" I asked.

"Haven is anyone's guess. Arvin, too. He wandered off when we crossed the dividing line."

"He does that," I murmured. Only now did any interest spark surrounding where he wandered off *to*. "He's probably on the streets, chasing the thoughts in his head."

The glass shard was still securely tucked in my pocket. I slipped it out, gingerly fingering the jagged edge. If only I had taken some of that poisonous plant with me. I didn't want anything to reach the point at which my glass weapon would be required.

"We'll split up," I announced. "Emry, Lizabeth, you guys take this stretch. I'll run down the next tier in the circle. Max, you can grab the outermost buildings. If you see either of them, bring them back here."

"What about me?" Adrienne asked. Her words were drowned out by the sound of a Level One streaking down the path, his naked flesh covered head-to-toe in a fiery rash. I winced, averting my eyes.

"Come with me. You probably don't have long, but while you're here, I need backup. These people want to kill me, don't they? They barely have the sense to identify themselves in a mirror, but if one of them takes notice of the elephant in the room, I'll stand a better chance with someone to accompany me. Do you know how to fight?"

Adrienne gulped. "Um… I took a martial arts course-"

"Excellent."

"…when I was five."

"Until we get to the bottom of this," I announced, "everyone who's reasonably healthy searches for a cure and a definite list of symptoms. Got it?"

Nods surrounded me. I gave them a small smile, relishing the feeling of leadership. I might have been given the boot from my Family, but in a way, this was better. I valued these nods. They were instrumental to a more significant plot rather than a mindless game devised to keep us entertained.

Maybe I wasn't done with adrenaline, after all.

I took my sweet time down the sector, welcoming the distraction of the chaos. Adrienne trailed awkwardly behind me, resisting the urge to scratch at her inflamed arms.

Instead of staring, awestruck, at the 2 burned into my arm, the inmates on the streets were too preoccupied with their own activities- small fistfights, significant shouting matches, and other daring feats like the nudist from a few minutes ago- to notice anything off about me. After all, *everything* was off about *them*.

Many people were unconscious, sleeping like a rock amidst a torrent of eardrum-shattering noises. Others retched, the first indicator of their descent into insanity.

I looked at my hands. The rash was already dying down. Why didn't it have an effect on me? Why wasn't I, like everyone else, baring my teeth and sharpening my claws?

I finally found Arvin in front of building 1-22, meandering around the perimeter and staring at the sky. I had fully expected him to be covered in a blotchy rash, perhaps only partially clothed, but he was in the same condition as always, staggering like a drunk man.

I ran to him, calling his name. He didn't notice me until I grabbed him by the arm, startling him back to reality.

"Cerina!" he exclaimed, overjoyed. "It was never my place to say, but I knew you would make it! What has it been… a day already?" He broke into a grin, leaning down to my ear. The next words he uttered came at a harsh rasp. "That's hard to do, you know. Good job. You've made it through two already."

I broke out of his grip. Adrienne looked as though she wanted to get in on the action, but she quietly stepped back after laying her eyes on Arvin's long, yellow fingernails.

"Arvin," I said, maintaining a firm, stern tone. "Who are you?"

"What kind of question is that?" He screamed, slamming back into the nearby building. "Instead of asking me something existential, you do the opposite! My ears are too old to hear wisdom and too shrivelled to leak it. So when it comes to a question that causes me to become immersed in myself, my limbs are raisins, and my heart is an empty pitcher of water! You *fool*! I am out of date, out of mind, and anything of value within me has long expired."

"We found the body, Arvin," my voice was deep now, speaking daggers. I rarely ever talked that way, and I didn't like to, either. When I snapped, I was quiet. When I was scared, I was loud. And when something was urgent… I made sure everyone knew it.

Arvin looked at me quizzically. "Too many bodies to count, too many to remember. Swallowed by the sea, swallowed by the ground, regurgitated into my ancient soul. Which one?"

"Yours."

Arvin's face lit up. "Oh! You did? Clever handiwork, wasn't it? Young mind, sharp mind. Sharper than theirs, anyway."

"Than whose?" Adrienne said, coming closer.

"All of them. All the ghosts. I see them from time to time. I think they're a bit envious."

I started leading Arvin back to building 1-3. "I don't understand."

"Good. You're not supposed to."

"The corpse at the bottom of that tomb had the same last name as me. That can't be a coincidence."

"And if it is?"

"Well," I grabbed Arvin by the arm, stopping him from stumbling away, "in that case, I'll be sorely disappointed."

"I bet your parents had a lot on their hands with you. You're mean when you don't get what you want."

I bristled at the mention of my family. "I'm not that petty. If you want me to be reasonable, though, you're going to have to be reasonable yourself."

Arvin scoffed, "if that's what you're looking for, you won't find it here. Haven't you realised, Cerina, that my reason for anything has long become irrelevant?"

I hefted Arvin up the steps. "I think you're lying."

Adrienne held the door open for us. Inside, I caught Jakson, Amélie, Farrah, and a tall man, the face of which I didn't have time to place, engaged in a lively discussion. They hardly batted an eye to Arvin's thrashing as they attempted to restrain a threat of their own. Haven, their uniform slightly torn, was firmly secured against the board of one of the bunks.

As soon as I stepped through the door frame, their head snapped up.

"It's you!" They cried through gritted teeth, "Cerina Rayz."

The reaction was so common, at this point, that I diverted to my habitual brand of snark. "I'm aware."

Arvin stepped in front of me. "Get away from here, Cerina. You made it out of the Level Two sector, but-"

Haven lunged out of Jakson's grasp, shoving Arvin to the side. They barreled toward me, hot rage in their dazed eyes.

I swerved, catching their wrist and using their momentum to shove their shoulder to the ground. They kicked, but I was faster, slamming them against the wall and pinning both of their arms behind their back.

"Bad idea." I booted the door closed. "So, Haven. You want to kill me."

"Wrong," they grumbled, their words muffled by the wood. "I *need* to kill you."

"Mhm… you might want to reevaluate your priorities on that one."

"This isn't a priority. It's an obligation."

Adrienne backed away. "Haven…" she squeaked, "what has gotten into you?" She stared at her arms. I couldn't see her from my position, but even on the other end of the room, I could hear her loud gulp.

"Excuse me," the tall man said. "What are you doing here?"

Using my elbow to keep Haven restrained, I turned around to face the man. Considering the guilty way in which Jakson, Farrah, and Amélie were staring at the ground, I was getting the feeling that my presence had already been revealed.

"Name's Cerina," I said, extending a hand. "But, I'm sure you already know that."

The man did not come forward to shake. "Get out," he ordered, "*now*."

For the past month, *I* had been the one to give the orders. Sure, before then, I was just another Level Two, obediently following the keeper of the key like any other hopeless prisoner. But I was not about to sit back and listen to a man whose name I didn't even know.

"Sorry," I said, before I could get a hold of myself, "you're going to have to tell me who you are first."

"Let go of Haven. Then we can talk."

Haven screamed something against the wall that fell along the lines of a swear word and a plea for help. I pressed their teeth further into the wood, and their cries were now beyond decipherable.

"I'm not sure if you've noticed, but I can't exactly do that right now."

The man sighed. "Look. I don't want to pick a fight with... someone such as yourself. But Haven is not an animal. Unhand them, or I will make you."

The door swung open, and Lizabeth, Max, and Emry stepped in.

"We didn't find-" Lizabeth began. She took a quick scan of the room, clamming her mouth shut. "Oh. Joe. Is this a bad time?"

The man, *Joe*, shook his head. "No, by all means, come in. It's dangerous out there."

I let the three of them step inside before slamming the door tight, adjusting my grip on Haven's shoulders.

"I think I remember you," I said, narrowing my eyes on Joe. "Right. You're the guardian of the Level One sector. I'm surprised. I thought you would be more of a pacifist."

Joe took a deep breath. "What do you know about peace? I'm going to say this again, and I'm going to say it slowly. I don't want to cause any conflict. Unhand Haven Magany and get out of this building before anyone else gets hurt."

Adrienne broke into a coughing fit, doubling over to hack out a string of phlegm.

"Er, with all due respect," Emry said, "if she leaves... things will not end well for her."

"Emry," Joe said, "I need you to listen to me. This Level Two has been manipulating you. She is here because she has no place in this world apart from the nightmare of this island. Cerina Rayz and the old man she brought with her are both murderers. I want to help you, but I can't do that if you aren't willing to step away and follow my lead."

My brows knitted together, and my muscles tensed. "May I remind you that I'm right here?" I said, "If you want to talk down to me, talk to my face. I'm the devil's spawn, aren't I? Don't you think I can take it?"

Joe looked at me with an expression similar to the one worn by Max. Pure, utter revulsion. "Get your bloodstained hands off of Haven. This will be your last warning."

Every nerve in my body screamed at me. I wanted to punch something, hurt someone, show them what a genuine Level Two looked like. I had half a mind to crack Haven's skull just to show this man what I could *really* do. By the look on Joe's face, I could tell that's what he expected of me. I could see in the way he stood that he was prepared to fight.

I sunk my teeth into my tongue, squeezing it between my incisors until a small trickle of blood spilt over my gums. That was what he wanted. My past was a taunt to me, a nagging presence in the back of my mind, but it didn't have to define me.

Slowly, I relaxed my grip, feeling the stares of everyone in the building like knives against my back. I wasn't like the others. *That* was what I would show Joe. Not for him and his self-centric ideals, but for myself, the only ally I had.

The moment I let go of my hands, Haven whirled on me. They swung the door open, shoving me back. My reflexes tugged at my arms like puppet strings, moving them into a fighting position. I stopped them at the last second, letting myself be knocked to the ground.

My eyes met Emry's. He had stopped watching, seemingly captivated by the floor.

Haven raised their fist, but I sprung up before a target could be acquired. I jumped back, righting my stance. Keeping my arms against my sides as though they were stuck by tight-binding glue, I shuffled backwards, knocked down the steps.

Haven's eyes were determined. "You're going to end this," they said. "I beg of you. Cerina."

At the mention of my name, every head in the immediate vicinity flipped my way. The people immediately stopped, ceasing their activity. They walked to me in a zombified trance, collecting in a tight circle.

I was trapped. Enclosed around me was a ring of people. They were strangers, and yet, I recognised them. Behind their eyes, each one had the same expression. It was the one I had seen in Irabella, the one I was watching now, buried behind Haven's irises.

"End this," they chanted. "End it, now."

From behind the door, all Joe did was watch. His eyes were downcast. He set his hand on the doorframe, and in one defeated motion, tapped it shut.

The click resounded in my bones, in my ears. My arms trembled, held still for too long. My head swam.

"End this. End it now."

"I don't understand what you want!" I shouted.

"Neither do we," said Haven.

A tremor passed through my veins. "What are you going to do to me?"

"End it."

"End *what*?"

"End you."

The people advanced, closing in from all sides. Only, they were not people anymore; they were a single, hate-driven entity. They were like the monster Joe had turned me into. The killer. The abomination.

"Don't you realise?" I said, digging my fingernails into my side to keep from raising my fists. "This will never end. As long as we're on this island. There will always be monsters. *We* will always be the monsters. Killing me will achieve nothing."

"We don't want to kill you," they said simultaneously. "We want to end it. We want to win."

The door to building 1-3 swung open. Flying against the wind, with his red hair flapping in all directions, was Emry. He burst through the crowd, shoulder-checking Haven and joining my side.

"Emry!" Joe cried, diving after him, "get back!"

The knot of people thickened, their blue and white uniforms blocking him entirely from view. Emry furrowed his eyebrows, crossing his arms.

"Not so fast," he said, crossing his arms. "I don't know what you want with Cerina, but you'll have to go through me first."

I would have laughed if I weren't so surprised. "Emry?" I exclaimed, "Why are you-"

"Because," Emry stuttered, "you're different. You could have left me to die in a dark basement. You could have killed me long ago, from the moment I had the nerve to steal your key and barge into your sector. And yet, of all the things you could have done, you *joined* me. You joined us in our mission for a better future even though you thought it was hopeless. You let Irabella live. Hell, you let all of us live. Maybe it's nothing more than a dumb gut feeling, but I trust you, Cerina. Can you trust me?"

I would have said no. But that was when I saw the look in Haven's eyes. They knew what was going through my mind. They knew what I was going to say because they were expecting to hear from a killer.

I was not a killer.

"Yes," I said, after a measured breath. "I trust you." Haven raised their eyebrows, completely flummoxed.

The crowd didn't advance, but it didn't back up either. They stood still, glitching, as though something in their commands had short-circuited.

I took Emry's hand, sending a deep blush up his face. If the prisoners around me were rage-bent robots, that simple gesture was enough to dump a massive bucket of water over their electrical wiring.

Arvin pushed through the crowd, breaking the people apart as though he were slicing through butter.

He grabbed my other hand, pinching it in a tight grip. "Come on," he said, "there's something I have to show you."

I slipped my hand out of Emry's, leaving him shell-shocked. As though I were moving through a sea of still-life paintings, I followed Arvin like a guiding light. He was the last person I could trust, but at least we were alike, him and I.

Dangerous.

Cerina Rayz

Long time, lost your sanity

Arvin didn't speak as he walked. He held the silence like a fragile, precious thing, cupping it between his wrinkled hands and passing it between us like a sacred chalice. We strode behind the buildings of the outermost circle, hugging the edge of the fence. We were in the last place I had expected us to be going, but I should've known, by then, that with Arvin, there was nothing I could foresee.

At last, he spoke, clearing his throat.

"They cut a hole so their essences could escape- but their sicknesses and naughty little voices stayed behind. They dug their bodies deep into the ground, maimed by my hand, cut by my blade. And the force that drove their hearts to beat was eaten up by the sharks. The sharks! To think that my digestive tract has something in common with an eater of souls- I can't even imagine."

A chill fell over my arms, sweeping up the tiny hairs lining them from top to bottom. Arvin put his hand on the fence's wire, dragging it along. We came into the central field. Guards were everywhere, and I was blatantly visible.

I ducked behind Arvin. "This better be worth it," I rasped.

We came to the dividing line. At least there, I had the cover of the wide signs. I hid within the folds of a giant 1 and 2, out of view of the guards positioned by the gate.

Arvin's fingers curved around the wire fence. His lips moved up and down, whispering to some imaginary ghost. Occasionally, the wind caught strings of his words.

"... it's all going to be okay... don't fear me... don't fear... sleep, rest... Be safe in the folds of my thoughts, be safe!"

Arvin yanked at the wire. Normally, the effort would have been in vain- the stuff connecting the chains was tough as nails. But with that slight tug, a whole section of the fence bent back. The gaping hole was big enough for a large dog or a small person to slip onto the beach.

Arvin ducked down, extending a leg through the hole.

"Stop!" I cried, leaping forward. I wrapped an arm around his midsection, and he landed flat on his back, crushing me under his weight. He flailed around, elbowing me in the mouth.

I rolled out from under him, shoving him back to the ground. "Are you crazy? The beach is *mined*!"

"Of course I'm crazy!" Arvin spat, heaving his tired joints up off the grass. "But that section of the beach is special. Would you blow up a grave? You can't shatter a heart that's already broken, so here they lie. Now *look*." Arvin pulled off his shoe, an ill-fitting work boot that had been long weathered down. He pulled his elbow back in a sweeping arch and tossed the shoe through the hole.

It clattered onto the rocks. It bounced once, twice, before settling peacefully on a large grey stone. I narrowed my eyes. Before I could make sense of what I had just seen, Arvin was already shimmying through the gap, planting his feet on the rocky shore without initiating a single land mine.

"How-" I stammered. Arvin, now all the way through, held out a clammy hand.

"Are you coming or not? I'm not wading in a pool full of souls only to freeze at the top of the high dive. Get over here, and pay your respects."

I swatted the hand away, manoeuvring through the hole myself. My balance faltered, and I twined a finger around one of the upper wires to steady myself. The ground was inches below the sole of my sneaker. If a single step was a leap of faith... then what would be expected of me when the time came to run away from this place?

Arvin drummed his fingers on the fence. "Where did the fearless Cerina go? Step onto the rocks. They won't cut you if you don't let them."

"If I didn't know you better, I'd mistake that for wisdom," I snapped.

"I thought you were *here* because you didn't know me. Stop being evasive and step onto the damn beach. They're waiting, and they lack patience."

More out of frustration than anything, I stomped my foot onto the rocky soil. A few stones leapt up in my wake. I couldn't help the triumphant smile that gnawed its way up my jaw.

From there, swinging through the hole was simple. Arvin urged me not to cut myself, and I did my best to take it slow. Regaining my footing on the uneven ground, I stared at the sea. There was no barrier between me and the limitless ocean. Nothing to stop me from jumping in. I wouldn't make it far, but, all things considered, being taken by the waves wouldn't be such a bad way to go.

Arvin pointed to a rock below me. I lifted the stone, brushing off a layer of dirt, sand, and other sediments that had been blown from the sea and tossed onto shore.

"May we honour the deceased," I read aloud. "Fallen in the trials, but never in spirit. Long live the guards and contestants, whose brutality built our country." I ran a finger over the last two words. "It's signed. By... Jezmon Tylor."

Arvin didn't respond. He was lost in thought, but he wasn't yammering anymore. His murky eyes were fixed on the ground beneath him. "It's high tide right now, but when the waves lower, the entire grave is visible." The sentence, so complete, felt odd in his mouth, imbalanced. His voice had a strange farawayness to it, but not the kind that materialised when he spoke in riddles.

"These trials..." I began, collecting the puzzle Arvin had laid out before me. "What were these trials, Arvin? What did they make you do?"

Arvin smiled bitterly. "I can't tell you that. All I can say is that before this Isle was a prison, it was an arena. There was more than one winner, and while we didn't fight to the death, many people preferred that route. And if they did, I was the one to deliver them there. I was allowed to stay, but I must seal my lips. The weight of those voices... those lives... it hangs heavy. And now... the Trials are happening again. Only this time, you don't know about it."

"What were you fighting for?" I pressed, smoothing my hand over the rock. "Please, Arvin. You must be able to tell me something."

Arvin shook his head, kneeling in a gesture of mourning. Grief shook his entire body. His chest heaved up and down as though he were crying, but no tears spilt from his eye sockets.

"I wish I could," he whispered, "but they listen, always. The only thing I can tell you is that the bronze key, the disease... they were all tests. And they're happening for you. I must warn you for your sake, but I must also be silent. Can you understand that?"

I met Arvin's solemn eyes, pleading with them.

"Please understand. I have no choice in this matter."

I looked down at the mass grave. How many bodies were below me? Two, ten? Fifty? How many of them had Arvin killed? How many of them had Arvin *meant* to kill?

How many, to this day, had haunted his every thought?

I grimaced, the reality sinking in. "You're a Rayz," I stated, looking out at the ocean. The waves splashed the rocks, giving the illusion of tranquillity. I could taste the salty spray on my tongue and hear the call of gulls and other sea birds. If the Isle weren't right behind me, the fence nearly digging into my back, I would have found it peaceful here.

Without outside intrusion, it probably *was* peaceful here.

Arvin gave me a single nod. "You can't be too surprised. Our family is messy, isn't it?"

"You're telling me."

"I'm your great uncle, Cerina. You have no reason to be proud of me, but I am proud of you every day. The voices have left me be for now, but when they come back, I don't always say what I mean. When the phantoms return, I hope you'll remember these words. They are the only important ones you'll get out of my mouth."

I gripped his hand, the worn-down calluses feeling familiar alongside my own. "We're getting out of here, Arvin. I promise."

***

When I returned to the Level One doctor, my head was clearer. My situation was anything but, but in the eye of the storm, I could maintain a level head.

Building 1-3 was out of the question. Joe had made that very clear. I couldn't blame the guy for his distrust, but part of me wanted to stab him in the throat with the bronze key just so he could know what it felt like.

I looked at Arvin, who was giving the ground a wistful smile. I pursed my lips.

"I have nowhere to go," Arvin muttered. The smile, I realised, was a grimace.

"You and me both," I said.

I held my breath as we returned from the field. A sudden change had befallen the sector. Not a single prisoner was out and about. There was a long way to go until light's out, but everyone was inside.

The way my footsteps echoed was like stepping into a ghost town.

As we rounded the corner, two singular figures came to greet me. At the front was Emry, which presented little surprise. But behind him was Jakson, a careful yet assertive look on his face. Their steps clattered on the stone, reaching a standstill as they approached us.

I stood in silence, waiting for them to speak.

"We've decided," Jakson said at last, "to hide you in building 1-10. Joe knows about the escape, and he doesn't want us going through with it. Nobody wants us to continue associating with you, but we still need your help… and, though I struggle to say this…."

"I need yours," I finished for him.

Emry prepared to talk, but Jakson held out a hand, cutting him off.

"I've never been the best judge of character," Jakson said, "and I'll be honest. This is a huge risk. But I'm willing to make a deal, and I am going through with this escape if it kills me."

"You're both fools," I said. Emry gave me a hopeless look.

"Well," Jakson said, "at least we're not the only ones."

Behind him stepped the others. Lizabeth, Haven, Adrienne. Even Max, Amélie, and Farrah were present.

"I-"

Words came easy to me, but these people had stolen them and buried them deep underground. They had claimed my voice for their own, and they had locked it away. For the first time, it was *they* who had the key.

Even my thoughts were scattered, thrown off-balance by a promise and a line of prisoners.

"We are willing to help you, Cerina," Haven said. Their rash had already begun to subside, melting in the strangest way.

No. They were not a line of prisoners because they were doing this of their own free will. They were the simplest of bonds, a puzzle piece I had been missing for years. They were the moment a tense silence shifts into a peaceful one, the brief instant where solitude becomes solidarity.

They were a line of allies.

Part 3- It's futile, this search

A communication

To: unknown client
From: R. Abbotsford, head of military strategy
Re: The winners

Edric Rayz- Final score, 7
Arvin Rayz- Final score, 7
Others of notable standing include; D. Savarin, F. Cramer, G. Brine, and Z. Amar.

The shipment and reintroduction to society of these winners will occur within the next week. The remaining contestants will continue to live at the Offshore Youth Rehabilitation Facility- perhaps, in a few years, their goals will meet our own.
Let's keep this brief. Your plan worked.

This message has been archived. The maximum security clearance to view this transmission is 1-A. If you have stumbled upon this message by accident, report it immediately to your local state representative. Any questions can be answered via the official government website.

Jakson Veer

The Incentive

"No way, no how," Arvin huffed, "I can't take the floor again. My back will shatter."

Cerina sighed for what seemed like the millionth time. "You don't really have a lot of options."

"There are always options! In this case, I can get the floor, or I can get the bed!"

"You can also sleep outside."

Arvin glared at Cerina, but the scowl was playful, not menacing. Out of nervous habit, I snuck a glance at the security camera. I had broken it myself before letting Arvin and Cerina in, but my gaze couldn't help drifting to that corner of the room, almost expecting that metallic eyelid to blink open, re-emerging from its sleep.

After a very long night, Cerina and Arvin, the newest unofficial members of building 1-10, were once again discussing sleeping arrangements with Farrah and me. Our situation was far from ideal- there was only so much space to go around, and two sudden arrivals, especially ones with recognisable faces, were always bound to cause a bit of suspicion. Farrah had offered to share her bunk with Cerina, which worked well enough to slip below the notice of anyone but Darby, who watched me like a hawk. However, he was getting closer to some of his other building mates, and now that he was occupied by interactions that didn't include vicious arguments and physical violence, his presence didn't raise too much concern.

Nobody complained, and even if they wanted to, everyone had been far too tired to put up much of an argument.

Except for Arvin. Nobody in any of the buildings seemed to have gotten a wink of sleep that night.

Why? I wasn't quite sure, but I had a pretty good guess. The contagion, rather, the *mindset* that had swept through the island had ended as quickly as it began. As soon as Cerina's display of humanity had snapped Haven out of it, the contagion had run its course, turning everyone into a mindless zombie as it flushed through the sector.

Observing this, Arvin had slipped below everyone's noses and, much to his chagrin, slept smack in the middle of the floor. The bags under my eyes might have been to do with the stress of the situation, but the more likely culprit was Arvin's gurgly snoring.

Farrah exhaled a heavy sigh. "We've been arguing about this for almost an hour. I need a breather, and Jakson's plant looks like it's on death's door."

I glanced at the stubborn sprout, lifting it up from its hiding spot under the bunk. I had given it a healthy dose of sunlight and water the day before, but already, the leaves were starting to droop.

Arvin scoffed. "You'd prioritise that thing over your guests?"

"The way this is going, the two of you might not be our guests any longer."

Cerina shuffled uncomfortably, giving Arvin a subtle pinch on his upper arm. He winced, swatting her hand away.

"We'll leave you two to work this out," Farrah said, holding the door open. A nervous energy caused my heartbeat to spike, shooting up to my throat and lodging itself there like a brick.

I gave Farrah a brisk nod, abandoning Cerina and Arvin to their own snippy argument.

No sooner had Farrah and I stepped around the side of the building that an abrupt rapping sound broke our awkward silence. Immediately, I froze.

The knocks, forceful yet formal, could only come from one particular party. I lifted JJ up, pressing my back against the wall. Farrah craned her neck around the corner, immediately whipping it back. "Guards," she rasped. "Two of them."

I peeked around the corner, risking a glance outside. Instead of carrying their standard brand of rifle, the pair of officers had long metal sticks over their shoulders with wire prongs on the end.

I narrowed my eyes, focusing on the tip of the rod. The metal wire was long and thin, but it resembled a familiar shape. My eyes flitted to the burn on my shoulder, then back to the stick. My brows leaned together in a confused knot.

"Open up," one of them grunted, "You have until the count of three."

Before I could come up with a good excuse to stall, Farrah was already in front of the door, shielding the building with her back. I shot my hand out to stop her, but she was too fast. I staggered forward, removed from my hiding spot.

With my other hand, I dropped the potted plant behind me, rolling it out of view.

"I'm in this cabin," Farrah said. "And you don't want to go in there. Trust me."

The officer in front was short and stocky. Her short tufts of red hair stood on end, jutting out as though she had experienced an electric shock. The man behind her looked to be about a decade older. His eyes were bored and sunken, a grim determination weighing down his hunched shoulders. He idly twirled his metal rod between his thumb and pointer finger, swearing as it clattered to the pavement with a loud smash.

"Get out of our way," the guard in front demanded, shooting an icy glare at the guy behind her. He promptly ignored her, returning to the act of staring into empty space, adding a little spin to his stick-twirling routine.

"The people inside are… uh, fighting," I said, spitting out the first excuse that came to mind. "And unless you're here to bet on a winner, they'd be pretty pissed with you if you barged in on them." Only then did I realise that was probably the *worst* excuse to give a prison guard.

Instead of bursting in to break it up, the woman only shrugged. "The sun could be tumbling from the fucking sky for all I care. Either way, you'd still have to let me in."

"If you don't mind me asking…." I blurted out, grasping at words. "What are you doing here?" The second guard, standing a bit further back, rolled his eyes.

"We're looking for a level 3. Now you, girl, take your dumbshit boyfriend and get out of the way."

Unable to help myself, a flush rose to my cheeks. I glanced at Farrah, who pursed her lips. For some reason, I had a very strong suspicion of who they were searching for. It was only a hunch, but we had a lot to base it off of.

I put my hands out, waving them in midair. "If there's a level 3 on the loose, isn't that a cause for concern? Shouldn't we all isolate ourselves in our cabins until the threat passes? I sure don't want to be killed in my sleep."

"That's exactly why we're doing this routine search. Now for the last *bloody* time, *get out of the way*."

"I'm not from this building," I announced, "but the people inside hired me to watch the door. And if I let you guys in, I won't get my payment. Would you really do that to me?"

Guard Number One grumbled in annoyance, but her ears perked up. It was only mild interest, but it was exactly what I was going for. "What could someone possibly be paying you with?"

Guard Number Two jabbed her in the shoulder. "Come *on*. We don't have time for this-"

"Wait," Guard Number One interrupted. "One moment. Kid, what are you being paid?"

"None of your business!" I was a terrible actor and an even worse liar, but the fear I forced onto my face was very genuine- just often suppressed. Now both of the guards had their curiosity piqued.

"Drugs?" Guard Number One guessed, her temper running thin. "Weapons? A free pass through the Level Two sector? Are you being blackmailed, bribed? Spit it out, kid, or we'll make you."

"Just… forget I said anything."

Guard Number Two tightened his hold on the pronged weapon, a sudden eagerness in his eyes. Finally, some excitement. I almost pitied the guy. No, not almost. I *definitely* pitied the guy. "Tell us what your reward is, and we'll let you go back to your building scot-free."

I shuffled a few paces away from the entry. Running was a no-go- they'd just lose interest in me, the mild but, for the moment, entertaining distraction. I couldn't make up some outlandish payment either- then they'd start searching the cabin for a meth lab or an arsenal of firearms, giving Farrah and me even more problems to deal with. On the other hand, if I gave them a lame answer, their anger would be provoked, and both us and Cerina would be in hot water.

In all honesty, it wasn't the guards that freaked me out. They were the lazy wanna be police officers of Sykona who got stuck with the crappiest job in all of crap city- floating around the Isle of Rebels as though they were prisoners themselves, with the occasional level 3 interrupting their monotonous line of work. They were nothing more than unfortunate civilians, and they probably wouldn't get any further in life than where they were now.

What scared me was what they were looking for. And while I couldn't be a hundred percent sure what that was, it was always better to play things safe.

The guards followed me as I moved backwards, turning their attention away from the door. Keeping my eyes on them, I motioned to Farrah, who nodded in my peripheral vision. I continued to step away until Farrah had a clear opening into the building. I shuffled even further back until the front door was out of view. I brought the guards behind the building, doing my best to feign desperation.

"I'll tell you," I shouted, masking the sound of the door's rusty hinges as Farrah slipped inside the cabin, "if *you* give me something in return!"

The guards both scoffed simultaneously. "Nice try, kid." The first guard advanced, taking a few calm and measured steps. At the last second, she doubled back, nudging her fellow officer, who dove through the now-unguarded door. I threw my arms out to stop him, but I only grasped at air. It was too late. Before I could react, the contents of the room were laid bare.

And those contents were Haven, Emry, Lizabeth, Adrienne, Max, Farrah, and Amélie. Cerina and Arvin were nowhere to be found.

There was no evidence of fighting, but both guards looked so satisfied with themselves that the credibility of my excuse was only secondary.

"Step aside," Guard Number One ordered in triumph, "we need to conduct a quick search."

Emry and Lizabeth, seated on the bottom bunk, made way for the guards to inspect. The man gave the underside of the bed a quick glance, feeling the sheets and pillows for any hidden items. Everyone else filed out of the room, giving me a nod as they passed by. I looked between them, confused.

By the time the guards had finished, only Emry, Lizabeth, and Farrah remained. The short woman rifled through the mattresses one last time before leaving, shaking her head in disapproval.

"I'll let you off with a warning," she grunted, "but if I catch you fighting again, you're going to regret it. There are ways you can punish people on this island that go beyond dumping them in with the Level Threes. Unless you want to find out what those ways are, I'd suggest you pay a little more respect to your superiors." She spat out that last statement with a cutting glance my way.

The other guard nodded, propping the metal rod onto his shoulder and correcting his posture. I could feel a retort bubbling on the tip of my tongue, but I shut it down before it could become a cohesive thought.

As soon as the door shut with a comforting tap, all four of us let out a collective sigh.

"They really don't care about whether or not we get hurt, do they?" Lizabeth said, her voice making me jump for a moment.

"Not in the slightest," Emry responded, hatred in his voice.

"What are you guys doing here?" Farrah asked, taking a few steps away from the door.

Keeping her eyes to the ground, Lizabeth answered her question with a brisk cough. "The guards came to our building too. They're looking for Cerina. We came to warn you, but at that point, it was already too late. It's lucky we arrived when we did."

Another, softer knock interrupted us from discussing things further.

"It's Arvin!" A scratchy voice called from the other end, "open up!"

I let the man in, followed by the rest of the gang, Cerina included. Even though the building layout was different, I could see people settling into their regular positions.

Emry sighed. "Well, I guess the band is back together. No thanks to you, Cerina."

Haven shut the door. "We don't have time to argue," they said, "Joe is hot on our heels."

Amélie laughed grimly, "that's so *like you*, Haven. Way to ruin the reunion."

"It's not a reunion," Haven said, "we're just picking up where we left off. As long as you're ready to continue, that is."

Amélie smiled. "You know I always am."

***

It was easy to forget that building 1-10 had loudspeakers. They were perched tightly in a shadowy corner, a cage with a black waffle-like pattern overlapping the grey underneath. Their presence was small and unassuming, and the one time I had heard any sound emanating from them was upon our first arrival. I frequently eyed the broken camera below them, but other than that, the only time the thought of the loudspeakers crossed my mind was when I considered their power supply, rooting out the best way to cut the communications. I had learned little about them, at least, little that could help me.

On that particular evening, after the group had dispersed once more and the sun was making its steady trek below the horizon, I was able to pick up on another notable fact. The loudspeakers were loud as hell.

"Attention, inmates!" A dull female voice announced, replacing the sudden jerk of lights-out with an even more surprising statement. Even from my lower bunk, the blaring sound waves pounded against my eardrums so aggressively they caused physical pain. "A recent program has been put in place throughout both sectors of the Isle. Presence at the centre field is mandatory for any and all prisoners. Arrive promptly after wake-up for further instruction. Anyone caught in their sleeping quarters at the time of the announcement will be harshly punished. Thank you."

The speaker crackled, and the room was shrouded by darkness.

***

At 6:00 AM sharp, I was on my feet and ready to go. Uneasy about what things at the centre circle would be like and how 'mandatory' their attendance actually was, I shook Farrah awake. She jumped at my touch, whirling around in a tangle of sheets and raising a fist, its trajectory pointed square at my face.

I placed a gentle hand on her clenched knuckles. "Calm down. It's just me."

Farrah settled, pushing her blankets back and brushing out the wrinkles in her baggy uniform. "Sorry about that," she said, "I just…" she trailed off, turning away from me. "Nevermind." An awkward silence dropped between us as our fellow building mates hurried to get ready.

"Have you given any thought to what to do about Cerina and Arvin?" I whispered, eager for a change of topic.

Farrah nodded. "They might be using this announcement as an excuse to draw everyone out and search the cabins again. But it's not as though we can bring Arvin and Cerina with us, either. We have to hide them somewhere, but if the cabins are a no-go, we don't exactly have a lot of options."

Farrah and I locked eyes.

"The washroom," we stated in unison.

Once an impressive number of people had filed out, taking the order of prompt arrival to heart, Cerina and Arvin emerged from their hiding places.

"You know," Arvin grumbled, "it's probably best if you include us in these plans of yours. Shouldn't we have a say on whether or not we get shoved into a toilet?" For once, Cerina didn't contradict him.

"You can't make an argument based on cleanliness," I said, "this whole place is an open breeding ground for all sorts of illnesses."

"I wasn't arguing with you," he muttered, "*this* time."

The bright wall of outside light took a moment of getting used to, stinging the back of my eyes as though it were a very mild form of liquid fire. I followed Farrah to the field, picking up the pace not because of the threat of punishment but because of my curiosity. Last night's announcement replayed over and over in my mind. A new program. What was *that* supposed to mean?

I stood on my tiptoes, picking Amélie's red hair out of the crowd. She was standing with the others, jumping to see past the tall heads in front of her. On the horizon, there wasn't much to look at. I could spot about ten guards lining the fence, keeping the crowd at bay and separating the Ones and Twos.

Behind Emry, on the fringes of the assembly, stood Joe. He surveyed the entire sector with a watchful eye, but the main focus of his attention was Haven and the group surrounding them. I felt guilt spike through me like a blunt-tipped needle- not sharp enough to draw blood right away, but bringing a slow and steady sting with it that couldn't be ignored. There was nothing for me to be worried about, not really. Cerina and Arvin were hidden as safely as they could be. Joe couldn't suspect anything from my presence with the group. We might have been planning trouble, but we were also… friends. If Joe saw himself as a parental figure, he certainly knew better than to deny the happiness of those under his guardianship.

"Come on," Farrah nudged, tugging me by the hand, "let's catch up to the others."

Numbly, I let her pull me away, unable to resist sneaking a glance behind me. For the briefest of seconds, Joe's eyes met mine. They flitted away an instant later, but I felt exposed. I had always been a bad liar. Even now, I could feel the heat rising to my face. While I could blame it on the summer sun or the crush of prisoners eagerly packed together to hear the news, the truth was still present and festering. And it was bound to reveal itself eventually.

"What do you think this is about?" I heard Emry question as soon as we were in earshot.

"Your guess is as good as mine," I said, jumping into the conversation. "It must be about the outbreak. It blew through too fast for a quarantine to be implemented, but the guards owe us an explanation."

Haven scoffed. "The guards owe us a lot of things."

A few impatient shouts began to rise from the crowd, the vast majority coming from the Level Two sector. The guards rushed to quiet things down, but all of us were restless. There were significant gaps between the various groupings of prisoners, but the idea of everyone smothered in the same space was making me uneasy.

Just as my misgivings started settling in, the loudspeakers lining the circular gate crackled to life.

"Attention Rebels, levels One and Two alike," a booming voice spoke through the intercom. Immediately, based solely on the chill it sent through my bones, I recognised who it belonged to. "My name is Jezmon Tylor, and you probably know me as the government's head of military defence. But never mind that title. Think of me as your guide, as your guard."

"As if!" Someone spat, letting loose a sea of booing and chanting. The guards adjusted the hold on their rifles. For once, the guards' attention spans weren't directed at an invisible force in the sky, dancing in their daydreams and driving their sluggish movements with a halfhearted hand- they were right here, right now, and they were ready to shoot.

Farrah tensed up beside me. She could sense it too.

"I have a directive for you- more of a proposition, actually," Jezmon spoke, shaking the very earth with the volume of his announcement. Cerina and Arvin could doubtlessly hear the call from their hiding spot- one could probably hear it from the mainland, the sound waves rippling over the many miles of sea.

"After the contagion outbreak that ran rampant a few days ago, four Level Threes were tagged. Their legal names are Zane Vanishe, Rosette Tamara, Irabella Redmond, and Cerina Rayz. Only two of them have been found and brought to justice."

A tremor went through the crowd. 'Brought to justice' didn't seem like a promising turn of events, based on who was speaking. "If you find Cerina Rayz, Irabella Redmond, or any other rebel who may be deemed worthy of the Level Three classification, you must bring them to the guards posted around the Inner Circle for inspection. You may only bring them in yourself, as the guards cannot leave their positions. If you can identify and capture said individuals, your sentence will immediately end."

A gasp rippled throughout both sides of the field. Over the intercom, Jezmon chucked.

"Yes, you heard that right. If you bring in a level 3, you got to go home."

Emry McLeod

If you can catch one

Lizabeth blocked my view, preventing me from tailing Jakson out of there. I hopped on my toes, but some of the heads towered almost a foot above mine- it was impossible to pick out one blond head with a dark streak in a sea of a thousand people.

Shouts rang out, but the guards clearly weren't taking questions. One of them fired a warning shot, scattering the crowd. Another turned the crank to the centre circle, pulling the gate open through a series of rusty clanks and scrapes. The rest of the officers pointed weapons at the crowd, eradicating any ideas of getting inside.

I didn't even try to peek over the mob. My eyes focused solely on who was in it and where they were going.

"Emry! This way!" Lizabeth grabbed me by the arm.

I swatted her away, and even amid the rush of the crowd, I could hear her grumble. "I said, get over here! You're going to get trampled!"

I couldn't argue with that logic. Picking up my feet, I made a beeline for the outlying sleeping quarters, a horizon I had become all too familiar with. I almost barrelled into the intimidating blue-haired guy who had been the cause of my missing glasses before Lizabeth yanked me by the tattered sleeve of my uniform.

The two of them, both Lizabeth and the scary dude, skidded to a halt. "Darby," Lizabeth muttered, the strength sucked from her voice.

"Lizabeth," the guy acknowledged. An icy claw gripped my heart. Was he going to beat her up? Was he going to beat *me* up? Taking inventory of all the potential things this guy could've broken, I might as well have hit the jackpot for my glasses to have been the only permanent casualties.

I cowered, staggering back. But Lizabeth faced the boy head-on, staring into his eyes. Then, only then, did I realise he had stopped. He wasn't fighting.

"You wouldn't… You can't…." Darby trailed off. I had never thought I could see him scared, but there he was, fear written on every inch of his face.

"I can," Lizabeth's tone was firm, "The message was clear. *'Any rebel who may be deemed worthy of the Level Three classification'*. We can bring you in."

Darby's eyes widened. "They didn't mean… They didn't mean…."

"People like you?" Lizabeth moved forward, and though Darby had about six inches on her, he moved back. My feet were screaming, begging me to run, but I stayed put, incapable of tearing my eyes away from the scene. The only thing missing was the popcorn and sugary soft drinks.

The two stood still for a moment, looking into each other's eyes.

Lizabeth, at last, shook her head. "I'm not like you. I don't hold a grudge. Jakson already showed you mercy, and now I'm going to as well. But this is your last chance. You're here now whether you like it or not, and I have the upper hand. Don't make me regret this."

Darby nodded, his eyes burning with loathing. "I hate you, Lizabeth Merrin."

"I pity you, Darby Olson."

With that, she departed, strutting away from him with a spring in her step.

"What are you looking at?" Darby grunted in my ear as he passed by, shoving me in the shoulder.

I raced back to Lizabeth, tripping over my own feet.

"I bet that felt good," I said, catching up to her.

She answered with a full, toothy grin that went all the way up to her eyes.

"You have no idea."

Haven, Max and Adrienne had already beat me to the building. All of them looked like they wanted to say something, and based on the energy in Max's eyes, it didn't look like something I wanted to hear.

Haven lunged for the door before anyone else could slip in, pressing their entire body weight on the frame.

"I know exactly what you're all thinking," they breathed, "and we are *not* turning Cerina in."

Max objected instantly.

"Why not?! The guards just handed us an easy solution on a silver platter. We get rid of the Level Twos, both of them, and we get home! No fake IDs necessary. No breaking into the inner circle, no hijacking the transport boat, *none* of that crazy shit we were all trying to plan. We'd be idiots not to take this chance."

Someone pounded on the door behind us. "Open up! It's us," Amélie, Jakson and Farrah shouted from the other end.

"Hold on a second!" Haven screamed, shutting them up. "There has to be a catch somewhere- they won't just let a bunch of people, a bunch of *prisoners*, walk home scot-free. Based on what we know about Level Threes, we must think about this for a second."

"I don't mean to interrupt!" Jakson yelled from the other end of the door. "But Haven's right!"

Haven tipped their head to the door, pointing at it in acknowledgement.

"For now, Cerina and Arvin stay hidden, and we escape as planned."

"But we could go home *now*," Max protested, "quick and easy. Cerina can't be trusted. Doesn't it make more sense to hand her in and pretend like this whole sucky endeavour never happened?"

Haven shook their head.

"Even if the guards *aren't* lying to us, here's the thing- do you really want to go back to living under these people? After what you saw in the tomb, with Arvin, with the mass grave Cerina told us about? Aren't you curious? I want my freedom as much as you do, but we need to think carefully."

I thought back to Cerina and how the wind had blown in her hair. How she had effortlessly broken into that building and outmanoeuvred all the rival Families in the Level Two sector. Haven's words registered, but they weren't what convinced me. I didn't know who Arvin was. I didn't know why Irabella turned against Cerina, and I didn't know what had made her sick in the first place. I didn't know what the deal was with the shrivelled lavender we had found in the tomb, but amid all of those uncertainties, I could be sure of one thing and one thing only.

Cerina was one of the good guys. No, who was I kidding? She was more than that. Much more.

Once, when I was a few years younger, I had seen an unsheathed kitchen knife and wondered, just for a second, what it would be like if I plunged it through my chest. It wasn't a suicidal thought, not at all. It was nothing more than a curiosity, a *what-if?* dangling in the forefront of my mind. I wondered if it would hurt, how much blood it would spill, and how long it would take before it killed me. Even hypothetically, the scene was enough to give me gooseflesh. I had banished it from my brain, ashamed that such an idea had ever crossed my mind. I pushed the thought of reporting Cerina down in the same way, so repulsed by it that I had resigned myself completely to the fact of its *wrongness*. There was no question in my mind about what came next. Not then, and, hopefully, not ever.

"So," Haven continued, letting Jakson, Amélie and Farrah into the building. "The real question is, what are they up to?"

"We don't have time to talk about this," Jakson said regretfully. "We have to split up again. Amélie can drift between the two groups as a messenger because she doesn't share either of our buildings. Cerina and Arvin will remain hidden- now, more than ever. People will be looking for every excuse to bring someone in- if they even bother to make an excuse."

"Farrah, Jakson, Amélie," Haven commanded, "grab Cerina and Arvin from wherever they're hidden. In five minutes, we will relocate to building 1-10."

The two of them nodded and rushed out the door.

"Now," Haven said, "with that out of the way… one of you has been spying."

Haven's eyes landed on me immediately. I blanched, grasping for words. "What are you talking about? It wasn't *me*. I wasn't even sure if the escape was still-"

"Relax," Haven said, holding a hand out. "I know it wasn't you. But it *is* someone outside this building."

I gulped. "You mean…" I trailed off. "Jakson, Farrah, or Amélie?"

Haven nodded. "Or someone else entirely."

"Please explain," Lizabeth urged, "did someone alert the guards about Cerina? What happened?"

"Yesterday, when the guards searched the cabins, they only examined buildings 1-3 and 1-10. The five of us had all been in here up until that point, grounded, essentially, by Joe. None of us could have tipped the guards off about Cerina's location. But there were only a few people with that information, some of which were elsewhere at the time."

When we had seen the guards walking up to building 1-3, we had known where they'd be going next. I had to admit- it was a little suspicious that Jakson and Farrah weren't around in the cabin for the inspection. Almost as though they knew it was going to happen.

"I don't think it's them," Lizabeth said. "I can't speak for Farrah and Amélie, but I know Jakson. He isn't like that. We're a team. What would they have to gain by becoming snitches? And why wouldn't they have turned Cerina in already?"

"You *knew* Jakson," Haven corrected. "But now, there's an incentive. We can't trust anyone outside of this circle, understood? Cerina will be watched securely until we get to the bottom of this new movement and figure out who the mole is. Until then-" Haven smiled, completely changing pace. "We have a talent show to plan."

***

The dark streak in my hair was fading. I noticed it only after we had dispersed and I had stepped away from the building to take a breather. Frowning, I picked it up between my fingers, some of the black residue rubbing off onto my hand. We were all due for a touch-up job.

As soon as I stepped outside, I was greeted by Joe's hawk-like stare. He was in front of a neighbouring cabin, his eyes glued to our door. A crowd of Level Ones from various buildings were assembled in front of him, asking a flurry of questions as though he had access to classified intel.

"Everyone!" Joe shouted, directing his attention to the masses. While his back was turned, Lizabeth and I slipped out. "You need to stop this at once!" I thought he was addressing me for a second, and I halted in my tracks. "I know just as much as you!" Joe continued, "if you have a little patience, I'm sure we'll get some answers."

That wasn't the response the crowd wanted to hear. I took advantage of the loud callouts, questions, and outright demands to slip away from Lizabeth. Leaving the amassment of people behind me, I sighed in relief. At last, some me-time.

Adrienne and Max were arguing behind building 1-3, so I opted out of that course of action before either of them could see me. I was alone for now, and I intended to keep it that way as long as I could. Until I found Cerina, anyway. I didn't want to be tailed, especially now. Who knew what that would entail?

My mind came up empty when I thought of the places Cerina could be hiding. My first thought was of the mass grave Arvin had shown her- there were no cameras, and it was also quite secluded. But something about that image didn't sit right. Cerina had a lot of respect for the dead, and I couldn't really envision her sitting among them to pass the time.

The only other places that came to mind were building 1-10 and the old mess hall, now reduced to a pile of ash. Both of those were obvious no-gos.

Near the gap behind building 1-10 and building 1-9, where the corner of the fence rounded off, I stopped. Usually, people were milling about, playing games, chatting, or doing morning exercise routines. But now, it was perfectly empty.

I basked in the solitude gratefully, expanding my lungs like a fish immersed in water.

Finally, introversion could reign supreme, if only for a short while.

Emphasis on the 'short while'.

Before any of my now-relaxed senses could spring into action, a rough, clammy hand clamped over my mouth. Something crumbly and sharp was crushed into my attacker's fist, grinding against my lips, my teeth. A second hand covered my eyes, plunging me into darkness. I screamed, kicked, flailed against the unseen menace, but I could slowly feel my consciousness ebbing away.

"Stop fighting," a voice snapped, "or I'll have to make this even worse for you."

Now, I recognised the dry texture jamming into my mouth. It was the poison, the crushed lavender that had knocked Irabella out.

Irabella. I recognised the voice, too.

"I said, stop *fighting*. Pass out already! Do you want me to use my bare hands?"

With the last of my fleeting energy, I dug my teeth into the leaves and bit down hard.

***

"Get up."

The words, distorted and gurgly, echoed against the rims of my earlobes.

"I said, get *up*, you little shit."

Groggily, I forced my eyes open. I was in a dark room- a sleeping quarter, it seemed, by the shadowy bunks. The smell of ashes was thick in the air. The windows and door were blocked, the only shards of light creeping through a little shaft at the bottom. My arms were duct-taped to the baseboard of a bunk, and my legs were stuck together by similar means.

Irabella's shadowy figure stood between me and the exit. Her forehead was caked with grime and ash, and tendrils of smoke wove through her hair, coming off in thick, fragrant fumes like a campfire gone terribly wrong. I stirred, adjusting my eyes to the dimness. The interior of every single sleeping quarter, with the exception of building 1-3 with its artistically decorated walls, looked exactly the same.

But it didn't take a genius to figure out that I was trapped in building 2-7.

"Whaddya want?" I slurred. The corners of my mouth, where I had bit down on the toxic plant, were numb. I massaged my cheeks with my molars, gnawing on them until the feeling returned.

"I'm going to spell this out plain and simple," Irabella looked me in the eye, a glint of refracted light flashing before me. In her hand was one of the glass shards from the wreckage. I gulped. Her face, only inches from mine, brought the smell of burning rubber even closer.

"If you want revenge," I spat, "go somewhere else. There's no dignity, or whatever, in beating up an easy target."

Irabella smiled. "I'm not looking for dignity. I want Cerina."

Now, the pieces started to click. "Good fucking luck with that."

"I won't need luck. I'll have you." Irabella's grin turned into a sneer. "You see," she said, "I don't *want* to go home. I'll only wind up here all over again, and while it'd be fun as hell to run away from the government, it's not the kind of lifestyle for someone like me. No, I want to rule this Isle of Rebels. And the only way for that to happen is if Cerina is out of the equation."

"You want to stay on the Isle?" Genuine bewilderment passed over my face. "You're an idiot."

Irabella fumed. "You're the one who's duct-taped to a bunk. So you're going to do as I say, or I'll cut you. Understood?"

Nodding vigorously, I listened intently to the rest of what she had to say.

"Now," Irabella continued, pacing back and forth on the shadow-draped ground. "She trusts you, which is why *you* must lure her to me."

"And what makes you think I'd help you?" For some reason, possibly from the poison or the darkness, my pulse maintained a steady rhythm. My composure was held together by a fragile thread, but it was stitched intact all the same. There was no doubt in my mind that I could stay loyal to my beliefs, and that devotion came with a weird kind of comfort.

"Because you don't have a *choice*, moron. Does it look like you have any power here? No. Does it *look* like you have any chance of taking me in a fight? No. Zip, zero, zilch."

"Look," I raised my eyebrows, illustrating the truth of my next statement, "I'm just going to establish, right here, right now, that I'm not going to help you. Okay? It's not going to happen. But I have to ask. Aren't the two of you friends?"

Irabella wavered for a second before covering it up with a brisk laugh. "You wouldn't understand. You don't have to fight for your position here. But I do. And I will. And you are going to listen to me."

"Okay, okay, I get it. But if you won't take the reward, who gets to go home?"

Irabella tensed her jaw. "Do I need to wave the answers in front of your idiotic face? There are two people here, and there is one reward. If I'm not taking it, then there's only one person it can fall to."

"You're giving me the reward? Are you *sure* that's a smart move?" I stared in disbelief, realising a second too late that I might as well have asked her to stab me here and now.

Irabella turned up her nose as though she had smelled something very foul. "I'm not *giving* you anything. It's just a win-win situation. Take it or leave it. Just remember who has the knife, okay?"

"It's not a knife. It's a piece of glass."

Even in the darkness, I could see Irabella's seething glare as clear as day.

***

I was only playing along. That's what I repeated to myself while Irabella gave me her first directives, the words playing over and over in the back of my mind. Still, every sentence she uttered was thoroughly absorbed by my hippocampus, my attention piqued. Sure, listening might have helped me stay alive, but I was making a mental picture of the plan, envisioning its course. If it was an impossibility, what could justify that?

Once Irabella was finished talking, it was a shock to go back into the daylight. Irabella slit the bonds with two quick strokes before dissolving into a shadow-laden corner.

Tentatively, I cracked the door open. Irabella's specific instructions were to *not get seen*, but the Level Two sector was even crazier than the Level One side. However, that wasn't necessarily a bad thing. A group of people I thought would blow my cover instantly turned out to be way too preoccupied to give me a second glance.

In fact, upon closer examination, I realised with a start that they were a large band of Level Ones chasing down a Level Two.

Maybe the tables had turned.

Something stirred inside of me. It was fear, yes, but it was also a terrible yearning. Not only that, but an impossible hope. That maybe, just maybe, I could go home again. It wasn't like the fantasy I chased with the Escape Artists; instead, it was a chunk of concrete evidence, a window of opportunity placed right in front of me.

Screw what Haven said. I would be an idiot not to take it. I did my best to lock that truth on an Isle of its own, but it wouldn't budge.

Deep down, I knew that Max was right.

Clearing my mind, I hurried through the rings of the circle. What was wrong with me? I couldn't abandon the others. I couldn't ditch Lizabeth, and I couldn't even *think* about burning the bridge to Cerina.

They were more important than my worthless freedom.

Right?

Something was clearly wrong with me.

Cerina Rayz

The warning

Jakson was right. Crouched in the outhouse with Arvin, I could hear the booming announcement clear as day. It was enough to stop Arvin's incessant complaining dead in its tracks, replacing his feebly-directed whining with a blank look.

Frankly, I wasn't sure why he was so surprised. I had known they were coming for me from the start. I didn't know why, exactly, nor was I aware of how they had come upon this information. But the target on my back hung heavily, and this announcement only stiffened its grip over my every movement.

I was so busy dwelling on this fact that I almost missed the second part.

If you bring in a Level Three, you get to go home.

We had to get out of there.

Wasting no time, I pulled Arvin out of the outhouse stall we had crammed ourselves in, assisting him down the wooden step. Hastily, I ushered him down through the rows of buildings, slipping between the gaps and fading out of sight. Once we were alone enough for comfort, I stopped in my tracks, bringing my voice to a low whisper.

"Where are we going to go?" I asked. Arvin looked back at me, an aimless expression on his face. For a dreadful moment, I thought he was about to ditch me. His name hadn't been called.

As though he could read my thoughts, he matched my tone, the words barely audible. "They're hunting me too. Always have been. Always listening."

"Where can we go?"

Arvin shook his head solemnly. "There *is* nowhere for us to go. Nowhere to escape the ear-voice. The only reason they haven't found you yet is because they want you to run." Arvin winced. His head shakes became more rapid, more violent.

"Arvin," I said, "stop it. You're going to snap your damn neck." I moved to place a hand on his shoulder, but as soon as my hand met the fabric of his uniform, he scampered back, looking at me with the eyes of a cowering animal.

"Don't-" he wheezed, "don't touch me. You mock them."

"Arvin…" I trailed off, "I can't help you if you don't tell me what's going on."

Arvin's breath came in heavy puffs, more choppy exhales following in rapid succession.

"I can't do that," he breathed, "you can only help me with your ignorance. And you're doing a fine job already. You have an ear-voice, but it's quiet now. It isn't active. I must keep it that way."

Again, this was an exercise in patience. I sighed, nodding even though it was the last thing I wanted to do.

"Okay. Back to the matter at hand. We can't go to building 1-3, where I'm sure they're readying their torches, ropes, and pitchforks. We can't go-"

Arvin put a hand up, stopping me.

"Didn't you hear me? We have nowhere to go. So pick a place and be done with it, or we'll wander forever."

"Fine. 1-10 it is."

As we crept between the buildings, a sudden flash caught my eye. A team of three people whizzed by, their shoes hot on the pavement. Something about them seemed a little off, but I couldn't quite place it.

Until the largest among them sprang on a Level One bystander.

The new target, a scrawny, malnourished boy who couldn't be a day older than fifteen, yelped abruptly. The attacker closed his fingers over the other boy's throat, shifting him into a headlock while the two other people surrounded him like a swarm of sharks. The skinny kid sputtered and coughed, kicking and flailing. Watching from behind building 1-5, I was able to hear the team's scratchy speech- another telltale sign of their young age.

"Keep struggling, and I'll choke you to death!" The aggressor screeched. Based on his airy, pubescent tone, it didn't sound like much of a threat.

But the bright red scratches on the other boy's throat told a different story.

The two other level ones pinned the boy's arms behind him, kneeing him in the back. "We're going to turn you in," one of them grunted, like it wasn't obvious already. "It's nothing personal, but we want out."

The fact that they were even willing to do such a thing clearly proved that they didn't deserve anything remotely close to freedom.

"Please!" The more-or-less innocent boy begged, pure desperation in his eyes. "I'm not a Level Three! You can't! You can't turn me in! They'll see through it immediately!" His dirty blond hair stuck to his sweaty brow as his wild brown eyes roamed the immediate vicinity for a saviour. "Please!"

My nostrils flared. So did the boy's. Our eyes met, and written inside of his was a feeling I knew all too well. A choked gasp emanated from my vocal cords, one I wasn't conscious of until I was tearing down the cobblestone path, ripping the boy free.

"Let him go!" I screamed, elbowing the assailant square in the jaw. The remaining members of the trio exchanged a glance before whipping around and fleeing. I gripped the boy by the fabric of his uniform while the other Level One doubled over, coughing blood all over the pavement.

"What's your problem!" He sputtered. The boy froze in my grasp, staring up at me wide-eyed.

"You're…" he squeaked, his voice barely above a whisper, "a Level Two."

"Wait a second-" the attacker regained his footing, wobbling on shaky legs. A giant welt was already forming where I had struck him, hitting me with the realisation that I might have gone a little overboard. "You're one of the bitches everyone's hunting down, aren't you?!"

I smiled grimly. I couldn't help but think about how Irabella would have loved such an intense spotlight- basked in infamy as though it were solid gold.

"Yeah," I spat, "that's me. Now run along, or you'll find out why."

The Level One didn't bother with a retort. He picked up his feet and bolted, gone from the scene in a split second.

"Why did you… help me?" The kid mustered. I loosened my grip, looking him in the eye. I had to peer down quite a bit to match his gaze.

"You reminded me of someone," I admitted. "Now go. Stay inside. Next time, you might not get so lucky."

He nodded, fumbling on the words for a thank-you. Before he could bother with an awkward reply, I was already gone, picking up Arvin's hand and jogging at an even pace to building 1-10. Arvin swerved in front of me before I could open the door, blocking my path.

"Why did you stop them?" He asked. "That wasn't your fight."

"He was innocent. It would have been ridiculous if the boy had been turned in when those who had falsely accused him went free."

Arvin shook his head. "No one here is innocent."

"You know what I mean."

"Do I? You're speaking loudly enough, but I still can't understand you."

"Then either listen harder or buzz off. What's done is done."

I lunged for the handle, but once again, he stopped me. "For a second, there, you looked a little scared. Has the big Cerina shrunk a few inches? Does she need a uniform re-sizing? Because I don't know when the last time was that I saw her get stitched up."

"And you tell me you don't understand what *I'm* saying."

Arvin gave me a knowing smirk. "You know what I mean."

"Don't use my words against me."

"Now I see why you like that Emry kid so much. *He* reminds you of someone too."

I gave him a deep glare. "We are not talking about this."

Arvin giggled, "*you* might not be talking about it, but *we* will be. We'll be hosting a great many thoughts."

I swung the door open. Now was not the time for a trip down memory lane.

***

Jakson, Farrah, and Amélie turned up at building 1-10 eventually. The three of them were obviously annoyed- I could only assume that the flush on all of their faces came from searching for the two of us. But as they entered, they didn't say a single word. Through chilly gazes and subtle nods, a mutual understanding was reached. We looked out the windows, and we watched the chaos unfold.

Amélie was the first to leave, fleeing the silence before it could consume her loud spirit. Jakson and Farrah slipped out shortly after, leaving Arvin and me alone once more.

"Well," I said at last, "do you want to go explore?"

Arvin shook his head. "You know that's a terrible idea."

"I do. But I'm bored, and if we stay here any longer, I'm going to come up with many worse ones."

Once I was breathing fresh air, it didn't take me long to get a sense of how this so-called 'reporting' worked.

The targets, many of which were brought in by the dozens, had to be present at the gate for the deal to be accepted. Once they were shown to the guard, a single nod sent all parties involved- both the potential Level Three and their reporter- through the gate and into the inner circle. The large steel barricade had been temporarily lifted, but even so, it was impossible to see inside. It appeared as though there were gates beyond gates- even behind the blockade, a screen made of black plastic that the captors and captives alike were ushered into prevented anyone from seeing the interior.

The situation was pretty grim. No one was asking for proof of any kind, and anyone brought in was thrown in with the rest of the bunch without so much as a second thought.

However, a surprising number of Level Ones were charging into the Level Two sector, armed with nothing but their fists. And the guards weren't doing a single thing about it. If they were trying to weed out the worst of us, I could in no way understand their reasoning behind this method of doing so.

I bit the inside of my cheek as yet another group of prisoners were ushered in. At this rate, the entire population of the Isle would be depleted to almost zero by the day's end. I wondered what was going on on the other side of the island. The mess hall had been reduced to a crisp. The bronze key was worthless. For a brief second, I wondered what would happen if a lowly spark fell the wrong way and the entire Level Two sector caught fire.

The guards would probably hide behind their walls and wait for us to figure it out. And if everyone burnt to a crisp, it wasn't like it would be the worst thing in the world.

"Don't turn around." A voice spoke, sending a chill shooting down my spine.

My nerves lit up. The voice behind me sounded strangely familiar, yet at the same time, I couldn't quite place it. It was neither distinctly male nor distinctly female, and the mechanical tinge that came with it made it bear the semblance of speech that was being run through a translator.

I curled my knuckles into a fist.

"And if I do?"

"Don't speak, either."

I laughed brittly.

"Who do you think you are?"

"Someone willing to hurt you. Someone who can hurt you."

"You're bluffing."

"Am I?"

"I'll see soon enough." With that, I whipped around, fist raised. But there was no target for my hand to meet. Behind me was nothing but empty air and the stretch between the buildings of the Level one sector. I dropped my arm, exhaling shakily. Maybe I, too, was starting to hear things.

***

I found Arvin as soon as I could, strangely comforted by his spaced-out face. I settled in beside him, on-edge and eager for the company.

"I think I've been hearing voices, too," I muttered.

Arvin turned to me. "Oh? It's spoken at last? A bit early for an ear-voice. Look at how old *I* am."

I smirked slightly, matching his ambling pace. "Again. I have no idea what you're talking about."

Arvin turned to the ground. "People rarely do."

"Do you ever wish the voices you hear would stop, Arvin?" I asked, "so you could truly focus on the world? Listen to your *own* voice?"

Arvin shrugged, shaking his head. "The ghosts are mine to bear. They're a part of me, even the unwanted ones. I'm too far gone to get help, but I don't think I care anymore. I've decided to help you, no matter what becomes of me. Wait here."

"Help me-"

My bemused question quickly faded from my lips as Arvin sped off, his mind bent on a new task.

I was torn. He had told me to wait for him, but I wasn't sure if it was the most incredible idea to do as he bid.

Walking off, I shook my head, smiling to myself. Weird as this predicament was, it was nice to have a friend. Arvin was a crazy, delusional, very old friend, but a companion none the same.

Lizabeth Merrin

Natural cycle

Haven ran their fingers over the cabin wall, a distant look in their eyes. I fidgeted with the corner of Emry's bunk, unsure what to do or say. Adrienne and Max were both in the room with me, whispering side-by-side. They were only a few feet away- in perfect earshot too. In theory, it would be easy to spark up a conversation.

But all they did was argue. And Haven's deep concentration on a faraway point in the distance sucked all the life out of the room. Really, though, it was more due to personal barriers that I didn't cross to that end of the room, instead resolving to silence.

My mind drifted between three things- Cerina, Emry, and Jakson, each one bringing an entirely new pang in my chest. Nothing was immediately wrong, per se, but the thought of them getting stuck here forever made my stomach plummet.

To think that at the beginning of this whole ordeal, I had been so full of hope.

"Life is brutal," Haven muttered, their fingers sliding into the crevices on the wall. "And I am *stuck*."

"What do you mean?" Adrienne asked, eager for an excuse to end her conversation with Max.

Haven glared, not at Adrienne but at the twisting vines marking the wall from front to back. "My poetry. Everything I come up with is hot garbage- because my life is going nowhere. It's infuriating."

"I can relate," I was surprised to hear myself, out of everyone else with much better things to say, open my mouth to speak. The others, by their raised eyebrows and questionable glances, appeared surprised too.

"I- I mean," I quickly covered up, blushing at the number of eyes suddenly pinned on my minuscule, formerly very insignificant presence, "I don't want to be trapped here either. Nobody does."

Haven looked at me as though I were a child, even though I was probably older than they were.

"Do you know what humanity's purpose is?" they asked, slowly, deliberately.

"I... well, I have my own interpretation of it, but nobody has a definite answer to that question."

"I suppose not. But do you want to hear my version?"

I had a feeling that I didn't. Before I could come to a decision, however, Haven was speaking.

"The thing is, there is none. But we've *created* enough meaning for ourselves that a detail like that one may be easily overlooked. I worry myself with the dealings of society. And the one true purpose, I find, within that web, is to make a place for oneself within it. My ambition is to carve a slot." Haven paused, planting their outstretched fingers over the etchings on the wall. "But of course," they grumbled, "it's fucking impossible to do that on a *prison island*."

A weight settled over the room. "Sorry," Haven whispered at last, dropping their hand in a defeated sigh. "There's no point in ranting."

Adrienne shook her head. I found myself mirroring the gesture.

"It's not wrong to be angry," I said, again wondering what mysterious fountain my words of attempted wisdom were spouting out of, "and honestly, if we escape, I don't know what's next for me. But if we can use our anger for the right reasons, then maybe we *can* carve a place."

The only thing I saw in Haven's round blue eyes was pity.

"Maybe we can sway Joe to our side," they mumbled, flipping back into strategy mode. "Let's find a way to get him out of the crowd. We need to talk to him, and we need to talk to him now- especially if there's a mole on the loose."

The door opened, letting in a rush of chilly air. And just like that, my floodgates closed as though the last moment had never even happened.

***

It wasn't hard to spot Joe in the streets, trying and failing to calm people down. Gradually, the mob had shifted closer to building 1-3, so close, in fact, that you could hear the sounds of their endless probing from inside the walls.

"Joe," Haven said, placing a hand on his shoulder. They were almost the same height. "We have to chat."

Joe faced us. "I'm a little busy at the moment," he grumbled, gesturing behind him, where somebody was screaming '*get him!*' at eardrum-bursting volume.

"You can stop a few, but more are going to come. We have a pressing matter to discuss."

"If this is about your escape plan, then I've already told Jakson exactly what I'm going to tell you- it's not going to work, and it's not going to happen."

"It's not about the escape plan. It's about the Level Threes. It's about the entire *island*."

"If you are fraternising with anyone *else* outside of this sector-"

"There's a mole," Haven interrupted, grabbing Joe by the wrist. Joe's eyes dropped to Haven's clammy hand, and he tensed his jaw.

Joe's eyes snapped back up, travelling to me. All of a sudden, an awkward tight-lipped expression crossed over his face. I surveyed him in bewilderment as the same expression crossed over the eyes of Haven and Max. Adrienne looked at the ground like it pained her to do so.

"Um, Lizabeth…" Adrienne muttered, "may I escort you to the outhouse?"

"What are you talking about?"

Adrienne grabbed me by the arm, pulling me away. Suddenly, the ground became very exciting to Max and Haven, whose attention was suddenly absorbed by it.

"Adrienne? What's going on?"

Adrienne gulped, leading me to the back of the line for the washroom. "Has this happened before?"

"Has *what* happened before? Is there something wrong with me?"

"No, definitely not!" Adrienne cried, "I mean, it can be… frightening or whatever, but it's just, um, your *introduction to womanhood*. It happens to everyone."

My entire face turned as white as a sheet.

"You don't mean-"

Adrienne gave me an apologetic grimace. "Yeah."

"Oh shit. Oh fucking shit."

Someone else joined the line, stepping behind us. I could feel a deep, plastery blush radiating through my cheeks.

Of course, it was nowhere near as red as the bloodstains on my sweatpants.

"Is this your first time? How old are you?" Adrienne asked, her voice a bit warbly.

"I turned sixteen last month. And, uh… yeah. This is my-" I gulped, wishing I could die here and die now. I wondered how that would look. *Level One prisoner mysteriously drops dead in a bathroom line*. Of all the ways the Isle could kill me, I had no idea this would be one of them.

"Wait, you're *sixteen*? You're older than I am! I mean, not that there's anything *wrong* with that, I just-"

"What do I do?!" I rasped in Adrienne's ear. "If they don't even have sinks on the island, they can't possibly-"

Adrienne bit her lip. "There are a few ways we do things. Some people use their backup uniforms- gross, but effective." She pointed to her own set of prison pants. I hadn't noticed it under her high boots, but the hem cut off below her knees. Rather, it had been *ripped* off.

"You can always wash it, but it's a pain in the ass. There's also the toilet paper method. I don't think I have to elaborate on that one."

Out of the corner of my eye, I spotted Cerina. It looked like she had just seen a ghost.

"Cer-" I started, "um, Mel!" The one name I could think of came to me in a moment's impulse. I kicked myself. Mel's name, a part of herself, was too important to me to be used as someone else's alias. But I couldn't bite back the words. The dude behind us in the line was already paying us a few side-glances.

"I'll go grab your backup clothes- you'll need them, regardless of anything," Adrienne said, speeding off. I didn't think it was a mere coincidence that she decided to bolt the second the runaway Level Two came into view.

Cerina spun towards me, keeping her head down. Her breathing, a heavy panting audible from a few paces away, took on a new sort of hitch when she saw the giant red spot that was only growing on the pants of my prison uniform.

She brushed beside me, but her pace didn't slow. "The hell do you think you're doing?" She rasped, "You don't *know* me. Shut up, and look ahead."

My heart sank. Of course I couldn't expect her to help. What could she do, after all? She was someone who only helped people if it helped herself. There was nothing to gain from getting me out of this incident.

Something dropped into my hand. I closed a fist around the crinkly plastic package, slowly releasing my fingers. Inside my knuckles was a tampon.

I slid the item into my pocket as though it were worth gold. It wouldn't last very long, and it was probably one of the last supplies Cerina had gathered from the mess hall- a sacrifice to her as well. But I wasn't going to forget the gesture any time soon.

Adrienne's brunette head of hair bobbed back into view. In her hands were my oversized backup clothes. I took them eagerly, hoping this awful day would hurry up and end.

Emry McLeod

Ulterior motives

I had no idea what the guards were up to. And honestly, their motives were probably the least of my problems. With the whole heap of trouble I had dug myself into surrounding Irabella, it was almost a relief to go to bed thinking of government conspiracy theories just like the good old days.

Unfortunately, said relief did not carry over to the next morning. I woke up in a sweat, grasping at the threads of a nightmare that had slowly dissipated. My dizzying headache, a constant reminder of my missing glasses, had only gotten worse. It felt like a nail was being shoved into my skull.

It was hard enough to think with the pounding in my cerebrum, let alone with the army of thoughts I had to face, wielding skull drills of their own.

"You seem distant," Lizabeth said the next day. There was something off about her, too- but I couldn't quite place it. It was probably none of my business. "How about we go on a walk?"

I shook my head.

"All there is to *do* around here is walk and plot. I'm going to find something better for once."

Lizabeth raised an eyebrow.

"I'm genuinely curious to see what you come up with."

"I was thinking about paying a visit to building 1-10."

Lizabeth's once-excited face immediately fell. "Absolutely not. As we speak, Jakson and Farrah are looking into a better way to hide her. It's a miracle that she's been able to blend in for this long as she has. If this doesn't work, the guards will pull something soon. I want to help Cerina, but it'll do more harm than good if we're caught in the middle of it."

"Frankly, it's pointless to try and predict what the guards will do next at this point."

"They might not be as thick-headed as we think, you know. Just- hear me out. I can't stop you from hurting yourself if that's what your heart is set on, but I don't want you to get hurt. Not to mention, where were you yesterday?"

"Where were *you* yesterday?" My lame attempt to deflect the question had more of an effect than I had been hoping for.

"I was thinking about a way to win back Joe's favour."

"Have you tried going on a walk with *him*, too?"

"Clearly you're not in a helping mood."

"You don't say?" I left briskly, invoking a slight air of disappointment over Lizabeth's eyes. I felt that familiar twinge of guilt again. Clearly, she had been hoping for a better conversation. And maybe, deep down, I wanted to stick around too.

But I didn't have the time to improve my social life. I had a dramatic psycho to deal with.

The note had arrived late last night, materialising under my pillow. Paper on the Isle was scarce, so the message was written on a scrap of cloth, in what was either a really low-quality brand of red ink or the swashes of actual blood.

Emily
I need you to write 3 messages. Scare her, and don't ask questions
Screw up and you die on the spot.
I'm watching.
-Irabella

The overall memo of the note didn't exactly reassure me. Irabella's plan had a lot of holes in it, which she passed off as 'things I was too much of a softy to hear.' For someone bent on becoming a social mastermind, she sure had a lot of hesitations. It was weird. I wasn't a pro at reading people, but it sure seemed to me like she didn't want to do this. Her motives were foggy, that was for sure.

I probably should have ignored the message and destroyed the fabric- dumped it in the outhouse, tossed it through the fence, shredded it into a million pieces using some unconventional method- but at the time, my mind had blanked, in part due to the distraction of the death threat, and I had shoved it into my pocket.

I wandered around for a bit, strolling aimlessly. For the most part, I was procrastinating. Irabella didn't necessarily give me a *time* limit for when I had to deliver these messages, warnings, or whatever they were.

My feet stopped for a second. Warnings. Irabella might have been a bit of a crazy person, but she didn't strike me as dumb.

Warning messages couldn't hurt Cerina, and they could accomplish exactly what I wanted. They would make Cerina wary. Irabella might as well have handed me an instruction manual titled 'how to play both sides' because she had given me all the ingredients I needed to succeed while continuing to be as big a chicken as possible.

The mission was settled. It was time to creep out Cerina Rayz.

Initially, Irabella's plan was to send some scary memos to her target; for what purpose, I didn't know. Then, after a specific time frame had blown by, I would lead Cerina back to building 2-7. Irabella would take it from there.

Of course, I had a plan of my own. But it was a lot easier said than done- and I wasn't even sure if I could get to building 1-10 without being picked off and reported for no reason. Even without my partial blindness, I was an easy target.

I tucked my hands into my pockets.

Keeping an eye out for Jakson, Farrah, and their weird plant, I carefully placed myself directly in front of a quiet building 1-10. Then, and only then, did I start brainstorming how the hell I was supposed to leave a dramatic message that could keep Cerina on-edge.

From my limited knowledge of Irabella, I figured she'd kill for something over-the-top, borderline cheesy. The note in blood might have been a suggestion to get me on my feet, but I wasn't eager to do the same thing. I had nothing to cut myself with, and I didn't dig the idea of slicing my hand open in the name of a theatrical display.

So I burst into building 1-10 ready to improvise.

Thankfully, the place was more or less empty. More or less, because someone had definitely just left. And, to say the least, they hadn't cleaned up after themselves.

A gaping hole was dug out through a big chunk of uprooted floorboards. I stepped forward cautiously, peering down into the chasm. I half expected to find another tomb, but all I faced was a tunnel of coarse dirt. It was barely big enough for Lizabeth to fit into, let alone Cerina. I hadn't a clue what the maker could have been thinking, but I didn't care. Because the hole and its surrounding wreckage had given me exactly what I needed.

Hurriedly, I collected some scrap wood and arranged it over the floor. I would've added the personal touch of placing it where Cerina slept, but considering my last name wasn't *Veer*, I didn't have the opportunity to see her rest her head on the rough, prison-issued pillows every night.

But if there was no point whatsoever to these 'messages,' it would probably satisfy Irabella, if not impress her, to see the word *DIE* in giant block letters, displayed to the whole of building 1-10 and any of its outside visitors.

I collected a handful of dirt before my next stop. Based on the sheer stupidity of my task, I wouldn't have been surprised if the stuff ended up coming in handy.

***

Two more stupid warning signs later, I'd had about enough. Supposedly, the whole point of being a Level Two was looking cooler than you actually were, but I didn't understand it- she *could've* just snagged Cerina here and now, in this time of turmoil. But no, of course I had to leave a message first, a signal that this was her work so she'd go down in history as the bigshot of the Isle of Rebels.

I was grateful, relieved, and still confused, but more than any of that, I was tired.

All I wanted to do was sit down and have a nap. There was another excuse for rage- why the hell did they have to wake us up at six in the damn morning? If all we ever did was sit around, there was no point. The only thing we lived for was to hurt each other. What purpose could that serve? A few people ran by, whom I recognised as the network of reporters, the huge group that had been going around kidnapping people. Why did the guards let this continue? Why did they send us here in the first place?

I jolted up. We got up early in the morning every day to do *something*. There was purpose in our pain. If there wasn't, we would have been killed. We were here for a reason…

A shocking revelation hit me over the head like a ton of bricks. It was a crazy guess. Frankly, I didn't even know where the idea came from, materialising in my mind as though it had dropped from the sky. But now that I had it in front of me, now that I was toying with the possibility of its existence, it seemed so obvious. The guards wore long sleeves. That could mean anything, but it was solid evidence. *The guards wore long sleeves*. My breath caught in my throat. It couldn't-

But of course it could. Of course, the government could do anything under our noses because we were a bunch of unperceptive little idiots, and somehow I, of all people, had just figured something out.

And there was one person I knew who could help me piece it together.

Jakson Veer

A brief meeting

"I'm telling you, the people in my building are *étrange*," Amélie kept a steady pace, jogging through the centre field. Farrah and I followed behind her. I was breathless and out of shape, but Farrah was able to keep up with Amélie's even treads. It was Amélie's suggestion to kick off the morning with a run, mostly because she was getting tremendously bored by our quiet plant-related conversations.

Did I love the idea of leaving Cerina and Arvin unsupervised? No. Did I have much choice in the matter? Also no.

"Oh yeah?" I panted, speeding up. "How so?"

Amélie laughed. "Well, for one, most of the place is taken up by this weird family- not a Level Two Family, but an actual group of relatives. All the members were involved in some messed-up drug scheme. Two of the wackos already made it through the gates. I wonder what's going to happen to them."

Farrah narrowed her mouth into a thin line, looking grimly at the path. "It's obvious that the guards are up to something. But not only that- Haven and the others in building 1-3 have been treating us strangely. It's almost as though we've been shunned."

"Why-" I began, nearly swallowing a lazy fly. "Why would they be treating us any differently?"

"Probably has something to do with Cerina. Or Arvin. Or both."

The way Amélie rolled the *r*s brought a smile to my face. I wasn't sure what I liked so much about her slight accent, but it had a certain charm to it.

Suddenly, my ears perked up. Behind me, I picked out the unmistakable sound of someone shouting my name.

I stopped running. We had managed to find ourselves quite far from the sector, and the figure racing after us appeared as a tiny dot in the distance.

"Cerina?" I asked, standing up a little straighter. "What's going on?"

Cerina hadn't broken a sweat from the trek, an enviable characteristic.

"Arvin's taking apart building 1-10," she reported. "I went out for a jog just after wake-up. He came with me for the first bit, but once he got tired, he set to tearing out the floorboards. I'm debating as to whether or not I should stop him."

"You should."

"Probably. But do I care enough to bother?" Another sentence was on the tip of her tongue, but she was cut off by Emry, who came barrelling down the field to join us, screaming as he went.

I had to admit- seeing his flushed face and hearing his exhausted wheeze made me feel a little better about my physical abilities.

"Jakson-" Emry huffed, bending over to catch his breath. "I need to talk to- oh." His eyes landed on Cerina. "You're here, too."

Cerina frowned. "Indeed I am."

"Okay, okay," Emry said to himself. "That's just as well. I need to tell you guys something- it might be completely stupid, but it's important. It's about the guards, the reportings. All of it."

"What do you mean?" My curiosity piqued as I looked into Emry's eyes, spotting the urgency written inside them.

"I think I might be able to understand a bit of what Arvin's trying to tell us."

I raised my eyebrows, but Amélie immediately shut down the conversation.

"No one can understand Arvin. Your best bet right now is to avoid the insane tattle-tales completely and try not to read too much into it."

"Tattle-tales?" I raised my eyebrows. "Is that what we're calling them now? It sounds awfully childish."

Amélie shrugged. "They need *some* kind of name."

"Whatever," Emry interrupted. "I saw the network of reporters, and I was just thinking-"

"Network of reporters?" I asked, "what are you talking about?"

Emry shrugged as though it were obvious. "You know. One of the many bands of crazy people who frequent the area. I've just been calling them that, but you guys are all geniuses in some way, shape, or form. You've probably thought up something catchier."

"Maybe we would have, had we known about this development," Farrah said.

Amélie moved to stand beside Emry. "I think I know who you're talking about. That's what I was getting to when I mentioned the psychopaths in building 1-1. They're experienced in this kind of thing, and, already, they've set up a whole system. I don't hang around the place due to the number of hostages, but I've gotten enough of the scoop to be wary. They're planning this big attack- if you could call it that. I'm not sure who it's on, but they're waiting until they can empty the building entirely. It's a bit suspicious if you ask me, but these guys are captured prisoners. They aren't exactly in here for their high IQ."

"What do you mean, hostages?" I interjected, a little ticked by the intelligence quotient comment. "They can't hold that many people in one building for long."

"Not unless they tie them to the bunks. Which they have." Amélie shrugged nonchalantly. "But it's not like we can do anything about it. Or, I should say, it's not like there's much point. They outnumber us four to one."

An idea sprang to mind. "Not necessarily," I muttered. "This could be an opportunity."

Farrah nodded. "Emry. Have those in 1-3 mentioned anything about getting Joe back on our side? If we truly want to escape, having him on board is a necessity."

"Well, yes," Emry said impatiently, "but that's not what I came to talk to you about-"

"Perfect!" Amélie announced. "If we stop these guys and restore order to the Level One sector, Joe will have to take note of our potential. He'll join us."

"Maybe," Cerina countered, "but it's not like we need him. He's just one guy. We have a whole team already. We didn't need him before, so why would we let him stop us?"

"Good point," I said, "but I wouldn't put it past him to pull out all the stops to end our operation. Ultimately, it will be well worth it if he's on our side. I can't think of anyone who will be a better help than the mom of the Isle of Rebels."

Cerina, losing interest in the conversation, walked off. "I can't help you there," she said, tossing a glance behind her. "He despises me. I'm going to go check on Arvin. Ever since yesterday afternoon, he's been fully absorbed by this construction project. We'll have bigger problems if building 1-10 gets torn to shreds."

I watched her leave, turning back to Farrah. "Let's consult Haven. They might be distancing themselves from us, but this is in all of our interests. We're much worse off divided like this."

Farrah nodded. "Thanks, Emry, for telling us about this."

Emry tossed his hands in the air. "I wasn't-"

Before he could finish that sentence, Amélie looped an arm around Farrah's good elbow. "Let's go stop some sociopaths."

We took off, again, at a brisk jog.

With the wind biting at my ears as I sprinted to catch up, I didn't hear Emry's shout of frustration or notice his ultimate defeat. I didn't watch him watch *us* leave, and I didn't see the look in his eyes. A knowing look. A visage indicating that only doom would follow.

The only thing I heard was the disgruntled patter of his footsteps as he stormed after me, catching up to the group.

"It's probably just a dumb hunch anyway," he muttered.

***

Lizabeth, Haven, Max, and Adrienne were just as surprised as I was to hear about the system in play within building 1-1.

"Amélie," Haven said after a long pause, "try to gather as much information as possible. Jakson, Farrah, figure out a plan to break apart their little organisation. I'll inform Joe."

"What about Lizabeth, Max, and Adrienne?" I studied Haven's expression. It was wary, much more so than the situation called for. Emry, his arms crossed in the back of the building, stifled a yawn.

"What about me?"

Haven's assertive gaze faltered, but only slightly. "Max, Adrienne, and Lizabeth will stay with me in building 1-3. We'll make a plan together. Later, we'll compare ideas."

"Wouldn't it be more productive it we all planned together?"

"When *that* happens, some of our voices get tuned out, and the ones that dominate don't always lead us in the right direction." Considering it was mostly Haven's ideas that stomped all over everyone else's, I couldn't help but take that excuse with a grain of salt.

"Are you angry with me?"

"No," Haven said, a little too quickly, "I'm just being cautious. You guys show us what you can do while we focus our efforts on Joe and the escape plan."

Haven wasn't a bad actor. Their passive-aggressiveness, therefore, was prominent and deliberate.

"Sure," I agreed, allowing myself to let it slide. "When Amélie gathers anything significant, we'll meet to discuss."

Leaving Haven with an unfinished idea and the tail end of a conversation, I joined Farrah and Amélie outside building 1-3.

"Was it just me," I said, "or was Haven acting awfully-"

"Psychotic? Yeah," Amélie interrupted. "They called me Farrah. *Me*. I mean, no offence, but we look nothing alike. Something's clearly wrong with them."

Farrah shrugged. "Either way, their idea makes sense. I'd suggest we get planning."

We walked back to building 1-10 with a slow, cautious gait. The three of us were lucky enough to be travelling in a group, but even in our triangular formation, with Amélie at the head, I still felt uneasy. The streets were eerily deserted, and it was no wonder why.

I looked at the ground. Beside the step of building 1-10 was a bizarre object. It was small, metallic, and very broken. The remnants of wires stuck out from the scattered shards, dispersed across the pavement. Before I could investigate further, Amélie was throwing herself at the door. I stopped her before she could barge in, pressing my ear to the wood and giving it a quick knock. No answer came, so I cracked it open and we all piled in, not even bothering to disguise our evident relief.

It only took a second for me to realise that the building was definitely not deserted. Soft tears came from the corner of the room, where Arvin was curled into a tiny ball. He sat in the centre of a cluster of uprooted floorboards, hugging his legs to his slender chest. His head was tucked in with such aggression that his kneecaps dug into his eye sockets. Though it looked like he was making a considerable effort to do so, his position did nothing to conceal his tears.

"Arvin?" I ventured, stepping closer. His sniffles were quickly turning into wheezes. If I didn't stop him, he was going to make himself faint.

"Are you okay?"

Hyperventilating, Arvin lifted his head up. Red rings were plastered around his eyes, and his teeth gnashed together uncontrollably.

"Take a wild guess, genius!"

I knelt down to help him, being careful to maintain my distance. "What can I do to help?"

"You can scram! You can go! You can take your friends and leave me to dwell! You did not earn my pain, and, likewise, you did not earn the right to hear of my toils!"

"No. But *you* have the right to accept my help. Which I am offering to you."

Arvin dug his fingernails into his scalp, tearing out a chunk of his thinning hair. It made an ugly ripping sound, but he barely winced. "I accomplished something, and it messed everything up. Who was I to know? I killed one voice, and another came in its place! Idiot, idiot! All I did was speed up the process! I am no liberator! I am a fool!"

"I bet you are sick of hearing this, but if you are going to talk to me, please do so in a manner I can understand."

"I'm *not* talking to you! Now depart! Scat! What is it you kids say? Fuck off!" He stuck up his wrinkled middle finger, the remaining hairs of his eyebrows knotting up into a tight glare.

In any other circumstance, I would have laughed at the thought of being flipped off by a seventy-year-old. Even despite the direness of the situation, I almost did. But another matter was brought to my attention before I could dig myself even deeper.

"Uh, Jakson?" Farrah said, turning my attention elsewhere. "The plant is… gone."

Cerina Rayz

Voices

Half an hour earlier:

It didn't take me long to notice the first message. Formed in large letters on the floor, the word *die* filled the entire room with the threat of violence. For a moment, I wondered if the shattering daggers, or another Family of the sort, were to blame. But that was ridiculous. The mess hall had been destroyed.

"Arvin," I said, picking up the pieces of wood that formed the misshapen letters and setting them in the corner, "do you know anything about this?"

Arvin answered me, but he clearly hadn't heard a word I said.

"It's done! You can hide here!" he shouted, gesturing proudly to the gaping hole in the building's floor. "Hide it!"

"I can't fit in there, Arvin," I explained as calmly as I could. I stepped over to Jakson's bunk, pulling his potted plant out from the underside of his pillowcase. I didn't feel particularly threatened by the message on the floor, but the feel of a potential weapon in my hands was grounding. The smooth-but-dry texture of the clay was firm and stable. I couldn't crush it easily. I didn't *want* to crush it.

Perhaps I held the plant in my hands because, when the world is ready to break you, it's reassuring to know that no matter how hard you try, any path of destruction is just a show. In the face of something bigger than yourself, it's up to you to hold onto your humanity. And it's also up to you to defend what you hold dear. With the power to do so, you could feel invincible.

And as much as I hated to admit it, that power was what I was used to.

"Not you!" Arvin cried, snapping me out of my wandering train of thought. "Little bird!"

"You really have a thing for avian fowl, don't you?"

Arvin smacked his forehead, drilling his palm into the space between his greying eyebrows.

"You think inside such a tiny box. It's a wonder you haven't suffocated in such a space- or maybe you have. Maybe when *they* were talking to me, I was deaf to the sounds of your choking."

"To the best of my knowledge, I'm alive and well."

"For *now*, anyway." Arvin let out a chortled laugh. "Now put it in!"

"For the last time, I have no idea what you're talking about."

"Nice little nest for a nice little birdy. Carrier pigeon number 2- unlocked by the key, brought on by the first bird."

"I get that you're trying," I said. "But if you want me to understand you, you're going to have to try a little harder."

Arvin continued to slap himself on the forehead. A red patch, sure to leave a bruise, bloomed on the area he continuously struck. I reached out an arm, staying his hand.

"Stop. You're going to hurt yourself."

Arvin spat into the miniature pit. "Pah. *You're* hurting yourself."

I dropped my arm, clasping Arvin's fragile-seeming fingers. They were cold and clammy, with long, yellow blood-encrusted nails. Revulsion swept through me, but I fought the wave down and looked into the man's eyes.

My voice lowered to a whisper. "I know you were one of the first prisoners on this island. And I know that you were put through a trial of some sort, where many people died. I also-" I paused, choking on the words. "I also know you're a member of the Rayz family and that you faked your own death. Now help me connect the dots. *Please*."

Arvin sighed. "You don't understand. I can't. I wanted to help you, but I have a birdie too. Must be careful."

I ran a hand through my tangle of hair. A bird. As soon as my fingers twined into the oily brown strands protruding from my scalp, Arvin's eyes lit up. I scrunched up my eyebrows, stretching my fingers until they touched the tips of my ears. Slowly, Arvin put a hand over his finger, nodding.

My fingernails traced my earlobes, passing over the long filled-in holes where I used to wear earrings. I had a prestigious lineage, but I had never thought of myself as 'cool' until I embraced the violence wrapped within it. That was before I got sent to the island. Before I acknowledged that such violence may one day catch up with my line.

As my right hand reached the centre of the ear, I tapped a tiny shard of metal. I tucked my nail under it, frowning in bewilderment. The chip was barely half the size of my pinky nail, but the skin around it was inflamed, swelling the surrounding area. What was more, the entire area was numb. I couldn't feel it in the slightest.

Arvin placed a finger over his lips. I understood at once. He had some sort of… earpiece?

"Do you understand now?"

I shook my head. Tears, welling up in Arvin's eye sockets, slid down his wrinkled cheeks. "Don't tell me I've failed. This is the best I could do. It's the worst I've ever done."

I made for the door. "I'm going to take it out, Arvin. Then you can explain everything."

Arvin shot his arm out. "No! Not like this! Not now! You have to put it in there, when the time comes!" I slipped out of his grasp, swinging the door open.

He pulled at my wrist, but I picked his gnarled fingers off with ease. I shut the door on him, holding it with unfair ease as he slammed against it, clawing at the wood.

I pressed my back to the door. "Sorry, Arvin. I have to do this."

Without hesitation, I clamped the chip inside my thumb and pointer finger, pulling with all my might.

Some sort of glue held it firmly, and a jolt shot through me. If the thing was permanently stuck... Before I could finish my speculative thought, the sticky filaments binding it to my face gave way, snapping off individually like tiny arms, a million broken links. Pain seared up my temples and into my skull as I yanked at it, bringing on a trickle of blood.

I bit my cheek, the numb feeling lifting with a searing-hot relief.

Plastered with sticky red and silver goop, I held out the extracted chip and gave it a precise look-over. Metallic indentations lined it from top to bottom, and the criss-cross pattern of an embedded microphone or speaker covered the side facing outward. A thin orange wire protruded from it. I held out a hand to stem the blood flow and felt something hard where the chip had once been.

Sticking out of the rough divot was the rest of the thin wire, the rough edges piercing my skin.

And yet, I did not feel the buzz of electricity or any other physical change. The one difference I was gradually beginning to notice was that a faint thrumming, white noise I had never paid any mind to, had receded. The world felt a bit quieter, more tranquil.

Or maybe that was just because Arvin wasn't there with me, nattering on about voices. I stood up a little straighter. *Voices.*

I thought back to the strange message I had received earlier.

Someone who's willing to hurt you. Someone who can hurt you.

Those were the only words of identification the person behind me had given, and they weren't much to go on. But I knew one thing now- the person who had threatened me earlier hadn't been standing behind me at all.

In one fell swoop, I tossed the earpiece to the ground and slammed it to the ground with the heel of my shoe.

I didn't return to building 1-10. I let go of the door, but Arvin didn't emerge. I needed to think. I needed to get *away*, but whoever was after me clearly knew something of my whereabouts.

On its own, I would have ignored the message on the floor, chalking it up to a shitty prank. But in light of recent circumstances, it seemed too well-timed to be a coincidence.

When I caught a glimpse of a second message posted on the wall of my new sleeping quarters, each letter formed with mud, I had to suppress a shudder. The gist of the symbol was the same, just a little more specific.

Die, Cerina

Hastily, I wiped it off, staining my uniform sleeves an even darker brown. That message might as well have been a neon sign, announcing my whereabouts to any and all desperate Level Ones hell-bent on getting home.

Before I could even think about where my feet were taking me, I found myself wandering the fringes of the Level Two sector.

The people in that sector couldn't care less about the reports, or me, for that matter. I hadn't seen Irabella, and I had to admit, I was impressed she had managed to stay hidden.

Assuming she hadn't died in the mess hall's fire.

I tried not to think about that as I passed the ruins. A circle of desolation radiated around it, the perfect place to be alone and below notice. The walls, the roof, every last foundation was reduced to a pile of black ash, charred to rubble. I thought I could peek out the faint decline that used to be the tomb. So much for respecting the dead.

Keeping at a careful distance- to avoid both injury and the fumes- I clambered around the perimeter. Nothing was salvageable, at least, nothing that remained. I hadn't been foolish enough to strike up a conversation that would give me the answers to what the Families and their new pastimes were, but it couldn't be good.

I could feel the weight of several different parties strategizing to gain a hold over the Isle closing in like a fist. It was only a matter of time before someone struck in some way or another, and what that meant for me, I could not yet tell.

I should not have come. Picking up my feet, I sped back to the Level One side, cursing my idiocy. What was I doing? The blood on my face was drying in the hot sun, sticking to my cheek in a heavy plaster seal. It had been an unshakeable force of habit that had led me to the ruins of the mess hall. I picked at the wire in my ear, stabbing it until the flesh went numb again from the white pain, where I diverted to pulling at the dark strands of my thick hair.

There was no room for breathers on the Isle of Rebels. Even if said breathers involved a stroll through the ruins of what was once the most high-status building on the entire island. Screw the inner circle. We had become so immersed in our own game that once it crumbled, there was no choice but to continue it. Now the game was everywhere. In the Level One sector, it was the reports, a time-killer disguised in the form of salvation.

And in my head, the aftermath of the Families was getting to me.

I hurried across the boundary line, and my heart just about stopped. As I darted forward, I glimpsed the rounded curve of the central circle's wall. Posted in front of the gate, as usual, were two guards. But instead of sitting by and chatting about the day's news, the two of them were stone-still, watching me like a hawk.

My feet skidded to a stop. I was *wanted*, and I was in plain sight of two guards who were surely aware of the bounty on my head.

I couldn't back out now. Both of them eyed me with unrelenting ferocity, and I visibly flinched.

"Keep moving," one of the guards said, fixing me with that same harsh gaze.

My feet shuffled forwards, but I didn't dare break eye contact. Did they even know who I was?

As if the guards could read my thoughts, the second one piped in. "*Move it*, Rayz. The time to collect you will come later."

"Collect me?" I said, giving voice to the whirlwind of thoughts wreaking havoc on my brain. "What the hell are you talking about?"

Both of the guards turned to each other, downcast.

"Just keep moving," the first one said solemnly. "Keep moving until you can't run anymore. Because eventually, your endurance will expire. Do you hear it? It's already begun."

"Piss off," I spat, reacting on pure instinct.

The guards looked at each other, then back at me. They nodded once, simultaneously. "Understood."

They whirled around, walking in a military-like procession to the other end of the steel wall, out of my sight.

I wasn't easily shaken, but their monotone voices and hard stares sent chills creeping up my spine. Not risking another word out of their mouths, I whirled and sped away, feeling for the missing chip. The blood flow had quelled completely, mottled streaks of red tying in with my messy hair.

It wasn't until I had returned to the still-unfamiliar Level One sector that I caught sight of the third and final message.

I'm coming for you.

This, too, was written in mud on the pavement directly in front of building 1-10. Below it was a scrap of fabric. I picked it up, smoothing out the wrinkles. In partially-smeared blood, it read-

Ily
I ne 3 messages. Scare her and questions.
Screw up die on the I'm watching.
-Irabella

I was not afraid. After all, the unknown was much scarier than anything in sight. And I knew Irabella like the back of my hand.

Yet, here I was. It should have been predictable- the messages were. But the guards? The chip?

I had never taken Bella for a criminal mastermind. Her heart was impulsive and exploded sporadically, but I had never taken it for such a hard thing. The vast majority of my 2-7 building mates were borderline psychopathic, but Irabella had room for compassion.

She wasn't working alone. And whoever she *was* working with knew exactly where I was. And it was precisely where they wanted me to be.

Slowly, I looked down at my hands. The pot was still clutched between my fingers. I gripped the stem of the young sprout and pulled it out of the soil, roots and all. It dangled between my index and thumb, swaying in the gentle breeze.

I threw the pot to the ground, letting it fall in an elegant arc. The bandages around it fell away, providing cushioning, but not enough to stop the clay from splitting open on the pavement. I set my foot on top of it, crushing the remaining shards into a fine powder.

"I suppose," I muttered, "in the face of adversaries, it's time to defend what I hold dear,"

Perhaps I would have said differently if I had known that the voices spoke through more than a mere earpiece.

Lizabeth Merrin

Recruitment Business, pt.2

Of everyone in the group- crafty Haven, outgoing Adrienne, observant Max- it was I, sensitive Lizabeth, who was tasked with going up to Joe and proposing our plan of action.

"Why me?" I had asked, plainly and simply, to Haven.

"Because you're innocent," they replied with nonchalance. "If I went up, Joe would be suspicious of potential strings attached. But you? You're hard to deny."

"I'm sixteen," I grunted, "and I'm not charismatic."

"Hold it-" Haven paused, looking genuinely flabbergasted. "You're sixteen? I thought you had just made the cutoff."

Mildly offended, I gave them the coldest look I could muster.

"I was a little surprised, too," Adrienne said, "don't get me wrong, it's not that I don't think you're wise. Far from it, actually. It's just, you're so *nice* for a sixteen-year-old. The majority, at least out of the ones *I* used to know, are complete jerks. I mean, not you, Haven. You're great. Sometimes."

Haven rolled their eyes, a small smile on their face.

I gave Adrienne a little grin. "I guess you found the best of the best."

She snorted. "Among the worst of the worst."

Max tapped me on the shoulder. "Lizabeth," he pressed. "Are you going to talk to Joe, or not?"

I turned to him, nodding. "Right, yes."

Adrienne pouted. "Way to kill the atmosphere, Max."

Max rolled his eyes. "Come on. If what Amélie says about their attack plan is true, then we don't have much time."

"You see what I mean about total jerks?" Adrienne rasped as I passed her on the way out the door. I stifled a giggle, and Max tossed me a dirty look.

"You'll thank me when something actually gets done around here."

Bitterly, I strode over a couple buildings down, where Joe was engaged in a heated debate with one of the Level Ones. I wanted nothing more than to turn back around, but Joe stopped me before I could chicken out.

Interrupting the plucky boy who had sparked up a lively conversation with him, Joe called out to me. "Lizabeth Merrin," he said, "what is it?" I was surprised, above all, that he remembered my last name. He spoke it as though I were a disobedient child, and my doubts about Haven's plan began to creep in.

"It's nothing," I blurted out instinctively.

Joe tipped his head to the side. "If it's nothing, then why are you standing here like you want to talk to me?"

"Well, there is… something."

"If it has anything whatsoever to do with the escape, I'm not hearing it."

I sighed. It was now or never.

"We've received word of an organised operation that captures Level Ones and turns them in upon request," I said, the words flying out at a reckless, impatient pace. Rather than stop and reconsider my actions, I continued to spew out a slew of vowels and consonants. So absorbed by my nervousness, I was barely even listening to what I was saying, unaware of whether or not I was leading myself to a conversational trainwreck. "They're on the hunt," I continued, breathing heavily, "they're going to get enough prisoners to bail out every last one of them."

Joe frowned. "Where did this word come from, exactly?"

"That doesn't matter. We're going to stop them."

"Define 'we'."

"Haven, Adrienne, Max, Emry, Jakson, Farrah, Amélie and me. We can do it, and we will."

"And you want my help?"

"In a manner of speaking."

Joe paused, pondering my words. "In a manner of speaking," he repeated. "I see. Look, Lizabeth. I don't doubt your determination- Haven's drive caught my eye the second they arrived at the Isle, and a similar spark lies in every one of you. Even disgruntled Max, believe it or not, possesses a strong light. But all those sparks do is start fires. This operation you speak of is a burning blaze, and I don't have to tell you what happened in Sykona's civil war."

"They fought fire with fire, and they all got burned," I muttered.

"Exactly."

I retreated back to the building. Everything I had predicted had come to pass- Joe had denied us help, but he was now acutely aware of the threat and probably preparing to deal with it himself. Everything was going according to plan... yet I felt a glimmer of dissatisfaction.

When I returned to building 1-3, it was almost deserted. Confused, I poked my head in, peering around the empty room.

"Ah. You're back." Haven's voice, coming from the corner, made me jump. I turned to them, bewilderment written all over my face.

"Where are the others?"

Haven leaned against the wall, slumping back from exhaustion. "They're looking for Emry."

"What happened to Emry?"

"He's looking for Jakson, Farrah, and Amélie."

"And where are *they*?"

"Looking for whoever stole their plant."

I sighed. "I'm surprised you aren't keen on helping."

"Right now, 'helping' is synonymous with 'joining the wild goose chase'. Eventually, they'll all run back here, ready for the slaughter. It's a lose-lose either way."

"That's an awfully pessimistic look at things."

"It's an awfully *accurate* look at things."

"I talked to Joe," I said, steering the topic as far away as possible from whatever rant Haven was preparing.

"And? What'd he tell you?"

"Nothing we didn't expect. Although, he's even busier than we thought. If we don't act now, he'll be so burnt out that he won't even consider our plan, no matter what we do to prove ourselves."

"And? Based on that, what do you think we should do?"

"What do *I* think we should do?"

"Yeah. You're smart. What should we do, Lizabeth Merrin?"

"Well… we should act now."

Haven smiled, giving me a knowing nod. "I don't trust Amélie, and this could very well be some sort of trap, but we can't act if we stay put. Let's go look for her, shall we?"

"No," I said, "not look for. *Find*."

***

Looking for Amélie proved harder than initially seemed in the confines of the Level One sector. Haven and I scoured the block, scanning the area for at least one familiar face. A few people paid me a cautious glance or a pitiful stare, but nothing beyond that. I knew what I looked like to them.

Like an easy target.

We searched the perimeter of Jakson's abode, unwilling to venture inside. Plastered in mud along the exterior was a foreboding message, and directly underneath it was a strange sight. I bent down to survey the item, doused in blood with various small wires protruding from the surface.

"Haven? What do you think this is?"

Haven bent over, surveying the minuscule disk. "It looks like some sort of computer chip. The remains of one, anyway."

The silvery pieces were ground so profoundly into the cobblestone they resembled metallic snowflakes. Curiously, I nudged one of them with my finger. The edge was sharper than I had first expected, and with a jolt, it dug into my finger, embedding itself between the lines of my handprint. I pulled my wrist back, picking the piece out. A small trickle of blood ran down my thumb.

"Lizabeth? You good?"

"Yeah. It's just a scratch. No big deal."

I didn't know how I was supposed to talk to Jakson about this. Did he know where this came from? Did it have anything to do with Darby?

I could almost guarantee he'd have an answer, but I had the strange, sinking feeling that it might not be one I wanted to hear.

Taking a quick mental note of the chip's location and physical description, Haven and I moved on to scouring the next street. I picked up the pace, watching my back.

"We should split up," Haven suggested, "we'll move faster."

"Good idea."

No sooner had I turned down the nearest street, away from Haven in the direction of nowhere, before cold, clammy hands were pressed over my eyes. I kicked, punching the air with my fists raised at my invisible assailant, but the veil of darkness had sprung on me at such unawares that my attempts were hopeless.

As if in slow motion, I was gagged and dragged like a limp doll to the hostile territory I had only just learned of. The hostile territory that should have been worrying me a lot more.

Building 1-1, home of the desperate reporters.

Jakson Veer

Moments of bravery

"It's pointless," Amélie said at last, voicing the thought that had been encircling all three of our minds for the past forty minutes. "The thief is long gone by now."

"Come on!" Farrah urged. "I'm sure we'll find them eventually!"

I shook my head. We had been running non-stop, and not only were we exhausted, but we were hopeless.

"I hate to say it, but I think Amélie's right. We've lapped the entire sector how many times now? Three, four, *ten*? Either we start searching some buildings, or this is a lost cause." I tried to contain myself but couldn't stop my voice from warbling. I pinched my arm, willing the despair from my mind. JJ was a *plant*. Not a *person*.

"You do have a point," Farrah said, the disappointment in her voice equivalent to my own. Hints of red trickled onto her face. "I'm sorry," she muttered, "this is all my fault."

Before I even knew what I was doing, my hand was on her shoulder. My heart skipped a beat, but I couldn't very well pull the arm away.

"It's okay," I said, a lot more awkwardly than I had intended, "it's not your fault in the slightest. If anyone's to blame, it's the jerk who made off with the thing in the first place."

Farrah nodded to ease my mind, but nothing about her hardened gaze looked convinced.

"How about we check in with Cerina?" I suggested, facing the inevitable, "I'd hate to find out that Arvin tore up every single floorboard of our building while we were away."

"Or," Amélie suggested, "we could meet back up with Haven."

"No. We were supposed to be coming up with a plan, remember? Look at where we are now. We don't have anything to contribute."

"Okay," Farrah said, "we'll come up with a plan. But if we can't think of anything, Haven's a good last resort." Her tone was soothing, and I realised with a bit of a start that my own voice was infused with an extreme measure of panic.

"We'll think of something," I said, my pitch slowly returning to normal, "we always do."

Haven took that moment to materialise from behind the nearest building, squishing our planning time to ruin. I exchanged a sheepish glance with the others.

"There you are!" Haven announced before we could come up with a reasonable excuse for our lack of plan. "You know, I appreciate your devotion to this plant, but you've already caused quite the stir."

"How'd you find out about the plant?" Amélie asked, suspicion in her eyes.

"Emry ran after you, took a wrong turn, reported back, then proceeded to run after you again."

"How'd he take a wrong turn? It's not like the sector's an impossible maze."

"He's Emry."

Amélie shrugged. "Fair point."

"Is Lizabeth with you?" I asked. Haven shrugged.

"She was. She went off in another direction."

"The two of you split up?!"

Haven looked at me in surprise before their face broke into a look of dread and shame. They brought their palm to their forehead, drinking in a good long face slap.

"That was a mistake, wasn't it?"

"Hopefully, it's nothing," Farrah said, stepping in before an argument could brew. "But it looks like we have some more searching to do, after all."

***

"I need you to lay out everything you know about building 1-1. That includes where they're keeping the hostages, who's in charge, and what their plan is. We need to learn the layout of the quarters and the guard placed upon them."

A good twenty minutes of pacing around the sector had turned up nothing, and after we had begun to spiral, I had finally called it. Haven, Farrah, Amélie and I were seated behind building 1-10, a map made from sticks and flecks of mud laid out at our feet. I sat cross-legged on the gravelly pavement, at the head of a sort of rectangle we had formed. Amélie was on the other end, staring directly at me. Farrah sat to my right, and Haven kept their head down at my left, gnawing their lip. My instinct told me to reassure them that this wasn't their fault, but my annoyance said the exact opposite. With both of those emotions held at a standstill, the only thing left for me to do was assume leadership and cross my fingers.

"Are you sure we should keep Adrienne, Max, and Emry in the dark about this?" Farrah questioned. "It seems like a bad idea to proceed without them."

"Usually, strength in numbers is one of our prime defenses," Haven said, "but not this time. We can't afford to argue." I nodded, though I kept my eyes away from them.

"Haven's right. We must act right now, or who knows what will happen to Lizabeth."

Farrah frowned. I couldn't help but pay close attention to the way our knees touched- casually but deliberately. Comforting.

"I know how close the two of you used to be. Are you sure you aren't being a bit hasty?" She shuffled away, and a chill crept up my arms.

"No," I reasoned, "I'm being logical."

"Perhaps you see that as justification," she argued, "but don't let your temper get the better of you. We could seriously use all the help we can get."

Something about her words infuriated me. "I'm not a child," I snapped. "I know what I'm doing. You're not helping."

A second later, my sense rushed back to me in a hot wave.

"I'm sorry," I stammered. "I didn't mean that. You're very helpful, *more* than helpful, valuable. Just... you need to trust me. Okay?"

Haven slouched over, fiddling with the hem of their prison uniform. Under their breath, they muttered something along the lines of 'here we go again'.

Amélie took the pause as her cue to start speaking.

"As for guards," she began, alleviating some of the tension, "there are two beefy guys posted at the front of the building. I'm sure you've seen them. Guy and a girl. They used to be shopping mall security guards until they decided that arson was more their style. A waste of muscle, really. You can be a human twig to start a fire. These guys are freaking *trees*." She brushed two clumps of mud over to the stick-model of the cabin, positioning them on each side of the door.

"Are those supposed to be guards?" Haven said, pointing to the globs with a sceptical finger.

"What *else* would they be?"

"Two birds. Raindrops. An artful decoration to this misshapen cabin model. *Literally* anything else."

"I don't know what I'm supposed to tell you."

Haven kicked the map aside, strewing the remnants of the image across the bumpy pavement.

"This map is dumb. What good is a visual representation anyway? It's not like we have anything to draw it with."

"Hey, don't insult the strategy plan! They always work in movies."

"Ah, yes, because *those* are the most useful source materials when it comes to freeing someone from a building full of criminals."

"Don't throw shade at criminals! *We're* criminals, but none of *us* have abducted anyone."

"Point taken. But, your crappy map aside, how are you actually planning on doing this?"

"So far, improvisation is our best bet," Farrah grumbled, not hiding her frustration very well.

Amélie shrugged. "I honestly don't think that's the worst idea."

Everyone turned to look at each other. "Absolutely not," we all agreed simultaneously.

Amélie's face fell. "Fine. Have it your way. But you're right about one thing- Lizabeth isn't going to be held there for long. I need you to hear me out. I'm not a great list-maker like all of you, but I have a couple… how shall we put it… suggestions. Ready to hear them? For Lizabeth?"

Everyone nodded.

"For Lizabeth."

***

Before we know it, I was positioned next to Haven peeking out from the side of building 1-1.

"You ready?" I asked. Haven nodded, but their expression was sceptical.

"I don't like this plan."

"Because you didn't make it?"

"No. Because it's terrible."

"By your standards."

"I don't think I'm wrong in my judgement. I mean, honestly, Jakson. You can't actually think this distraction is going to *work*."

Before I could answer, Amélie strode forwards, her flaming hair fanning out behind her. She dragged Farrah at her side, pinning Farrah's good arm behind her back but walking carefully enough for comfort.

Amélie walked directly up to the guards, who placed their muscular arms over the door, barring it from access. I couldn't make out their words from that distance, but Amélie's charismatic attitude and pointed stride appeared to be working.

"If all goes well, they'll let Farrah and Amélie inside. Once the two of them get a sense of the layout, they'll give us the signal, and we'll be good to go," I muttered, pressing my upper lip between my teeth.

"You just re-stated the plan without giving any opinion whatsoever."

"I don't have much of an opinion either way. It either works, or it doesn't," I muttered, the words blending together in a rapid slew.

"Liar. You're worried as hell."

I grit my teeth, annoyed that they could spot it so quickly. "So? I have reason to be."

I watched as Amélie and Farrah slid into the building, disappearing behind the wooden doors. Both the guards resumed their positions in front of the entrance, looking on at the quiet block.

"Maybe it's just because of *those two*," Haven said, "but I have a bad feeling about this."

"You don't say."

A loud crash whipped both of our heads around. The door burst open, and Farrah was pushed outside, tumbling onto her back like a capsized turtle. Immediately, I shot to action, ditching the hiding spot and coming to her aid.

The guards, momentarily bewildered, stepped back to survey the scene. Amélie stood on the other end of the doorframe, her hands outstretched.

"Serves you right for insulting me!" She shouted to Farrah, who groaned from the ground. She tilted her head up to me and gave me a slight wink.

My brain registered the message, but the memo didn't compute to my feet. *Farrah has a bone condition*, I recalled.

Trapped in a psychological loop, my joints were held firmly in place, fixed, as though, by a mental brand of adhesive glue.

"Jakson! The hell are you doing?! That was the signal, dummy!" Amélie shot forward and grabbed me by the collar of my uniform, tugging me into the dark cabin. The guards behind me, however, were faster. One of them yanked me back, stopping me from moving any further than an inch.

They didn't utter a word, but their firm grip said it all.

"Hey! Big guy!" Haven's voice, the scratchy chant of an angel, rang out with the volume of my old high school's fire alarm. "Over here!" They kicked the guard behind me in the shins with their full force. As if propelled by a gust of steam, the guard's hands flew off my shoulders, bound for Haven's neck.

Haven proceeded to take off running, with both guards, their pride insulted, trailing after them.

"You're welcome!" they cried. I bent to help Farrah, but she swatted me off, shooting up on her own. I heard her stiff joints crack as she stood, but she gave me a reassuring smile.

She might have been faking it, but she did too good a job.

Just as the guards were beginning to lose interest in Haven, Amélie pulled the both of us into building 1-1, slamming the door and plunging us into darkness.

It took a couple seconds for my eyes to adjust to the dim light. I blinked, allowing my pupils to dilate.

The first thing I noticed about the interior of building 1-1 was that they had broken the lights- each bulb was shattered, and no glimmer emanated from the dead metal wires. Like Cerina's old building, the windows were blocked off by people's uniforms, casting an eerie glow over the scene where the sunlight filtered through the fabric.

We were completely surrounded. Half the population of building 1-1 watched us from their bunks, their eyes narrowed. Of course, it could very well have been less than half, but the intimidation they expelled carried the force of a hundred people per glare.

I caught a whiff of stale urine, tasting decay on the tip of my tongue. My joints stiffened.

"Welcome," Amélie said, taking a few steps forward, "to my humble abode."

I groped for the door, but my hands came up empty. Someone stepped behind me, blocking the exit.

"Okay..." Amélie said, gesturing to the bunks and their beady-eyed inhabitants, "I know how this looks. But I can explain. This guy is an ally, too."

My eyes rested on a large shape at the end of the room. No. It wasn't a singular shape. Rather, it was a *collection* of shapes tied together in a giant cluster. A long cord of uniforms slithered around legs and torsos, forming a giant, smothering cage. People struggled against the bonds, picking at the tight knots, but their only result was snapped fingernails.

The shape did not make any noise. No wonder zero people were trying to speak- the awkwardness, I could imagine, was unbearable. But even more unbearable was the silence, closing in like a vise and smothering the room in hopelessness.

So many people were pressed into that claustrophobic tangle that I couldn't even pick out Lizabeth's eyes.

One guy stepped forward, his arms crossed over his chest. "*Sure*, they're allies. Allies who just *happened* to be there when you tried to make off with our merchandise." His voice was surprisingly gentle, but it had an underlying scraping quality, like chalk being slowly scratched across a board.

"Woah," said Amélie, "You are jumping to the *wrong* conclusion, my friend. I live here. You have to at least-"

"Save it. Since you're a member of this building, we're willing to make an exception for you. You get to walk free, as long as you don't show your face around here ever again."

"And my friends?"

"Think of them as payment for this freedom."

Amélie didn't think twice before shaking her head. She held her head up, giving chalkboard-voice an assertive glare. "No deal."

"Wrong choice, bitch. Wrong choice."

Amélie's nostrils flared. Something glinted in her hand, peeking out from beneath her closed knuckles. I tilted my head to get a closer look. It was one of the glass shards taken from the mess hall's window. She must have obtained it from Emry or Cerina.

My stomach stirred. I didn't have high hopes for where this encounter was headed.

"*What* did you just call me?" She moved closer, neck and neck with chalkboard-voice.

I stepped toward her. "Amélie-" a hand caught me from behind, stopping me in my tracks.

"Can it, blondie," my captor grumbled. Farrah gave me a warning glance, searching for my hand. She clasped it with a firm grip, sending a ray of warmth to my veins.

Chalkboard-voice smirked. "Do you want me to repeat myself? Maybe I could spell it out for you. B-i-t-"

Amélie sliced the air as she raised her fist.

The blade travelled in an arc. Rewound in slow motion, the strike would've been elegant, gracefully and deliberately aimed for chalkboard-voice's chest. In the moment, however, with the promise of bloodshed dancing on the blade's lips, the trajectory looked a lot more ugly.

Chalkboard-voice swerved at the last second, the glass shard embedding itself in his shoulder. A gasp came out of him in a short puff, his temper pushed to the limit and howling like a boiling kettle.

"Now!" Amélie cried.

Sprinting like a shot, Farrah dropped my hand and made for the cluster of prisoners trapped on the other side of the room. Amélie ripped the glass shard out of chalkboard-voice's shoulder, tossing it to Farrah with a throw so measured that even the strictest of gym teachers would've raised their eyebrows at its precision. She sliced the cord in one stroke, the thin fabric falling away in one clean sheet.

The group of captives exploded like a bomb. But as the group dispersed and the members of building 1-1 swarmed to block the exit, another sight was laid bare. There was still another cluster, fixed in the same sort of bondage, stuffed into the back corner of the room.

The next seconds were blurs. Farrah was taking me by the hand, and we were running deeper into the building, running into the dark. Amélie was by my side, spattered with blood and covered in sweat.

A moment later, the shard had transferred to my hand, and I was cutting the rope, slicing each thread as though my life depended on it. Lizabeth's voice rang in my ears. In that moment, I couldn't care less about what she had done, how she had stuck us here. I only cared about her. Despite the panic racing through me, despite everything, I only cared about her.

When it came down to it, that was the true test.

"That's good! You can let go!"

But I didn't. I continued to saw, and when the fabric snapped, the shard of glass was still in motion. It nicked Lizabeth in the arm before she had time to swerve, bombarded by an onslaught of fleeing targets.

"Thanks," she muttered, her teeth clenched.

"Was that sarcasm?"

"Was it *supposed* to be?"

Lizabeth only had time to shoot me an agitated scowl before it was every person for themselves. The army of 1-1's blocked the door, their fists flying this way and that. Farrah's hand slipped out of mine once more, the thick knot of people smothering the room.

I had never had much of a way with words. My vocabulary was expansive, but more often than not, my thoughts came out in a clunky, straightforward manner. With numbers, there was always a right and wrong. With actions, there was a do or do *not* do. But words were messy things. They meant one thing to one person and a different thing to the next. They were a cacophony of thoughts condensed into the feeble strand of a sentence, a whirlwind of emotions set loose to play with the fragile constructs known as vowels and consonants. They were a blender of everything and anything, where every surface was reflective, and every mirror was distorted.

But things need to be said, sometimes. And I could feel words rising to my throat. I could feel them coming prematurely, like a high tide, and while I regarded them in fear, I didn't run from their power.

"Everyone, stop!" I shouted, pushing a gasp of air from my lungs.

When I had pictured a fight scene, I had always expected it to be loud. In movies, where every moment was tied together by dramatic music that thrummed in tune with a racing heart, there was little room for talk. Only screams and chords. But the quiet ensnaring us was much worse than a loud brawl. It was all-consuming and unexpected. My words carried, but nobody heeded them. I tried again.

"EVERYONE! LISTEN TO ME!"

That got a few people's attention, but the captives continued to scrape their way out, completely uncaring as to where their outstretched fingernails scratched.

"Don't you see what you're doing?!" I cried, "we are *all* in the same boat. We are all awful! You can argue about the ethics of this system; you can debate about who deserves to be here and who doesn't. But at the end of the day, we are, each one of us, prisoners. It doesn't make sense for us to fight when we have a common enemy. The guards have tried as they might to weed out the worst of the worst, but here's the thing- we have bigger problems on our hands than each other."

Many people had stopped, pausing their fight and holding back their cries of victory.

"I have a question for all of you!" I continued. There was no holding back now. "What do you think they do with the Level Threes? Do they kill them? Do they torture them? What do they do with the people who report them, and what will they do with *us*? That is the question you should be asking yourself. Not 'how do I get home,' but 'why do I *want* to get home? Why the *fuck* would I want to go back to Sykona?'"

I gasped for air, a stunned silence penetrating the atmosphere. Farrah found me amid the turmoil, and she pulled me forward.

"We need a guard," she whispered in my ear. "We need answers. And we also need a leader."

A hand shot out to block me. I looked at its owner with pleading eyes. The hand belonged to chalkboard-voice.

"Get back," he snarled, a ketchupy pearl of blood running down the side of his bare arm.

"No," I objected. "You don't have to do this. Things don't have to be this way."

"Oh yeah? What can *you* do?"

I pushed past him, flying out the door. He called after me, a torrent of spit flying out with the rest of the words.

"I'm not going to listen to some idiotic kid!"

But clearly, he had, since I was outside, and I had a path to follow. Everyone flooded onto the pavement, leaving a bubble of space around me. Haven had circled back to us, waving in greeting.

"Jeez, Jakson! I hadn't expected you to make friends so quickly!"

Farrah joined my side, determination in her eyes. Amélie advanced as well, her hands still soaked crimson red.

"Go back to building 1-3!" I called, "Find Max, Adrienne, and Emry! We need to get them over here."

Haven was about to protest, but the crowd, fueled by the momentum of rebellion-born violence, pushed me on. Just like that, we were moving. *I* was moving. *I* was moving *them*.

"Where are we going?" I asked Farrah, a little breathless, as we led the crowd, stomping forward in a military like march.

"The centre circle."

I stole a glance behind me. The group I led consisted not only of my friends, but also the vast majority of building 1-1's sunken-eyed members. They blinked profusely, their eyes unused to the searing daylight, and out of their mouths flew cries for their freedom.

I bit my lip. This group was definitely more on board with Darby's brand of full-scale anarchy than they were with the prospect of social reform. In situations like these, anarchy could be suited to a purpose, even though assigning it to a cause would mock its very existence.

We walked a fine line.

My pulse pounded all the way up to my ears, and I could practically hear the sparkling crackle of my nerves. In a flash, whatever attack force this was had adopted me, of all people, as their spearhead.

We stomped into the centre circle with our fists raised, in some cases, quite literally. My thought process had yet to come full circle. Were we going to storm the place, forcing ourselves in and kicking them out? Would we offer demands? What leverage did we even have? Was I going to see the inside of the gates?

As we approached, I, along with all of my worries, came to a skidding halt. One of the guards at the gate was unconscious. I blinked, unsure of what I was seeing.

His long red hair captured by the wind, Emry McLeod held the guard's rifle between his trembling arms. The second guard was alive, with Emry's gun pointed at her skull.

Emry was choked up, his eyes stricken with tears.

"For Cerina!" he cried.

Emry turned suddenly, jumping at the sight of us.

"Jakson! Farrah! Amélie!" He cried, taking in our presence. "I... I have made a huge mistake."

Emry McLeod

A little idiot in a big-kid cage

Irabella's final message could not have come at a worse time. I mean, there was probably no good time for a message such as that one to arrive. However, if anyone ever got bored enough to create a list of *worst times to betray someone out of fear for your worthless life*, the moment I landed myself in would definitely make the top three.

The message came when I was on my way out of the washroom. Of course, when it comes to awkward timing, the involvement of a washroom is never a good sign.

On the way out of said washroom, there was a small step down to the pavement. It was a small, insignificant thing. It was nothing more than a shifted piece of concrete jutting out of the base, and while the edges were sharp, it was prominent enough not to be too much of a tripping hazard.

Unless, of course, you were me.

I was very much aware of the step, but thanks to my lack of spectacles, I hadn't been correct in my guess of how far away the step *was*. I had largely overestimated the distance, extending my leg only to plummet from an unexpected drop.

My foot slid, and, in an almost graceful plummet, I was on the ground with another scraped knee and a hole in my uniform, attempting, with no success, to stop my angry mouth from spewing a load of incomprehensible swears.

That was how it had begun. And things were about to get a hell of a lot worse.

"You done?" A voice, impatient and gravelly, cut into my miniature temper tantrum. I looked up, staring into the face of a bored-looking sixteen-or-seventeen-year-old with a buzz cut and a strong jawline. It took me less than half a second to notice the prominent 2 branded into his arm.

I hobbled up, just about tripping a second time and cracking my skull on the cement.

"Who's asking?"

"Name's Wes. Irabella sent me. She told me to look for a clumsy redhead doing something stupid. You look like you fit the bill. I assume you're Empty?"

"For the love of *decency*, it's *Emry-*"

"And I care because…."

I crossed my arms, tucking my scraped leg behind the other one to hide the depth of my injury. "What do you want? To report me to the guards? Or did you just come to piss me off?"

"I'm supposed to deliver a message."

"Another one?"

"Yeah. *Another one*. And you'd better listen to it, because she's waiting for you as we speak." He pronounced his 'er' sounds like 'ah,' indicating some sort of accent.

"Waiting for me to do what?"

"Waiting for you to bring in Cerina Rayz."

In his voice, 'Cerina' sounded more like 'Seena.'

"And how, do tell, am I supposed to do that on such short notice?"

Wes shrugged his shoulders. "I dunno. You're supposed to figure that out yourself. I heard you had a plan? If you want my advice, stick to it and listen to her. If not, well, she'll probably send me to snap your neck."

As it turned out, there was no faster way to kill a conversation than to end it with a literal death threat.

After Wes had disappeared, I covered the scrape with my hand, doing my best to stem the blood flow. After a while, I gave it up, letting it blister naturally. The benefit of getting scratched up on the Isle was that I could always blame it on something way cooler than a stumble on the way out of the outhouse.

While I walked, I was thinking about two things. First of all, there was my excuse for the scrape. Weighing the options, I decided to attribute it to a minor scuffle. Nothing *too* bloody, but something I could boast about.

Then, of course, there was Cerina.

A shudder crept up my spine as I recalled Wes's words. It had been, what, an hour since I had written the threatening notes? How had Irabella found out about them so quickly? And, what was more, how could she ensure Cerina had noticed them?

If she had spies like Wes, then it was equally probable that she had hidden snipers, waiting to shoot me in the back the second I fell out of line. I glanced up at the rooftops, just to be safe. I couldn't see anything, but I supposed the whole point of *hidden* snipers was for them to be out of sight.

"Fuck you, Irabella," I spat, hoping whatever stalking method she was employing had the ability to pick up audio. For good measure, I stuck up the finger, waving it around the immediate vicinity. The few people with the courage to roam the almost-desolate streets shot me a couple odd glances. In response, I extended the gesture to them as well. I was done with the world.

Surprisingly enough, like the bubbles of a carbonated soda, a laugh wafted up from somewhere buried deep in my chest cavity. It was a snorty laugh, and, in my near-delirious state, it sounded more like an agonized wheeze. I sputtered, hysteria pounding at the thin wall that reinforced my thin scraps of sanity.

Somebody on planet earth thought they could take down Cerina. No. They thought I could take down Cerina. Me. Based on what Wes had told me, I didn't exactly stand high up on the podium of Irabella's esteem. And yet, I had been tasked to take Cerina to her. They had entrusted their hope in me, and the plan hung in the balance of *my* actions.

It was hilarious.

I tucked my hands back into my pockets, snickering as I paced back and forth.

A thought I didn't even want to consider nagged at the back of my mind, but with this justification, this comedic failure on the part of the entire Level Two sector, I was able to push it down with ease. I could save my skin, and Cerina would be fine. I had warned her. If I did my part, no one could hold anything against me. Not even Cerina. Because she knew how strong she was. Everybody did.

I was never that great of a strategist. Not like Jakson, whose help I desperately needed. Not like Haven, whose help I *also* desperately needed. Not like Cerina herself.

As I had done with everything in my life so far, I would improvise. And if it got me sent home, could that really be the worst thing in the world?

Damn. There was that thought again.

I raised my fist, giving the door to building 1-10 a rapid set of consecutive knocks. They rang out, their echoes travelling far, but nobody answered them. I frowned, trying again. No reply.

The main thing I had taken away from my one failed junior high school relationship was that if someone leaves your text message on 'read', sending *more* messages isn't going to help. If you're being ignored, you're being ignored.

And if the only person inside building 1-10 is a temperamental old man, then you're out of luck. Because unless you've conveniently mastered the power of teleportation, you're going to have to work a little harder to find what you're looking for.

A jet of air streamed from my nostrils, my jaw clenched in frustration. "Cerina?" I called to no one in particular. "You around? I have to bring you to your doom. No biggie or anything."

***

I had walked almost a full mile before I found her, both of our aimless paths intersecting at last. Her head was held down, but her attempt at passing as a Level One was like a dark roast coffee trying to pass for a mocha. You didn't need a label to tell that the two of them just weren't the same.

"Emry," she said, spotting me before I could think of anything witty to say. "What's up?"

I swore under my breath. She would be fine. Whatever she did, whatever *I* did, she would be a hundred percent *fine*.

"You have to go to the Level Two sector," I said. The words tumbled out of my mouth the same way my little sister attempted to perform cartwheels- with false confidence that would have been cute if she hadn't knocked into my grandmother's vase, sending it pinwheeling onto her skull and leaving her with three stitches.

Cerina furrowed her eyebrows.

"What are you talking about?"

"Those people in building 1-1?" I said, Amélie's words coming back to me. "They've found out where you are. They're coming for you, and they want to turn you in. They aren't working alone, either. Jakson's got more intel than I do, but I heard their whole building is coming after you. The only place you'll be safe is the Level Two sector."

"I don't need to be safe. I'm bad enough at that on my own, but I certainly don't need you 'helping' me," Cerina said, the snarl in her voice unmistakable.

"I'm going to pretend I don't take offence to that," I grumbled under my breath.

"I spoke to Irabella," I continued. Maybe I was pushing my luck, but Cerina didn't look like she would be moving anytime soon. "She agreed to take you in. You have to go, now!"

I'd never been a great actor, and my legs were shaking violently. If my goal was to look like a helpless kitten dumped in a bucket of icy water, I'd accomplished it tenfold.

Cerina stood up a little straighter, raising her eyebrows.

"Irabella wants to help me?" Her right hand fidgeted with something in her pocket. I glanced up to meet her eyes, regretting it immediately. Her pupils swallowed me whole. I could lie to my shoes, staring at the ground while I dug myself in a hole of falsehoods to save my skin, but I couldn't lie to those eyes.

Cerina whispered something under her breath, and I noticed a trail of blood creeping out of her right ear.

"Irabella wants to help me," she repeated. I gave her a robotic nod, staring intently into empty space.

Cerina then proceeded to do something I hadn't expected. She stepped forward, placing a warm, calloused hand on my shoulder. This time, it was her gaze that found mine, latching onto my line of sight, my attention span, and my fluttering, helpless heartbeat.

"I hope you know," she said, dropping her voice to a whisper. "That I'm defending you, too."

I nodded again, and as soon as I blinked, the moment passed.

"Walk to the border with me," she said, beginning to stroll. "I would like to see you one more time, like this. Before it takes hold, I want to remember you."

The silence we walked in was like a conversation of its own. I had heard of the companionable silence two people sometimes found, the sheer peace of not needing to say a thing to enjoy each other's company. This wasn't that. This silence was agony. But it was an unspoken message nonetheless, a resounding thought passed between two people in an almost telepathic way, a sentiment that weighed much heavier than any word.

In the oddest way, it felt like a goodbye.

Before I knew it, we had crossed the field and were standing at the line. I had the sudden, overpowering urge to stand on my tiptoes and kiss her, to clasp her hand and tell her that I was here, and I was here for *her*.

But based on the look she was giving me, I figured she already knew that.

"You should go back," she said.

"I know."

Cerina gave me a soft smile.

"I'll see you soon, okay?"

"Okay. Be… Be careful."

***

After those moments had slipped away, ebbing into the house of my memory, I watched Cerina depart. She was a silhouette slowly blurring between the foggy lines of my screwed-up vision, and she was all I could think about. A recollection of her words murmured in my ears, repeating and repeating until they sunk into my soul, losing their meaning entirely and leaving me in a state of suspended animation, watching and waiting and doing nothing, doing *nothing*.

A sinking realisation dropped onto my gut like a thousand-pound weight, and I snapped back to reality. I gasped as though I had just emerged from the bottom of the ocean, grabbing the first breath I could get my hands on.

My voice came back to me.

"Wait!" I cried, speeding past the border. "Cerina! Wait! Stop!"

Her figure had already passed into the row of sleeping quarters. She was long gone, but my feet kicked hungrily at the grass.

"Stop! Wait!" My lungs, already exhausted from walking, burned with exertion. "Cerina! Don't go!" My feet gave out, stopping me halfway down the remaining stretch.

"Cerina!" I wailed uselessly, halting in the middle of the field. A tendril of something, guilt, regret, pain, gripped me and pulled. It strangled me like a rope, slipping down my throat and seizing my airway like an invisible hand.

I first thought that it was a visceral reaction to my hopelessness. It was a snake, coiling around my internal organs and constricting them with the binding weight of my mistakes. But it was also a revelation. An urge. An idea.

My eyes widened. My theory. I had to confirm my theory. My feet, guided by an unseen force, turned back to the centre circle. My only half-functional eyes narrowed on the silver gate.

"What the hell am I thinking?" I whispered to myself. A new ambition drove my feet, propelling me forward, moving me back to the border, to the food station. My limbs were on fire, but they were barely an afterthought. I had a target. I had a goal. I had a reason.

Two guards were in front of the open gate, waiting for another group to arrive. They wandered aimlessly, not bothering with so much as a conversation. I was sure they were bored to death.

Death. What I was about to do would probably get me killed. To think- I was more curious about death than what would happen if I managed to escape it.

And so, without another thought, I ducked behind the uniform washing station, my muscles contracting like a wire spring. In one swift strike, I jumped out, raised my fist and struck the first guard from behind his skull. He cried out, scrambling for his rifle. I kicked the back of his knees in, elbowing him hard in the jaw. My arms looped around his gun, and I wrenched it out from under him. Giddy energy surged to my brain, tugging up the corners of my lips. Was this what it felt like to fight? Was this what it felt like to win? With the loaded weapon in one hand, I used the other to grip the guard by the long sleeve of his uniform. I sank my nails into the thick fabric, and I ripped it as hard as I could.

I shouldn't have been shocked to see what was burned onto the skin of his bare shoulder. But the blistering 3 staring back at me ensnared my breath all the same, dissipating any and all other thoughts. My mind slowed until it reached a complete blank, a state of sheer awe.

"It's true...." I gasped. My fingers slipped on the gun, my entire hand weakened by the startling revelation. What had I done?

I had been correct.

In seconds, the other guard was on me. I gasped, lunging out of her grasp. My sudden movement caught her by surprise, and I managed to get my hands on the rifle once more. For a third time, I smashed the back of it onto the head of its previous owner. We both winced. He let out a low moan before collapsing to the ground, a trickle of blood mottling his dusty-blond hair. His shoulder, and the scarred burn on it, were still visible for all to see.

The guard was a Level Three.

The second guard held up her rifle, digging it into the back of my neck. "Put that down immediately."

I hefted up my own rifle, readjusting the handhold. I had never held a gun before- let alone shot one. It felt strange in my arms, almost electric. Something about it reminded me of a squirming cat, except this time, if I dropped it, it wouldn't land on its feet, and no one would walk away unscathed. I spun around, dodging before she could shoot.

We both stared down the barrels of each other's guns. The guard's crystal-blue eyes had no fear; if anything, they ached with boredom.

"I bet you think you're awfully tough, carrying that thing over your shoulder," she stated. "But I'll tell you this- you don't know the first thing about strength. Now hand over the rifle, or you'll genuinely regret it."

"Will I be herded off into the centre circle?" I spat, "with all the other unstable minds?"

The guard was smart. She didn't fall into my conversation, maintaining even eye contact.

"Put the gun down," she repeated. "I won't ask again."

Shooting was a lose-lose. I'd probably miss, and even if I didn't, we'd both end up with bullets in our skulls. Running was equally out of the question. I'd be dead before I made it back to the Level One sector. The only option was to stall until Cerina arrived. I didn't know what shape she'd be in, and I didn't know who would be with her. But when that time came, if the situation called for it, I would fire the gun as if there was no tomorrow.

Stalling, however, was getting harder by the minute. I was in the guard's crosshairs, and I had lost the element of surprise. Now, I was nothing more than a scrappy Level One with a scraped knee, a vision problem, and a rifle too big for my body.

My odds weren't looking good.

There was maybe about a foot of distance between the guard and me. For now, I only had a single advantage- it was her against the wall, not me.

I stepped closer to the guard, and she started to turn. She wanted to swap places, taking my one bit of leverage and leaving me cornered. I kept my eyes forward and gritted my teeth, continuing to advance. Once I had narrowed the gap between us, so close that I could smell the guard's breath, I made a decisive strike.

My leg shot out, and I kicked the guard's legs. She was ready for me and easily dodged, knocking me to the ground and pinning me there. She wrenched the rifle from my hands, swinging it over her shoulder. The other gun was still pointed at my head.

"You're a little idiot," she snarled. "But who knows. Maybe you're a useful one." She fumbled for the radio at her belt. With a click of a button, everything would go down. With the click of a button, I'd go to the same place they were trying to send Cerina. I couldn't let that happen. Not now, not yet.

With my last shred of determination, I kicked and writhed like mad, head-butting the guard square in the forehead. Stars swam through my field of vision, but it wasn't like my sense of sight had ever been on my side in the first place. I lunged, jumping out of my position and grappling for the guns. My feet flew off the ground and connected with the guard's kneecaps. She swore, spitting curses.

Somewhere in the fray, my tear ducts let loose. I had never fought another human before, and I had never thought of myself as a criminal. Yet here I was, a victim of circumstance. What an impressionable, gullible individual I was to succumb to the world's dark places and kick a person, a living, breathing *person* like there was no tomorrow and no escape.

It was because of Cerina, but more than that, it was because I was a little idiot in a big kid cage, and I had forced myself into growing up. Now I knew what the fingers were that had gripped me before. They were the prison bars.

I couldn't even see what I was hitting anymore, my punches raining down like hail. I think I might've screamed, or maybe the guard did, or maybe it was us both, a choir of agony mixed in with the smell of blood and sweat. My hands were sticky, but I couldn't force myself to look at what had made them that way.

"For Cerina!" I mustered.

I was fully prepared to continue, but something made me stop. On top of the guard now, I paused, panting heavily. Her gun had flown about a foot away, and she groped for it madly, spitting in my face. She was more resilient than the man who was with her, and even though the both of us were on the brink of consciousness, she continued to struggle.

A familiar sound lit up the field. It was a shout. My head turned, and a series of shapes started to come into focus.

At first, the figures on the horizon were nothing more than shapeless blobs, drawing nearer with each miserable beat. I wiped my tears in an aggressive swipe, and the scene eased into focus. At the front of the charge, a giant *army* of prisoners, was none other than Jakson.

My relief was hardly containable.

"Jakson, Farrah, Amélie!" I shouted, digging my nails into the gun. "I- I have made a huge mistake."

Arms closed over me, and I only realised they belonged to Lizabeth after I was dragged away from the guard, peering into her turquoise eyes. She was… hugging me.

"Lizabeth," I rasped, clutching her hand. I backed away, wobbly on my feet. "We have to go to the Level Two doctor, now! I- the guards, they're-"

"It'll have to wait," Jakson said. "We, too, are busy doing something terrible."

I looked back at the guard. She was wholly outnumbered, her face pressed to the metallic wall of the centre circle. Jakson picked up her rifle, wielding it like a natural. Lizabeth lifted the other one from my hands while Farrah placed her hand on the guard's back, keeping her from getting any ideas. The rest of them stood at attention, a ferocity in each of their eyes.

The second guard's body was thoroughly trampled. His chest heaved up and down, but his breaths were shaky and clipped. I ran to him, parting the crowd. Grabbing the man from under the armpits, I dragged him out, propping him upright against the wall and away from the mob.

"You're welcome," I whispered pointlessly to his unconscious body.

Jakson adjusted his hold on the gun, giving the guard the deadliest look I had ever seen.

"First," he commanded, "you're going to head back to building 1-1 with us. Then you'll answer our questions. Got it?"

"Wait!" I cried, shoving to the front. "We don't have time for a full interrogation! We have to save Cerina!"

Jakson looked at me in annoyance.

"I don't know what you did, Emry, but whatever it is, Cerina can take care of herself."

"What are you doing with the prisoners who get reported?" I blurted out, giving the guard a tiny punch that was supposed to be threatening.

Jakson placed a hand on my wrist.

"We can't do this here," he said, his voice low. "They'll send out reinforcements if we delay any longer. If, no, *when* they do so, it's the chopping block for all of us."

"I don't care," I snapped. "Answer me, guard! What are you doing with the people who are reported!"

The guard laughed. "Your friend there is onto something." She whipped out her radio and clicked the button. "I need backup, now-"

Farrah shot out her hand, snatching the radio and flinging it to the ground. She brought her foot upon it, snapping the device in two.

"You have about a minute before they show up," the guard chortled. "A minute I will spend here, with my lips sealed."

"If you don't talk," Amélie snarled, "we shoot. Plain and simple."

The guard began to laugh even harder. "Do you think I give a living shit about my life? We live in an awful world filled with awful people. I'd be happy to get a ticket out of it. Please, blow my brains out. I will welcome it."

"If you hate your life so much," Farrah said, her voice so quiet that I had to strain to pick out the words, "why live it?"

"Wouldn't you like to know?"

Farrah kneed the guard in the back, bringing her to a wince.

"You're going to have to do better than that," Farrah fumed, "if you live without a purpose, why live at all?"

"Don't lecture me about 'purpose'. What are *you* living for? Freedom? Money? Your own petty selves? There is no meaning to any of it, only give and take and endless control. They weed out the bad ones and worship the worst. Not everyone gets a proper burial."

Jakson jammed the rifle into the guard's head. "I'm not going to ask again. What are you doing with the people who get reported? Why is your partner tagged as a Level Three?"

The guard rolled her eyes. "The reported people aren't the ones we're looking for. You'll see eventually. If you play your cards right, that is."

"What are you saying?" I pressed.

"It's sad, honestly. We've amassed quite the collection of useless fools. But we're one step closer now. Soon, the crowd will thin."

Between her tortured gasps, she was starting to sound like Arvin.

"I'm taking her back," Jakson said, wrapping an arm around the guard's shoulders. He paused for a second before handing me the rifle. "Don't make me regret trusting you," he whispered, the words reaching my ears only.

His second announcement came as even more of a shock.

"Everyone from building 1-1, come with me! Lizabeth, go with Emry."

A girl I didn't recognise grabbed onto the guard's other side, helping Jakson carry her down the field. I watched them depart, still trying to grasp the situation.

Lizabeth tapped me on the shoulder.

"Well?" she said, "what did you get yourself into this time?"

I fiddled with the gun's strap.

"Come with me," I said. "We have to hurry."

Cerina Rayz

The illusion of childhood

I knew what I was in for the second I was out of Emry's line of sight. In fact, I had known long before then, before I had discovered the earpiece, discovered anything. The facts were always there; they were only out of reach. But once I had liberated myself from the metal device, something within me had snapped. I was free, but I was also even more of a prisoner. It was difficult to explain. I already knew the answers to many of my questions, but with the same certainty, I knew that such knowledge would be my undoing.

The uprooted fibres of the deadly nightshade plant barely weighed more than a feather. But in my pocket, I felt like I was carrying a metric ton. Something about the earthy texture brought me back to reality for a split second. I squeezed my eyes shut. Was I really about to do this?

A shout snapped me back to life, and I retreated to the shadows of the Level Two sector. I thought of the earpiece, and I thought of Arvin. Hell, I thought of Emry. I pressed a hand to my cheek, scratching off the flaky layer of dried blood. Irabella's betrayal stung, and the barb had a sharper bite than I could ever have imagined. To me, she was an enemy. My rage was a blue flame- controllable, small, but hot and deadly. I could feel it consuming me, eating away at my insides. I had always been in control, but this time, I felt possessed. I knew I needed to stop. My set of beliefs was a vast lake, and the water within it, like my reason, had completely evaporated, laying bare all the sharp rocks underneath.

"I don't understand you, Arvin," I muttered under my breath. "But I think I'm about to. I think that's what you want."

I drew in a shaky breath. "I've done this before."

Irabella lived her life on sparks, and when those embers were extinguished, I would make sure she went out the way she hated. Unnoticed. It was a reflection of my hopelessness, a shard of my spite.

I was trapped. I could either embrace that or break free. Relishing the taste, I bit down on my lower lip.

"I hate you," I whispered.

The funny thing was, I had no idea who I was addressing.

My hand reached inside my other pocket. Within it was the day's meal, the soup intended for my consumption. Soon, it wouldn't be edible to anyone, imbued with a toxic plant.

My feet guided me to building 2-7 based on muscle memory. I stood before the structure, my eyes following an invisible line up the steps and through the doorway. I wondered what would happen if I knocked. I wondered who would win if we fought fairly.

The route I took, creeping up to the edge of building 2-7, was a blow to my pride. But it would also be a blow to Irabella's. And I was not doing this for glory. I was doing it for balance, for sick justification, and because I had to. Whether I wanted to or not was irrelevant.

I crouched below the windowsill, pulling the can open with gentle precision. The scent of cold soup wafted up to greet me, and I resisted the temptation to take a sip. My stomach growled, hungering for even just a tiny taste. Even the bitter whisper of death could not quell my biological instinct.

Each fibre of the deadly nightshade plant would need to fit inside for the silent killer to do the trick. I pulled the sproutling open with my two fingers with the cold touch of a vivisection, grimacing at the sight of its delicate structure. It seemed too fragile, too young to take a life.

Not like I could throw the blame on *it*. But it felt a little better to know I wasn't the only one at fault. After all, it wasn't as though I'd be murdering anyone with my own bare hands.

The threads of the plant dropped into the soup, and I swished them around for good measure. I had to hurry.

The structures around me seemed to close in. The salty sea breeze had a bit of a kick to it, reeking of blood, filth, and dead fish. I hiked up my sweatpants, the searing heat radiating off the paved pathways. To think that I had once called this place something similar to a home.

The familiar window above me was cracked open, blocked off by the newly implemented shutters. Sure enough, the cold can of Irabella's soup still sat there. She had a habit of forgetting her meals, but the location of the soup can was a new development. Should I have been flattered or insulted with the knowledge that Irabella had taken up residency in my old bunk?

I swapped the containers with ease, closing my fist around the cool, serrated metal. I brought Irabella's can under my nose. It was open and partially eaten. I frowned at the brown broth. I would have to hope Irabella wouldn't notice any difference in her meal.

Of course, it wasn't like I was familiar with the taste of deadly nightshade.

My stomach grumbled. I looked down at the soup and pressed my lips to the jagged edge where the lid had been ruthlessly torn off. Why let a good meal go to waste?

I downed the container in two gulps. The broth slid smoothly down my throat. It tasted bland, like watered-down vegetables and a measly sprinkle of some sort of spice, but my taste buds welcomed food with a dangerous eagerness.

For a moment, I could forget about the cup on the windowsill and sit in the sunlight, basking in the rays. Cerina Rayz. I laughed to myself, both as a lighthearted chuckle and a curse to my family name.

As if on cue, the curtains were pulled back. I crouched low, holding my breath. My heart rate sped up, though I wasn't sure why. *I* wasn't the one who was about to get poisoned.

The can scraped above me, and I heard the unmistakable sound of slurping. I could listen to the soup travelling down Irabella's gullet with every starved sip. I shut my eyes, though I wasn't sure what would cause such action. I wasn't the one who was about to die.

Irabella sighed in relief, but her breath took on an abrupt hitch. She began to cough. I stepped back. Her hand was at her throat, and her eyes were pointed down at the empty can of soup she had just inhaled without a second thought.

Her eyes didn't have time to meet mine before I was running to the door, flinging it open and barrelling inside. I *wasn't sure why*. I had been confident of everything up until this point, but now, the only desire I had was to protect this ailing person, to save my friend.

We locked gazes. Her face was already starting to pale.

"Y… ou…" she rasped, leaping down from her bunk with a thud. She swayed violently, clutching the railing. Her coughs grew louder, and a thick wad of phlegm spattered on the ground. "You did this to me!"

I walked forward. There was a hairbreadth of distance between us, and I could feel each of her pained breaths as though they were my own.

"Shh…" I muttered. "Be still."

Her heart thumped at a maddening pace, and her eyes were wild. Her lips were bared in a snarl. "I… I am going… to kill…."

I placed a gentle finger over her mouth. "You were going to kill me. I know."

"I... AM going to kill you."

I shook my head. "What happened to you, Irabella? You weren't like this before, were you? You had some compassion left."

She dove away from me, but I shot my hands out, clutching her by the shoulders. I dug my fingers into the soft flesh, and she winced from the pinched grip.

"I never knew you hated me so much. But look at us! I know you hate me now." My voice rose, a madness consuming me entirely. "For I," I continued, staring deep into her desperate eyes. She had stopped coughing, and her cheeks were turning blue. "I gave you the one thing you never wanted from me. A quiet parting."

She lunged again, but the struggle was futile. I could feel her muscles relaxing, her last ebbs of strength fading out. Her eyelids sagged, and she stared at me with a look I could only describe as pure, unequivocal sorrow. Her fingers brushed the long hair away from my face, the most delicate touch I had ever felt.

With her last breath, she raised her fist and drove it into my skull. She knocked me back, stars swimming in my vision. I didn't let go of my grip on her shoulder, tightening it instead, feverishly clawing at the sleeves of her uniform. She opened her mouth in a silent scream and punched me again.

I didn't stop her, didn't fight the black wave that consumed me as I spiralled into unconsciousness. We dropped to the floor at the same time, a tangle of arms and lost hopes. My last glimpse was of her eyes, the life, the colour, the spark finally drained out of them.

The edges of my lips pulled into a smile.

Now I knew I deserved to die.

Cerina Rayz

Is this the future?

When I was younger, it was easy to pretend I didn't live in luxury. I went to public school against my family's best wishes, prepared my own meals, and made my bed in the morning even though I didn't have to.

When I got older, it was harder. Once the world so rife with suffering began to steal my youth away, plaguing my innocence with the inevitable, it wouldn't have taken much to simply turn a blind eye to it all and live in a little bubble, basking in the fruits of other people's labours.

I couldn't allow myself to do that. My family, on the other hand, had no trouble giving into the good life. That bothered me, but at least they left me alone. My brother, who was a full seven years older than I was, moved out when I was eleven and seemed to have forgotten he even *had* a sister in the first place. My mother disliked my baggy clothing and shouted when I tracked mud into the house, but it wasn't as though she could stop me from befriending the kids in my class. After all, was it so wrong to want a normal life?

My father was never around. He was too busy working as the president of Sykona.

We kept our history tightly under wraps. Everything about the government was highly classified, and the only people who were ever allowed to enter my father's study were himself, my mother, and Jezmon Tylor, head of military defence. They had no government building, which they framed as a way to avoid creating a target for violence and attacks, but the real reason was likely due to Sykona's pitiful size.

We lived in a high-class mansion in a wealthy neighbourhood, and in that same mansion, my father ran a country. It was the most posh undercover operation I had ever seen. As a child, I would clutch the bronze railing of our house's top level and sneer down at Jezmon's balding head as he waltzed into my home and strolled so seamlessly into the one place I was forbidden. Maybe I envied him because he got to spend a lot more time with my father than I did. Or perhaps I was just following a gut feeling.

I had tried to spy on their meetings since I was eight, with missing front teeth and a few plastic gadgets that were supposed to listen through the walls. But the only time I had ever actually managed to catch a snippet of one of my father's conversations had occurred when I was fifteen.

The funniest part was that my case of eavesdropping had happened by accident. I had been walking past the study when I noticed the door was slightly ajar, spilling a thin shaft of golden light past the polished exit. Voices flooded through it. Unable to help myself, I had pressed an ear to the wall and listened.

"...the new batch isn't coming nearly as fast enough... the trial program was more successful by far... yes, but we aren't in the midst of a war. There's no need to rush."

I caught my father and Jezmon drifting between a conversation. My lungs had burned with the breath I was holding, but I had managed to keep myself there for a moment longer, peering into the room. I could still recall the faint silhouette of my father standing behind his impeccable desk, fixing Jezmon with a hostile glare.

"We need more intelligence on the Offshore Youth Rehabilitation Facility. Arvin has been virtually useless, and we've only been able to turn out incompetence... Yes, if that's what it takes, I am suggesting we distribute a pool of the ones we collect *back* to the prison."

Looking back, I realised that if things had gone differently during that encounter, the course of my life might have taken a drastically different path. If I had held myself together and stayed below notice, I could've made it past undetected.

But it's often the little things that we regret the most.

When my idle-minded foot had bumped against the door, my father shut down his conversation immediately, shooting his head in my direction. My eyes widened, and although it was my father's face staring back at me, I had recognised him as something wholly different. Edric Rayz, president of Sykona, was no father of mine. We maintained eye contact for about half a second, and in that time, the only sight I registered was the face of a perilous person.

I turned and ran without a second thought.

Neither Jezmon nor my father gave chase. The only sounds that followed were the stomping of my feet on the carpeted stairwell and the buzzing in my ears as I stormed out of the house, hit by a wall of crisp evening air. I walked up and down the block, processing what I had heard.

It wasn't the information I was worried about. I was completely in the dark when it came to anything my father worked on, so the scraps I had been offered were useless to me. What I feared was my father's anger, which seemed to be an imminent prospect.

After I had exerted myself, I concluded that I was being ridiculous. Instead of pacing around the street like a coward, I would go home and face whatever punishment awaited me.

For once, I was extra careful to take my shoes off at the welcome mat. It was late spring, so I hadn't bothered with a coat. My mother detested my sweaters, however, so I reluctantly shrugged that off as well before taking my spot at the dining table.

My mother had given me a weird look, immediately seeing through whatever I was trying to play at. I wasn't as cunning back then, but my mother didn't call me out on it.

I didn't see my father once for the rest of the week. My mother was in a sour mood, but that was a regular occurrence. I kept to myself, as always, and dismissed the eavesdropping incident as something I was playing up in my head. After all, it wasn't as though I had stumbled upon anything classified. I was just being dramatic.

Everything was comfortably boring until my last week of school, when my father emerged from his study, confronting me as I came down the hallway. Panicking, I had sped up before shoving the fear away and slowing down again.

"Dad," I said, turning around. "How are you?"

A small grunt escaped him, and he strode towards me.

I backed up, slamming into the wall. My heart skipped a few extra beats. My father was a big man who took up the entire width of the hall. His arms were strung with tight muscles, which housed a big chunk of his pride. He insisted he didn't need security guards due to the number of hours he spent at the gym, and there weren't many people who could contradict him.

At home, he didn't look much like a president. He was wearing a faded t-shirt from a decades-old TV show, and his eyes were the same yellow colour as his coffee-stained teeth. Pyjama bottoms were tied at his waist, and his fist was clenched around something. Standing so close to me, his breath bore the unmistakable whiff of mint gum.

"Cerina," he said, holding out his palm. His voice was deep and sincere, and inside his hand was a small item. Tentatively, I picked it up, examining the smooth metal surface. It was a pocket knife. The blade itself folded into a compact rectangle, hanging from a metal chain attached to a thin ring. It had quite the weight to it, I realised, balancing it in my hand. The thing must have been made of pure silver. "Congratulations on your report card," my father continued, "straight A's. MVP on the volleyball team. Very impressive."

Pleasant surprise coursed through me. Never once had I been asked about my grades, much less congratulated on them. For all I knew, my parents didn't even glance at my report cards. As long as they didn't get any phone calls from the teacher, I was fine.

Suddenly, I felt bad about how I had crumpled the certificate of academic achievement and tossed it carelessly to the bottom of my backpack.

"Thanks," I choked out. "This is a very pretty… knife."

"Interesting comment you make," my father said with a smile. "It used to be mine, many years ago. Few people see the beauty in violence. But I think there is something to marvel at in everything. Don't you agree?"

"I… guess? I'm not sure I understand what you're saying."

My father chuckled. "You will. Time reveals all ends, and you'll figure that out far sooner than you think. Be prepared." He winked, retreating behind his towering doors.

Those were the last words he'd spoken to me.

The next day was grey and cloudy. Technically, there was still one more pointless day of school, but I couldn't bear the thought of sitting in a stuffy classroom any longer, even though it was technically my last day of junior high school. I had already cleaned out my locker. There was no reason whatsoever to walk through those crowded halls any longer and watch G-rated movies for 7 hours straight to occupy the slot of our mandated instruction time.

I felt the strong urge to get up and do something. My father's words had been circling through my head all morning, and they were driving me insane. I needed a breather.

Time reveals all ends, and you'll figure that out far sooner than you think.

I hadn't realised I was shivering until I had stepped outside, my knees trembling as I walked down the block, loading up my jogging playlist.

Brushing off the chill, I hurried to my usual running route. With the rush of air tunnelling around me, all my problems were long gone. I could leave them in the dust and think of nothing but the wind in my face and the path at my feet.

Shutting my eyes, I let myself be swallowed up by the summer breeze and the steady thrum of cars and cyclists whooshing by. Leaving the tree-lined path behind me and turning into an alleyway, I was fully immersed in my own peaceful world until a pair of figures stopped me in my tracks.

Two men- boys, I should say, they only looked about sixteen or seventeen- spotted me in that alley and gestured my way with a dazed stagger. I halted, tugging out one of my earbuds. That was when they closed in. The two men backed me into a corner, one of their meaty hands landing on my shoulder.

The duo didn't quite fit the stereotypical picture of two guys who would corner you in a back alley, but appearances were misleading. They both wore finely-clipped suits, their greasy hair pinned flat to their heads with an excessive amount of gel. The stench of alcohol was on their breath.

It appeared as though they had just failed a fancy job interview, drowning their sorrows in something a little stronger than beer. Something was very off about them. Back then, I had attributed it solely to their drinking. And, it was true, some people, the lowest of the low, had so many screws loose that they possessed only their animal desires and nothing else. But, in hindsight, something about their presence in that moment, with my father's knife in my hand and his words echoing through my mind, seemed a little too calculated to be coincidental.

"Where do you think you're going, little girl?" The first one, a heavyset build with a squeaky voice asked, tightening his grip on my shoulder. He swayed to the side, and his friend, a taller, leaner guy with a scraggly attempt at a beard, helped steady him. The friend's hair was a light blond colour, and if it weren't for his dishevelled appearance, he would have been moderately handsome, cute at least.

When I was ten, people had always told me I looked old for my age. That was about when I got my first period, so I guess it made sense for them to mistake me for a thirteen-year-old, frustrating as it was. But when I actually *turned* thirteen, I didn't look much older than I had in fourth grade. Perhaps I was a few pounds heavier, but over the course of almost six years, I had maintained a steady height of five feet and five inches.

Even before my time on the Isle, I had kept a habit of working out and keeping healthy. I might have been young, but I certainly wasn't little. And those two men were about to learn that.

Forcefully, I swerved, ducking out of the sweaty hand's grasp. The second man shot an arm out, grabbing me by the hood of my sweater.

"I *said*, where do you think you're going?"

One of his hands twined around my waist while the other man restrained my flailing arms. "We've had a bad day," he said, a drunken slur, "what about you? Do you want to make our days better?"

His greasy fingers reached out, and with that single touch, something within me ignited. Time seemed to slow as I drew the invisible line between my foot and the blond guy's kneecap. I kicked as hard as I could, and he doubled over with a sharp crack.

He let out a moan, but his friend, whose hands were still all over me, did nothing but laugh. "She's a feisty one! Woah, woah, calm down, now. You wouldn't want to get hurt, would ya?"

I didn't have time to think, time to process, before my father's knife was in my hand. The man's eyes widened in surprise, but he didn't even get the chance to blink before the blade was embedded into his heart.

Horrified, I leapt back. The man's fingers groped for the blade, a choked gasp wrangling free from his lungs. The metal chain at the end of the knife snapped off, clattering to the pavement. His friend looked between me and the gaping wound before turning to flee, tripping over his own feet. I couldn't react, couldn't move.

With a trembling hand, I picked up the chain. The man clutched the knife in his chest and ripped it out with a gasp, staining his suit crimson red. His eyes darted around madly, their trajectory drifting slower and slower, moving from a feverish sprint to a slow float in a matter of moments. The blood continued to pour, collecting in a pool at his feet. Red streaks ran down his entire arm, each individual muscle tensed up and ready for a fight.

"You'll get what's coming for you, girl," he slurred, raising the knife. "You'll get it a million times over."

Part of me wanted to let his stroke fall. My knees quaked, my feet glued in place. As if in slow motion, he brought his hand down, aiming for the throat.

The next second, the chain was wrapped around my knuckles, and the man was on the ground, a gash running down his forehead. He writhed, spitting up blood and mucus.

"I'll kill you! I'll fucking kill you!"

I couldn't tear my eyes away. His hair was stained, and a red blotch was blooming from my sharp punch. His nose was bent at an odd angle, and blood covered his cheeks like war paint. But the true horror was his chest. Blood pumped out of the wound at an alarming rate, dousing his entire body in scarlet waves. Nausea cycled through me, and bile rose in my throat. The knife was still in his hand.

Think about what he would have done to you, I told myself. I bent down and pried his fingers open, wrenching the metal out from the tight vise. He rolled to the side once more, stretching his fingers out. Their bloodied tips managed to graze my arm, leaving three red strikes.

"You…bitch…"

I knelt down, looking at him with soft eyes. He dropped flat onto his back, staring up at the sky. His breath came in short, pained wheezes. He looked like an ant that had been crushed under a toddler's foot, struggling with its insides half-ground into the cement but continuing to live on and flail its tiny limbs as though it still had a chance.

Even a toddler would know that the only merciful thing to do at that point would be to stomp on the ant even harder and put it out of its misery.

In the same way the four-year-old would raise their sandal-clad foot, I set the metal tip of the knife against the bottom of the man's chin. He didn't even fight it, having already succumbed to his fate. The final cut was soft, and the knife broke the skin with a faint pop, the rough screen of flesh bearing the texture of coarse bread. My eyes stayed wide open, but they didn't register what I was seeing. Everything was a white flash, and in the span of a second, my seething hatred had replaced itself with pity.

My hand was shaking beyond control. The knife clattered to the ground, bouncing once, twice, three times before it settled at last.

The man's eyes finally shut, his limbs dropping to his side. Shuddering, I prodded at his neck, drawing back a second later. There was no pulse, but the skin was still warm. Of course it was. Would it have been better if it were cold?

I didn't know how long I stood there, mesmerised, entranced, by the brutal scene I had just invoked. Long enough for my white sneakers to be permanently stained. Long enough for the man's blood to soak into my hands, permanently stuck there no matter how hard I scratched at each crevice, unearthing the agony in each line in my fingerprint.

Long enough for me to wretch all over the corpse, emptying my upchucked breakfast all over his cooling carcass.

I didn't stop the cops when they arrived. I let them handcuff me, and though my feet felt like they were blocks of cement, I let them drag me away from the scene. When they burned a bright-red 2 on my shoulder, I didn't even feel it.

I didn't even flinch.

The last thing I remembered before I was taken to the Isle was a ringing in my right ear and the smell of rotting wood.

***

I woke up, the taste of cold soup still fresh on my tongue. For a second, I was confused, staring into the white light above me. Moments flooded back to me in snippets. I was in building 2-7. No, I had been booted *out* of building 2-7. But why was I here?

Bulging against my wrist, I felt the shape of Irabella's knee. I scampered up, reality crashing down like a thousand-pound weight.

Irabella. I shuffled away, tearing my eyes off of her. No. Not *her*. Her *corpse*.

There was no time to waste. The next evident course of action materialised before my eyes, but I couldn't bring myself to follow through with it. I hopped onto my bunk, putting as much distance as possible between myself and the body. It couldn't have been real. I couldn't have *done* such a thing. Not to anyone, but especially not to her.

The window was still open, letting in a gust of air. My fingers danced along the ledge, tapping it furiously. I looked out at the path below me, at the wall of building 2-8 to my right.

If only I could run again. I thought back to my old jogging playlist and started humming to myself. The upbeat music sounded brutally distorted beyond all recognition, but my scratched vocal cords did the best they could. The sounds they produced were unsatisfactory- raw, guttural bellows instead of sharp, snappy chords.

Like a drumbeat to my lament, someone knocked on the door.

I waited a moment longer, letting the soft tapping flow in tune with the rhythm I created. *Knock. Pause. Hum. Knock. Hum. Pause.*

Unsatisfactory.

The door burst open, and I rolled to the side. My eyebrows furrowed in confusion. Instead of being greeted by the group I had expected, I was looking at two guards.

They both stared, stone-faced. Completely ignoring Irabella, they shut the door behind them. They exuded a different demeanour, setting them apart from the other island officials. This pair stood straight-backed, marching like soldiers to my bunk, where they cornered me. Both men had pointy chins and firm jawlines, lips pressed into a tight line. They could have been identical twins with similar bald heads and flaky skin.

One of them reached into a black messenger bag at his side. He produced a small grey box, the edges smooth, polished, and pointy. It was only made of cardboard, but those edges could probably draw blood with so much as a prick.

"Miss Rayz," the bearer of the bag said, holding the box out to me. "Your father has a message for you."

I snatched the box from his hands, flipping off the lid. It thudded to the ground as I tore out the contents, looking at it in bewilderment.

Inside the box was a single silver earpiece.

Part 4- It's inevitable, this fate

Promising Candidates

Cerina Rayz. Level: 2 Age: 16
Emry McLeod. Level: 1 Age: 14
Jakson Veer. Level: 1 Age: 16
Hannah Megany. Level: 1 Age: 16
Lizabeth Merrin. Level: 1 Age: 16
Adrienne Jemmott. Level: 1 Age: 14
Max Lavino. Level: 1 Age: 15
Amélie Archinauld. Level: 1 Age: 15
Farrah Vanyis. Level: 1 Age: 16

Jakson Veer

Interrogation

"How about we try again, but with a gun," Amélie smashed the guard's head against the wall of building 1-1 for what was probably the fifth time. "Tell us what you're doing with the Level Threes."

"Give it a rest, Amélie," I said, resting a hand on her shoulder. "She's almost unconscious. We're not going to get anything out of her if you beat her to a pulp."

Amélie shrugged indifferently. "I'm offering her an incentive. I'll *stop* whacking her head to bits if she gives us information."

"Should I be concerned by how much you're enjoying this?"

"Probably. I'm on the Isle, after all," she smirked. "Now, hand me that rifle."

With great hesitation, I passed her the weapon.

Knowing that the endeavour was pointless, I stepped out of the building to take a breather. The sun was starting to sink below the horizon. Soon, lights-out would fall upon us. We had gotten nowhere, and the day was drawing to a close.

The tables, indeed, had turned.

"You look worried," Farrah snuck up beside me, breathing in the cool evening air. "But that's pretty much a given, isn't it? We're all worried."

"The worst part about it," I admitted, "is that I don't know what to be worried *about*."

A long moment passed before I continued to speak.

"I'm sorry about earlier. When we were planning. I was being stubborn." The words slipped out with little to no planning, but I didn't immediately regret them. Farrah looked at me, her gaze softening. Maybe I was imagining it, or maybe it was just the light, but I thought

I saw a rosy flush covering the light brown skin of her cheeks.

"There's nothing to apologise for," she said, moving to my other side so she could grab my hand. "Forgiveness is the most important virtue. Nobody can change the past, but if they accept it and live with the present, they can go on to live a good life, free of grudges."

"Forgiveness," I muttered. "I mean, it sounds easy in theory, but-"

"It takes time."

I laughed, "I'm sure you've noticed, but I'm not particularly good at patience."

"Sometimes, you don't get the choice to do what you're good at. You can only do what you have to." She paused, turning toward me. Her deep brown eyes met mine, and I felt my heart flutter as though a bunch of agitated butterflies had been released inside my stomach.

I flitted my eyes away, glancing at the ground. I hated to break her gaze, but I couldn't face her like this. I felt like a lovesick thirteen-year-old.

As though she could sense my misgivings, Farrah smiled.

"You know," she said, "don't get me wrong. There's always a choice. There's something I'd like to try, and I'll need your help. Can you do something for me?"

"Anything. Just name it."

"I'd rather not."

One second I was standing with my hands in my pockets; the next, her lips were pressed against mine. My nerves shot up, completely frozen. A moment later, I bent down, leaning into her and pressing my eyelids shut, moving a hand to caress the side of her face. The kiss was soft, delicate and completely out of the blue. Until it was over, I hadn't completely registered what it was at all.

I only knew it as the happiest three seconds of my life.

She drew away steadily, maintaining level eye contact. All the surprise that had flooded my face vanished away, leaving only the expression of pure bliss mingled with utter loss and poorly-disguised confusion.

"Can we… do that again?"

Farrah smirked. "At this point, you don't have to ask."

Our second kiss was cut short by Amélie's not-so-subtle cough.

"Break it up, lovebirds," she interrupted. "I'd be teasing you like crazy right now, but we have other things to deal with. Our guard friend is finally ready to talk."

***

The guard was not in good shape. A few fresh cuts speckled her face, and the swollen welts lining her jaw were sure to leave bruises. Her formerly neat hair was now dishevelled, and blood poured over her stained teeth like coffee on ice.

Chalkboard-voice from building 1-1 had taken over the interrogation. He gave me a few hostile glances, but with an outlet other than myself upon which he could direct his hatred, he had been compliant thus far.

The guard wasn't struggling anymore. More than anything else, she looked bored and fed up.

"I wish I had a cyanide pill," she grumbled, "but there wouldn't be much sense in giving us those. We'd all drop like flies."

The eyes of the inhabitants of building 1-1 watched me carefully, posted at their bunks and ready to lash out at any moment. Chalkboard-voice stood beside the guard with a prideful smirk.

"I've finally made her crack," he boasted. "You here to swoop in and take all the credit once again?"

I tried to ignore it, stepping in front of the guard and meeting her eyes. She was kneeling in the middle of the floor while chalkboard-voice pinned her hands firmly behind her back.

Chalkboard-voice wasn't much to look at. At her full strength, the guard could have easily taken him out. Frankly, I was surprised she hadn't tried.

"Ah, you're here at last," she spat, looking up at me with her venomous cat eyes. "I take it you haven't come to do me any favours?"

"Maybe. That depends on how you answer my questions."

The guard scoffed. "If it's earned, it's not a *favour*. It's a payment. And it looks to me like both of us are short on coin."

"Don't start speaking in metaphors. That won't change your treatment."

"Damn," she grimaced, "that usually works. But at least I'm still sharp. That's defiance in its own right, isn't it?"

"Why would you need to defy us? You're a representative of authority."

"A pretty laughable authority."

"Amélie told me you were ready to talk. Spill, or you'll regret it."

The guard gave me a one-sided smirk, as though I had just butchered an inside joke. "Pro-tip," she said, "never give a prisoner their torturer's name. Granted, the little French girl is a pretty crappy torturer, but a name gives someone humanity. People are afraid of monsters. Not *Amélie*s."

I squared my shoulders, recalling the vital task at hand. I wasn't going to let this distract me. "What are you doing with the Level Threes?" I asked, narrowing my eyes. "You can give me another one of your smart remarks, but that doesn't change the fact that, for once, you're on the other side of the rifles."

The guard paused, heaving a deep sigh. "You're going to wish you never asked, my friend."

"People only say that when they want to stall. Your time is up. 'My friend'."

The guard smiled. "The Isle has taught you well, I see. Now, in my delirium, I already revealed this to your buddy over here, so keep in mind that this knowledge doesn't make you special. A turning point in the government has come upon us. I know little about it myself, but I can tell you this. The people who were brought in aren't Level Threes. In fact, they're the complete opposite. Real Level Threes don't get themselves caught, and real Level Threes wouldn't fall for our incentive, either. Both the reported and their reporters are nothing more than unexceptional scum. Normally we'd let the true Level Threes stand out naturally, but, well… the Isle's population is growing, and circumstances are unforeseen. We have to rush it and weed out the useless space holders."

I heard a gulp from chalkboard-voice. A 'useless placeholder' who had just about met the same fate as the people he had held captive, ready to report.

"What do you mean by 'weed out'?" I pressed. "Is that why you're sending them home?"

"Nothing like that. Could you imagine how much paperwork would be involved? How much distrust would be sent our way? Sykona is a shit show, but it's not *that* big of a shit show. By weeded out, I mean cut down. Removed from this plane of existence. How much clearer can I make it?"

"You're killing them?"

"Not me specifically. I'm just a pawn. *Everyone* is just a pawn."

I looked up. A creak sounded as Farrah stepped inside, joining me next to the guard. Perfect timing.

"Farrah," I said, trying to soften my voice, so it didn't sound like an order. The urgency in it, however, clearly had the opposite effect. "Go to the Level Two sector, now. Find Emry, Cerina, and Lizabeth. Get them back here."

Farrah nodded, whirling back around. "I'm guessing they can be found around 2-7," she estimated. "Good luck, Jakson. I'll be back in a few minutes."

I waved at her back as she closed the door, the weight of the kiss still on my shoulders. There had been words on my mind, but I had found myself unable to compute them.

"I'm not done with you yet," I said, looking back at the guard. "What are the *real* Level Threes used for?"

The guard sighed in the same way a parent would to a disgruntled child. "They become a part of the government. It takes a little persuasion, of course. More than a little. I can't tell you about that part, as much as I would like to. I worked my way around this part of the web, but I can't give you the source code of my real restraints. The good ones get the good jobs. They are fearless, cold-headed, and cold-*hearted*. Perfect soldiers, right? But since we aren't in the midst of a war, there's a lot of surplus. That's how I got stuck in this shit hole and regained a bit of my humanity."

"The Level Threes... become government officials?" I repeated, sure I had misheard. "Why would-"

"Maybe you're not done with me. But I'm done with you. Done with you and the useless placeholder behind me."

Chalkboard-voice grunted. "My name is Dawson. You'd do well to remember it."

"Did you literally not just hear the advice I gave your buddy here? Not only are you weak, but you're stupid, too."

I placed a hand on Dawson's shoulder. "Dawson-"

He swatted the hand off, rage steaming from him. He was a ticking time bomb.

"Say that again," he snarled, snapping the guard's arm at an unnatural angle. She barely winced. "I dare you."

"Dawson-" I pleaded, a disturbed laugh at the absurdity forcing itself up. I shot it down at the last second, disgusted with myself. I kept my own arms a safe distance away. This Dawson guy might have been a spaz, but no one could be so brash as to act on that rage. "Please, calm down-"

Dawson reached up, pulling out a big chunk of the guard's maroon hair. "Well? I told you to do something. *Say it again.*"

"Sure. You're-"

"Dawson!" I commanded, "don't be petty! Can't you see what she's doing?"

Dawson turned to me, fury radiating off of him like hot coals. "She's insulting my pride. *That's* what she's doing. We got the information. You hear that, guard? You're useless to us."

"No! She isn't!"

"Maybe she can help *you*," he snarled. "But I don't take orders from ya! And I'm fucking sick of hearing her voice. *And* yours."

"That's not-"

I took the snapping of the guard's neck as my cue to leave.

***

I couldn't have stumbled into building 1-3 fast enough. As promised, Haven had gathered Max and Adrienne, but they had left it at that. In fact, they had almost seemed surprised when I stomped inside, as though they'd been expecting me to be gone a good half hour longer. Their eyes were downturned, and they were gnawing anxiously at their cheek, still beating themselves up about abandoning Lizabeth.

Amélie came in next, shutting the door behind her.

"It's official," she said, "the 1-1s are pissed."

"How bad is it?" The fact that Amélie wasn't lifting her hand from the door wasn't a sign that boded well.

"We're not under complete siege, but 'ticked-off' is too light a term to describe it. They're in no rush to grab another guard, so either they're going to give up or come for you. I'm betting the second one is the most likely probability."

"That's promising. Is Farrah back?"

"No. I don't know where she is."

Two voices in the back of my brain were engaged in a screaming match. One of them wanted to sort things out here and now with Haven, and the other wanted to run off to search the Level Two sector.

"I don't know," I repeated to myself. I dropped my voice, whispering in Amélie's ear. "Haven's a bit of a train wreck right now. I can't leave them to this, but if I don't, Farrah and the others might be in trouble… if they aren't back-"

Adrienne tapped me on the shoulder, cutting off my monologue with a disapproving glare. "You know," she said, "you and Haven aren't the only people in the room who can fix things. We aren't sheep. You can trust us."

"That's easy for you to say."

"Is it? You sound like a second grader trying to justify a temper tantrum. Sure, you're very competent, but you're not the only one."

"People need leaders. And I'm terrible at being one."

"Nobody *asked* you to be one. The fact that you took that on willingly is an admirable trait. But remember- we're the escape artists. A few weeks ago, our minds were bent on breaking out of here. If you thought we could do that, well… what makes you think we can't do this?"

Adrienne's forehead creased in determination. I let out a loud huff.

"I'm going to make sure the others are okay."

I stepped past the threshold, jogging into the fading sunset. I had to trust them. Coming to a realisation, I stopped in my tracks. I had to trust Farrah, too.

Now I knew why I had felt the need to apologise to her earlier. Because I hadn't given her my full respect. Because I hadn't given *anyone* my full respect.

What a surprise. The star student had been a bit arrogant in a new classroom.

I couldn't let myself be useless, but there were some things I didn't need to help with. Some things I could step away from. Breathing in the evening air, I channelled the measly ounces of zen floating through my veins.

My eyes were about to close when I spotted something, rather, someone, dashing urgently toward me.

It was Arvin. Of *course* it was Arvin.

"Jakson!" He wheezed, gripping onto my arm. "Bad things on the other end. Bad things! People… people are going to be killed. More blood. More voices. The escape has to be moved up. They're going to take Cerina!"

Why couldn't I just catch a break?

Cerina Rayz

Disillusionment of the purest kind

I fumbled with the silver device, sliding it into my earlobe as I would a headphone. Jam-packed with the clotted blood and mottled glue left over from this morning's little extraction, I had to prod the ear cavity with my fingernail to get it to close over the metal.

Immediately, the speaker inside crackled to life.

"Cerina." The voice on the other end matched my father's deep rumble, but there was something off about it. It was stretched thin, a little wispier than the boom that used to come straight from his chest.

"Father," I answered, keeping my voice as steady as possible. My eyes lingered on Irabella's motionless body. Her mouth was still open, bringing my mind back to the threats that had died on her lips. My breathing sped up. *Died. Dead. Finito*. The words echoed in my headspace, but none of them resonated as anything more than an abstract concept I had yet to wrap my head around.

"I'm surprised to see how rapidly this plan of mine moved forward," my father continued, wasting no time cutting to the chase. "But I'm impressed. You're a Rayz, after all. I knew you had it in you. Now that I think about it, I never properly thanked you. The information you gave me was vital, and due to your… accomplishments, I now have everything I need."

I wished with every fibre of my being that I could transmit glares through a phone call.

My father chuckled a little, as though he could read my mind. The two guards began chatting, and I covered my ears with my palms to stay focused on his ailing voice.

"I suppose I owe you some answers," he said, "after all, you've more than earned them. I've always mentioned that your family has a history, but I've never explained that history to you. You're a lot like me, you know. And I've never liked to be talked about behind someone's back. I'm not the kind of father who reads their children bedtime stories, but would you like to hear one?"

"Make it quick," I snapped, my teeth gritted.

It was as though I could feel the creases in my father's face turn up in a slight smirk from the other side of the communication.

"First things first," he said. "You are completely surrounded. The friends who went after you are being restrained as we speak, and you have utterly no chance at stopping them or saving anyone. So sit back and relax. I'd like all our secrets to be on the table before we dine, don't you think? And yes, I mean that literally. In a few minutes, I invite you to a meal in my Central Circle."

"I told you to make this quick."

"Yes, of course. I suppose I was getting ahead of myself."

"Start at the beginning. Then we can talk."

My father inhaled deeply. "As you wish. It all started many years ago when the war had ended and Sykona had been split off from the rest of the UK. Our government was unstable, and the condition on the streets was worse than the chaos of the Level Two sector. It was a strange time to grow up in and an even harder time to *thrive* in. But nobody thrived better in the early days of Sykona than your grandmother, Rhina Rayz.

"She was the head of a criminal organisation known as the *Spark*. But that's a detail that has been overlooked by most of society. The point is, her chief rivals were the members of a second gang, which went by the name of the *Igniters*. They both claimed vast territories located in various parts of Sykona. The fights that occurred between them weren't mere street squabbles. Both groups were so powerful that the government could no longer turn a blind eye to the crime running unchecked down the streets, and when both groups got their hands on high-tech weapons, it had to step in."

I finished the sentence for him. "And so began the civil war. Excluding the bit about my grandmother, I've heard a lot of this before."

"Allow me to finish. As it turned out, the government had more in common with the two gangs than they thought. The leader at the time was a rebellious person- unsurprisingly so, of course, considering they managed to rise against the nation and create their own country that wasn't bound by the new worldwide currency plan. The President was offered an ultimatum- to join the *Spark* or be trampled by criminals with weapons as big as their egos. Without much protest, they agreed, and the *Spark* seized political control. The *Igniters* struck back, however, with their own arsenal. It was all-out war."

"I'm aware," I grumbled, "the Sykonan war was fought due to the sudden shifts in worldwide currency, and from there, things went to hell in our little corner of the world. It's a big part of our history, and I paid attention in class. Didn't you praise me for my straight As?"

"How many times do I have to tell you this? You're so impatient, Cerina."

"You've never told me I'm impatient. You've never been there to tell me anything." My hands clenched into fists. I closed my palm over the splintery bar of my bunk bed, feeling a few slivers of the unstable wood sinking into my skin. Now I had *literal* blood on my hands.

"Back to the issue at hand," my father went on, "I know there's one thing your teachers didn't tell you about. One thing the heavily biassed curriculum, *my* heavily biassed curriculum, made sure to leave out. Well, one or two things. The first of which being the Trial system.

"You see, the *Spark* was very selective about who could join them. To become a member, or at least a respected one, you had to master a certain... diabolical nature. It was how Rhina rose to the top. She possessed a spirit that belonged only to a select few individuals. To weed out these individuals, young inmates would be stolen from local penitentiaries and shipped to the Offshore Youth Rehabilitation Facility for their potential to be assessed at an early age.

"The prisoners sent there were put through a series of rigorous tests to calculate their level of cruelty and potential usefulness. These trials consisted of three main tests, which I'm sure you have grown familiar with- the Bronze Key war, the Infection, and the Reporting. I was entered into these trials with my uncle Arvin, who barely made the age cutoff, and we scored exceptionally well. What more could be expected, after all, from the successors of Rhina Rayz? I was overjoyed, but Arvin was haunted by the experience. He faked his own death on the frontlines of the war, sneaking back onto the Isle with the next batch of Trial candidates. The coward."

"Arvin is no coward," I interrupted. My father promptly ignored me, continuing with his tale.

"Rhina was growing old. Even with the government on the *Spark's* side, the war had been raging for quite some time. Peace was long overdue. In Rhina's dying breaths, she appointed me the successor of the *Spark*. I built a new government. I changed the world."

I grumbled under my breath. "You sure are modest about it."

My father laughed, a tone much unlike the mocking chuckle he'd used before. "Humility won't get you very far in the world of politics. I offered the Igniters, whose army was starting to crumble, a deal. The fighting would stop, and I would seize control. In exchange, they would get a seat at my right hand and a loud voice in federal decisions. Oh, and, of course, we would stay our hand in obliterating them."

He paused, as if expecting me to laugh along with him. My stern expression didn't budge.

"Reluctantly, the Igniters agreed with my motion. I took executive control, and as promised, I granted their leader, Jezmon Tylor, a position of power. He was given oversight over all defences, and over the Trial system. But as for the general public, things weren't as easy. We had to craft a lie- a new government rising like a phoenix from the ashes of two criminal organisations. It wasn't far from the truth, but it cut away the messy bits. They ate it up eagerly. The only thing left to deal with was the Trial system, because I, too, had standards for my military officers. Jezmon and I agreed that we would resume the trials, or rather, something like it. If I wanted more soldiers for my army, more officials for my country, I would have to grow the pool of prisoners I was collecting."

"This isn't your country," I snapped.

"No? Then whose is it? It belongs to the *Spark*; therefore, it belongs to me. As the only one with diplomacy, it is my right. You're still a child, Cerina. Before you take over, you'll have to learn what's yours and how to take what isn't."

"When I take over? What are you talking about?"

"The Level Threes my guards tag are forced to serve me. It's hard to get them to do my bidding, believe me, but everyone has a weak spot. The only reason the *Spark* has survived for this long is because of a… skill that we have passed down for generations. But this skill takes years to hone. Right now, the Level Threes serve little jobs. Some are repurposed as prison guards, others go on to serve in the streets. It all depends on the person. Thanks to the intel I've gathered from you, I have a whole batch of prime specimens. Jakson Veer. Amélie Archinauld. Emry McLeod. The late Irabella Redmond. But the best, or should I say, *worst* of the bunch? That's you, Cerina. I've rushed things on this Isle, eliminated the useless ones, because I need a successor. I'm sick and old, you see. I may not look like it, but I will die soon. And you will fill my place."

I had stopped listening after he said the word 'eliminated'.

"What do you mean by 'eliminate the useless ones?"

"The people who were reported, and their reporters. Pointless garbage. If they haven't been disposed of already, they will be soon."

"Those are innocent people. How many others have you killed?"

"As many as I need to. And I take pride in my list of kills, as should you. The Rayz family legacy is a bloody one, and there is no one better to carry it out."

"I beg to differ."

My father sighed. "I want you to get changed into something a little more presentable. Then, we shall dine. Let's just see if I can't change your mind."

The transmission cut out. The two guards had stopped their conversation, looking up at me. The bearer of the earpiece produced a black box from his backpack, turning away from me. Carefully, I lifted the lid. Inside was a dress made of dark blue silk. It matched the guard's uniforms perfectly. Most notably of all, it didn't have shoulder straps, exposing the bright number 2 burned on my skin to the entire world.

"Once you have changed, get down and follow us," the two guards said. "If you do not comply, we will use force."

I reached into my pocket and squeezed the silver chain. Hopefully, my father wouldn't mind if I tweaked the outfit a little.

"Don't worry," I muttered, "I'm coming."

Lizabeth Merrin

Inside the Circle

I ran with Emry down the stretch of grass, keeping an even pace with him as he rapidly explained the shameful details of the last forty-eight hours.

"You're an idiot," I told him, panting. We swerved into the Level Two sector, skidding between the buildings. "But I can't blame you. Fear makes you do crazy things."

Emry blushed. "I'm not *afraid*-"

"There's nothing to be embarrassed about. I've been afraid this entire time. And as reluctant as everyone is to admit it, everyone in building 1-3 has been afraid. Hell, even *Cerina* is probably scared to pieces."

Emry began to speak, but the words died on his tongue as building 2-7 came into view. It was surrounded by guards, each one carrying a gun on their belt. Not a military-issued rifle, but a sleek pistol that glinted in the fading sunlight. I stopped in my tracks, grabbing Emry's wrist.

"We have to go back."

Emry stopped moving, looking me in the eyes. I might have been older than he was, but he still had to bend down to match my gaze. He pried my fingers off, stalking ahead. "Maybe I have a death wish. I don't know anything anymore. But the one thing I do know is that I'm getting Cerina out of there, even if it kills me."

"Emry!" I cried, launching after him. "Wait! What the hell do you think you're *doing*?!" Emry only sped up, completely ignoring my words. The guard's heads turned, but Emry didn't back down, pushing forward.

A calloused hand caught me by the arm, stopping me from moving any closer. I twisted around, catching the merciless stare of a stone-faced guard with a pair of handcuffs dangling from his fingers. Through gritted teeth, I swore. I knew better than to put up a fight, but the nagging urge to smack the officer square in the face was overwhelming. This was just like getting arrested all over again.

Before he could get even remotely close to his destination, Emry's wrists were bound and cuffed, his pitiful struggles completely useless.

"What are you doing with her?!" He grunted, "let me go!"

The guards stood stoically, not responding to a single one of his pleas. Emry wrestled through the guard's grip, whipping his head in my direction. I raised an unimpressed eyebrow. Honestly. How had he *thought* this was going to go?

Emry looked up at the guards, thrusting once more against his bonds. "Let go of me," he snarled. "Take me to Cerina."

"Are you shitting me, Emry?!" I cried over the wall of uniformed haircuts. "*That's* what you're concerned about right now?"

Emry gulped, his eyes drifting from my eyes to the veiny hand encircling my arms, clipping a set of handcuffs around my wrists. As he made the connection between those two sights, I watched his face fall and his eyes widen.

"I-"

"Cut it out, chatterboxes," the guard behind me interrupted. "Commander Abbotsford. Where do we take them?"

An old man advanced to the centre of the formation, sizing us up.

"Lizabeth Merrin and Emry McLeod," he grunted, "they match the descriptions to a tee. Take them to the central circle, but keep them separate from the captives. We don't want them accidentally getting killed."

Emry visibly gasped. I understood exactly what was going through his head. People, no, *high-ranking guards*, were familiar with our names. Not only that, but they had been hunting for us, and us specifically.

We were, at least in some way... *valuable*.

My face lifted in relief, even though we had just been ordered to our doom. Both the people who had been reported and those who had reported them were alive. We could save them.

If we could get inside... maybe the escape mission was still a go.

As long as there was a link to the others, this could work. I looked at Emry, who appeared to have similar thoughts playing out in his head.

His thoughtful eyes snapped to life, and he shot me a semi-subtle wave. With the tips of his handcuffed fingers, he gestured to two of the guards in front of us. Their hands were empty, but a walkie-talkie was in each of their pockets.

"Oh, Emry," I muttered under my breath. "You embody an oxymoron. And I mean that as a term of endearment, you clever idiot."

Giving Emry one last glance, I stepped up to take my turn as the holder of that title.

"Hey!" I shouted. No reaction. "What are you doing with Cerina? What are you doing with us! I demand answers, now!"

"Shut your mouth," the guy behind me snapped, "or I'll shut it for you."

The old man, Commander Abbotsford, looked down at his clipboard. "Patience. We are not to harm the prisoners."

"That'd be easier to do if the prisoners weren't asking for it."

"I think you mean 'yes, sir.'"

The man behind me fumed.

"Apologies, commander," he mumbled, although his words weren't sincere. Maybe I could use that. A knot of guilt twisted in my gut. Even though I was doing it to people I had every right to hate, I still didn't like what I was about to do.

"I didn't know commanders cared so much about their captives," I said with as much nonchalance as I could muster. "Or is this guy an exception?"

"This pig's about as stuck up as all the other senior officers," the guard remarked, loud enough for the commander's ears to twitch. "There's nothing special about him."

"Watch your tongue, soldier," Abbottsford snapped. "You forget who you're speaking to."

I felt the guard's grip on me tighten, fueled by fury. This was working. I couldn't believe this was actually working. I had barely needed to give them a nudge, and already, they were scuffling like wild dogs.

"I thought when I joined your stupid military, I'd get paid actual respect," the guard spat. "But all you do is dangle threats over my head and treat me like shit. I can't be the only one who's a little pissed with you, *commander*. Am I right, soldiers?"

Nods and mutters of agreement flooded the group. All eyes were on the commander, whose face hadn't so much as reddened.

"If you think you're superior in every way, how about you talk to my fist. Come forward, guard. Receive your punishment. Unless, of course, you're too cowardly to face it."

The guard dropped my hands, handing me off to one of his companions, an equally sour-faced woman.

"You're on," he challenged, stepping up to face the commander. It was as though Emry and I had disappeared entirely, every pair of eyes fixed on the two officials. A few Level Twos had even stopped along the edges, curious about the commotion. The first fist to swing was that of the plucky guard. It missed by a mile, letting out a loud series of whoops and booing.

Now was Emry's chance. He shimmied his arms out of the guard's grasp and, fighting against his restraints, looped his fingers around the antenna of one of the walkie-talkies. It clattered to the ground, but the noise was lost amid the brawl. The commander struck back, landing his knuckles right in the centre of the guard's face.

The guard moaned, a trickle of blood streaming from his nostrils. Emry slipped the second walkie-talkie into his pocket. I tried to hide my excitement behind a slightly bemused expression. I had actually done it. I had started a prison fight.

Abbotsford punched again, leaving a giant bruise on the guard's forehead. The guard staggered back, slurring a string of curses.

"Let this be a lesson," Abbotsford barked, "to all who dare go against my order. You are mere guards, but I am under the direct employ of His Honour, the President of Sykona. This man will be demoted as soon as we get off this Isle, as will any whose ideals match his. Understood?"

I could hardly contain a smirk.

Emry mouthed a *thank you* under his breath.

We were herded off to the centre field without so much as another word. I resisted the urge to look behind me at the walkie-talkie Emry had dropped. I could only hope somebody would pick it up.

For some reason, I had expected a more subtle approach. But the same warning sirens that had once driven fear to my heart lit up the peaceful silence.

"LEVEL 3 TRANSPORTATION. PLEASE CLEAR THE FIELD IMMEDIATELY."

How was I dangerous? I had always been wary of those announcements, but I had been safely withdrawn from them amidst my misgivings. To be the cause of them... was unthinkable.

I pinched myself through my handcuffs. This had to be some sort of ridiculous dream.

"LEVEL 3 TRANSPORTATION. PLEASE CLEAR THE FIELD IMMEDIATELY."

I had to get a grip, keep it together. There was no way this was happening. No possible way.

Emry glanced at me; the same thoughts echoed in his visage.

Skies above, this was actually happening.

The giant metal gate sprung to life. A separate set of soldiers rushed to collect us through the plastic screen, but commander Abbotsford held out a hand to stop them.

"These ones are special. They go with me."

He pointed to a pin on the front pocket of his uniform. I squinted. The small golden pin held a circular insignia, with a large *R* in the middle, surrounded by little dots that reminded me of sparks. The other guards straightened their backs, nodding vigorously.

"Of course, commander. Please, come in."

As I passed, I caught snippets of their conversation.

"...one of the big leagues... what could they be doing here? I thought the routine check-up wasn't for another two months...."

The blare of the alarms faded out as we passed through the plastic screen, several layers of vine-like strips dangling from the ceiling like a synthetic jungle. In that world, we were the animals.

When the last layers faded, I squinted against a bright flash of sunshine. Instinctively, my hand shot up to block my eyes, but the cuffs made any attempt to do so virtually useless. As we walked forwards, the scene came into clearer view.

That was when I noticed how the shiny metal wall at the other end of the circular plateau reflected the light from the open sky, sending beams of light straight into the prisoners' eyes. That had served as disorientation enough, but what I found in the centre circle threw me off even further.

The circle was nothing like I had pictured. For one, there was no roof. A wide hallway curved around the court, dotted with doors bearing a chain-link screen and an ID scanner. In those hallways, records would be stored. Somewhere in there, the meal chute was operated. And somewhere in there, all the reported inmates were stashed away, awaiting their deaths.

But that wasn't the part that had surprised me.

The real sight wasn't the barbed wire that somehow looked more intimidating from the inside than it did from the exterior. Nor was it the gleaming surface of the walls, or the wide hallways riddled with unknown variables. It was the house that formed the centrepiece of the grand layout, sticking entirely out of place among the iron bars and chain wire.

The ground was paved in the same style as the Level One sector, with neat cobblestone tiles leading up to a broad set of brown-painted stairs and an intricate railing. Putting our insignificance into perspective, a Victorian-style mansion that had been shrunk to fit the circle's boundary stood in the middle of the vast area. The stained-glass windows seemed to look us in the eye. An old beauty I had never expected to find was rooted right here, deep in the belly of the beast and out of reach to everyone around it.

The roofs were pointed and triangular, little metal spires jutting out of the top. Every door knob was forged in brass, the surfaces polished to perfection. A small balcony stuck out of the second floor. The metal bars that encircled it were nothing like the steel barricades that kept us prisoners inside; instead, quite the opposite. They were purely decorative, looping and swirling over the overhang like elegant brushstrokes. Tones of white, pink, and deep blue splashed the building with colour, the grey shingles completing the palette.

Max would have to see this. Even *he* would hardly be able to contain himself.

The barrel of a gun digging into my shoulder blades brought me back to reality. While Emry and I had paused to gawk, the guards were snickering.

"Keep moving, Merrin," my new shepherd commanded, giving me a second jab for good measure. Emry closed his gaping mouth, shuffling forward. It pained me to tear my eyes away from the sprawling mansion, stopping their careful journey over each immaculate line in the structure.

Commander Abbotsford opened one of the iron doors, the gate swinging with a mechanical buzz. I was prodded into a dimly-lit corridor, jam-packed with an entire fleet of guards. The overhead lights flickered as we moved down the claustrophobic enclosure, stuffed together like sardines. A heavy stench of B.O and blood hung in the air, none too different from the reek of the Level Two sector. This stink had a certain edge, though, a rusty stain. The Isle's suffocating odour came from years of breaking points being met, from hundreds of scuffles and zero victories.

This hallway was different. The smell was fresh, the torturous epitome of every prisoner's suffering. Instead of a smothering reminder of where and who we were, it was a landslide of doubt, worry, and fear, all crashing into one hideous aroma.

It didn't smell like an unhygienic prison block. It smelled like fifty people packed in a single room, about to be massacred.

At long last, the dense crowd thinned. A second door blocked the path, and the commander whipped out an ID card, shooing everyone else off except the two guards handling Emry and me, their fancy handguns tucked into leather pouches.

"Put them in here. We're rushing the initiation process."

The guard behind me loosened her grip. It might have just been me, but I thought I heard her gulp in anticipation.

Her head dropped beside my ear. "I'm sorry," she rasped, "do your best to comply. There's no backing out now."

She snapped back up, practically shoving me through the door frame. She pulled out her walkie-talkie, speaking into it.

"The two targets have been moved to the Viewing Cell. I repeat, the two targets have been moved."

The sound of her voice bounded in waves out of Emry's pocket. I coughed to cover up the sound, but there was no need. The slamming of the door and the darkening of our surroundings provided plenty of distraction.

The room we were ushered into was dimly lit, and within it, the stench had thickened. I coughed, for real this time. The suffocating aroma was enough to bring tears to my eyes. For one unbearable moment, all I heard was Emry's panicked breaths.

Then a second light blinked on. We were facing a different room, stuffed with Level Ones and Twos alike, united by the sheer terror rampant in their eyes. A thick pane of glass separated us from them, stained with fingerprints and red stains. The prisoners shrunk back from the bright light ignited over their heads, while shadows still lurked in the corner of the tiny room Emry and I could only watch from.

"Welcome to the Viewing Cell," the commander explained. "If you'd kindly pay attention, I've booked you front row tickets to a good show."

The Viewing Cell's walls were painted black. There were no lights in the room itself, all the illumination emerging from the captive's chamber. That light displayed a shelf positioned in the corner of the room, with three familiar metal rods hanging on hooks. One of the sticks had a 1 on the end of it. Another bore a 2. And the third, which the commander picked up and fingered, had a 3 attached to the tip.

Nails and hands tore at the glass. The chamber on the other side was pure white, with a wide drain in the centre. The prisoner's fists were useless against the barricade, but I could hear their screams crystal clear from a loudspeaker positioned overtop of the glass window.

"What…" Emry stuttered, his voice hollow, "what is this?"

"This is your final test. Normally it only requires a single subject, but this method kills two birds with one stone, so to speak. By joining up with a group bent on defiance, you have shown aptitude in many of our tested areas. But that does not quite suffice, does it? In this last trial, you will be closely monitored. If you show any reaction whatsoever, so much as a *twitch*, you will join these subjects." He lifted up a small portion of the division window, a tiny one-way slot, similar to a doggy door, that opened in the viewing deck and led into the chamber.

As soon as it cracked open, the people sprang. The fastest person to react was a girl by the edge. Desperation seeping from her hands like ooze-dripping talons, she clawed through the gate and stuck her fingers through the opening, crying out and kicking the other prisoners behind her who fought for a space by the slat.

The door was slammed shut instantly, slicing off three of her fingers. They dropped to our side of the floor, and a bloodcurdling scream lit up the loudspeaker. My stomach turned, but I forced myself not to flinch, not to recoil. Keeping my back straight as a board, I pressed my lips together and maintained a monotone expression.

Emry struggled to do the same.

The commander stood up.

"Good. Consider that the first part of your test. Now, wait here while I prepare the remainder of it. And remember- we're watching!" He pointed to two cameras, each on separate ends of the wall. They pointed directly at us, the red lights peering down with a menace they weren't even trying to conceal.

The commander left the room, slamming the door behind him.

Immediately, Emry whipped out the walkie-talkie. I put my hand over his, shoving the device back into his pocket.

"What are you doing?" I rasped, "we can't use this here! It'll be confiscated before we figure out how to use it!"

"Come closer. We can hide it."

I shuffled towards Emry, my nose inches from his face. He brought the walkie-talkie up again, and I glanced at the cameras. Holding the device between us, it was safely concealed between the fabric of our uniforms. Only from that distance did I notice how filthy Emry was, how filthy *both* of us were. The crooks of our elbows were plastered with grime, and dust had managed to fill every possible crevice it could find.

Keys listing the numbers one through twenty lined the top of the walkie-talkie, with a final button labelled 'all.' I thought back to the one we had left behind, visualising its surface. On the top of the one clutched in my hand was a white sticker with the number four.

The details came back to me, flooding my memory. If my recollection served correctly, a similar sticker with the number five had covered the other one. I hoped for the best and pressed the fifth number on the dashboard.

A speaker crackled to life. The link had been opened.

"Hello?" I spoke softly, "this is Lizabeth. Can you hear me? Press the number four to talk, number *four*."

I let go of the button, glancing at Emry.

"I wonder what this looks like from the cameras," he said, his gaze darting to the mechanical eagle eyes.

I shot up my eyebrows. "I think you know what it looks like."

A blush crept up Emry's face. "I-"

"Just for clarification," I said, "I'm into girls."

Emry's blush deepened. "Don't worry. It's not, you're not…"

"Good. Now keep that in mind as I solidify this charade."

Throughout my time on the Isle of Rebels, I had learned many things about Emry McLeod. He was a convenience store robber. He had no impulse control. He was blatantly head-over-heels for Cerina Rayz.

He was also a horrendous kisser.

I leaned in while he held himself slack-still, mortified and frozen as I bridged the distance. His lips were rigid and awkward, and he almost let the walkie-talkie slip from his hands in sheer surprise. I pulled away immediately, leaving a hairbreadth of distance between us.

Before he could speak, I pressed the button on the walkie-talkie once more.

"Hello? This is Lizabeth. Emry and I are being held captive. You can reach us at number *four*."

Our audience on the other side of the glass stood still, momentarily distracted. I wasn't sure whether or not they could see us, whether or not they were looking at a one-way mirror. Frankly, I wasn't sure which would be worse.

Emry grimaced. "I'm not sure this is a good time to mention this, but I feel like I should inform you that... whatever the hell that was... was my first kiss."

My stomach plummeted, and a blush of my own rose to my cheeks. "Oh shit. I'm so sorry-"

"Don't be," he cut me off. "As far as awkward, romance-free first kisses go, this one was pretty dope. I mean, how many people get to say that their first kiss was in a high-tech prison cell? Not very many."

I laughed. "I mean... it could've been a dare."

"Good point."

The debate of what we had to do next plagued the forefront of my thoughts. Did I have to kiss him again? Would I be safe to pull away? Had anyone picked up the walkie-talkie in the first place?

Before I could consider even more dreadful possibilities, a voice on the other end of the walkie-talkie rang out, bringing the device to life.

"Lizabeth? It's me, Farrah. Where are you?"

I had to fight the urge to cheer. "Farrah!" I cried, shouting at the first sign of a communication link. "We're in the central circle. I'm here with Emry-"

"Hi," he butted in clumsily.

"Where are the others?" I asked, "we don't have much time."

"It's just me right now. Everyone else is okay- apart from minor scrapes, there are no injuries on our side."

A tide of relief flooded over me.

"Farrah. You have to listen to me. All the people who were brought in are right in front of us. The guards are going to kill them. You have to cut the comms, cut the power, do *anything*. Do you understand? You have to climb the tower Max talked about. We have to get out of here. The escape mission begins now."

"Understood." Farrah's voice wobbled, but there was comforting certainty within it. "Do whatever you can to buy us time. We'll do the same for you."

The speakers crackled as our connection cut, my finger lifting from the button.

Emry wrenched the walkie-talkie from my hands, holding it to the cameras. I grabbed his hand, tugging it away.

"What the hell are you *doing*?!"

"Buying us time." he pressed the *all* button, speaking into the intercom with an authority only Cerina could ever truly master.

"Attention, scumbags," he spat. "We are currently in possession of a bomb, taken from one of your stupid explosive escape deterrents. Yeah, that's right. My friend Lizabeth is holding a land mine. And if you don't let us go right now, I'll set it off and blow this shithole sky-high. Got it?"

He held the walkie-talkie high over his head and brought it to the ground, smashing it with his worn-down heel. Pieces flew everywhere, and the crowd of prisoners looked at us in confusion. They could see us, then, but they couldn't hear our words. That was probably for the best. It meant there were probably no microphones close enough to pick up our speech.

The door flew open, and in stomped a red-faced Commander Abbotsford.

"What do you idiotic kids think you're pulling? That's the oldest trick in the book. No one's going to buy into your little prank. Now hand me the walkie talkie."

Emry picked up the pieces, depositing them into a neat little pile. "Here you are, commander." He topped it off with a mock salute.

The commander looked at the pile, then back at Emry. "You're too dense to be a Level Three. But maybe you're cruel enough." The commander seized Emry by the collar of his uniform, cutting off his airway. He picked up his own walkie-talkie and held his finger over the *all* button. "Begin the-"

Something inside me burst. Seeing the commander's carefree chokehold set off a cannon of rage, aimed for my skull and weighed down by the pressure of a million people who deserved my anger. I lunged at the commander, knocking the device from his hand.

"We still have another call to make." I raised his device, smashing the *all* button. "Fuck the government. Emry and Lizabeth out."

The commander let go of Emry, diving for his walkie-talkie. I tossed it back to Emry, who repeated his swift stroke, bashing the electronic to minuscule shards.

"You *fools*," the commander snarled. His temper hadn't quite flared yet, though. He stepped inside the room, shutting the door behind him. "You have a rebellious nature. That's good. But the first thing you'll learn is that lashing out gets you nowhere. You two are partners in crime, yes? Let's see how you do when one of you gets thrown in with the reporters."

He glanced between us, his eyes settling on my lean frame. "How about you? You're not meaty enough to get fed to the wolves, so you'll get thrown in with the slaughter instead. It's only the way of the world. You can test your friend here. Sound like a plan?"

I backed up, slamming into the wall. The questions he was asking clearly weren't ones I was allowed to answer. He looked at my cuffs, grabbing me by my bound wrists. "How shall we get you in here? It shouldn't be too hard, should it?"

Emry dove to stop him, but the commander kicked him hard in the ribs, sending him flying across the room. He clattered into the shelf of burning tools, and the numbered rods tumbled onto his head, singing his red hair. What was at first a tiny spark quickly caught fire, spreading over his long locks. The flames burned up at an alarming rate, and he screamed, swatting at the fire.

The commander stopped, his focus pulled away by Emry's burning scalp.

When the last of his hair strands were smothered, Emry's formerly shoulder-length head of hair was nothing more than a ragged swash that ended at his ears. He ran his fingers through it, and, shockingly, he started to laugh. A bright red burn was on his cheek, flooded by tears of hysteria.

"I've always hated this stupid hair!" He wheezed between giggles, coughing and chortling in disbelief. "But now, look at me! I got a free trip to the fucking salon!"

I didn't know if I should have been amused or concerned that Emry cared about his hair at a time when I, along with a bunch of others, was about to get brutally murdered.

The commander didn't know what to say, tightening my handcuffs as Emry collapsed to the floor, full-on belly-laughing in a wild mess of the fallen rods and his burned arms.

Just as Emry was coming to his senses, the commander shoved me through the door.

A wall of people obscured my vision. There were hands everywhere, my torso stuck between the narrow opening. I couldn't breathe, suffocating in the throng. An icy hand seized my lungs, squeezing all the air from them. My mouth opened to scream, but the dark spots swimming in my vision were the only answers to my shouts.

The prisoners on the other end were pushing me back. My arms flailed around, wrestling with air and an immobile might. The commander shoved me forward, jamming against the flood of a million hands pulling at my limbs, my face, my battered uniform. They were playing a great game of tug-of-war, and I was the rope.

My eyelids sagged. I was about to drop into unconsciousness, dangling at the edge of a precipice, when a cold breath of air seeped into my lungs. I clung to it, pushing above the crowd. It was like quicksand, pulling me deeper and deeper. Now, my airways were open, and I could shout to my heart's content.

I screamed and screamed. I couldn't tell whose shouts were mine and whose belonged to the prisoners, to Emry. I was blind, deaf. I felt my legs jam against the door. I was almost all the way through, with nowhere to go and no room to fight.

With one last breath, before I plunged beneath the waves, I gave in. My arms and legs went slack, pulled and pushed in each direction. The bottoms of my shoes hooked on the base of the hole, working as my last defence. Blood rushed to my head, and I shut my eyes. My toes were pulled up and pushed, at last, through the opening.

In pure defeat, the arms around me released. I dropped to the ground, stomach first. Winded, I pushed myself up. The prisoners had put a great distance between them and myself, leaving me a huge room to get up. I rubbed my eyes. Why, only now, was I just starting to realise how tired I was?

My head turned over to the glass. On the other end of it, a silent movie was playing, starring Emry McLeod. He pounded his fist against the glass, screaming his throat raw. But, of course, I couldn't hear a thing. Tears streamed down his cheeks.

The commander lifted up one of the sticks. I pressed my fist to the glass, letting it unfurl into my empty, useless palm. The small door was closed.

Emry winced, cringing back from the commander. The end of the metal stick was pressed against the bare flesh of his right shoulder, going directly below the 1. The torn sleeve of his uniform was ringed with blood, the fresh burn steaming. My cheeks were hot, wet, and sticky. I was crying too.

All of a sudden, a hand touched me on the shoulder. I looked behind me, and my heart almost stopped. Standing right there was none other than… Mel.

My former girlfriend, here, with the reporters, in a Level One uniform.

"Lizabeth," she spoke, her soft voice as gentle as I had remembered it. Without a second thought, I flung my arms out, wrapping them around her and burying my face in her chest.

"Mel…" I sobbed, "how…." The moment before she spoke seemed to stretch for an eternity. Maybe the not-knowing was better. Maybe I didn't-

"I got caught. When we were separated, the cops saw me leave… I was taken here, but my boat got delayed. I got captured by the reporters the second I arrived. Oh, Lizabeth-"

I clutched her tighter. It had all been for nothing. The rift between me and Jakson, my place with the Escape Artists. This. *All* of *this*.

She bent down, and I pressed my lips to her ear.

"How… how could you?"

Jakson Veer

Escape Artists

Arvin and I were almost barrelled into by Farrah, sprinting and speaking into a device at the same time.

"...we'll do the same for you." As she drew closer, I noticed that the shape in her hand was a walkie-talkie. She lifted her finger off the button, shoving the device into her cast.

"Jakson!" She cried, shouting even though I was right in front of her. "Lizabeth and Emry are in the centre circle. I don't know all the details, but something terrible is about to happen."

I broke away from her. "What do we do?"

"You'll think I'm insane when I tell you this, but we have to cut the comms. We have to start the escape plan."

"You are insane."

"I know. With that out of the way, I'm going to get Haven. The escape is back on, and you're climbing the wall." She went over a plan in rapid detail, my thoughts racing a mile a minute to keep up.

Without waiting for my confirmation, she started to speed off, but I caught her by the shoulder. "I can't climb that thing! We don't have a rope, let alone a good climber!"

"Wrong," she said, "we do have a rope. It's in building 1-1."

My memory flipped to the string of uniforms that had bound their captives. The 1-1s weren't very happy with us, but they were all surrounding building 1-3. Their building was empty.

"I stand by my previous statement about your insanity," I said, "but you're also a genius."

Leaving Arvin to choose his own path, I made for building 1-1.

I was in and out in a flash. There were still a few stragglers, but they comprised the undetermined population, who would rather bum around on their bunks than stay mad at anyone.

Retrieving the rope, which was bunched up in the corner of the room, I dashed off to the centre field, running as fast as my legs could take me. On the way, I tested the strength of the fabric. I wasn't sure if it would hold. Dread twisted in my gut as firmly as the knots in the rope.

The guards at the front had yet to be replaced. I didn't let that fact deceive me, though. Behind the plastic curtains covering the gate, I could see the ghostly images of dancing silhouettes.

They weren't watching me, but they were definitely listening.

I snuck a glance over my shoulder. Far behind, I caught a glimpse of Haven, Amélie, and Farrah running up to meet me. There was no room for relief. I couldn't wait for them.

I thought back to all the phys-ed classes I had rushed through, devoting my life to academics to prove… what, exactly? That I was worth a place in this world? Now, at the bottom of this wall, my dreams of success seemed ridiculous.

I reached into my pocket. The only weighty object I had in there was my meal card. Hastily, I tied it to the end of the rope, bunching it up in my hand. I wound up my throw. I stepped back, getting a good angle. An angle. This was nothing more than math with high stakes attached. And if there was anything I knew I was good at, it was math.

Adrenaline surged through me. I had one shot, and I couldn't afford to miss it.

Setting my mind on my target, I aimed, and I threw.

The rope of clothes made an arc across the painted sky, falling against the setting sun. My breath caught in my throat. I clenched my hands into fists, crossing my fingers. I had never believed in luck, but if there was any time I needed it, it was now.

A sigh of satisfaction heaved against my chest. The bundle sailed over the thick knot of barbed wire, wrapping once, twice, around the small metal pole of the antenna. The knot slid down, catching in the tangle of wire, which only reinforced its grip. I pulled my hand up, looking at my crisscrossed fingers.

I ran to the wall and ripped off my shoes, using my bare feet to push myself up. I used the top of the uniform washing station as a platform, clasping the rope with both hands and moving up the first section of tied fabric. Sticky with sweat, my toes had a great deal of grip, and the unstable knots provided excellent handholds. I was just above halfway when the four people arrived. I didn't stop, barely paying them a second thought.

Looking down, I met Haven's eyes. I had many questions, but I couldn't afford to ask a single one. If the guards turned, emerging from their concealed posts, we were done for.

"Adrienne and Max are inviting people to the performance," Amélie said casually, in a way that would appear to anyone else as nothing more than the tone of an average person reporting on current events.

The performance? They were pushing the talent show to *tonight*? There wasn't much time left before light's out. Would we even get the chance to?

Panting and breathless, I reached the top of the enormous wall. Well, I had *almost* reached the top of the enormous wall. There was... a slight roadblock.

Right over my head was the knot of barbed wire. The rope had slipped, hanging by a thread ensnared in the tangle. What was more, I couldn't very well swing myself over. The barbs were sharp as knives, and they were everywhere.

I scanned for a path through the hopeless minefield of sharp edges. There was none.

In the silence, I could hear the threads above me snapping. The rope sagged, and I came close to losing my balance completely.

Biting my lip, I plunged my hand into the thorn-covered knot. The wire tore at my skin, digging in deep. My fingers, stained crimson, twined around the base of the antenna. I had it.

Killing off any shed of the triumph that had begun to blossom, the rest of the rope snapped off, tumbling to the ground. I forced myself not to look down, putting all my ebbing strength into my right hand, the one thing holding me upright. I stole a peek at the ground below. My stomach plummeted. The fall had to be at least 20 feet. Unless I somehow mastered the ability to land like Lizabeth, there was no way I'd make it without serious injury.

I looked back to the antenna. My second arm flew over the wire. I winced with pain as I brought it over the scratchy barbs, wrapping my hand around the base of the thin metal outcropping. The very thing I was supposed to destroy was the very thing keeping me from plummeting to the ground.

I only had one option- to climb over the barbed wire. The metal roof upon which it rested extended a while past it, giving me a suitable enough platform if I could get to it. I had to be smart about this. I slid my hands further up the antenna, swaying dangerously. My angle wasn't terrible. I could do this. I could do this, and if I died trying, well, there were worse ways to go out.

The cold night wind whistled in my ears as I swung a leg up, balancing in the thin gap between the barbs. Teetering on one foot, I hoisted the other leg over, easing out of my crouch. I was standing on top of a hallway.

Using the antenna for balance, I hopped to the centre, collecting myself. My breaths came in jagged puffs, riddled with disbelief.

Now on two feet, I turned my attention to the blinking white light on the top of the antenna. My foot was raised to stomp it to dust, but something stopped me. I furrowed my brows. It would put the enemy at an advantage, but the makings of a plan were slowly clicking into place. For what I was about to do, I needed a comm link.

Instead, my attention shifted to the trapdoor next to the antenna. If this was a maintenance ladder, it probably led into a maintenance closet.

Which meant I was right above the breaker box.

The square door was controlled by a big wheel, painted bright red with jagged indentations. My arms were noodles, but I still managed to twist it open.

It cracked open with a satisfying snap. I kicked it up, and a shaft of white light streamed through. Sure enough, there was a ladder below. I shimmied down with no time to lose.

This hallway was moist and musty-smelling. I climbed down, leaving the trapdoor open above me. The only light came from an eerie red bulb on the ceiling, surrounded by metal wiring.

It was as though everything was behind bars in this place.

A clunky furnace chugged next to a hot water tank. On top of the cylinder was a sticker with the check-up schedule, noting that the tank was long overdue for maintenance.

Next to the heating system was the slot for meals. Cans of soup were stacked along the wall in a neat mechanical assembly line. The tangled wiring of the meal card scanner stood beside it. Like the Isle itself, it looked a lot more polished off from the outside.

The wiring led to nothing other than the breaker box. I ran to it, my hopes dropping as I scanned the exterior. Of course. It was locked.

I hiked up the sleeves of my uniform. It was hot in here, and time was not on my side.

Something, just then, occurred to me. There was a person who was supposed to be operating this room. And they had to be around somewhere.

I grabbed a can of soup off the wall, using it as a doorstop as I slipped out of the room. The hallway opened up, a barren stretch of beige tiling, flickering lights, and white walls. A sign hung above the door, reading *boiler room*.

Next to it was a washroom.

I pulled the door open to the men's side, stepping inside. Two urinals and one stall lined the wall, with a sink and a dryer in the corner. There were more flies than people buzzing around the empty room. The realisation sank in that unlocking the breaker box wasn't an option.

I had to destroy it and somehow avoid getting electrocuted in the process.

The first place I looked was the cabinet under the sink. There were a few spare rolls of toilet paper, a tissue box, and wet wipes lining the bottom of it. I was about to abandon hope completely when my hand found something tucked in the corner.

Triumphantly, I pulled a wrench out of the compartment. It was a small thing, most likely used to repair the pipes. But it would do the trick. It would have to.

"Ey, kid? Whaddya think you're doing?"

A gruff voice froze my speeding pulse. I looked up with my lips pressed into a sheepish line, the wrench still in my hand. The man standing over me was a giant. He had a big red beard, strong meaty arms that could probably knock my head off with a single swipe, and, at his waist... a ring of keys.

I had time to take two deep breaths before I struck, hard and fast like a viper. In those two deep breaths, I leeched all the tranquillity from the room, succumbing to the very essence of the raspberry air freshener situated in the corner. I harnessed the calm rooted in all the terror, letting it surround me for a few brief seconds.

Then I tucked it all away and ran.

Snagging the loop of keys, I bolted down the hall, slamming the bathroom door behind me. My doorstop hadn't moved. I flew into the boiler room, kicking the can of soup free just as the guy from the bathroom came to his senses, figuring out what had hit him. He came careening down the hallway, beating his huge fists against the door.

His attempts were in vain. Without his keys and security card, he was trapped outside.

And I was trapped in.

I fumbled through the keychain, trying the lock. The first key was too big, and the second didn't fit. But the third slipped in with a satisfying click. I ripped the box open, fingering the wires. There it was, the master switch.

The light above blinked out. The clunky furnace came to a halt. With giddy energy, I pushed open the flap that the meals came from, letting loose a flood of soup containers.

On the other side, Farrah was still watching the roof.

The moment she saw me, all the worry melted from her face.

Haven cheered. "Jakson! You did it! You actually did it!"

"Climb in," I instructed. "Now. We're running tight on time."

Amélie scoffed. "You can't be serious. There's no way *I* can fit in *there*."

Farrah cleared her throat awkwardly. "I could. I wouldn't want to risk the drop, but I'd fit." Farrah's brittle bones bulged against her shoulders, and I pushed down a gulp.

"Are you sure there isn't another option?" Amélie said, voicing my similar concerns.

"I don't think there is," I admitted. "Farrah. Are you sure about this?"

She nodded, placing a tentative hand on the hatch. "Yes. I've got it."

I held my arms out, propping the shaft open as Farrah stuck her head in. The blood rushed to Farrah's face as I eased her in, slowly but surely steadying her as she balanced precariously on the ledge between the walls.

She thudded to the ground, getting up with a slight wobble on her feet.

"See?" She said, a quiver in her voice, "that wasn't so bad? What next?"

The beefy guy punched the door, shaking the entire building. Farrah flinched, and dread pooled in a murky sludge at the bottom of my stomach.

"We deal with that guy."

***

"Okay," Farrah recapped. "Your plan… is to use me as bait, then bean the tough guy on the head with the wrench?"

"Yes."

"That seems like…."

"A terrible idea? I'm fully aware."

"I wasn't going to critique your reasoning. It's not like we have a better option. It's just, you know, the whole being-used-as-bait thing-"

"I can be the bait."

"Are you sure?"

"Yeah. Why not? I'm the one he's angry with." I handed Farrah the wrench, and she weighed it in her palm.

Farrah set her hand on the doorknob, clutching the metal tool. "Are you ready?"

"Not in the slightest."

"Same here."

Leaving me on that reassuring note, Farrah pulled the door open with one swift tug. The man's eyes locked with mine, and his wide hair-lined nostrils flared with a spastic rage. He stalked forward, his broad-shouldered shape seeming to grow.

"I'm gonna get those keys back-"

Farrah jumped up, bashing the guy's head with the sharp, silvery wrench. The man yelped in surprise, flinging me onto my back. Farrah's stroke fell hard, but it wasn't enough to knock him out. The man picked me up by the collar of my uniform, pressing me against the wall.

"Give me those keys back, you little shit." His grip tightened, but as he scrunched his eyebrows, a brief realisation caused his hand to go slack. "Wait a second… you're a prisoner. Oh. *Oh!* This got interesting." He grabbed my hand, wrenching the keyring out of it. "This just got very interesting indeed-"

The man's head connected with mine, shoved forwards. As his colossal form slunk to the ground, I lunged out of the way. Dizzily, I got back up, massaging the spot where the giant bone in his nose had smashed against my forehead.

Farrah stood over the unconscious body, the corners of her mouth turned down in a reaction that was part surprise, part horror, part victory. The wrench was in her hand.

"Thanks," I said. "Next time, though, don't give *me* a giant bruise."

Farrah gave me a slight smile, allowing a bit of blush to creep into her cheeks. "Come on… let's go save a shitload of people."

"Now *that's* a plan I can get behind."

Emry McLeod

Why we celebrate

Everything hurt. My arm, with a fresh 3 stamped onto it. My face, which felt like it was still on fire. My eyes, from crying over someone I had been so bold as to call my friend.

I didn't want to die, but then and there, I was starting to sense that death was the only outcome my future had on the horizon.

When we plunged into darkness, I thought the world had ended. In the dark, punches could come from anywhere. Shadows could come alive and mess with your head, and forces entirely out of your control could move you like a puppet. But when I found my instincts driving me to kick Commander Abbotsford's kneecaps in... I realised that maybe the darkness had a few advantages.

We both shouted. His cry declared war, while mine came from a mixture of shock and terror. Somehow, though, I caught my arm reaching for his pistol. Somehow, my fingers got a hold of it. And *somehow*, despite everything... the fear helped me.

I dove, jamming the barrel into the back of the commander's neck. He froze. We were in pitch darkness, but the shadows still had texture. I could see the shape of his hands in the air.

"Don't do that," he said. "You *really* don't want to do that."

"Name one reason why." I switched the gun to my left hand, scanning the wall with my right-hand fingertips. I felt the shape of the door popping it open. The prisoners on the other side clasped it eagerly, surging through the opening.

On my unsteady feet, the commander swung at me. I flailed my arms, toppling onto my back. I felt the cold metal of the pistol against my chin, cutting off my airway. I choked, struggling to draw in a wheezy breath.

"One reason? Here are three," the commander found my hand, squeezing my fingers. "One-" he snapped my pinky. I screamed, a shrill wail, the sound distorted by the lack of air. My head hurt, and it wasn't just because I had lost my glasses. The commander laughed, his chest heaving giddily. "Two!" the bone of my ring finger broke like a twig, crumbling backwards. I shrieked, but the pistol dug in harder, cutting off my oxygen supply. I kicked my legs, but they found no target apart from empty air.

"I won't kill you," the commander giggled, his voice shrill, filled with maniacal energy, "I'm just teaching you. Are you ready for your final lesson?"

With a smack, the tension on the pistol dropped. I sucked in a breath, drinking it in. Sweet, sweet air.

"Three," Lizabeth snarled, standing above the commander's slack figure. She tore open the main door to the Viewing Cell, a faint shaft of natural light flooding through. Her fist was outstretched, and blood dripped from her knuckles.

"Come on, everyone! We have to get out of here."

The prisoners flooded out one by one, shoving through the slot and jumping to their feet. I didn't see any of their faces, but I could sense a mutual emotion spreading over us like a wildfire. These people weren't innocent. Some were reported for good reason, and others had taken random inmates out of desperation. Nobody here was a good person, but we were all enslaved by the same thing.

The girl Lizabeth had briefly reunited with on the other side of the glass clung to her arm, leading the front of the crowd. I ran up to them, breathless. I didn't know where the walls began, much less where they curved. We had just moved into another cage.

"What do we do?" I followed Lizabeth down the only available route- further down the hall. The pistol was in my hand, but it was useless to me. Even if I could somehow bring myself to use it, my aim was utter garbage. Add in the darkness, and I was a bigger danger to myself than to anyone in my path.

"Does anyone here know how to shoot?" I asked. I didn't love the idea of handing the gun to one of these people, but we were out of options.

"I do," said Lizabeth's girlfriend. I hadn't gotten a good look at her before the lights went out, but I had remembered a streak of pink hair and a double set of silver earrings. Everything about her screamed 'cool.' It only made sense that she'd know how to shoot a pistol.

A bit reluctantly, I handed her the gun.

"How did you learn, Mel?" Lizabeth asked, her tone numb.

Mel. So *that* was her name.

"My sister taught me. I could show you sometime."

I felt the path turn. Lights blinked on in the distance. A shout of alarm rang out, and all of us froze. The guards had come.

"Focus all priorities on defending the House! His Honour is inside!" One of the guards barked an order, and the others nodded, scampering off to some unknown location. The guard turned to us, a flashlight at his hip. "Commander Abbotsford-"

Mel rushed up to the guard, pointing the gun at his head.

"You…" the guard trailed off, taking his hands off his rifle. "You aren't the commander."

Two more figures rounded the corner. I prepared for the worst, shielding my face. But the two people weren't guards. One of them grabbed the guard's flashlight, and the other took his gun.

Holding the flashlight was Farrah, with Jakson at her side.

"Let's find a door," Jakson said, not even bothering with a catch-up, "we've got to run. The roof isn't an option anymore- the next hallway is crawling with guards."

"Okay," Lizabeth said, picking up her feet. "If we get out of here, we'll find ourselves by the mansion. From there, we'll have to run like hell."

Jakson paced along the length of the wall, locating a door handle. He placed his hand on it while Mel continued to threaten the guard with her weapon.

"Line up behind me," Jakson instructed. "We have to do this carefully. Is everyone ready?"

"Yes," everyone around me chanted, our collective whispers blending into one loud shout. Under my breath, I muttered a different sentiment.

Are you ready? What a dumb question. Whoever said yes was a liar, but if you opposed the popular opinion, you were a chicken. "Of course not," I whispered. "But the thing is, none of us have ever had much choice in the matter."

Before I could continue with my complaints, I came to a realisation. People weren't saying 'yes' because of their pride. They were saying 'yes' because it was better to pretend than to cower in fear and await your demise.

At least if you were confident, you stood a chance.

Jakson held the door open, hitting us with a rush of night air. As we broke into the circle, cries of alarm rose up, both from our side and theirs.

Every guard was positioned around the sprawling house, a gun pointed at each of us. A collective gulp came from each of the prisoners, myself included.

Three seconds of silence passed as our gazes drifted between each other. Jakson was the one to break it.

"Run!"

No one had to be told twice. Bolting for their lives, the prisoners darted for the gate. A beat later, the guards caught on, and the terrace turned into a battlefield. I stood in place, unable to think as gunshots lit up the night. My ears rang, and the scene blurred. I couldn't tell who was a corpse and who was still running.

"Emry!" Jakson screamed, keeping the door open for the last few stragglers. "What are you doing? You're going to get shot!"

"So are you! Why aren't you moving?!"

"I have something else to do!" Something popped up in my field of vision. Sprinting across the bloodsoaked tiles was a singular figure dashing *toward* the fight. Their brow was lined with a sheen of sweat, and in the glimmering scrap of ebbing sunlight, the fading black streak in their blond hair waved behind them like a flag.

Barrelling towards us was none other than Haven Megany.

"Jakson!" Haven exclaimed, "Let's go! Did you find it?"

Jakson nodded. "Get back, Emry, now, while you still have a chance! We're going to find the records. Go!"

I put a hand on Jakson's shoulder. I had envied him, distrusted him. Same thing with Haven, perhaps even more so. But now, I was sickeningly worried about them both.

"Shit," I said, "please bo okay."

"We'll bloody well try to be," Haven said. "The same goes for you."

I nodded once and bolted into the fray.

Bullets whizzed past my ears, but there were too many targets for a solid mark to be made, and the group was running fast. The guards, I noticed, weren't shooting to kill us. They were shooting to threaten, to drive us away. These were the people like the woman outside, who'd wished for her own death more than anything. Although it ran thin, these people still had regained some shreds of common decency.

Even still, some hadn't managed to escape the firing. I could count at least three corpses lining the pavement, one of which I almost tripped on.

Morally, it could be called selfish to wish that my own friends made it out. After all, who has the right to decide whose life has more value? But as I sprinted, I crossed my fingers and prayed like hell, even though I had never really believed in a higher power. The whole island could implode for all I cared, as long as Lizabeth, Cerina, Jakson, and all the others made it out okay.

I ran the final stretch with the last of my energy, breaking into the field. A massive crowd, composed not only of the newly-escaped reporters, but of what looked like half of the Isle's population, had gathered around the open space. They were assembled into a large circle on the Level One side. Some were sitting down, and others were standing on their tiptoes on the fringes of the crowd.

Seemingly oblivious to us and deaf to the gunfire that lit up the night, their eyes were directed to the middle. The dots between the crowd, the guards, and the focus of attention connected. The prisoners were an audience.

In the centre of the ring stood Adrienne, Max, and a kid juggling bundles of socks. The talent show had begun.

"Emry!" Amélie caught me by the arm, pulling me away from the crowd. "We have to trigger the land mines! Jakson, Farrah, and Haven are getting the records. The escape plan is a go. Where is Lizabeth?"

Where *was* Lizabeth?

Amélie and I looked at each other, searching the giant crowd. But it was impossible to pick out a single person in those numbers. Adrienne had truly outdone herself.

"What happened in there?" Amélie asked, worry creeping into her tone.

"I-"

The awful thoughts racing through my mind were interrupted by a voice at my side. Lizabeth and Mel rushed towards us, gasping for air.

"Lizabeth!" I cried, impulse tugging me in her direction.

Without even thinking, I was hugging her.

I pulled back all of a sudden, embarrassed. "Sorry-" I said, my face turning tomato-red. "I just-"

I didn't have time to finish that sentence before Lizabeth was hugging me back.

"Thank you," I whispered, digging my fingers into her uniform. "Thank you so much."

Lizabeth pulled back, giving me a pat on the head.

"You did well, Emry. Nice job."

Amélie cleared her throat. "I need you guys to come with me. When Adrienne finishes her routine... We have to blow up a beach."

Roarous applause exploded from the crowd like multi-coloured fireworks. The juggling kid had just finished their routine.

Adrienne took the stage, peering up over the sea of people to catch Amélie's eye. Amélie stuck her hand up, giving Adrienne a thumbs up across the giant assembly of people.

"Excellent, excellent! And for our next performance...." Adrienne didn't have a mic, but she didn't need one. There were probably two hundred people, if not more, standing and watching her. But each of them was held by her voice, listening carefully to the show. They were all here by choice. And they were enjoying it. I saw different burns on different shoulders, 1s and 2s gathered together.

We were standing with murderers, but we were having a good time.

"Give it up for Savannah from the Level Two sector, here to show us a… modified baton twirling routine. Judges? Do you have the baton?"

The singular judge, Max, produced a stick. It was no metal baton, but it sufficed.

This was exactly like the talent shows at my school, right down to the types of acts and the nervous smiles of the people performing them. Only, this was the last place I would've expected to find that awkward charm.

Baton girl held up the stick. "I confess," she said, "I'm a little rusty after two months on the Isle. I didn't get any notice about this beforehand… but I hope you all enjoy it! I've heard this show is a little tradition, and I'll be sure to do it justice!"

The crowd gave her a round of applause. Before their clapping had died down, she started twirling, using their applause as music. I caught Mel smiling.

It seemed unfair to celebrate at a time like this when minutes ago, I had stumbled through a torrent of gunfire. But I supposed, in the thick of everything, that those moments were *why* we celebrated.

Because they were worth more than our sorrow.

"I'll be back soon," Amélie said in a hushed whisper, keeping her voice down. "I have to sort the details out with Max. There are three more acts before Adrienne closes us off. Until then- enjoy the show. It might be the last time you get to."

With that, her red hair bobbed away.

I glanced at Lizabeth and Mel, shifting uncomfortably on my feet. There was obvious tension between them, but their hands were locked together.

I moved forward, burying myself in the crowd and allowing the intoxicating crush of bodies to pull the air from my lungs. In this sea, it was almost as though I could withdraw myself forever.

Which was just as well. I was here to enjoy the show, after all.

Cerina Rayz

Diplomacy

I had made one single tweak to the midnight-blue silk gown the guards had handed me. It wasn't even that much of a difference, but I found comfort in its instalment. The only other person who would notice it was my father, but hopefully, it would be enough to send him a message.

At the waist of the dress, a black belt of fabric wrapped snugly around the centre, tying off at the side in an elaborate bow. I hated the frilly embroidery, but I had to work with what I was given. I worked my silver chain bracelet into the bow, weaving it through the fabric. It looked like a silvery flowerhead bursting out of black plumes. Not exactly the look that I was going for, but it would do.

The pocket knife was long gone, but my father was sure to recognise the chain he had attached to it.

Below the waist, the fabric sprawled out, layers of silk cascading in a waterfall of threads. I had to admit, the dress was beautiful.

I ran my finger over the smooth metallic rings. Why? Why was it worth it? Maybe my father wanted the leader of building 2-7 to be his successor, but he had pushed me to my breaking point, and I was a leader no more.

One winter, when I was considerably younger, my mother took my brother and me up north to the mountains for a family vacation. Since trips away from Sykona were expensive and complicated, it was one of our only family outings. We had aimed to spend most of our time skiing, but our time on the hill lasted only two hours.

My mother insisted that, since I was a beginner, I start out on the smallest hill. It was a joke, really, to call it anything larger than an insignificant pile. Compared to the towering mounds that disappeared far into the clouds behind it, it was nothing more than a blip on the horizon.

The ages of its users ran, for the most part, from five to six years old. I was twelve.

My brother had scoffed at me, proceeding to travel up the chairlift with my mother, who insisted I stay back and meet them when they were done. I had a cellphone to text them with, but it was virtually useless since my data plan had been cancelled two months prior.

After I had watched them leave, I had gone down the bunny hill once before deciding I'd had enough. I had picked up my feet and skied over to the chair lift, ascending the mountain with nothing but the wind in my hair and a pair of ill-fitting rental skis.

I had dismounted the chair with ease, surveying the different runs that snaked past both sides of the hill. The brown chalet was so far below I could barely see it. It was merely a speck behind the fog-shrouded mountains below, the frozen-over rivers painting icy lines over the silver horizon.

I felt no fear on top of that hill. It was as though I owned the entire mountain. But the thing I had yet to learn was that once you were on top, it was impossible to stay there.

My skis had slipped on a thin sheet of ice, choosing a route for me. I tried desperately to swerve as I careened towards the black diamond, skidding down a hill so steep you could simply roll down at lightning speed. In the distance, mounds of snow were piled up in front of me. Later I would learn that they were called moguls. But for the moment, the only thing I could refer to them as were enemies.

Just as I hit the first one, I gave up. The only thing I could do was watch my skis drag me onward, bracing myself as they curved up the jump in an abrupt jolt.

They flew off the first pile in a sharp arc. I landed at an angle, if you could be so brash as to call it 'a landing'. My feet smacked down with a sharp thud that sent a tremor up my ribcage, threatening to snap every bone inside. I didn't even have time to register the impact before I was up to the next one.

This time, my feet were pointed to the side. I shot like a bullet, colliding with the wall of sharp snowflakes below. My tailbone connected with the top of the next obstacle, a white-hot burst of pain flooding up my spine. But it didn't stop there. I tumbled, face-first, onto the next stretch of hill. My helmet slid up my forehead, the strap briefly cutting off my airway as it slid up my chin.

My elbows splayed out to stop my fall, embedding themselves into the surface of the tall, menacing bump.

My weight shifted helplessly, but I didn't fall again. I dangled there, suspended in time for a good fifteen minutes, with my elbows holding me up like ice picks. My arms were on fire, and all my muscles were so shell-shocked that I was in a temporary state of complete paralysis. It felt like every bone in my body had snapped.

It was then that my skis decided to pop off my boots, sliding down the rest of the hill until they reached the bottom, eventually finding their way to a member of the first-aid patrol.

My mother had used a deceitful web of false identifications to get me into the nearest hospital. When my report came back, it showed two broken elbows, a sprained ankle, and a minor concussion.

From that point forward, I had never skied again, but I had never stopped being brave.

"Have you changed?" The guard behind me asked, losing patience.

"Yes," I said, "you can turn around." Now, I felt like I was on that ski hill once more. Only this time, my wounds wouldn't heal. I could only stand there as my skis, like balls and chains clamped to my ankles, dragged me to wherever I would face my undoing.

I could continue, but I didn't know what I was continuing *for*.

The guards looked at me, nodding their approval. "I almost forgot," the guard with the backpack said, "he gave us footwear, as well."

I slipped a velvety pair of uncomfortable heels over my bare feet, sliding down from my bunk. I teetered, swaying like a poorly-built skyscraper. A black ribbon fastened the shoes to my ankles, and the wobbly things were like stilts.

It seemed utterly ridiculous for me to be decked out in fine apparel, regaining my balance on absurd heels next to my former friend's cooling corpse.

Once I was on my feet, the guards swung the door open. As I had predicted, a sea of uniformed people crowded the building. They straightened up when they saw us, parting for me.

I wobbled my way down the steps, covering it up as smoothly as possible. Once my feet were on the cobblestone, we stopped.

"Where's Commander Abbotsford?" The guard behind me asked, frowning slightly.

"He went to take two Level Threes to the centre. Our orders remain the same."

The two guards behind me nodded. "Understood."

I was prodded in the back, sticking out my toe to avert a guaranteed faceplant. My foot felt like it was being constricted, and I could almost feel the bones grinding against each other. "Well, Rayz? Get moving."

The walk from building 2-7 to the centre circle took an eternity. The air outside had cooled considerably, but that didn't stop sweat from collecting on my brow. I looked ragged, and my now-muddy shoes did nothing to conceal it.

If my father was trying to teach me some stupid lesson, it wasn't working. Unless he was simply trying to piss me off. In which case, it was *definitely* working.

The guards, as well, were rapidly losing their temper.

"Pick up the pace, Rayz. We don't have all day."

"Oh? How about *you* try walking in these things."

One of the guards sighed. "You can take the shoes off for now. Just ensure they're back on before we reach the centre circle."

Eagerly, I tore the dastardly things from my feet.

Once we reached the gate, the guards at the front, who were all in a scramble, rushed to meet us. I was glared at, scowled at, shouted at. One of them even had the nerve to spit in my face. I kept walking through the plastic screen, ignoring every one of them.

But I remembered their features. I would hold a grudge, not of my own will, but inherently. I could understand why they hated me, though. They had been put through hell and back just to qualify as guards, and here I was, my father's heir by nothing more than birthright.

They all wanted their hands on presidential power. And I was getting it freely, even though it was the last thing I wanted.

It was unfair, this life.

The last of the plastic curtains fell away, leaving me to behold the mansion. I was led towards it, keeping my head high. At the base of the steps, I slid the shoes back on, climbing the steps with as much grace as I could muster.

Every guard on the Isle, just about, had filled the central circle. I felt every last one of their stares.

A man dressed in a white shirt with a black tie opened the door for me. He didn't carry a weapon, so I could only assume he was some sort of assistant. On the knot of his tie was an emblem with the family seal, an *R* surrounded by sparks.

Was he, too, a Level Three? Probably.

Taking a deep breath, I stepped into the mansion.

A carpet of deep red was laid over the dark wood floor, curving through the house. I passed by portraits and golden wallpaper, table lamps and a room with an old piano. This house belonged in a museum, not an island. It had an ancient quality, and the old-fashioned walls appeared as though they would crumble if someone hit them too hard.

A few lucky guards milled about, walking alongside me or darting to and from the kitchens, bringing in meals on trays. I crossed the final door frame, and the walls opened to a massive dining hall.

The long table was covered in a white cloth, which spilt over the edges. In the centre of it was a candle holder, where three flames kept the piece alight. I had to squint in the darkness. A few oil lamps were positioned on little side tables in the corners, but the lighting was dim.

It was weird to imagine my father spending any hour of his day in a building without electricity. I thought back to our mansion and its sprawling stairwells and gilt balconies.

Maybe he had always been classy.

"Take a seat." My father, wearing a sharp suit, was positioned at the head of the table. He looked as though he hadn't aged a day. His hair, perhaps, was a little scruffier, but apart from a chin of stubble that was a few days due for a shave, he looked exactly the same. My breath caught in my throat. I collected myself, surveying the room. I wouldn't let myself be daunted. Not here, not now.

At my father's right was Jezmon Tylor, whose lips were downturned in a disapproving frown. The table was long, with space for almost fifteen guests, but only three other chairs were set out.

The first was on my father's left, where he gestured for me to sit. The other one stood beside Jezmon, and the third was next to mine.

Awkwardly, I smoothed down the dress and took a seat amidst the billowy fabric. I inched my chair away from my father's, fidgeting with the fork and spoon that had been set out.

Not even a butter knife, I noticed. Such a precaution was probably wise.

"Sir," Jezmon spoke, shooting me a patronising side-glance, "where are the other two?"

My father smoothed out the table cloth, pausing a moment before he spoke. It was funny. Through the distortion of the earpiece, I hardly remembered what his actual voice sounded like.

"The commander has just returned to the centre circle, so I've heard. He has the right to go where he pleases, but if he abuses that right, I suppose we will have to start without him. He is in high esteem within these walls, but not high enough esteem to be waited on."

I brought up the courage to voice my concerns, my worry for the others overpowering my fear.

"Why did you bring me here?" I asked, interrupting my father. Jezmon gawked at my lack of courtesy.

"Cerina," my father said calmly, "you were *not* given permission to speak."

Just then, I spotted the steak knife mixed in with his utensils.

"If I can't speak," I stated plainly, "why have me around at all?"

"You're here to *listen*. You can speak later."

His fury was quelled by our next guest. Coming down the hall in street clothes was a sight that made me stop breathing for a second, tightening my fist.

Taking the seat next to me was my mother.

Her outfit did not fit the occasion. Unlike my father, lines of age were wearing on her face, and her brown hair had greyed considerably since I had last seen her. She wore a plain blue cardigan with a white shirt underneath it. A necklace hung at her shoulders, and her grey eyes were downcast. Her age, all of a sudden, was slipping my mind. Was she in her forties or her sixties? She had turned into a shallow husk, a turtle shrinking into its shell.

"Hello, Cerina," she said, taking her seat. I felt sandwiched between them, letting out a heavy exhale.

"Hello, mother."

My father waved his hand, "there is no need for titles at this table. Her name is Laure, I am Edric, you are Cerina, and this is Jezmon. The commander who lacks punctuality is named Randevald."

"With all due respect, sir," Jezmon huffed, "Cerina may be your daughter, but I am a respected member of this government. I outrank her; therefore, she must address me as a superior."

"If you would prefer to use formalities," my father said, "*you* should address *her* properly as well. After all, if all goes as planned, she will be taking up my position."

Jezmon scoffod. "You can't be serious."

"Mr Tylor, I suggest you lower your voice. We wouldn't want to say anything drastic, would we?"

I bit my lip, forcing down a torrent of thoughts. My father had set up this argument so I couldn't object to anything. If I were to take my father's side, I would be giving in. But were I to take Jezmon's side, I would be openly denouncing myself. The only option, in this case, was to stay shut up and wait for the food to arrive.

My father cracked his knuckles, leaning back in his chair.

"Now, Cerina. As I'm sure you're aware, you were brought here to take up an offer."

"No way," I snapped. "I wore your stupid dress and went to your stupid dinner. I am *not* taking your stupid title."

"You're going to have to think of some stronger adjectives," my father laughed, "the fastest way to be made into a laughing stock is to let your rage fly freely. Soon, people won't fear it anymore. You don't want that, do you?"

"I don't want any of this."

"That was a trick question," my father smiled, revealing two rows of uneven, yellowing teeth. "Nobody gets what they want."

I resisted the urge to stand up, calming my nerves. I couldn't be rebellious. I couldn't be foolish.

"What did you *really* bring me here for?" I asked. "I don't know you as a father, but I know you as a strategist. You can't possibly be handing me your position. Why the dress? Why the formalities?"

My father sighed.

"In a couple minutes, I am going to read you an oath. Said oath was originally taken by all members of the *Spark*, both soldiers and leaders alike. While it varies depending on the context, its principle remains the same as it was many generations ago. If you sign it, the power will be shifted to you. I have already put my name on it, giving you permission to take my place. We don't live in a democracy, Cerina. This is nothing but another choice to make, for you, and only for you."

"What makes you think that the second I agree to this, I won't abolish all of your customs and blow up the Isle of Rebels?"

My father smirked. "Because there is a need for diplomacy. And I am here to convince you of that."

He lifted his arm, checking his watch. "It seems we'll have to start without the commander. Pity. Antonio, bring the meal. We are ready to discuss matters in full."

The man from the door had reappeared at the corner of the room. He nodded, disappearing down the hallway.

"Oh, and the dress?" My father said, another chuckle between his teeth. "It's to show you that society is all about appearances. If you want to navigate it, you have to do so slowly, and you have to look the part. I can't take you back to the mainland in a prison uniform, now, can I?"

Something in his sentence sparked a memory. *Take you back to the mainland.*

The escape plan. I had almost forgotten. I didn't know if the group was still together, but either way, they soon wouldn't be. If we were going to act, it would have to be now.

But where could we run?

"Take me back to the mainland? Do you have a boat?"

"We do, but when and if we board it all depends on you. This meal will take about half an hour. And after that thirty minutes is up, you will be signing my oath with your own hand, driven by your own free will."

"Why are you so eager to give up your position? And what makes you think I'll cave so easily?"

"Oh, believe me, I'm not willing to give up my position. But, you see, the wielder of the power has to remain young. It's another tradition, one you will only understand when you, too, take your place in the family tree."

A beat of silence radiated through the room before the guards came in, wheeling a cart bearing five plates. The man in white, Antonio, began laying them out. My father put a hand out to stop him from setting down the fifth. "Nothing for the commander. His tardiness should not be rewarded."

"What should I do with the meal, sir?"

"Whatever you wish. Now leave us be, and close the door behind you." He picked up his steak knife and looked at his food. An entire feast was laid out- ribs, mashed potatoes, steamed vegetables, and a side dish of bean soup. I sunk my fork into the food, marvelling at the mere texture. I hadn't eaten a proper meal in a long time.

I dropped the fork, shuffling back. My father knew how tempting the food was to me. Across the table, I fixed him with a cold stare.

Wine glasses were set at our sides. I turned my nose up at the smell, but I didn't bring up the fact that I was technically still underage. I also neglected to mention the detail that I had never once drank alcohol before.

Looking my father straight in the eye, I held up my glass and took a long sip of the acidic beverage.

My father smiled. "Now. Let's talk."

Jakson Veer

How it ends

I slammed the door, jamming all my body weight against it to seal it shut. Haven and Farrah joined me, their heavy panting muffling the torrential downpour of gunfire.

Tentatively, I stepped away from the exit.

The barred window let in a small shaft of natural moonlight, but Farrah had given the flashlight to one of the fleeing prisoners. We'd have to do this in darkness. "I've made a small change to the plan," I began, "Haven, we'll need you for this part."

"Perfect," they said, clapping their hands together. "Let's clear some criminal records."

The hallway was eerily quiet as we made our way across the metallic floor. Every guard had been stationed outside, guarding the house in the middle. To the best of my knowledge, anyway. We had to be on high alert. I led us from memory, feeling alongside the wall's edge. The records room was close.

"Farrah," I said, "you don't by any chance have a light-emitting device stashed in that cast of yours, do you?"

She shook her head. "Sorry. I'm empty-handed."

"That's okay. There's a computer in the records room that I might be able to get into."

Haven eyed me doubtfully. "You know how to hack?"

"I mean... I know how to code."

"You're quite the scholar," Haven said, "but I'm not sure it's the same thing."

"I've done it before," I explained with a sigh. "I can do it again."

I *had* done it before, with Lizabeth and Darby, but ultimately, I had failed. I had managed to get into a fifteen-year-old's laptop, but his parents' passwords were uncrackable. I'd managed to create an untraceable banking identity, but I had never actually gotten the chance to test it out.

I'd have to do it again, and I'd have to do it better. Which was virtually impossible, considering I was far out of practice and this was a government building.

I didn't mention this fact to the others, however. I couldn't stand false hopes, but I couldn't stand to crush them either. Especially theirs.

"Follow me," I said, distracting myself from the issue ahead. Right now, our only goal was to get to the records room and destroy our identifications. Destroy our existences. Whatever came after came after.

We dashed down the hall, the rifle heavy at my back. I adjusted the strap around my shoulder, but that didn't stop the gun from digging into my uniform.

It was nowhere near the worst of my wounds, however. Both my arms throbbed from the barbed wire, a few of the cuts still trickling blood. I clenched my teeth, stalking forward. The sides of my uniform had been stained a muddy crimson.

My hand latched onto the doorknob of the records room. In the dim light, I could faintly make out the lettering on the wall. *Archives*, it read. I rummaged through my pocket for the maintenance worker's key card. I fished it out, holding it over the scanner.

Nothing happened. I cursed my idiocy, shoving the device back into my pocket. The power was out. Of course, the scanners wouldn't work.

Farrah tried the knob, but it had locked automatically, refusing to budge.

"Shit," I muttered, rifling through the key ring. "There must be some sort of manual method." I fingered the knob, feeling the bulge of a keyhole at the bottom of the handle. "If we want to make it on that boat, if we want anyone to make it on that boat, we have to do this before Adrienne's performance. And if Adrienne doesn't perform soon, everyone is going to get caught."

"We know the stakes, Jakson," Haven said. "Do any of those keys work?"

"No!" I tossed the keychain to the ground in frustration. "Do you think-"

All of a sudden, an idea sprang to mind. We looked at each other, holding a gaze.

I was the first one to speak. "That guard. The man from before. He can't have gone far."

We took down the hall again, retracing our steps. Sure enough, we found the guard next to the door, debating whether or not to exit the deserted corridor. Once he saw us, he stopped, his eyes flitting in two directions.

I held up the weapon, pointing it at his chest. "Open the records room," I ordered, "now."

He shot his hands up, backing away. "I can't. I'm not authorised."

"Who *is* authorised?" Haven asked.

"Only the high-ranking officers."

"And where can we find those?"

"Everyone is outside. You won't make it two steps out there without being caught or killed."

"Do you know where they keep their keys?"

The guard bit his tongue.

"I *said*, where do they keep their keys?"

"I'm not telling you anything," he stuttered.

I handed Haven the gun.

"Are you sure about that?" they repeated, holding the weapon with a natural, relaxed stance.

"I don't fear death. But I know you do. Unless you want to be met with that fear, you'll put that thing down. Slowly."

"Not a chance."

The two of them held a tense stare, testing the other's will.

The guard smirked. "There's no way you'll shoot me. Your branding says it all. If you want to get into the archives, I'm your only chance."

"Never say never. We're being hunted as Level Threes, after all."

The guard stepped closer. "I *was* a Level Three, kid. You don't know what you're dealing with."

Haven slipped their finger over the trigger. In one abrupt motion, they jerked the gun to the side, shooting the guard in the centre of his hand. The blast shook the walls, the vibrations rippling up to my eardrums and pounding on them with a frantic, merciless beat. The guard held out his bleeding hand, examining the gaping bullet wound without so much as a wince.

He looked at Haven with raised eyebrows.

"I can do a lot worse," Haven said. "Now, I won't ask again. *Will you open the fucking archives?* Or are you going to stand there and die?"

The guard took a deep breath. "I'm going to get the key from the commander's station."

"Alone?" Haven said, "I don't think so."

"I can take you with me."

"I'll go," Haven said. "The two of you, stay here."

Before either of us could argue, they were racing down the hall, following the guard's lead.

Farrah and I were left in silence.

"So," I said, "alone at last."

Farrah laughed. "Normally, that would be a good thing."

"I'm worried."

"Your worry is justified."

"What do you mean?"

"That's why you told me, right? So you could justify what you were feeling by seeing it in my own eyes?"

"That's not-" Farrah's features were warm, not accusatory. I stopped myself, taking her hand. "I told you I was worried because you have the right to know what's going on inside my head. Is it wrong to recognise things like that?"

Farrah's grip went slack. For a moment, I feared she would drop my hand altogether. But a second later, she was squeezing my fingers.

"Oh. Well, now I look insensitive."

"Not to me."

She smiled softly, brushing the long bangs away from her face. "Just so you know... I'm worried too."

"At least we're worried together."

She shuffled closer, resting her head on my shoulder.

"At least we have that much."

We stayed that way for a moment that was both too long and not nearly long enough. If reality could be an optional cruelty for just one sparing moment, I would be open to any alternative. Farrah was right. We had this much. And if we pretended, we had more. We had everything.

It was nice to lie, whether it was consequential or not.

Very nice indeed.

Haven and the guard returned in minutes, finding us hand in hand. We stepped away from the door as the guard unlocked it, holding it wide open for us. His hand continued to drip blood, hanging by his side like a dead fish.

"I'm not taking you any farther," he said, "you can tell this psycho to put her gun down."

Haven's expression tightened, and, just as a precaution, I slipped the rifle from their hands.

"Those aren't my pronouns," they said, defiance in their tone.

The guard stood there, confused. "What do you mean?"

"I'm not a girl. I'm not a guy either."

"You know what you are? Overdramatic. You won't get very far in there, but you can't say I didn't help you. Sayonara."

The guard turned, fading into the darkness. Haven stared after him, glaring holes into his back.

"At least he was smart enough not to ask for his gun back." Haven hoisted the rifle back onto their shoulders, leading the way inside.

From what I could decipher in the limited light, we were standing in a wide chamber. Rows of tin filing cabinets ran from wall to wall, hosting our distorted reflections in their rippled surfaces. I barely recognised myself. Backlit by the narrow shaft of ebbing sunlight, I looked like I had just stepped out of a war zone. The wounds running down my arms looked superficial, but they were bleeding like crazy. Some blood had transferred to my white-blond hair, speckling my cheeks.

Haven bumped straight into a set of wooden desks, screaming a string of profanities too harsh to be directed at a table. The desks were plain and undecorated. A few had nameplates, but most were bare of everything except a charging cable, curling up the table legs like slender black snakes.

"There are laptops on the desks," Haven recovered, once their incomprehensible rant had died down. They flipped one open, revealing a plain white lock screen. The bright light bathed the room in colour.

Illuminated by an eerie glow, the letters and numbers labelling the filing cabinets formed a clear organisational system. The files were arranged by last name, one side housing Level Twos and the other, which filled up a considerably more significant portion of the room, belonging to Level Ones. My eyes stopped at the cabinet labelled 1-V. Somewhere in there was my whole life.

Class pictures.

Medical records.

Contest certificates that meant nothing, perfect test scores that led to nowhere.

I couldn't wait to burn all of it.

"Hey, Jakson!" Haven shouted, "what are we going to do about this computer? These files aren't going to destroy themselves."

Dread crept through me. I turned back to the desk, where Farrah and Haven were huddled around the bright screen. "Is the laptop password protected?"

I hurried over before they could answer. Sure enough, I found myself looking into the face of a login page.

"Dammit."

"Can you hack it?" Haven asked. "It says 'user login-'"

"I can *read*, Haven," I snapped. "I can't just put on my nerd pants and hack a computer. This password could be anything, and I don't have the software on me. This takes technique. Technique I don't possess."

"Great," Haven said, stepping back. "Just great."

A tide of frustration pushed to the surface.

"You don't have any right to act like that," I snapped, "what have you done here? Argue with me and point the gun around. And mope. Yes, you're *great* at whining."

"I've done more than your girlfriend here, and you're not bugging *her* about her contributions. Stop trying to pick a fight. I get that you don't trust me, and frankly, I don't trust you either, but you don't have to be a dick about it."

"It isn't that. I do trust you. You don't trust me?"

"I mean..."

I whirled on them, fixing them with a tight glare. "You led us here, Haven. We were taking a risk when you brought us in on your plan. If you don't reciprocate trust, maybe you aren't someone I should trust *in*."

I wrenched the rifle from Haven's arms, slinging it around my shoulder.

"Hey!" they cried, lunging for me. "The fuck are you doing?"

I shoved in front of Haven, staring at the blank computer screen and letting the white light sear my eyes. I had to fight the urge to snap the device in two.

"Give the gun back, Jakson." Desperation clawed at Haven's voice. It was insulting.

"It doesn't matter," I snapped, "we shouldn't even have to use the thing. Our biggest enemy is this lock screen."

"If it doesn't matter who holds it, why can't I?" Haven pulled the gun away from me, tugging at the strap. I whirled on them, prying their fingers off.

"Stop." They didn't obey, grappling for the handle. "Hey! Stop!"

We wrestled for the gun, and I felt the strap slide off my shoulder. Haven's elbow flew at my face, which I narrowly dodged. I shoved them forward, sinking my nails into the handle and yanking it back. The barrel pointed every which way, the trigger just in reach.

"You're forgetting who put the Escape Artists together! You're forgetting who started this whole thing! It's me! It's always been me! Give the gun to *me*, Jakson!"

I gritted my teeth. "I can't believe how selfish you are, Haven."

"*I'm* being selfish? Get a mirror!"

The gun was snatched from both of our hands and lifted above our heads. Farrah steamed with fury, her eyebrows knotted in a scowl.

"Stop this, both of you! We can't afford to fight with each other! *I'll* take the gun."

"You're right-" I began, but my words were cut off by the sound of Haven propelling themself at her, flinging their arms in the air.

Farrah cried in alarm, dropping the weapon. I lunged at Haven, sticking my arms out. "Get out of the w-"

The rifle bounced once, twice. Then it fired.

I rolled, bringing Haven down with me. The bullet ricocheted off the cabinet, sinking into the desk. I panted, taking heavy breaths. My hand reached to brush the spot where it landed, inches away from Farrah. The bullet hole steamed, faint smoke wafting from the gap. A crack that trailed down the leg of the desk chair had been produced by the chasm. Farrah grabbed the laptop just in time, yanking it up before the desk collapsed, crumbling to a pile of splinters and rubble.

Haven grunted, pushing me away. The sharp bang continued to echo, reverberating throughout the room.

The light on the computer had gone out.

Haven ran a hand through their hair, muttering. "Shit. *Shit*. Is everyone okay?"

"Not a scratch on me," Farrah confirmed, tapping the mousepad on the screen.

"Jakson?"

"I'm fine," I said hollowly, a faint ringing in my ears. "But we just announced our presence to every guard in and around this building."

Haven's eyes flitted between us. They ran forward, kicking the remnants of the desk. A chunk of wood split off, flying across the room. Haven grumbled, raising their leg to kick it again.

Farrah swooped in just in time. "Haven," Farrah said, setting her hand on Haven's knee. "Stop. What do you think you're doing?"

Farrah stepped away, and Haven collapsed to the floor, their head in their hands.

"Dammit, Farrah, I'm just fucking more things up. It's all I ever do; it's all I *can* do. You're right, Jakson; I'm a selfish asshole. All I've ever wanted to do was make an impact on the world. Everyone tells kids that they can be anything they want to be, do anything they want to do. I really took that to heart, didn't I? Ever since I was ten, I wanted to do *everything*."

They smashed their fists on the ground beside them. "Do you know how I got arrested in the first place? It was early fall. In a too-large coat, selected specifically because it would blow in the wind, I read a poem about social injustices on the roof of a building. I was speaking my mind about identity. No, not just anyone's identity. *My* identity and why it mattered. Max and Adrienne were at my side. We vandalised that building to make a statement. I thought I was supporting a cause, but really, I was flaunting my ego. I just wanted to be noticed. The building's staff eventually saw us, and I beat the shit out of the worker who tried to stop me. I thought my punches were driven by the fuel to lead society. Now, look at me. The two friends I'd swore I'd die with, gone, at my side no longer because I wanted to claim the heroic deed. Breaking everything in my path because all I care about is getting to the end of it. I thought the two of you were spies, you know. For the longest time. Thanks to my paranoia, I could've killed one of you."

"Don't say that," Farrah said. "You were angry. That's okay."

"No, it isn't. I'm an impulsive piece of shit, and I just gave us away. We're doomed, and it's all my fault."

"You know," I stated, "that's probably the most egocentric thing you've said all night."

"Jakson!" Farrah cried, "you're not helping!"

Haven waved their hand. "Nah. He's right. He's irritable, but at least he's not basking in self-pity. There is no emotion more narcissistic than that. I'm sorry, you guys. I truly am. And I think the best way to make it up to you-" they shot up, grabbing the device on the table, "is to help you get into this computer."

I smiled. Something about the quiver of my lips was uneasy, unsure.

But if Haven was willing to change… so was I.

"Now we're talking."

***

All the laptops in the room were exactly the same, with the password-protected screen and the profile known as 'user login' staring at us in mockery. Haven was incredibly efficient in opening them all, checking for differences.

We found none. Nothing about these supposed 'users' was apparent from their profile screen. One of them had a small sticker of a forest landscape on the back of their computer, but that could mean absolutely anything.

On the plus side, the open screens lit the room up a lot better. Although, since the only things it clarified were everyone's hopeless expressions, the light didn't do much.

"Try 'password'," Haven suggested. "A lot of the guards we've run into are pretty dense. You might as well give it a shot."

Doubtfully, I typed it in.

Nothing.

Farrah frowned. "Password 123?"

It was truly grasping at straws, but I tried it anyway. Sure enough, a red error message looked back at my dirt-covered face. *Too many failed attempts. Try again in two minutes.*

"It's hopeless," I resolved, slumping into the spinning desk chair in utter defeat. "If we keep trying, the system will lock us out forever. It could be anything-"

From the other end of the room, a tiny creak cut into my train of thought, bringing my words to a screeching halt. With a faint tap and a couple of footsteps, the door swung open.

I shot up, knocking the rolling chair aside. Farrah and Haven gasped, stepping back and huddling closer. I eyed the gun, where it sat uselessly on the floor. I debated running to get it but settled on the decision that such an endeavour would be pointless.

Because the figure who had entered the room had already crossed the floor, placing their finger on the trigger.

Of its own accord, the door swung shut. We were trapped. Slowly, I put my hands in the air. I heard Farrah gulp.

"Joe?" I ventured, narrowing my eyes.

Everything about the person in front of us *resembled* the Joe of building 1-3. He had the same creases around his aged brown eyes, the same bald scalp. His stature was identical to that of the man we all knew.

But from the moment he stepped into the records room, trapping us with him, I could tell something was wrong.

His eyes, dark brown irises that had once appeared wise and cautious, looked pained and regretful. His rough hands clasped the guard's loaded gun, resting over the trigger. But the most telling sign was his wardrobe change.

Instead of his prison jumpsuit, Joe was wearing a uniform. The long sleeves were navy blue, and black buttons with gold fringes around their edges ran up to the collar. A single pocket was placed over the heart, with an *R* embroidered into the middle.

The sleeves were rolled up slightly, stopping at his wrists. One of the buttons was undone, an indication that he had changed in a hurry.

Normally, there was no way I could believe it. Not Joe, the caretaker of the Level One sector. He couldn't be a guard.

But the name embroidered above the R led me to believe otherwise. Stitched with the gleaming threads of betrayal was a single title.

Officer Joe Lopez

Haven balled their fists. "You-"

"Put your hands in the air, Haven. I don't want to hurt you; I only want to negotiate."

Haven, along with the rest of us, glared daggers, but we all solemnly obliged.

"Step aside," said Joe, slinging the rifle onto his back and lifting up the computer. My eyes darted to the sheath on his belt. There was a second pistol inside.

We were absolutely done for.

The laptop was plugged into an outlet on the far side of the wall, but Joe let the charger drop out of the side. "You want the password," he began, "and I want my efforts to pay off. I want a promotion, and you want to derail my career. Right now, our goals don't align."

"You're telling me," Haven said. They were fighting to keep their tone even, pouring confidence into their words, but even I could see through them. They were barely holding it together. "So *you* were the mole."

"No," Joe explained, "that was Cerina. She didn't intend to spill your secrets, but her earpiece gave them all away. I never lied to you, Haven. I was a monitor, and I still am."

"How could you do this?" Haven shouted. They dropped their false bravado, letting their voice shake. "You were a guard this whole time?"

"The first thing you need to know," said Joe, "is that I never tried to hurt anyone. People are complicated. You should know all about that. I chose to help you for a reason. Before you began your disastrous operation, before you allied yourself with Level Twos, the two of us were friends. I cherished that time, and I tried to keep you safe. It's not my fault you had a death wish."

"Don't make this personal," Haven snarled.

"When has it been anything *but* personal? I was sent to the Level One sector to pick out the Level Threes mixed in with the bunch. But that doesn't mean I don't care about each one. I'm still Joe. I'm just in a different uniform."

"How can you care about us? You're a *guard*."

Joe sighed. "I don't know if you've learned this yet, but the Level Threes *become* the guards. And right now, you are wanted for that exact purpose. We're exactly the same, so, please… just listen to me."

Words were on the tip of Haven's tongue, but Joe cut them off before they could start.

"The Level Threes are chosen because they are strong souls. But even the strongest of spirits can be bent. I need you to join me. I have been *commanded* to get you to join me, but I'm allowed to do so on my own terms. If you give your heart and will to Sykona, I will give you the password to these laptops in exchange. You will be able to erase and alter the records of all the prisoners in this establishment. You can read them and decide who goes free- who is actually dangerous and who never earned this punishment. Whoever you choose gets to escape. The only exceptions are the three of you and the friends who came to your aid. It doesn't seem like too much to ask, does it?"

"It makes sense," I said, "more people get freed, and we stay behind. We don't really have many other options."

"From a logical perspective, it seems like the obvious choice," Haven said, their hand on their chin. "But consider this- where can the captives go? And who are we to decide who makes the cut? I would rather die than serve as a mindless pawn. And that's exactly what will happen if we stay."

"We'll be mindless pawns either way," said Farrah, stating an accurate point. "But this option frees a bunch of people."

"But will those people truly be free?"

"I thought you were the one campaigning for an escape."

"I know... I was. But I don't know anything anymore."

"Think about it morally," I said. "It's not right to sacrifice the livelihoods of hundreds, if not thousands of people, to save our own. Plus- we get taken either way. This isn't a decision. It's an order. We have no other option."

Haven raised their eyebrows. "Weren't you just trying to break into that computer? And don't bring morals into this. I'm just as confused as anyone on those grounds. We're not in the right state of mind to judge people."

"In that case," I argued, "we should do what Joe is telling us to."

"Did you *literally* not just hear a word I said?"

"I did. And you're right; your words do carry weight. Where the weight swings is just up for interpretation."

"Shut up," Haven grumbled.

"Great argument."

Joe cleared his throat. "While this is amusing to watch, I am still pointing a gun at you, and you still have to make your choice. I don't want to shoot you, but nobody cares about the desires of people like us. You can play by the rules, or you can get caught in the brutal crossfires."

Haven shook their head. "Who said *we* can't make the rules?"

"It's sad. I can't be angry with you because of how little you understand, but I pity your naivete. I would have tried to keep you from this sooner, but my previous statement stands true in all accounts."

"If you're keeping something from me, spill it," Haven said, their words like acid. "I can't agree to any of your terms until all the facts are in front of me."

"Don't play this game with me, Haven. Do you or do you not agree to hand yourselves into Sykona in exchange for the freedom of others of your choosing?"

"Are we really worth all of them? Are we really more valuable than hundreds of people who have done things much more ruthless than we ever could?"

"Yes," Joe said. "Yes, you are."

"But you're not going to tell us why?"

"No. Because there's nothing to tell. You'll see it for yourself."

"That isn't reassuring."

"It's not supposed to be. Nothing in your lives will ever be reassuring again."

I never knew stares could have so much effect. I knew they were powerful, but standing in the weight of the gaze between Joe and Haven, I felt like I would collapse from its sheer intensity.

Haven took a deep breath. "Fine," they surrendered, kicking the table one last time. "I give myself up to Sykona, or whatever the hell else you want me to submit to. Congratulations. You've won. Now unlock the computer."

"You made the right choice."

Joe stepped closer, setting the laptop on the table. No sooner was his finger on the keypad than Haven's hands wrapped around the rifle, the barrel pointed at Joe's side.

"Step back," Haven said, grasping the weapon. "And put your hands up."

Joe looked at Haven with a gaze that could only be described as genuine disappointment. I bit my tongue.

"Oh, Haven," Joe said sadly, speaking, as though, to a child that had misbehaved. "I thought you were finally starting to learn something."

He flipped out his own pistol, swinging it casually around his fingers. He let go of the laptop, moving further down the line of cabinets, both of his hands on the gun.

"You can't always overpower your enemies. The best solution to that problem is not to make them in the first place. And here I thought we could be friends."

"We *were* friends, allies, at least," Haven bit. "Before you betrayed us like a backstabbing craven."

"I think you're confusing rationale with cowardice."

"Since when do rational people betray the individuals they swore they'd care for?"

"I still care for you. But I'm starting to reconsider if you're suited for this."

"Suited for what? Becoming a slave?"

Joe sighed. "I wish I could tell you, but I have been commanded not to. If the general public were to find out about this, everything would spiral into disarray."

"You're telling me."

Joe's pistol was now pointed directly at Haven's face. Any pretence of friendliness had completely evaporated.

Farrah placed a warning hand on Haven's shoulder. "Haven. Think carefully about this. Let Joe type in the password. It's for the good of all of us."

"Farrah's right," Joe said, "it's for your own good. But unfortunately, Haven has proved they can't be trusted with the code. They are unsuited. As sad as it makes me, orders are orders."

"Please, Joe," I begged. "We'll do whatever you say. Just put away the weapons."

"I really wish I could. But I care too much to stop myself. I care too much about *you*."

"Haven," I warned. "Think carefully about this."

"I care, too," Haven said. "Step back."

I stood my ground.

419

Farrah spoke softly at first, but spiking in intensity. "Haven, stop. You're losing control of yourself-"

"I have never *been* in control of myself. But you've taught me something. The world doesn't revolve around me. For once, let me do something for you. Let me fight for *you*, and Jakson, and Lizabeth, and Amélie, and Emry… and Max, and Adrienne, who have never deserved any of this. I need you to tell them. Tell them that I'm sorry for everything. Tell them they've been the most loyal friends anyone could ask for. Can you do that?"

I swore under my breath, stepping beside Haven. "If you're going to dig in your heels, then I have no choice but to stand with you."

In an instant, Haven's eyes widened. They pushed in front of me, sprinting forward. "Jakson, I told you to get ba-"

Haven hadn't even finished speaking when two bangs rang out in rapid succession. A hand I realised seconds later was Farrah's pushed me back, landing me on my tailbone. The three of us fell on top of each other, one after the other, our knees buckling. Farrah's palm covered my eyes.

"Don't look," she rasped. I started to push her hand away, but she replaced it with the other one. "Fuck, Jakson. Don't look. Don't look. Don't look. Don't-"

The room went silent. When Farrah peeled her fingers away, the power had gone back on.

Industrial-style lights blinked on overhead, temporarily blinding the two of us. Farrah and I sprawled out on the white tile floor, along with another crumpled figure.

It was Haven. In the centre of their chest was a crimson red bullet hole, streaming blood. They sputtered and coughed, getting to their knees and flailing their arms to steady themself. I shoved them back down. "Don't move. It'll only make the bleeding worse."

Haven wheezed. The bullet had sunken into the bottom of their ribcage, on the left side. It had aimed for the heart, but it had probably gotten a lung instead.

"Please understand," a voice spoke, deep and raspy. "I only did this to save Haven. To save you. Both of you are unfit, Jakson and Haven. This wasn't an order. It was supposed to be your salvation."

Farrah and I stood up, whirling around. Joe was standing on his two feet, holding himself up perfectly steadily.

He would have appeared perfectly normal was it not for the gaping gunshot in the middle of his forehead. Unfazed, he pulled his hand up, smearing away the torrent of blood.

He crumpled to the floor with his fist over his heart.

"Know this," Joe whispered, "I regret nothing. You will thank me later, when you're the regretful one." His breathing stilled instantly.

Haven had aimed for the brain, and they had struck. They hadn't been lying. They were an excellent shot.

And they had been merciful enough to provide a quick death.

Haven's hands gripped my pant leg, clawing at my ankle in a frenzy. "Tell them! Promise me! Promise me you'll tell them! Jakson! Farrah! I need you to promise!"

"I promise, Haven," I spoke softly, letting them bleed out all over my uniform. "I promise not to let you die before you tell them yourself."

Haven's chest heaved slowly, once, twice. "Not yet. Not yet."

Haven Megany

This moment is my worth

The therapist's office.
Pens, neatly stacked. A clipboard, covered in childish designs.
Scratching.
Scratch, scratch, scratch.
I smell antiseptic and lost hopes.
For someone whose job is to help people with anxiety, this room paints a picture that can be summed up by only three letters.
OCD.
"Hannah," she says. Her voice is supposed to be comforting.
A grounding force.
A music note.
To me, it sounds like nails on a chalkboard.
"Do you know what a mood disorder is?"
I had played dumb, but I knew my worth all along.

"Not yet." I sucked in a gulp of air, bringing me back to life. I was in the records room, and Jakson and Farrah were in front of me. One of them held my hand, blurred out of focus. Every breath hurt, and the air stung like poisonous gas.

My legs looked like blobs. Abstract blurbs that only Max could see the beauty in. I appreciated broad concepts, but meaningless splotches on a canvas seemed to me like nothing more than low effort projects, made to look deeper than they actually were.

Few things deserved a philosopher's appreciation.

I teetered on my feet. Once, I could count on my legs to support me, but I swayed like a flag in a thunderstorm. An out-of-control symbol attached to a lightning rod. I couldn't trust my depth perception, so I stuck my hands out blindly, finding the laptop by feel.

My fingers closed around it just as my legs caved in, sinking back to the ground.

The world was a pit of quicksand, dragging me deeper and deeper. I had spent my life trying to wade through it, but I had never realised that maybe the only place to go was down into the abyss.

My fingers, which looked long and spindly in this distorted fish-eye view, were useless to me. Farrah only had one hand to use. I needed Jakson to do this.

"Jak...son..." I wheezed. "Guest login."

"I don't understand," Jakson's voice was gurgly. I couldn't tell if he was crying for me -probably not- or if it was nothing more than a figment of my imagination. I had always been overly creative. Lost in thought, but never schizophrenic. Now I knew what it was like to hallucinate.

For a brief period in fourth grade, I had gotten lucid dreams almost every night. This was something like that.

Except if I wanted to make myself fly away, I could never come back.

"We can't access the passwords with a guest login," Jakson explained, "much less the records themselves."

"Vi-" I choked out. "Video. Wasn't that..." I trailed off, gasping for air. "Wasn't that your plan? What you need me for?"

Typing. Jakson was typing. The ghost of a smile traced my lips. I *knew* I could be smart.

"I got in with my school account," Jakson said. "There had better be a camera on this thing."

My eyelids drooped, tugged down so fast they might as well have been attached to weighted strings. My whole body felt like it was being crushed by an elephant. I pictured that scene, and a sputtery laugh bubbled up my throat and out of my mouth like bile.

"I've got it!" Jakson announced. "But we have a problem… you see, in court, videos don't count as permissible-"

"Too much…" I gasped. "To turn a blind eye to. Now let me speak-" I coughed, each puff shaking my brain against my skull. "Let my words have meaning."

Jakson sighed. "As you wish."

My bedroom.
A mix of movie posters and LED lights.
A nauseating disco party.
Frankly, it looks more like a marketing scheme than a place to sleep.
One moment, I'm crying into a pillow.
The next, laughing at a computer screen, probably reading a gratuitous fanfiction, a level of over-the-top that I can't help but find hilarious.
Then I'm scribbling furiously in my notebook, jotting down nonsense poetic babble and listening to motivational music.
The scene is a sports movie montage gone terribly wrong.
It is wrong because there is no victory.

"Haven?" My shoulders were being shaken, and Farrah was looking down at me. I blinked groggily. There were those weights again. "We're recording."

I struggled to sit up, picking apart the fuzzy landscape for the camera. I settled my eyes on a white-blond patch that faintly resembled Jakson's head.

"My name is Haven Megany," I slurred. I found my shoulder, pulling up the sleeve of my uniform and bending my torso, so the bright red number 1 fell into the shot. "But you know me as a Level One rebel. Another part of our society that you'd love to overlook, just like world hunger and climate change. Ah, yes, political issues. But I'm not here to talk about those." The whole sentence came out in a fast, airy string. Black spots were beginning to float in my vision.

"The truth is," I said. "We are not bad people. I sound like a hypocrite, saying that in a prison uniform, but don't take my word for it. Take his-"

I swatted the laptop, indicating for Jakson to move the camera to Joe. He did so, a bit reluctantly. I continued the monologue, a barren voice-over.

"This man, known as Officer Joe Lopez, or simply Joe, was a prisoner just like us. He was tagged a Level Three and became a soldier. He was bred here and went up to form the authority. Much like every other military official you've encountered, this man was a former inmate on the Isle of Rebels." I didn't know how my tone sounded now. Perhaps I wasn't even speaking the phrases, suffocating on my own words. I didn't care if I was eloquent as long as the truth got out.

"Haven," Farrah repeated, her tone ringing in my ears. "We're recording now. You can begin."

The camera was still pointed at Joe's body, blood trickling out of the hole in his head. I reached up to touch Farrah's shoulder. Initially, I had pictured my hand over hers, speaking my last words like a wise mentor, gone to the grave after many long years of passing down the wisdom I'd acquired.

But instead, I clutched at empty air.

"You do it," I said. "It's inevitable, this fate. I can't have my dream, so I'm giving it to you."

Farrah and Jakoon's faces came into focus for a brief second, their expressions blank. My lips had gone still. Inside, my thoughts screamed against the cage of my skull, pounding on the bars. No answer came; no words rang out.

I could not speak. I could not breathe.

I shut my eyes again, putting my face into its resting position. If I could convey anything, it had to be my resolve.

I wanted this.

I

Wanted

This.

Adrienne Jemmott

Steal the show

"Thank you, thank you!" I shouted, applauding the second to last act- a girl from the Level One sector showing off her ventriloquism skills with a puppet made from a dirty sock. It wasn't the most thrilling act, but it was lengthy, which bought us time. Plus, my upcoming performance would be more than enough to kick this show up a notch.

The girl took a bow, a faint blush plastering her face. We were in the heat of a very volatile situation, and the sounds of claps, however loud they were, hadn't *quite* drowned out the rumble of gunfire from afar. But I couldn't help myself. I loved this.

It was everything I looked for in a party- adrenaline, enthusiasm. The surge of a crowd and my absolute control over it. I felt powerful, invincible. If the guards stormed the talent show, they couldn't lay a hand on me.

I didn't have a stage to stand on, but I felt like I was on top of the world.

Maybe I was kidding myself, but a little encouraged happiness didn't always have to be a bad thing.

"Next up, we have our final performance!" My lungs ached from screaming, but it was a burn I welcomed eagerly. I stood on my tiptoes, looking above the sea of people. Emry, Lizabeth and Amélie were all together, forming their own stand-out cluster on the very edge.

I nudged Max. He snapped out of his space-out daze, jumping above the crowd and shooting Amélie a thumbs-up.

Amélie matched the gesture, and their group moved around, evading the guards who were starting to join the audience, searching faces.

I was ready to begin my performance, but something stopped me from bringing out the song I had prepared. It didn't quite fit the mood.

No. A smirk came to my face as I settled on a song. The lyrics were a little too vague for me to truly appreciate, but the song had a good beat, and it would work to the soft music of a ukulele.

Haven would be overjoyed to hear one of their creations serenade our grand escape.

I stepped into the centre, gesturing for everyone to sit down. The change in movement rippled through the crowd as they followed the direction, leaving me standing. The guards stayed up, their uniforms painting ugly splotches in an otherwise beautiful painting.

The scene didn't have the upbeat music of a rave, but I felt just as empowered, facing the crowd of the hundreds of people who had cared enough to show up past lights-out.

"This is a song that... I didn't write," I introduced, laughing a little at the second part. "But it means a lot to me because of who *did* write it. They're here now, at least; they're about to be. And you're going to help me out with it."

Nods rippled through the crowd. I smiled in satisfaction. When I got off the Isle, I'd have to become a DJ. Or a party planner. Or a singer, once I could afford a better instrument.

"This song is dedicated," I began. "To my best friends in the entire world. Haven and Max."

I pulled out my ukulele, plucking the opening chords, coming up with them as I went. Haven's words guided me, and as I repeated the intro, I opened my mouth to sing.

My voice sounded better than ever.

***

Halfway through the song, when I had sung my vocal cords hoarse, Jakson and Farrah appeared. The two bedraggled forms, helping to keep the other upright, were easy to spot amid the assembly of prisoners. My chest tightened, and I missed a note, my voice cracking.

The third figure was missing.

I sang on, but my heart wasn't in it. Where was Haven?

The chorus rolled around again, carrying me with it. I moved around, craning my neck. Did they stay behind to finish something up?

Suddenly, over the crowd, I caught Farrah's eye.

Inside it was a dark shadow. The same one was mirrored in Jakson's face. My breath caught in my throat. *Where was Haven?*

I stopped singing.

The audience looked around, unsure of what to do. Slowly, the echo of my background music died down, leaving only me and a field of silence.

Vomit rose up in my stomach, pooling in the back of my throat. I knew that look. It was the same one I had seen on my parents' faces when they returned from the hospital the day my grandmother passed away.

I dropped my ukulele.

When the first explosives went off, they swallowed me whole, dragging me up to the starry sky. They were the only sound to be heard, alone in the dark of night.

Part 5- It's how we (burn)

Alight
By Haven Megany

In a dark night
You aren't blind
For the sky is only new
Come rising sun
When the day's begun
All the roads will lead to you

Take a sword
Take a heart
Do what you must
Take your aim
Take your shot
You're the only one you can trust
Only you can burn
No other fuel's enough

In fragile waters
You aren't broken
Yet on the cliffs
You're strong
No wonder why nobody knows
Where the fuck you belong

Take a sword

Take a heart
Do what you must
Take your aim
Take your shot
You're the only one you can trust
Only you can burn
No other fuel's enough

When you rest your tired eyes
Will the silence console you?
When you go to sleep at night
Does your past come back to haunt you?
A haunt or a taunt, no one can say
The only choice is up ahead
To burn it all away
You're hanging by a fragile thread
So burn it all away

Cerina Rayz

Under the Isle

I could only stomach about three bites of the meal. My father dug in generously, helping himself to an enormous platter of meat. My mother took sizable portions, and Jezmon didn't eat at all, focusing all his energy on staring at me until his rage burned a hole into my skull.

"The thing that you've probably realised at this point," my father began, "is that everyone needs an incentive. There is no better incentive than one that can be guaranteed and easily delivered. There are three parts to the Level Three indoctrination. The speech, which I am giving you right now. The show, which I am about to present. And the selection, where those who have successfully shown their aptitude are given the reward they desire, beginning their service. Some Level Threes don't make it that far- they're only deluded into thinking they have. It's quite easy to do, actually."

"I suppose you've already made up your mind that I'm fit to receive this 'reward'."

My father shook his head. "Oh, not entirely. You've complied with my demands so far, but to receive the Level Three classification, you must possess a very specific set of qualities."

"Right. Psychopathic and sadistic qualities. Understood."

Again, my father gave me a patronising *no* and a pitiful glance.

"If sadists ran the government, we'd be in big trouble. Sure, the inclination of a person's moral compass is a key factor, but it doesn't define the candidate. I could brag all night long about the criteria, but it's time we move on."

He held up his arm, checking his leather wristwatch. "Ah, yes. Five of our thirty minutes have already flown by."

I set my utensils down, and my father frowned. "Keep eating, Cerina. You're muscular in stature, but it isn't healthy if there's nothing in between those bones, sturdy though they may be."

We both knew that any concern of his was bullshit. He wanted me to eat because that made me vulnerable.

Still, I did as he bid, not wanting to risk a fight.

I was halfway through the plate of steamed vegetables when he spoke again.

"Power is a tough thing to understand," he said. "It may seem simple at first. It's total domination; it's the presence of authority. When you get into the nitty-gritty, it's often hard to understand why people do what they do. But there's always a reason, always a motive. Power is the ability to bend those motives, so they fit your own will. It's the most important skill anyone can develop."

"The most important skill anyone can develop? You don't say. It's not like you've been going on about it this entire night or anything."

My father laughed. "Is that sarcasm? You certainly are my daughter. I bet you think you're funny, but you must learn to appreciate your elders."

"I'm really not *appreciating* your words of attempted wisdom."

This meal had taken a turn. The mood had suddenly shifted, and now we bore the semblance of a family gathering. It didn't have the convivial atmosphere of a New Year's Eve feast, but something about it reminded me of the dinner parties I'd see on TV. Grandparents droning on about politics and healthcare, small children helping themselves to a small selection of the grand buffet, gravy on their faces. Adults sipping wine in a corner, having civilised conversations about how much their children had grown. Teens in the corner of the room, staring at their phones and wishing they were anywhere but that overcrowded living space, even though such events were obligations they were old enough to be familiar with.

Jezmon's glare immediately killed any sense of family or familiarity that might have considered springing from the table.

"Sir-"

"Edric," my father corrected.

Jezmon Tylor huffed. "*Edric Rayz*. This has gone on long enough. I insist you do what you came for and stop delaying us."

"You don't like the food, Jezmon? You could've said something when Antonio was still here. Just look at you. You haven't even touched your plate."

"You know perfectly well what I mean."

My mother cleared her throat.

"Jezmon isn't mistaken, Edric. We don't have all day. Show Cerina what power is, or risk losing it completely."

That seemed to win him over. He pushed his chair back, sighing through his nostrils.

"Fine. Cerina, come with me. You two, please stay here and finish your food. If Commander Abbotsford graces us with his presence, give him a talking-to that's as stern as the look Jezmon is fixing my daughter with. Thank you. We'll be back shortly."

I had expected my father to make for the door, but instead, he strode away from it. He stopped at the edge of the room and ran his hand over the olive green wallpaper adorned with shades of gold and black. Gently, he tapped it with his knuckles, and I heard a loud, resounding echo.

The wall was hollow.

"This variety of hidden room presents tedium for my construction team," my father said. "But a door would be too obvious. I'd advise you to step back, Cerina. Wouldn't want to ruin that dress."

He raised his polished shoe and kicked the centre of the wall.

It crumbled, and the memory of the mess hall's supply closet flashed before my eyes. This pseudo-wall fell the same way the plaster had, collapsing in a waterfall of dust and rubble.

My father brushed his hands off, stepping back to the table. He took the three-branched candle holder from its perch on the thick tablecloth, using it to light the way. He stepped over the wreckage, his footsteps reverberating through the opening of a dark hall. The glow of the candle lit up his face in an ominous shade of flickering white.

"Cerina? Are you coming?"

His feet started moving, not waiting for an answer. My shoulders slumped. I lifted the corners of my dress and stepped over the rubble, taking tiny, careful steps in my unstable heels.

The hall closely resembled the cement stairwell to Arvin's tomb, the stone walls seeming to close in on each side. We were still in the centre circle, I reminded myself, still inside the Victorian-style mansion.

A clinking sound made me jump, scampering back. My father held his hand out, blocking me from going any further. Illuminated by the soft glow emanating from the candles was a deep shaft plunging into the very depths of the earth.

Its sides were lined with ropes and cables, joining up with a small crank fastened to the wall.

"Do you want to do the honours?" My father stepped back, and I curled my fingers over the brass handle. Nothing seemed to use electricity in this place. I couldn't tell whether that was a clever and sneaky ploy or yet another layer of extra effort meant to appear articulated.

I had to heave to get the gears moving, but eventually, I found a rhythm. The lift clanked, slowly but surely chugging up to us.

At long last, it settled on the platform, clanging to a halt. The crank auto-locked in place, and I heaved a breath of relief, stepping back. My father climbed onto the lift, the unstable structure sagging under his weight.

The lift looked like it had been built a century ago. I tested the ground with my foot, hesitant to step onto the platform when the only things stopping me from falling to my death were my father and an aged bundle of rope. One was an inanimate object, and the other was a slimy politician whose ideals I couldn't be further from understanding. I could trust neither of them.

I couldn't help but notice that my father in no way tried to reassure me. I had to at least give him credit for that- he was smart enough to realise that any words of his in this situation would just be twisted against him.

The lift stank of machine oil, along with an earthy, acidic stench I couldn't quite place. My father took up most of the space, leaving only a claustrophobic bubble for me to fit into.

Resolving that there was nowhere to go but further down, both literally and figuratively, I ducked to fit inside the elevator.

The guardrail slid shut with a metallic clang. I could feel the pulse of the candle's warmth, hear every one of my own heartbeats. A second handle was stationed inside the lift, which my father did me the courtesy of operating himself. The cables scraped as we began a steep descent into the core of the Isle. Sweat pooled beneath the folds of my dress, and I caught my own reflection glimmering off the unpolished brass.

I looked like a complete stranger. Of course, I hadn't gotten a good look in a mirror since I arrived at the Isle.

I had always tried my hardest not to care about superficial appearances, and stopping to check my hair in the midst of an all-out war over the bronze key had always seemed petty and unnecessary.

But when I noticed my defined cheekbones, my dirt-plastered forehead, and the dried blood that had managed to slip into every crevice unoccupied by filth and grime, I couldn't hold in my gasp. My dress was a mockery of the dishevelled girl underneath, the ridiculous heels perfecting the look.

Now I understood the purpose of the outfit. It was a reminder that if I wanted respect, I not only had to look the part, but I had to care about the impression I made.

Otherwise, I'd be nothing more than a sixteen-year-old hobbling around in shoes too big for her feet.

My eyes flitted away from the reflection. I squared my shoulders and looked my father in the eyes.

"Are you going to tell me where we're going?"

His look betrayed the inevitable answer. Of course he wouldn't.

"You're fairly observant," he said, "I was hoping you would."

"We're riding in an old-fashioned lift down a deep, dark shaft. There isn't much to observe. I can't predict the future, which means whatever's at the bottom is anyone's guess."

"That bothers you a lot, doesn't it?"

"Of course it bothers me. I could be riding to my death with nothing to prevent it. You've put me in a situation where I'm completely powerless."

The honesty of the statement surprised me, possibly more so than it did my father. But his answer was the real shocker.

"You are never powerless. Now that you have let down your pride, you have proven yourself. Congratulations, daughter."

"I thought we weren't using such titles."

The elevator jerked to a halt, knocking me off my feet.

"No," my father said, a faraway look in his eyes. "No, I suppose we weren't."

He pushed by me, sliding his fingers through the cage-like railing. He pulled it open, wrestling us free using a hinge in dire need of greasing.

With one soft puff, he blew out the candle, plunging us into darkness.

A cold wash of air hit me suddenly, the chill sweeping over my arms. With it came a new light, enveloping the chasm.

The stone walls around us seemed to glow, lighting up the cavern. We were standing on top of a jutting dais made of solid rock, the edges crumbling away like a cliff. At the bottom of the precipice, sharp rocks submerged in fresh seawater surrounded our little oasis.

We were on an island under the island.

"Get off the lift, Cerina," my father commanded. "It's time for the final step."

Lizabeth Merrin

What comes next

On the crowd's edge, I balanced restlessly on the balls of my feet. Amélie tugged me by the hand, shuffling through the group with our heads down. I was getting tired of this. The longer we stayed, the more likely we'd be recognised and bumped right back to square one.

I tugged at Mel's sleeve, getting her attention.

"We have to go. That gun you're hiding isn't very subtle, and you're very… noticeable." I clenched my jaw. Way to go, self. Could I have been even *less* smooth with that word choice?

"Stay down, Lizabeth. We have to wait for the signal."

"But-"

"I know."

A tense moment of silence passed between us. I bit my lip. I still didn't know what to feel about Mel- if I should hate her for getting herself sent to the Isle or feel relieved, selfish as it was, that she was with me at last.

Comforting words were on the tip of my tongue, but I swallowed them at the last second, focusing instead on the back of Mel's head, where the pink streaks faded into their natural black. When I met her, Mel hadn't dyed her hair yet. Funnily enough, our first date took place somewhere similar to this.

Although maybe it was a bit of a stretch to try and find a similarity between a local band's small concert and a prison revolt.

I was snapped out of my awkward daze when applause broke out, congratulating the previous act. I hadn't even noticed what it was, though in my defence, doing so required me to see over the thick wall of people.

Standing on her tiptoes to look for Adrienne's signal, Mel gave us a little thumbs-up, waving to Amélie. We were good to go. I found Emry and gestured to the edge of the crowd, whispering the plan into his ear. He nodded, his eyes travelling along the edge of the beach.

When the first audience members began to sit down, we took that as our cue to leave. We fanned out in different groups, splitting off to give the guards a more challenging time. Amid the blackout, the only light came from the sliver of the moon and the guards' flashlights. We had an advantage.

Of course, we had about a thirty-second window before all of that would change.

Something about this side of the fence felt strangely familiar. I couldn't place it in the dark, but it matched a description I had heard about...

I gulped. This was the entrance to the mass grave Arvin had taken Cerina to. The one with the prisoners who hadn't survived the trials.

The thing was, they were probably awful people. Back then, in the Isle's early days, the selected criminals were charged fairly. Even though I was about to destroy the resting place of murderers and thieves, I was about to destroy a resting place none the same.

And maybe I was being unfair. After all, they were nothing but shrivelled corpses. Did they not have the right to the benefit of the doubt?

Some unseen urge compelled me to stay Mel's hand before she pulled the trigger, activating the land mines that would disturb their years of peace.

"Wait-"

I was knocked back by a fiery glow as the pistol fired, coming into contact with the first mine. It sprang into action immediately, pelting the fence with a torrent of rocks as a grey cloud settled. Amélie whooped in triumph. Mel cheered as well, loading up her next bullet.

Emry looked queasy. He shot me a knowing look, and I realised the feeling was mutual.

The blast lit up the night, turning the guards' focus all one way. Like a deer in headlights, I watched as their heads shot simultaneously in our direction. I felt like a guilty little kid caught in the act of stealing a cookie from the pantry.

The next blast fired, and we started to run.

Amélie and one of the guards spoke simultaneously. Their words garbled into a blend, but Amélie's was the only phrase that mattered. The other part was relatively self-explanatory.

"Split up," she ordered, "then meet up at the spot! They don't know which of us has the gun!"

Emry ducked one way, and Amélie and Mel went the other.

The guards charged as well. I still hadn't moved.

I wanted to go with Mel, hear her voice, drink in every moment between us. But I couldn't leave Emry alone for the wolves.

At the last second, I swooped, careening after Emry's dark blob of singed hair. The guards barked orders to follow, breaking into two groups of their own. I felt the rush of air behind me as they gained on us. My hours of sprinting around the track in phys-ed class had paid off, but Emry was running out of steam.

We didn't have much time.

In the thick of the sprint, an idea popped into my mind. I thought it over, weighing the risks as my feet started to slow. I could only hope Emry would figure out what I was doing.

"My name is Lizabeth Merrin!" I screamed, the roar of the wind carrying my words in a swift current, "and I am proud to be free!"

I veered off course, splitting away from Emry and drawing closer to the fence. Two guards were tailing us, but both of them seemed much more interested in me than they did in Emry. Emry flung himself the other way, rearing back for the crowd. Another explosion shook the earth, its pulse matching my own. I breathed a sigh of relief- Mel was still hanging in there.

The guards whipped their heads around, drawn to the noise.

There wasn't much point in following Emry back to where we had come, considering the guards likely had backup on the way. But options were running tight. Technically, I was on the Level Two side of the fence now. I had to get back to the crowd, where I would be able to blend in. I had to find Mel again, or none of us were getting out of here.

My zigzag motions occupied the guards on my tail long enough for me to make one final sprint, taking me to the densely packed group. The music had stopped, and everyone was wandering in confusion. People lept back in surprise as they saw us charging through, forming a wide path.

Blending in was going to be harder than I thought.

I could feel one of the guards breathing down my back, expelling a moist texture of unbrushed teeth and stale saltine crackers. My jaw clenched, and with one giant leap, I swerved left, diving into the mob.

My short, lean complexion worked to my advantage. I slipped through tightly-packed clusters of flailing arms, broad shoulders, long legs, and tall heads. On a mission, I weaved through the crowd, using the chaos not as my sword but as my shield. The guards beat furiously at it, but they couldn't pick me out of the sea of bored inmates, unable to distinguish between a confused Level One and a small figure running for dear life.

Sucking in a deep breath, I burst through the wall of people, following the trail of explosions. Yet another flare sent my ears ringing. They were close to the dock, and the fence was in sight.

We had skipped past the fence factor in our hasty plan, concocting nothing more than a half-baked goal. As far as our strategy meetings were concerned, we had never thought very far past the records room.

In my mad rush, I hadn't been able to spot Jakson, Farrah, or Haven. I could only hope that our preparations had gotten them that far, at least. I had plenty of my own problems to worry about. Problems such as figuring out how to hotwire a *boat*.

I snuck a glance behind me. Adrienne was still in the centre of the field, but she wasn't moving. She wasn't singing, wasn't laughing, didn't possess the usual fire in her smile.

Instead, she stood slack-still, staring into space.

The crowd was already starting to thin. People were either bored, confused, or scared, dipping out of the audience and calling it a night.

For some reason, it made me sad, just then, to think that I would never see the intricately designed walls of building 1-3 again.

"Hey, everyone!" I didn't quite possess Adrienne's natural charisma, but not for lack of trying. A few heads swivelled my way as my reckless plan came into action, but not nearly enough to count for something.

"People! Levels One and Two alike! I need you all to listen to me!"

My second announcement perked up a few more ears, but no one seemed keen on hearing the rest of what I had to say. A few people snickered, which made me fume. Sure, based on looks alone, I was a little harder to take seriously. Long ago, I had given up trying to be the kid whose voice always gets listened to, resolving that I'd never want to be selfish enough to drown out other people's thoughts.

I hated public speaking, but right now, this was another question of priorities.

Either I could be shy and never embarrass myself, or I could take a risk. One of them would end with me behind bars, trapped, persecuted, or maybe worse. The other one had two outcomes- freedom and torture, polar opposites but equally probably alternatives.

They didn't call it the risky option for nothing. I drew in a deep breath, digging my knuckles into my skin. There was no better time to be selfish than right now.

"Everyone! If you want to get off this island, you'll have to help me!" The weight of what I was doing hit me over the head like a bowling ball. I was about to liberate tons of prisoners. Only those who had been willing to watch Adrienne perform would go free, but a vast chunk of those people were Level Twos.

If I set murderers free, did that make me as bad as they were?

And it wasn't just that. I had made a huge mistake before, making a call that sacrificed both myself and Jakson, not to mention Darby. I had doomed all three of us on a whim because I had been stupid enough to take a stand because I had followed my moral compass until it led me off a cliff.

Could I really trust myself to make that kind of choice again?

My tongue froze, the reality flooding like a waterfall. I stood still, petrified, my face blank and indecisive. The spotlight was finally on me, and I didn't know what to do.

I didn't know what was right anymore.

The guards' heads snapped in my direction, making a decision for me. I was being pursued. The very thought made me sick, but there was no doubt about it-

I was on the run. I had no time to think about what was right and no time to worry about what was wrong.

"Hey!" Max cried at the top of his lungs, storming to my side from the centre of the crowd. I had never heard him utter more than two words at a time, let alone scream them. "Shut up and listen to her, you idiots! Do you want to escape, or not?!"

His voice carried, stopping everyone in their tracks at the mention of the word 'escape.'

"We're going to charge the fence," I announced. I had never been more confident of a single thing in my life. "Did you hear that? You have to follow me!"

The last explosion fired, the starting pistol in our great race. Shouts came from behind me, mutters of confusion blending in with battle cries. The guards were pummelled over, swallowed up by the push of the crowd. Max ran at my side, sprinting surprisingly fast. The fence came into view, the metal wires closing in like the walls of a trash compactor.

Mel, Amélie, and Emry were all there, hands pinned behind their backs. Mel's pistol was in a guard's hand, glinting in the moonlight. Their faces lit up when they saw us, but that expression quickly faded into horror. The look was mirrored in my own eyes.

I had unleashed a tide, a thick, unstoppable wave of angry prisoners, angry *rebels*. And the three of them were caught in the crossfires.

I felt people at my back, their arms and legs pressed against me, faster feet nipping my heels. My head swivelled, and I almost smashed my nose into someone's skull. The crowd was behind me, knocking the air from my lungs and forcing me forward. We were a giant, human battering ram.

My hands just had time to shoot out before I was slammed against the fence. The bars cut into my palms, my muscles wobbling to keep my head away from the bending metal. My chest heaved laboriously as people pressed on every end, kicking, clawing, and pounding at the barricade.

At first, I thought it was all in vain. It was all-out madness. People were getting trampled, squished, and stepped on in a hopeless fit. But then the chain links began to give.

I kicked the gate, reinforced by the might of hundreds of inmates, liberating the Level One sector. Locating anyone was a fruitless search. I only knew three things- kick, push, and break.

With a satisfying creak, the fence bent.

People started climbing it, forgetting the threat of the barbed wire completely. Now that the beach was partially secure, nobody had to worry about who dropped where. Already bent askew, the fence sagged under the weight of the prisoners. Someone used my head as a stepladder, pushing me deep into the pit of the crowd.

Grabby hands and kicking feet blocked the moon, plunging me into a darkness that reeked of sweat and stung of blood.

Then we were moving. I couldn't see, but by the chants of triumph, I was able to understand well enough. We had broken past the fence. *We had done it.*

I struggled to keep myself up, tripping over the fallen links and stumbling over the prongs of barbed wire. Something, rather, *someone* pushed against my back, and I tumbled to my knees. Winded, I got onto my hands and knees, lifting up my head. The rocky beach was in sight, freedom only inches away.

But the mob was stronger.

Kicked around like a punching bag, I had to struggle to keep my head afloat. Suffocated screams, not of liberation but of exertion, filled the air. My breaths came in sharp wheezes, both my knees scraped.

"Lizabeth! Grab on!"

An unfamiliar voice pierced the loud backdrop. I whirled around, nearly getting mauled over a second time.

When I saw the swash of blue hair, my heart skidded to a stop. I had to pause to register what I was seeing- the wound on his leg, the mischievous green-eyed gaze. Perhaps I had been kicked in the head harder than I thought.

Tenderly, I reached out to clasp Darby's calloused hand, puzzled by the firm, very much real texture of his palm.

He pulled me up to my feet, and I dusted myself off, unable to break his gaze.

"You-" I said. "Why did you help me?"

Darby dropped his hand, a little bit flustered.

"Because *you* helped *me*. You chose not to turn me in. This seems stupid and cheesy, and I'll deny I ever told you about it, but what you did… when you continued to lead those people…" he took a deep breath, babbling quickly. His words came out in a rushed, garbled string, but I could tell by the red on his face that he meant every one of them.

"You changed me. Now come on, or they'll trample you again."

He didn't have to tell me twice. We sprinted down the charred remains of the metal dock, and I caught sight of Emry. I ran to him, grabbing him by the wrist. His eyes lit up the moment he saw me.

"Lizabeth!" He cried. "There you are!"

"Emry! Is Mel okay?"

"I saw her a few minutes ago. She and Amélie were trying to pick the locks to the boat."

The thought of Mel alone with another girl made me bristle with jealousy. I quickly pushed the feeling aside, jogging ahead. The thin metal dock, rather, what was left of it, ran all the way to the small briefing room.

Beside it stood the huge transport boat, towering far above us.

Amélie was at the top of the deck, throwing a rope down to Mel. A few of the others had assembled beside them, and I noticed, with relief, that among them were Jakson and Farrah.

As for the rest of the prisoners, the initial craze had passed. The vast majority of them had stopped moving, completely shell-shocked. The less rational of the group were throwing themselves in the sea, screaming prayers or insults or both, slurred together in an incomprehensible medley.

Suddenly, I considered something. *This* section of the beach had been blown up, but we hadn't managed to complete a full circle. The mines on the right-hand side of the briefing room were still very active and just as deadly.

The remaining guards were still desperately trying to handcuff people, but they were severely outnumbered. Darby left to join the thick of it, kicking a guard in the stomach and tossing their gun into the ocean.

I turned to Emry.

"Do you know where Max, Adrienne, and Haven are?"

A shadow passed over Emry's face.

"Max is over by the boat, with the others. Adrienne is here too; I just saw her. But Haven... they never came back from the centre circle."

I gulped. There was not the time to think of the worst.

"Let's go. We have to get people on this boat, and we have to do it now."

Jakson gave Farrah a hand up the rope ladder before jumping down to aid the others, who were patiently waiting below. Max hesitated at the bottom, biting his lip and rushing back to look for Adrienne.

I hopped on, clambering up the web of ropes.

"Hey, Lizabeth?" Emry cried, "I just wanted to say thank you! For everything!"

I furrowed my eyebrows in confusion. What was that supposed to mean? I shrugged, turning around. I had probably misheard him.

At the top, I caught up with Farrah, who was opening the hatch below decks, a shadow hanging over her face. Steadily, I brought up the nerve to ask the question nobody wanted an answer to.

"What happened to Haven?"

She turned her eyes to me, and the shadow darkened. I bit my lip. I had expected to feel sad, and of course I did. But I also felt angry and exhausted. I was burning, but I was burnt out at the same time.

"Were you close with them?" I asked, unsure of what to say. She had known Haven longer than I had, after all.

Farrah shook her head.

"Not particularly. Not in the way Max and Adrienne were, anyway. I feel like I stole Haven's last moments from them. I have no right to those memories."

"You didn't steal them if you didn't choose them. I know I'm giving unsolicited advice here, but I feel like the only way to deal with that burden is to share it with the people who deserve to know the truth. I'm so sorry-"

"Don't be. Nobody could've known..." she trailed off, pulling in a deep breath. "We didn't even destroy the records. But Jakson recorded a video of Haven's dying breaths and sent it to all the major news stations in Sykona. The world is soon to find out the truth. Although, I can't say I'm completely clear on what the 'truth' even is."

"The only thing that matters right now is that we're on this boat, about to sail to freedom together."

Farrah sighed. "But we *aren't* all together. Not only that, but we just liberated a bunch of criminals. That thought makes me uneasy."

"There's no going back now. Frankly, I don't think there ever was."

"I'd attribute that comment to nothing more than pessimism if I didn't think you were onto something."

Everyone else was starting to board the boat. As the deck filled up, Farrah, Jakson, and I moved to the captain's control room, where we met with Amélie and Mel. Max and Adrienne were nowhere to be found, but I had seen the two of them going up the ladder.

I looked at the controls. The room was bare apart from a leather-lined steering wheel, a panel of confusing mechanical readings, and a coat hook. On the hook, a blue rain poncho with the label *captain* on the front sat next to a formal-looking sailor's hat.

"I don't know about you," Amélie said, picking up the hat and twirling it around her finger, "but I don't have a *clue* how to pilot a boat."

"We're on this ship with roughly two hundred prison escapees," Mel said, "I'm sure at least *one* of them knows something about sailing."

"Operating a cargo ship is a little different than paddling a canoe," Amélie cut in.

"Even that's better than any experience I have. Do you guys mind going around looking for someone? I'd like to chat with Lizabeth in private."

Everyone nodded, dispersing.

Mel stepped closer, and for a fleeting second, I both hoped and feared that she was about to kiss me. But all she did was close the door, heaving a deep sigh.

"I'm so sorry, Lizabeth. You put everything on the line for me. And, even after everything you did, I got myself caught."

I found her hand, taking it gently between my fingers. I recognised the light touch, my nerves lighting up as our palms reconnected like the broken shards of a puzzle. My grip tightened.

"I missed you. Every day. Even though it was selfish. So, of course I forgive you, even if that's the worst part of me talking."

Mel smiled, her eyes softening. She stepped closer, her warmth radiating up to me. After a long moment, she spoke.

"Are you sure we did the right thing?"

I dropped her hand, and she visibly winced.

"What do you mean?"

"Well-" she stammered, catching herself. "If this boat thing goes according to plan, we're about to let a ton of inmates loose. The government is… problematic, to say the least, but the guys that got me sent to the centre circle in the first place could be on this ship as we speak. Sure, people are complicated, but some of us were taken to this island for a reason. Are you sure we should be here at all?"

"No. I'm not. But a couple of minutes ago, I ran into Darby."

A flicker of worry passed over Mel's face.

"Shit. Did he hurt you?"

"Quite the opposite. He helped me. I don't know why or how, but he told me he'd changed. That *I* had changed him."

"And you believe that?"

"If he were truly a terrible person, he would've left me to get trampled. But if he can change, even a little… I think these people can too."

"Some of them are *Level Twos*. They took people's *lives*. Can you really get over something like that?"

My mind immediately shot to Cerina. Oddly enough, the first memory that sprung up wasn't of her harsh words or her terrifying leaderly presence. It was a set of two flashbacks. The first was the painful memory of my awkward washroom incident and the tampon she had slid into my oblivious, mortified hand. The second was a reel of the day she had been turned out of building 1-3 by Joe. *This Level Two has been manipulating you. She is here because she has no other place in this world other than the hell of this island*. That's what he had said to Emry, wasn't it? And even then, we had all gotten up to defend her.

I had gone with them because, like all of us, Cerina was human.

Drawing a shaky breath, I gave Mel the best answer I could.

"We'll have to see."

Tense silence, a thick, murky haze, blanketed the room. I couldn't stand it in the slightest, especially not between Mel and me. We, along with everybody else, hung on a fragile thread.

"Well, then," Mel said, meeting my eyes. I stared into her crystal blue irises. They matched the sea we floated on, perfectly at home. "If that's the case, we probably have a few minutes before the others return."

I hesitated before smiling, hesitated before pulling in close. Mel's arms wound around my waist, her breath hot against my neck. I shut my eyes, leaning into her.

I felt the shadow of her lips as they moved closer, waiting for me to complete the gap. There was so little space between them.

I only had to move an inch.

Half an inch.

A quarter inch.

At the last second, I stopped myself, pulling back. This was exactly like the times before, the beautiful moments I had struggled with all my might to regain. But it didn't feel right. Not anymore. Not like this.

Hurt passed over Mel's features. I owed her an explanation, an excuse. But I couldn't form words, struggling for air, drowning in a current.

My actions would have to speak for themselves.

I turned away, shutting my eyes as I stepped into the night air. My eyes stung, and I slipped out of the room, scanning the deck behind the glossy film of my watery eyelids.

My lungs burned as though they were filled halfway with water. There was enough room within them for me to cough and sputter but plenty of space for struggle.

I spotted Jakson perched on the top of the ladder below deck, balancing on the topmost rung. Dashing ahead, I caught him just in time.

"Jakson," I panted. A single word. He stopped, looking up at me. For a brief moment, he frowned in confusion. A second later, understanding sunk into his eyes.

Briefly, he glanced down at Farrah, who was managing quite well on the ladder with a broken arm. He cleared his throat, informing her that he'd be right back. Then he reversed his course, hopping up to meet me.

We took a few steps away from the hatch, avoiding any unwanted eavesdroppers. Jakson twitched awkwardly, waiting for me to speak the words both of us grasped for.

"When Darby attacked me... back on the Isle, all those weeks ago... you told me that we should spend some time to grow apart," I said, the delay in my phrases shining with prominence.

Jakson's throat tensed up. He nodded tersely.

"I do recall saying such a thing."

"Well-" I continued, "I'm not sure how to say this. A lot has happened. I'll regret what I did forever, but... I can't change the past. However, I *can* choose what I do in the present. Something Darby, of all people, said to me made me realise that. And I feel like I'm ready to forgive myself. It might be a long shot or a hopeless cause, but... would you consider being my friend again?"

Jakson's face was unreadable.

"I've figured out some stuff, too, you could say," he muttered. "And I think I'm the one who should be apologising. Of course I forgive you, Lizabeth."

A small smile crept up to my face. "Friends?"

Jakson nodded.

"Friends. Shall we shake on it?" He held out a hand, but I didn't take it.

Instead, I wrapped my arms around his shoulders, pulling him into a tight hug. Surprised for a moment, he tensed up, straightening his spine.

But then he relaxed, pulling his arm out and hugging me back.

We faced each other, and I found, to my surprise, that the ocean of guilt stirring in my ribcage had spilt out, letting me drink in a glorious, untainted mouthful of air.

We could never go back to the past, I realised, but maybe this new future wasn't so bad.

***

Not only could he draw, but Max could pilot a ship. He was our best bet, anyway. Adrienne settled him into the captain's chair, placing the white hat hanging in the corner on the top of her friend's head for extra moral support.

Max swatted it off his brow, seizing the controls. We all held our breath. He muttered an instruction to Adrienne, who took off to the engine room, wishing us good luck.

Then we started moving.

Everyone cheered, not just the few of us crowding the captain's room but the entirety of the ship. I peered out the window as we left the dock, biting my lip as I noticed a few prisoners still struggling with the guards on the beach. I spotted somebody on the edge of the boat, winding up a throw. Inside their hand was a rock.

They tossed it over their head, completing a magnificent arc across the sky. It clattered to the beach, rolling once, twice-

I closed my eyes as the last explosion went off, instantly killing those on the shore and giving us an extra push. Silent tears streamed down my cheeks.

There was my farewell to the Isle of Rebels. An explosive blast, a killing blow.

Two salty tears.

I turned to face the others. Adrienne returned promptly, sitting next to Max with a solemn veil over her once-bright eyes. Jakson squared his shoulders, walking over to the two of them. He started to speak, and I caught snippets of their hushed conversation.

"...Haven's last words...."

Picking up the start of the conversation, I tuned out their chat. I had no business hearing whatever message Jakson was passing down.

I took in the sight of the room. Adrienne and Max comforted one another, the tears in their eyes drying slowly but surely. Amélie paced back and forth, plotting our course for the future, anxiously muttering in French. Farrah stood in the other corner, deep in thought. We were the Escape Artists. We had done it, and everything was as it should be, at least, as close enough as possible.

Except-

"Hey," I ventured uneasily, "where's Emry?"

Everyone looked at me, then looked around the room. He wasn't with us.

"He could still be on the boat with the other prisoners?" Amélie suggested, doubt creeping into her tone.

But I knew, in my gut, that she was only grasping.

Now I understood his words to me as I climbed onto the ship. I hadn't misheard anything. While I was on the ladder, his message half-muted by the wind in my ears, Emry had delivered his parting words. His goodbye.

The idiot had gone back for Cerina.

Cerina Rayz

To break the chain

"Step off. I don't have all day." My father looked at his watch, tapping it with disapproval. "We only have twenty more minutes together. I wouldn't want your dawdling to put that time to waste."

I steadied myself on the edge of the lift, gripping the bronze bar. Gingerly, I planted my foot on the ground, descending onto the cold stone.

"Whatever ends this abysmal ordeal," I grunted, pulling the stubborn folds of my puffy dress out of the shaft.

My father smiled, although, in the dim light of the cave, it looked more like a grimace. "That's the spirit."

He moved away from me, stepping back so I could take it all in. Only then did I notice what was in front of me, tied to the rock. Still in his faded prison uniform was a captive Arvin. He shot his head up, wincing against the strain on his wrists. Two wires jutted out of his wrinkled ears, attached to a dangling black earpiece. They bobbed back and forth on a pendulum, each pull initiating a wince.

"Ce- Cerina!" He cried, bursting toward me. His ropes caught him, and he yelped, flung onto his back like a capsized turtle.

Ignoring my father completely, I grabbed Arvin's hand and pulled him up. His skin was dry and exfoliating, reminiscent of snake scales long shed.

"What are you doing here?" I asked, "how did you… how did you *get* here?"

"There's another access point via boat. Do you see that little tunnel over there?" My father pointed to a shaft partially submerged in water, stepping agonisingly close. "He was taken in by one of our guards." He laughed. "I'm surprised he didn't drown.

But my uncle was always second only to me. He might have given himself up, but even now, he has guts."

I looked between my father and Arvin. I could certainly see the resemblance. Their eyes were the same dull grey; however, the shade was very different. In Arvin's case, his eyes looked like shimmering pools of wisdom, dimmed with age but as expansive as ever.

My father's eyes, on the other hand, possessed a maniacal sheen.

"You know, Arvin, I used to look up to you," he said, disappointment dripping from his tone. "Until you faked your death. Broke into your own tomb and lined it with poisonous flowers. You must have thought you were quite clever, old man. But your strength was a more admirable trait than your intelligence. We found you. We let you go back to the Isle with your earpieces and the madness they fed you, and, like Cerina, you became quite the useful spy. You'd be amazed by the commands that can be passed down through speech. But even those pale in comparison to the feats that can be accomplished face-to-face."

Arvin lashed out, lunging against his bonds and putting his face inches from my father's. "I have never served you," he cursed, his words infused with acid, "and I never will."

My father chuckled. "Fool. You've been serving me this whole time."

My father turned back to me, putting Arvin behind him. "Where were we?" He said. "Ah, yes. Cerina. May I direct your eyes to the ground?"

Puzzled, I glanced at the smooth stone beneath our feet. Etched into the glossy rock were the distinct lines of neatly carved letters.

Below the crisp, chiselled message, was a far more chaotic stone-based drawing board. Underneath the words, at least twenty, possibly fifty names had been carved in by hand, scarring the rock slab with their handwritten tendrils.

Many of them had been worn with age, but I could still make out the texture of the most recent names.

Before I could read the list, my father brandished an item from his pocket. He handed it to me, and I ran my fingers over the ice-cold, metallic surface.

I had to bite back a laugh. Once more, my father had given me a knife.

Only, this time, the blade was double-sided.

"I've appointed you my successor," my father continued, "but the choice is yours- you can inherit my power and position, or you can stay down here and die like your great uncle Arvin is about to, now that he is useless to me. He might have passed the trials, but he was too good to be made into a soldier. He had no remaining weaknesses. I stole his freedom, and, through his earpiece, I stole his secrets. Do you really want to join him when I steal his life as well?"

"It doesn't seem like much of a choice," I muttered, "does it?"

"That's what you'd think at first. But one of the options enslaves you, while the other sets you free. Really, you could flip it both ways. You'll have to pick soon, though... our time is running out."

I pursed my lips, grazing the sharp blade with my thumb.

"What does this transition of power, or whatever you want to call it, entail? What does it mean to be your successor?"

"Read the slab."

My father stepped away, and my eyes skirted over the sculpted surface.

The criteria for our ranks, written by Rhina Rayz

-The individual is strong of will and strong of spirit. They are not daunted by bloodshed and are willing and capable of making any sacrifice for the good of their master.

-The individual has an appreciation for violence; however, they are not too drawn to the concept. They have a commanding presence but understand obedience.

-The individual is witty and capable of navigating both social and physical challenges with ease.

-The individual is capable of leadership and can harness power of all kinds.

-The individual cannot be cowed by anyone other than a Rayz.

This signature certifies the permanent and irrevocable loyalty of the subject and offers the candidate's service to Sykona, the Rayz family, and all of its successors.

. This was no transfer of political power. It was a transfer of physical, immeasurable strength.

An individual cannot be cowed by anyone other than a Rayz.

What the hell was that supposed to mean?

"Normally, you don't get a choice in the matter," my father said. "But you are no ordinary individual. You are a Rayz. If you inscribe your name onto this document, the guards will obey you. You will have absolute power over their actions, over their thoughts. Rhina's power was hypnosis, Cerina. And its reach traverses generations."

My fist clenched. "What's the catch?"

"I am on my deathbed," my father said in a careful, measured tone. "But even the commanders have people they obey. Orders they follow. Even if the givers of those orders are long deceased, rotting in their graves."

Words began to float up to my ears, reverberating around the chasm. I looked up, searching for the source of the noise.

It was an echo, and a powerful one. Was I just imagining it, or was it repeating in my voice?

Dizzy, all of a sudden, I took a step back, nearly plummeting to the jagged ground below. I caught myself just in time, staggering forwards.

My eyes settled back on my father, zeroing in on his face.

His mouth was moving.

Like a mantra, the words repeated over and over.

The individual is witty and capable of navigating both social and physical challenges with ease. The individual is capable of leadership and can harness power of all kinds. The individual cannot be cowed by anyone other than a Rayz.

The individual cannot be cowed by anyone other than a Rayz.

The individual cannot be cowed by anyone other than a Rayz.

I screamed, breaking the stream of words blaring into my eardrums. I took the small knife and plunged the blade deep into the fleshy muscle below my thumb, twisting it for good measure. The noise stopped, fading out. Replacing it was the white-hot flash of pain and the wail of my vocal cords.

The searing jolt was intense, incapacitating in its own way, but it didn't daunt me.

I surged forward. *The individual cannot be cowed by anyone other than a Rayz.* I called the words back now, finally understanding their meaning.

My father was no diplomat. He was a manipulator.

"Hypnosis," I rasped, "I should have known."

I thought back to the strange incident at the centre circle. I had told the guards to get away from me, and they had obliged without complaint, stomping off to the other side.

Without even knowing it, I had given them orders. I thought of Irabella. Her ruthless, uncharacteristic actions. *My* ruthless, uncharacteristic actions. My mind drifted to the sickness that had spread across the sector. It had placed us under a firm hold, but in the end, it had stopped. In the end, Haven had resisted. I had resisted.

I lunged, driving the blade towards my father's neck. He knocked it back with ease, and it flew from my fingers, clattering to the rocks. He laughed, the chortle rebounding off the walls.

"You can't kill me, Cerina. I made you."

He gripped my wrists, forcing my flailing hands to my sides.

"Do you need me to go over our agreement again?"

With a sharp jab, I kicked his kneecap. He doubled back, winded.

"I never signed shit," I bit, advancing. My father stepped back in a gesture of surrender, throwing his hands in the air.

"You're feisty," he stated. "That's a required trait."

"It's also an awfully inconvenient one."

I went for the kneecap again, but he anticipated it, dodging effortlessly. Thrown off, I recovered just in time to duck before his right hook made contact, beating at empty air.

"If I commanded you," my father shouted, "we would be unstoppable! You would learn the art! We would continue the line!"

"There is no *we* in that scenario."

My father shook his head slowly, as though I were failing to comprehend a very important point.

"You're only looking at my role, Cerina. You will have the power. I… will be a corpse."

I evaluated my options. I didn't have many at the moment, but I had a very short window to make a choice. My father dropped his hands, tapping his watch.

"I haven't made this difficult for you. Don't make me do things the hard way."

"Why did you bring me to this place?" I spat, continuing to stalk forward.

My father pressed his lips into a firm line. "Because it's not a natural beauty. It was carved below this house, and it served as a meeting place. It was where I got my first orders, and it's where you will too. Very few things of true beauty came into this world the way they are. They were sculpted. Controlled."

"Commanded," I finished for him.

"Exactly," he said.

It was where I got my first orders. The words repeated in my head, not as a motto but as a revelation. He wasn't the first to use the Trial system to get things done.

He was merely filling out his role in a cycle before it was too late.

"I pity you," I said. "You have never been free once in your life, have you?"

"That depends on how you look at it. If you crave freedom so desperately, all you had to do was stab that blade into your neck. Slice the jugular. It's not too late, you know. If your soul is truly beyond redemption, then let it go. You've never been free, either. None of us have. We might be guards; we might be inmates. Either way, everyone on this Isle is a prisoner."

"Doesn't that make you sick?"

"No. It makes me happy. It's a beautiful, methodical system, and we are at the top of it, able to watch and spectate as order runs its course. All I am is proud.

Proud of myself. Proud of Sykona. And I can be proud of you, too."

My fists weren't raised anymore. I dropped my defences, narrowing my eyes into slits.

"Power is nothing more than an illusion," I said. "You command nothing."

My father shook his head, laughing under his breath. "Who cares if it's an illusion? As long as people believe it, it's the same as reality. No one will be able to touch you. If freedom is your incentive, what's more liberating than that?"

"If I listen, no one will be able to command me," I snapped, "except you. And your commander before that. And the commander before them."

The individual cannot be cowed by anyone other than a Rayz.

Perhaps my father thought that by exposing me to the world's cruelties, he had been preparing me. But before he had pushed me over the edge, I had seen beyond the brutal cycle of violence. I had led a Family. I had belonged to a group. I had met Irabella, Emry, and Arvin.

I understood the guards, now, and the brutality they served. That brutality wasn't strength. But what I had? It was.

"This is mercy," I said, voicing my thoughts aloud. "Not weakness."

Without waiting for a reaction, I placed my palm over my father's heart and pushed him into the chasm.

He jolted, his feet skidding over the rock. He turned back to me, his eyes widening in shock and terror.

Then he smiled. Not in the coy way I had come to recognise, but in a soft, peaceful line. Calm resolve. As he toppled over, like a tree struck by an axe, he didn't fight his fate, spreading his arms like wings.

His final statement echoed across the walls.

You made your choice.

A second later, he was gone. A painful second stretched as he fell, disappearing from view.

The thud that followed was inevitable. I had expected to hear the crack of his ribs, anticipating the feel of the shaking ground as sharp rocks jutted into his back. But I hadn't prepared for the chill that hit my bloodstream, sending an earthquake up my arms as I untied Arvin's bonds.

Goosebumps pricked my skin. I slid Arvin's ropes off his wrists, pulling him to his feet. He staggered, wobbling slightly. Slowly, I brought him to the lift, our footfalls echoing against the rocky walls. I helped him up the step, and as soon as he reached the golden platform, he sagged to the ground, wheezing.

Instead of seeing relief in his slumped features, I was looking at a reflection of my fear.

"What-" Arvin rasped, "what have you done?" He tugged at the wires dangling from his ears, ripping out the plastic-coated coils. They popped out with a series of slow, agonising snaps, clattering to the stony ground beneath him. At long last, the ghosts lurking in his headspace were gone.

I left Arvin in the elevator, walking to the edge of the precipice. I couldn't resist one final look. Trodding on top of the oath, I teetered on the rocky cliff, staring at the shadowy form splayed over the rocks. It wasn't bloody, which, in a way, was worse than any gore.

Fixed in that position, my father could have been sleeping. His end was nowhere near satisfactory, but his features were perfectly still. Perfectly resolute.

"I hope you find your freedom," I called, choking on the words.

With a last, parting effort, I kicked off the wobbly shoes, tossing them on top of my father's body. They barely made a sound as they landed, cushioned by his suit.

From there, I didn't look back.

I closed the door to the lift, wrapping my fingers around the crank's handle. The brass was still warm from my father's touch, contrary to the ice-cold metal underneath my bare feet. I wound up the crank, stone-faced, taking us back up.

The first explosion from above sent a tremor through the earth. With my other hand, I smoothed down the dress, adjusting my hair and checking my reflection in that same brass piece. Fine-tuning my features, I lifted my shoulders, correcting my slouch. Against all odds, I would be composed.

Because it was true. They didn't call this place the Isle of Rebels for nothing.

Maybe, in the end, this was what my father had wanted.

Emry McLeod

The things we do

Adrenaline. From the mere scrapings I had picked up from science class, I had learned that it was a hormone that makes you excited, anxious, and ready to run for your life. Its chemical composition was $C_9H_{13}NO_3$, and when you broke it down like that, it almost sounded boring. But when you truly got to experience it, those moments were anything but. For me, adrenaline was a cocktail of fear, invincibility, and an odd sensation of guilty pleasure. I felt as though I were about to get caught doing something terrible, but was off the hook for now.

The surprise explosion on the beach shook the ground, skidding my feet to a halt. My legs argued with me, eager to get moving again, but I couldn't stop myself from stealing a glance behind me.

On the rocky beach, the few stragglers that had remained, mostly guards, lay decimated in a spread of carnage. Most were in several pieces, knocked back by the blast. The prisoners that lay dead next to the uniformed officials had either been complete idiots or brave heroes. Either way, if it weren't for them, the huge cargo ship drifting off down the horizon would never have been able to set sail.

With my limited eyesight, the boat was nothing but a grey blob on a midnight-blue backdrop. But the second chemical that entered my veins painted more of a picture than my beat-up eyesight ever could. I couldn't tell what the chemical was. All I knew was that it was uninvited, clashing terribly with the jittery stream of adrenaline and fading into a gross blend of two polar opposites mushed against each other.

The last shards of excitement ebbed away as I thought of everyone on that ship, sailing out to meet their futures.

Farrah.

Amélie.

Jakson. *He'd* know what the weird hormones were called.

Max, Adrienne.

And Lizabeth. Something gnawed at my heart, the same sticky, unpleasant ripping sensation I had felt when I was taken away from my family. I didn't know where it came from because the two situations were completely different. All those weeks ago, all I had cared about was getting bailed out.

But right now… fuck it, I was sad.

I hadn't even gotten to say goodbye. Pangs of guilt seized my lungs, sucking the air right out of them. What had I been thinking? Cerina might not even be alive, and there was no way I could find her, let alone break her out, all on my own.

I had done the right thing. I repeated that mantra to myself over and over again as I forced myself back to the beach, watching where I stepped. I hated what I was about to do, but it wasn't like I had much choice.

There was no one I could depend on now. If I was going to free Cerina, I was the only one who could do it.

***

From the wreckage, I managed to scrape together a guard's uniform. Or rather, the pieces of several guards' uniforms, some of them with *pieces of the guards* attached. The slightly-tattered uniform shirt I'd managed to gather fit well enough, but the pants were a lost cause. The best I could do was roll up the legs and hope they wouldn't fall down, silently cursing the previous owner for not using a belt.

I had even managed to acquire a pair of gloves, although three of the fingers on the right hand were singed off. The ID card I'd picked up looked nothing like me, but it was the only one that hadn't been melted beyond recognition. At least the barcode wasn't obstructed, although if someone checked the photo, I'd be done for. Sure, my style had changed a bit since the hair-burning incident, but not enough for me to pass off as a strawberry-blond girl with functional glasses. If I was even seeing the fuzzy picture correctly. I smeared some blood over the photo, hoping it would be enough to mask the identity of its real owner.

I was a bedraggled mess, but on the plus side, everyone had been fighting. I'd hardly stand out. I looked like I had barely survived a landmine explosion, but... that explanation checked out.

The last thing I was missing was a rifle. That and a decent alias, but the latter was more or less impossible. A few guns had been tossed in the sea, one of which I picked up easily, dampening the cuffs of my already-too-large pants. They tugged at my waistline, threatening to fall down. I hiked them back up, tucking in my shirt and puffing out my chest. The last thing I wanted was to make a pantless appearance in the centre circle.

The name of the guard whose card I had stolen was Amanda Smith. It was an older name, which worked to my advantage because that meant it was probably fake.

I left the beach behind and began the sprint to the centre circle. The adrenaline was back, and it was stronger than ever. I ran as fast as my legs could take me. There was no point in pacing myself because I was inspired. There wasn't a chance on this earth I could just start strolling.

I came to a halt at the open gate, nearly toppling over from exhaustion. Nobody stood in front of the plastic screen, which was more foreboding than relieving. I risked a glance through the opening. I couldn't believe I was returning to the mouth of the horrors.

Through my brief glance, I noticed that the setup hadn't changed. Every single guard, the vast majority of them struggling to stay awake, was still positioned around the house.

I tried to reason with my gut feeling, but deep down, I knew that Cerina was inside that building, and would *remain* inside that building for an indefinite period of time.

The only question was how the hell I expected to get in.

I pressed my back up against the wall. It wasn't a *super* inconspicuous move, sure, but I had been conspicuous from the start. As long as I wasn't seen yet, I was fine. I could think.

The same mental block that had been set in front of me when I was dealing with Irabella had returned, this time worse than ever. I was hyperventilating, the sweat mixing in with the various shades of blood speckled over my uniform.

High-pressure situations were definitely not my thing.

I fought down the jitters. What would Jakson do? What would *Lizabeth* do?

They certainly wouldn't be doing this, hiding like a chicken and wishing they could be anywhere but here. I let go of the wall, strutting forward with my head up. Might as well face the music. Sneaking wasn't an option anymore.

With mild interest, the first guards at the gate turned their eyes to me. I grinned out of awkward instinct, looking way too jovial for a guard whose companions had just been maimed and ravaged. I dropped the goofy smile and thought of the first depressing thing that came to mind. Cerina dying. Of course, that made me think of situations that could lead *up* to her death, and if I were to watch her *die*, it meant I would have to *get* to her first. Which would mean swooping in and saving her and watching her grateful reaction-

"Hey, dude, what's your problem?" A very insensitive guard clapped me on the back of the head. I stumbled. Behind me was a very tall, broad-shouldered woman with a no-nonsense attitude. I gulped. Behind *her* were two other guards who were very similar in appearance, eyeing me as though I were a toddler who had stumbled in on a private discussion.

"I, uh…" I scrambled, holding my ground. I couldn't run now. Cerina was still here. I had to play it cool.

I had been called 'dude'. That was, oddly enough, a good sign. You didn't call potential assassins 'dude', no- you slapped them in chains and sent them on their way. This guard thought I was one of her own.

Although from her face, I could tell that my guise was quickly slipping.

"Um," I stammered, "the prisoners! They- they got away. We, uh, have to go after them?"

I phrased the last bit like a question, trailing off. The guards looked at each other. I was sure they didn't buy it. The one in the middle stepped closer, narrowing her eyes.

Cho grunted, and I pressed my eyelids shut. Maybe if I didn't *see* the wound she was about to inflict, it wouldn't hurt as much.

"You're lucky you made it out," she said. I breathed a huge sigh of relief, barely hiding it behind a quick cough. "Stupid commander," she continued, "posts everyone important here to watch the house while idiots like you get to run amok. No wonder something happened. 'Bout how many got out? And why aren't you following them right now?"

"They got away on one of the boats. The rest of the guards got blown to pieces by the mines. As for the prisoners, about half the island's sea-bound. I- I tried to stop 'em-"

"You're shitting me, right?" The guard's attention was now grabbed. Her nostrils flared, her fingers tightening on her rifle.

"I wish I was."

"What's your name, boy? Normally I wouldn't bother with someone of a lower rank, but if you're the only survivor, I owe you that much."

I gulped. "Amand…o. Smith. Amando Smith. That's me. What about you?"

She scoffed. "I'm not giving that to you. You might be pitiful, but you don't deserve *that* much of my sympathy. Now find your captain and get into place. We're gonna be here for a while."

"We're not going after them?"

"The hell are you talking about?"

"I mean, why aren't you going after them?"

"Shut up. You know perfectly well why we can't. You're the only one who hasn't been commanded."

"Commanded?"

"Are you dense? We have to follow orders. Now piss off and find your captain before I lose my patience."

With a nod, I scurried off to nowhere in particular. I circled the house, guards' stares following me at every turn. I looked more out of place than a rainforest bird flapping its way through a blizzard.

"Hey! You there!" I froze, slowly turning my head. A man with a round face and sagging, wrinkly cheeks pointed a stubby finger at me like the cops on TV. My adam's apple bobbed. With a quick glance, I surveyed the area.

I was on the far end of the circle. Not close enough to the door to make a run for it, and, now that I had caught the guards' attention, too obvious to slip away unseen.

"Yep?" I squeaked.

The guard's nostrils flared.

"Can I see your ID card?"

I held out the card, noticing that some of the blood had smudged. Amanda Smith's forehead was clearly visible, and it looked nothing like my own. The guard came closer, squinting to take a look. As he approached, two things went through my head.

The first: undeniable terror and dread. (Maybe that was two things in one?)

The second: a terrible but unfathomably brilliant idea.

I dropped the card before the guard had time to put two and two together and whipped out my rifle. With it came the drawing of every other weapon in the vicinity, but by the time my gun was out, I was already running.

The house's back window was broad and beautiful, the stained-glass panes reflecting the moonlight into a brilliant mosaic of beams. It was also just an inch taller than I was.

A weird sensation of guilt plagued me as I smashed the window with my rifle, not daring to risk shooting the thing. Not only did the purple-stained glass look great, but it also blocked my view of what was happening inside. For all I knew, there could be people on the other end, and whoever's side they were on, I didn't want anyone else getting hurt.

Not to mention that if I loaded the thing, I'd be more likely to accidentally shoot myself in the head than actually succeed in doing my target damage.

The brittle panes broke without strain, the old glass crumbling under my strokes. I ducked at the last second, swerving out of the way as the first shots began to fire, decimating the window completely. Panting heavily, I leapt through it, landing on my hands and knees and skidding through the frame, not stopping to assess the damage. I was in a dimly lit hallway, a soft carpet underneath me.

The scent of burning candles reached my nose. I looked up as I ran, resting my sights on the oil lamps fastened to the ceiling, their flames swaying in the newly let-in breeze.

Footfalls pounded, and I skidded down the next hallway, swerving as I blew past closed doors. Cerina could have been behind any one of them, locked in chains or worse.

Aside from the gunshots announcing my pursuers, the house was eerily quiet.

What if she was being tortured? What if she was dead?

I continued on, searching for a living room, an entryway, a creepy basement, *anything* to get me on my feet. The hallway before me was long and sprawling, and the guards, angrily cursing my fake name, weren't far behind.

As far as mansions went, this one actually wasn't that big. But if I continued down this path, I'd be a corpse in a matter of seconds.

I shot a hand out and twisted the nearest doorknob. The door popped open, revealing a small bathroom.

I tumbled in, just barely getting the door closed behind me.

The sound of a mini-stampede shook the house, rumbling at the same speed as my racing heart. I wiped my forehead. Not even ten minutes had gone by before my cover had been officially blown. I slid the silver chain into the old-style lock, catching my breath. At least I wouldn't need this ridiculous uniform anymore.

I had left my prison shirt back on the beach, but to prevent the guard's from falling, I had opted to keep the bottom half of my prison uniform on. I looked ridiculous in the full-length mirror positioned on the other end of the wall, but mobility was far easier without the baggy trousers.

Even though the baggy prison sweats *definitely* clashed with the collared guard's shirt.

I slumped against the door, taking inventory of my brief refuge. I hiked my bunchy sleeves up, peeling the gloves from my fingers. I didn't have long. Sooner or later, the guards would complete their sweep and figure out I'd hidden somewhere. Then, it would only be a matter of time. The flimsy lock would be useless against bullets and kicks, and in the cramped room, I would have nowhere to run.

The bathroom contained a single toilet, a wooden sink with exposed plumbing, and the mirror, propped against the wall. The toilet's flush handle hung from the ceiling, dangling on a chain like the kind you'd see in old-fashioned movies. A lonely, unopened bar of soap sat on the counter. For a brief moment, I debated swallowing the thing whole. *Something* in there had to be poisonous, and a quick death at the hands of a chemical concoction would be preferable to the guards' brutal punishment any day.

I searched the area for anything that could be used as a weapon. Amid the window-smashing dilemma, I had dropped the rifle, which meant I certainly didn't have the upper hand in that department. But I did have the element of surprise working for me, and if I could get my hands on a crowbar or a conveniently-placed scalpel, I might just stand a chance.

Unfortunately for me, none of those items could be found in a bathroom.

Hastily, I rifled through everything that opened—which wasn't a lot. I considered the pipes to the sink, but there was no way I could take apart a plumbing system bare-handed. Or with any kind of tool, for that matter.

There was no medicine cabinet, no drawers. There wasn't even a toothbrush, which could at least be used to gauge someone's eye out.

I bet the bristles would hurt a lot.

Shoving my disturbing thoughts aside, I re-focused on the task at hand. There was no shower, nor was anything attached to the toilet seat. All I found behind the mirror was a boring-ass wall, and the only piece of furniture that wasn't fixed to the ground was the metal roll that made up the middle of the toilet paper holder. I unfastened it, balancing it for weight.

It wasn't plastic, I had to give it that, but the thing wasn't heavy in the slightest. As an inherently weak individual, I'd have a really tough time bashing someone's head in with that thing.

Although I seriously hoped that things wouldn't come to that.

Sighing, I picked the metal tube up anyway, concluding that it was my only option. The footsteps in the hallway had stopped. They were either waiting to draw me out, or they had left, soon to return.

Before braving the unknown, I checked myself in the mirror. In my eyes, I looked just as terrified as ever, but I had to admit that my new hairstyle made me look way cooler than I felt.

Hand on the doorknob, I paused for a second.

The mirror. Of course.

Abandoning the door, I crossed the room, inspecting the reflective surface. My hand glazed over the smooth, chilly plating.

Mirrors were made of glass. As I had already seen from various misadventures, glass could be broken and used as a blade.

Without thinking, I swung the toilet paper holder like there was no tomorrow.

The mirror cracked with a satisfying split, but that didn't stop the shatter that came along with it. Some of the glass pierced my thumb, and I shouted, unable to help myself.

Shards tumbled everywhere, and the crash echoed through the halls, creeping past the door.

I scooped up a set of glass pieces, taking one in each hand.

The footsteps were quiet at first. Shuffling feet, barely a whisper. But they were drawing closer.

A fist pounded on the door, trying the handle.

I clenched my teeth, sucking in a jagged breath. My blood pumped up to my head, making me dizzy and coating my arms in sweat.

My good friend adrenaline had returned. Although in this context, it felt a lot more like an enemy.

I had heard about fight-or-flight in school. Strangely enough, neither of those instincts had kicked in. All I could do was stand as my blood froze, the seconds until my inevitable doom ticking by.

My knuckles clenched around the shards.

I owed my useless self this much- When I died, it would be at my hand. The guards had enough blood to take. I deserved to be my own killer.

Lives were precious things. Before, I might've thought that was a dumb statement. Of course lives were precious, but they were undeniably present. They were the constant reality, and who could question the solitary constant of existence? But after seeing death up close and getting to know someone who had taken it… it might have seemed silly, but I couldn't stand the thought of mine being stolen away by anyone other than myself.

I could hear breathing on the other end of the door. I brought the glass to my neck, resting it against my perspiring flesh. The second that door opened, I would do it. I would slit my own throat and hope to cut deep. I would do it for everyone I had foolishly abandoned, but mostly for Lizabeth, mostly for my family, and, for some reason, all for Cerina.

No. Not 'for some reason'. Because, sure, she was strong, smart, and super hot, but not only that… she had shown me to appreciate why we do the things we do.

Her past was still a mystery to me, and maybe it always would be. But if I ever found her motivation, I would cherish it like a prized painting, the final piece to a puzzle.

Because she had helped me find *my* motivation.

And while I would never win any awards for 'determined person of the year,' it was nice to know that I was acting for a reason.

The door jolted forward, held in place by the small chain. I scampered back, pressing my back to the wall. The serrated edge of the makeshift blade dug into my neck. All it would take was one slight push. I could do this. I *could do this.*

The chain struggled to hold under the pressure, and I could hear it beginning to snap. The seconds felt like hours, each following a steady drumbeat, playing the intro to my funeral march.

Kicks beat at the wood, and I pushed the glass a little harder. I squeezed my eyes shut. In the movies, they made this look so *easy*.

I felt the chain give, and along with it, so did my knees. I drive the blade home, one last stroke of power to end my useless existence.

One last push to end all pushes.

It felt… good.

***

"Emry! No!"

My grandmother wrapped her hands around my waist, pulling me back from the road just in time. The bus swished by, mottling my already overgrown hair.

I gasped, my glasses dropping down the bridge of my nose. I was unsure of what exactly had just happened.

My feet were planted on the solid ground of the sidewalk, and my grandma was beside me, breathing hard. She pushed me back, blocking my view of the road, the cars continuing to whoosh past us.

"Emry Terris McLeod!" my grandmother scolded. I stumbled, my huge backpack catching the fall. My grandma's hair flew in the harsh wind, blowing behind her like a cape.

She was my hero, but she was also my worst nightmare.

I got up, dusting off my shorts, which had been a poor choice of clothing, all things considered. Technically, it was almost summer, but I had been overly ambitious. The wind still had quite the bite to it.

I turned to leave, but my grandmother stopped me, grabbing onto my backpack.

"Wait a minute! Don't you see what you just about did to yourself?"

Half-stunned, half-annoyed, I mumbled the first response that came to mind.

"I- I almost got hit by a bus."

My grandma circled around, crouching to meet my eyes.

"It's simple, Emry. Don't rush things. The crosswalk is at the end of the street. I can't watch you every morning on your way to school, so you have to learn to be safe."

I nodded, mostly just wanting to get this over with. I wasn't in the mood for a lecture. It was the first day of third grade, and so far, it wasn't off to a great start.

"What will you do next time?" My grandma asked, standing back up.

"I will use the crosswalk."

My grandma smiled, the wrinkles reaching all the way up her cheeks.

"Yes, you will. Make sure to protect yourself."

I had then proceeded to go off on my way, eager to be done with the conversation.

At the time, I had dismissed her words as a bunch of overprotective jabber.

But in the end, her lessons had worked.

Her lessons had worked, because I hadn't been able to bring myself to plunge the glass shard any deeper.

Emry McLeod

This moment and forever

My eyes blinked open, lowering my hand. I clutched the shard so hard my knuckles turned white, little cuts forming in the divots. I would stand. For once in my life, I was going to fight.

With one final, resolute kick, the door flew open, spraying wooden splinters every which way.

The airflow to my lungs severed as though a giant blockade had been stationed in my throat.

Was I dead, after all? I had never believed in an afterlife, but from what I had heard, I would've thought the ascension process would have been a little more… ascension process-like.

In front of me was Cerina, in a billowing blue dress that trailed behind her, the hem stained with dirt and blood. Behind her was a sick-looking Arvin, who swayed at the edge of the doorframe, uneasy on his feet.

"Am I…" I ventured, waving a hand in front of my face, "seeing things?"

Cerina clamped her hand around my wrist, a grim expression on her face. "Sometimes, I really wish I could attribute everything to that. But no… I'm here."

I sighed, nearly collapsing. "Thank everything."

"I wouldn't say that. There are a lot of people who aren't very happy with me at the moment."

I climbed up to my feet, pausing as we reached the door.

"What happened to the guards?"

"They're all in the dining room. I'll catch you up on the way."

***

I arrived at the dining hall behind Cerina, my mind thoroughly boggled. She strutted in with complete confidence while Arvin and I kept a safe distance back.

All the guards, whose weapons had so eagerly been trained on me mere minutes ago, were standing unarmed against the wall, seething with pure hatred. Cerina gave everyone a long look, setting her hands over the chair at the head of the table.

The two people sitting at the long table, one of which I recognised as Jezmon Tylor, hadn't budged, eyeing Cerina as though she were insane.

"Attention, everyone," Cerina said, speaking with the authority of a true leader. "I can guarantee, right now, that every single person in this room hates me."

I was ready to object, but she held out a hand.

"And if you don't hate me, you have every reason to hate my predecessors. But none of that matters much, does it? I don't need your loyalty. I only need your obedience, and I can get that with a flick of a finger."

Murmurs of uncertainty filled the room. What kind of speech was *this* supposed to be?

"But," Cerina sighed, "I've learned that you can't just eliminate your problems. You have to face them head-on and reason with them, agonising though it may be. And on this dreadful Isle, on the *Offshore Youth Rehabilitation Facility*, problems have only grown. You might not agree with me on every front, and I, likewise, might not agree with you. But we can all agree upon this cold, hard fact. Edric Rayz is dead, and it is time to begin a new legacy. I know better than to try and assume control, which is why we must take this step together. Without a chain of command, but as human beings."

She paused, allowing that to sink in.

"The Trial system all of you were put through was brutal and inhumane. I, too, have done terrible things to be where I am. I stand now, in front of you, a sea of people who have been through hell. Maybe you would think it insensitive if I claimed to understand you, but if you won't meet me in solidarity, at least fight for yourself. I am not going to give you an order. I am, instead, going to allow you to join me. Not as soldiers, not as pawns. But as partners. Allies. Individuals."

Her final words echoed throughout the chamber. People turned to each other, casting doubtful glances.

I stepped forward, and Arvin abruptly followed.

"I don't know if there's much point in it," I announced, "but *I'll* join you." I loosened my grip on the mirror pieces, letting them drop to the floor. My support didn't count for shit, but I would cheer Cerina on until the very end. And maybe that made me crazy. But we had all gotten ourselves here, and I would never allow myself to see us pushed back.

Arvin joined me, nodding his agreement.

The room stirred, all eyes pointed our way. For a terrible moment, I worried this wasn't going to work. That these born-and-bred murders would mutiny, and everything would come crashing down.

But it didn't.

The first person to step forward, albeit reluctantly, was the first guard I had encountered in the inner circle disguised as Amando Smith.

"I will join you," she muttered, staring at the ground.

That was all the crowd needed.

Clamours of agreement rose from every corner of the room. Commanders and soldiers alike, all stepping forward to give their solemn support to this single, unified cause.

Our enemies. Our greatest fears.

The two figures at the end of the table looked at each other, weighing their options. The woman who bore a surprising resemblance to Cerina stood up, facing the room head-on.

"You-" she huffed, "you monster." A heavy second passed where the two of them held a gaze, entirely at each other's mercy. "You are not my daughter," the woman spoke, crossing her arms, "but we have a lot of common ground. I will ally with your cause if you can prove to me you know what you're doing."

Cerina gave her a terse nod, challenging her mother with her eyes.

"That will suffice."

The only one left in disagreement was Jezmon Tylor, staring daggers at Cerina's head.

Sighing, he shuffled out of his chair and rose.

"I suppose," he grumbled, " the only reason I'm here is because of a diplomatic agreement. The turning of a tide. So who am I to go against an evident change? I am with you, Cerina Rayz, on this matter and this matter only. What will happen next is left for the future to decide."

Cerina nodded once.

"Understood. At your own discretion, I ask you all to follow my lead."

***

We got organised at an incredible pace. The guards, newly determined, worked quickly. Soon enough, we were walking down the beach of the Level Two sector, loading Cerina's father's private ship with the remainder of the prisoners.

Cerina, Arvin, and I stood together on the top deck while the guards, our temporary allies, herded the inmates down below to await fair trials when we got back to the mainland.

I supposed it was a good thing Jakson, Farrah, and Haven hadn't managed to destroy the records.

We weren't the only ones at the top. Joining us were Jezmon Tylor and Laure Rayz, Cerina's mother. Both of their mouths were pressed into firm, sour lines. Clearly, neither of them were very pleased, but this was the only happy medium everyone could settle for.

And don't get me wrong. I wasn't content either. Cerina had given me the full recount of her past, and honestly, her actions would take me a while to process.

But maybe that was okay. Change took time, and perfection was impossible. All the alternatives were still unexplored, but we had something right now, and we had to hold onto it.

Once the last of the prisoners, which I realised, with a pang, could easily have been me, were loaded onto the ship, Cerina lifted her hand, fingering something clasped inside of it. The object in question, I noticed, was something that resembled a metal bracelet. She aimed her pitch and, with that, gave her first real order.

"Take us away from here."

The ship chugged to life, and Cerina launched her throw. The bracelet sailed in a wide arc, crashing into the dark blue waves.

A wave swept us from the harbour, pushing us off to sea. The guards shouted, chanting up screams and curses, prayers and pleas. It all sounded the same to me, in this world of blinding light and sea-salt air.

I found Cerina's hand, not daring to clasp it. She patted the back of my wrist, a gesture of comfort.

That familiar red blush crept to my eyes. The world was confusing, but maybe...

Maybe that was okay.

Arvin joined her side, twining his aged fingers with hers. They looked at each other. Two fighters united at last, in a gesture of peace.

I smiled sadly. Now I knew what I had to do.

On the private ship, it was a little harder to find the hatch to the bottom, where the prisoners were being stored. But eventually, I located it, resting my palm on its heavy handle.

I thought back to what I had seen on the beach. Darby helping Lizabeth up. Arvin and Cerina, joining arms and finding their place amidst the chaos.

I had a place too. I was a Level Three, and I knew why. Surprisingly enough, I knew why.

With one thrust, I pulled the hatch open, stepping down the ladder. My feet found the floor, and my eyes adjusted to the bright hall below deck.

Under low ceilings, most of the prisoners were sitting on the edges and keeping to the outskirts, divided into their respective groups.

I cleared my throat, and their heads turned. All kinds of eyes focused my way. Level Ones. Level Twos. Dangerous people. Scared people. People like me. People like Lizabeth.

People.

It was a known fact that I didn't have a clue what I was doing. But I had been tagged in the first place because I had the nerve to try. Because I could unite *people*.

"Excuse me," I began. "I have something to say."

Not much of the chatter died down, but a few inmates were looking at me, their interest temporarily held.

I took a deep breath.

"This might sound a bit ridiculous. But I'm not going to sugarcoat anything or pretend to be cheery. Our predicament sucks. And, yeah, I said 'our'. Everyone is in the same boat, literally. Now, I'm not big on metaphors, but if we don't want to sink, we're going to have to pull it together, and you're going to have to listen to me."

Pausing, I half expected to blink and find a knife embedded in my back. But the strangest thing occurred. I wasn't mocked, wasn't shoved out of the deck like the chicken I was, still wearing the ill-fitting guard's disguise. The prisoners didn't try to kill me, they didn't even mock me.

They listened.

And as we sailed into the night, I told them a story about the Isle of Rebels.

***

The waves pushed the boat forward as it began its course. A light breeze skidded over the upper deck, bringing a scent of saltwater and ashes. Overhead, the stars twinkled, navigating us through the violet sky.

Looking at those same stars were the passengers of another ship, a silver dot on the horizon.

The two boats were very different. One was filled with criminals, their possibilities boundless but only starting to open up, and the other was filled with guards, inheritors, winners.

Everyone on those ships had different goals, different stories, different reasons to stay alive, but the waves pushed them all in the same direction.

The unknown.

It was never my intention to become a rebel-

But I had found myself none the same.

Acknowledgements

First and foremost, I would like to thank my family. Your readership and support has been instrumental to me. I would also like to thank my cat, Ollie, aka my unofficial brother, for the unwavering and unconditional love as well as the soothing purring sounds.

Second of all, my thanks go out to all the fantastic writing mentors I have had over the years, along with the wonderful writing community I have been able to connect with. Without you, I never would've gotten the chance to improve my work and put myself out there. You have all helped me in many ways at different periods, but without your feedback and instruction, I never would've been able to do this.

Thirdly, I would like to thank my friends. To everyone who has touched my life and read at least one page of this in its early draft stages, you guys have no idea how much you amazing weirdos mean to me.

About the Author

Willa Holmes grew up in Alberta, where her love of dystopian fiction was born as she secretly read *The Hunger Games* in her desk during math class. Apart from writing, Willa adores coffee, cats, guitar, scouting, and spending time with friends. She is currently completeing junior high school, and this is her first novel.

Manufactured by Amazon.ca
Bolton, ON